GIVE UP ON ME

Part 1

Sam Douglas

Copyright © 2024 Sam Douglas

All rights reserved

The characters and events portrayed in this book are fictitious. Any similarity to real persons, living or dead, is coincidental and not intended by the author.

No part of this book may be reproduced, or stored in a retrieval system, or transmitted in any form or by any means, electronic, mechanical, photocopying, recording, or otherwise, without express written permission of the publisher.

Cover design by: Sam Douglas

Dedicated to my husband. Thank you for your support

CONTENTS

Title Page

Copyright

Dedication

Content warning

Chapter 1	1
Chapter 2	57
Chapter 3	95
Chapter 4	134
Chapter 5	164
Chapter 6	210
Chapter 7	259
Chapter 8	289
Chapter 9	328
Chapter 10	376
Chapter 11	420
Chapter 12	472
Chapter 13	515
Chapter 14	547
Chapter 15	584
Chapter 16	611
Chapter 17	666

Chapter 18	699
Books In This Series	727

CONTENT WARNING

'Give up on me' is a contemporary romantic love story between a drug dealing pimp, his high flying mogul brother and a naive prostitute.

While gripping, the story does include elements that might not be suitable for some readers.

The content includes, but not limited to: references to kidnap, drug use, rape, suicide, abortion and murder.

References made to real life locations and references are fictitious and while the Author has attempted to keep the story realistic. The content is not to be taken seriously, as there are many elements that have been created to enhance the narrative.

CHAPTER 1

"Good morning, Jasmin." My overenthusiastic therapist beamed, taking his seat in front of me in his worn-out, beige fabric recliner with more stains than his underwear. The hinge groaned in protest as he sat back, the sound of which never failed to bug me.

I managed a small insincere smile. *Ugh—I hate these sessions.*

"As you know, we have come to the end of your regular programme. And now that you're twenty-one, we can start transitioning you into adulthood. Isn't that awesome?"

"Um, sure." I murmured as I played with the hem of my skirt, flicking the thin fabric with my index finger.

"Fantastic! I'm glad you're on board." He fidgeted on his foam cushion seat pad with disingenuous overexcitement.

I glanced in his direction, greeted by his belly roll perched on the desk and his idiot moon-shaped face grinning at me.

"Is that all you wanted to tell me, Dennis?" *It better be.*

"Stay focused a little longer for me, Jasmin. Just to be

clear, we aren't going to kick you out of the foster system, so to speak." He steepled his fingers in front of his mouth as he contemplated his choice of words carefully. "When you turned eighteen, we extended your stay due to, you know, the circumstances that landed you here. So, in order to continue providing you support, we can schedule regular sessions with me, and put you forward for some job interviews."

Interviews?

I glared at him square in his deep-set hazel eyes. "I already have a job?"

This man was all too familiar with my career of choice. In fact, he'd previously sampled the services I offered.

"Yes, indeed, Jasmin," he cleared an obstacle in his throat. "But aren't we hoping to see you away from that line of work?"

I smirked, crossing one leg over the other before fluttering my lashes at him. "Are you saying you didn't like the blow job I gave you, Dennis?"

With my lower lip caught between my teeth, I struggled to disguise my enjoyment in toying with him. Like a rodent's tail pinned under a cat's claw; he played victim well, but my patience was wearing as thin as his hairline.

As neither of us could turn back time and erase our brief

encounter, we mutually agreed to keep it to ourselves. He knew as well as I did he'd be going to jail if I blabbed about the ill thought out orgasm he received last summer, which afforded me an advantage I often exercised.

He stared down at his desk clock, restlessly twirling one thumb around the other, recognising the session had just begun. Pained by his own misfortune, a heavy droplet of sweat formed against the dampening skin of his balding head.

With intrigue, I watched closely as the bead slithered towards his eyebrow, eventually dissipating into the fine grey hairs.

The hands of the clock ticked louder as silence descended upon the room, where dust particles caught the light through the window behind him, whirling around one another, forming intricate shapes. It was mesmerising, and I could sit in quietude for as long as required.

Dennis, however, had other ideas. With a burst of energy, he clasped his hands together as he leapt from his chair.

"Let's call this session over, shall we?" He reached for the door handle. "I'll be in touch soon. Happy birthday."

Back at my foster parents' house, I sat in front of my

vanity mirror, preparing my hair and makeup for the most important celebration of my life. Twenty-one was a year to welcome, after all.

Not quite believing I'd lived in Los Angeles longer than my home country, time had flown by so fast.

I'd never fully embraced my transition from England to the USA during the whole mess with my parents dying and my step dad bringing me here—but that was a topic I saved for therapy.

As of today, I was technically free of the foster system, so it was about time I made some effort to embrace what life offered in America.

Sure, life had thrown me a few curve balls along the way and some might say that the questionable choices I had made resulted from that. But I preferred to view my situation in a more positive light, and being blessed with my mother's beauty didn't need to go to waste.

Never shy of improving my skill set, the lengths I'd gone to in honing my craft over the years earned me more cash than a nine-to-five desk job ever could. And now, at my coming of age, I planned to leave my foster parents' home and spread my wings, which was the American dream I'd clung onto since the day I arrived.

In an ideal world, I'd love nothing more than to forget

about the past—traumas and all—but who said life was that easy? Put up or shut up. That's always been my motto and absolutely nothing was going to ruin this day for me. After all, tonight was my night and I couldn't wait!

Turning up the sound system, my greatest hits playlist repeated within the confines of my minimalistic bedroom.

This room had seen some tears and tantrums during my stay with the couple who had given me a chance. But as my safe space, it was where I relaxed when I wasn't working. A place of solitude in a crowded world of disturbed people.

One attribute my foster parents possessed that I appreciated was their giving me freedom to decorate my own space. So aside from a few polaroid photos of the people I cared about tacked along the headboard of my bed, the whitewash walls were exactly to my taste.

With my blue eyes wide and my mouth open against the mirror, I applied mascara to complete my natural makeup. My silver hooped earrings and fine chained white gold necklace completed the look.

Still in my underwear, with not much time left to get ready, I rummaged through my closet in search of the sexiest outfit I possessed, settling on my favourite red dress with spaghetti straps that showed plenty of cleavage.

Countless clients had fucked me in this innocuous little

number that hung so innocently on its hanger more times than I could remember. She was my money maker, and the crowd loved her.

Inch by inch, I shimmied into the thin fabric that hugged my body like an extra layer of skin and turned to look over my shoulder in the floor-length mirror at the young woman staring back at me. *How did you get so grown up?*

My blonde hair styled into beach waves fell midway down my back, and my bottle tan gave a summer glow, neutralising my pale skin, affording me the confidence I needed to keep up with the pace of the evening.

I checked the time on my Casio wristwatch to see how long it would be until my bestie Hanna would arrive. Whenever I checked the time, I smiled internally as it meant a lot to me, being the last gift my mum had given me back home in England before her passing.

My treasured timepiece informed me I had thirty minutes remaining until the party really started, so I slipped on my high-healed matching red shoes and checked my purse to see how many drinks would pass my lips.

The clasp fell open to reveal a sorrowful sight indeed. Empty; not a penny remained.

Shit.

So how was I going to celebrate my birthday without a dime to my name?

Hmm, maybe I could message one of my tricks?

There wasn't a single girl in the game worth her salt who didn't have at least half a dozen men she was using for money—or tricks, as we affectionately labelled them.

I happened to have a couple of them on the go myself and now was the time to call upon their favour.

The most obvious choice in my contacts was Troy. A weird character, he spent more time showing me his figurine collection than anything else, but he was a great payer and an easy target. If I could rely on anyone to help a girl out, it would be him.

<Me> Hey Troy. Wanna chat?

So why then, had five minutes gone by and he hadn't messaged me back?

Impatience grew like weeds around my moral compass as I waited for a reply to my text that never came.

When will I ever catch a break? It's my bloody birthday!

Left with no other choice than to take matters into my own hands, I resounded myself to the notion of actioning plan b.

I crept down the stairs, hoping to remain unseen, as my eyes honed in on the old satchel sat upon the small telephone table by the front door.

Legend has it that Nancy, my foster mother, had more money in that bag than her humble abode suggested.

Not that holding my breath helped as I tiptoed along the creaking floorboards, but regardless, I championed through until I made it undetected where I waited a moment, listening for movement from the living room before I executed my plan.

Old-fashioned music echoed throughout the house, the sound of which emitted from the very room I suspected the troll was dozing, likely in her rocking chair with a small glass of sherry in her claw-like grip.

Now!

My freshly painted red finger nails snaked their way into the opening of the bag in blind search of her wallet. The telltale sensation of wrinkled paper against my digits afforded me a smile as I pulled out what I suspected to be a one hundred-dollar bill. *Bingo.*

"What are you doing hovering by the door?" Nancy popped her head around the living room's mahogany-stained door frame with an empty glass in her hand.

"Um, nothing." I slotted the note between my cleavage before turning to smile at her. "I was just about to leave."

Her eyes followed the curves of my body as she scrutinised my outfit. "You look like a tart in that dress," she croaked in a way that made my skin crawl off my bones.

She'd had many an opportunity in our forged relationship to say something nice to me, but I was still waiting for pigs to fly.

"Oh, be quiet, Nancy. I can smell your decomposing body from here."

The wrinkles above her thinned lips stressed as she scowled at me. "You're nothing but a brat. I don't know why I bother."

Fact was, she never did bother with me. Not that I could remember, anyway.

I glanced at my watch impatiently. If Nancy had her way, we would be at this for hours.

"Don't think I'll put up with your crap for much longer. The worst mistake I made was agreeing to take you on."

"Yeah, yeah." I rolled my eyes. "I knew it was just about the money with you."

She placed her mottled hand against her chest and took a step back, creating a distance between us.

Nothing new there.

She detested when I stood up for myself and this time, the old hag didn't have a comeback. Everything I'd said was true.

A car horn hooted in the distance, announcing Hanna's arrival.

We remained at a standoff for a moment, sharing an evil glare until finally I relented, storming over to the front door while her stoic expression watched me leave.

Hanna continued impatiently hooting her car horn when I made my way out of the house as I slammed the decrepit front door a little too hard behind me to finalise my point. The sooner I could move away from that bitch, the better.

As I sashayed away, I sensed Nancy twitching the drapes at the window before I turned around and caught her scowling at me with resentment.

With a wry smile as I etched her expression into my memory, I raised my middle finger to her, where the sense of gratification it gave me produced a buzz of adrenaline like no other.

Not wishing to give her satisfaction in ruining my birthday celebrations, I shook off the negativity and heel-trotted over to Hanna's car cheerfully, feeling a flutter of excitement at the prospect of spending the evening with my best friend, getting up to no good like we always did.

We beamed at each other when our eyes met through the windshield.

On cue, her car rattled in protest as it idled at the curbside, waiting for me to embark upon the birthday express. The tin can on wheels wasn't actually roadworthy as per its last vehicle inspection, but who was I to judge? There wasn't much chance of me buying my own car anytime soon.

"Hey, Han!" I beamed, feeling instantly at home in her presence as I took my seat beside her.

Hanna was like a sister to me and we shared the same passions in life; sex being our number one bestseller.

Prostitution was the only way women like us who came from nothing could survive the streets of L.A, and we wouldn't stop doing something we were good at just because society deemed hookers as lower-class citizens.

Whether tricking would be my lifetime career, only time would tell, but for right now, I was proud of the woman I'd become and I knew she felt the same way, too.

Hanna looked me up and down with a smile. My girl understood my intentions.

"Ooh shit, you're in the moneymaker." She eyed my dress in appreciation. "You're going to pull tonight, Babe. That dress never fails!"

I peered down at my red satin finery and caressed the material that skimmed my thighs. Feeling classy and beautiful, confidence radiated from me when I was in Hanna's company.

Close in age, we'd known each other since high school and worked together occasionally with clients. It wasn't however until we worked on a particular job that we actually became best friends.

Hanna had organised that client—a close call that neither of us wanted to repeat—and it affected us more than we cared to acknowledge.

You see, back then, she also was a renegade girl, choosing to exchange her services for money without protection of a pimp in order to keep her earnings for herself.

However, that encounter changed everything for Hanna, and her confidence hit rock bottom until she enlisted the help of a pimp, or daddy as she called him.

I didn't understand why she chose the guy she did. Well

known, he spent more time in the news with his latest sluts than he did focusing on keeping his women safe, but I guess his good looks played a part in the final decision.

Of course, I was too stubborn to follow suit, and despite her best efforts to persuade me otherwise, I truly believed that I would be better off going alone.

It was common knowledge that pimps were more trouble than they were worth, anyway. And I'd seen too many girls come undone by such overbearing, powerful men who promised protection but rarely followed through with it in favour of intimidating vulnerable girls into giving up a huge cut of their earnings for nothing in return.

"You OK there Jassy? You seem preoccupied."

Hmm?

I looked over at my girl with adoration as she skilfully navigated from the driver's seat, cruising along the highway at speed towards the partying hotspot in downtown Los Angeles.

Her gorgeous supple skin shimmered in the late evening sun, rocking her magazine cover glam with conviction, and with her gold heels and accessories complimenting her dress, she was chefs' kiss perfection. Together, we were an unstoppable team.

"I'm fine. I was just, um, thinking about what happened in that hotel room."

She cocked her head and scowled at me. "Why would you do that to yourself?"

"Do you never think about it?"

She shook her head, her eyes back on the road.

I placed my hands in my lap, feeling silly for overthinking again. "Oh. Nevermind then."

I wanted to tell her that each time we planned to find a client together, my mind would fixate on the man that nearly killed her. But as Hanna wasn't a talker, I guess that purge would have to wait.

"You know I don't do emotions," she chuckled, grabbing my thigh. "Tonight we're gonna earn big. I can feel it."

I placed my hand on top of hers. "Absa-bloody-lutely." I winked, flicking my hair dramatically.

"I love your British accent." She smiled, shaking her head at an internal thought.

Matching her grin, I poked her arm. "Come on, what are you smiling at?"

"Oh, nothing," she turned up her retro-fitted sound system, "nothing at all."

We lined up for what felt like an eternity to get into the

nightclub, ironically named 'Easy Access'.

"Daddy should be here by now." Hanna's teeth chattered as she huddled into herself.

We hadn't come prepared for the chill in the evening air and our hardened nipples showcased the fact.

She glanced over her shoulder anxiously, waiting for the pimp that was allegedly providing her and a few other hookers' protection tonight at this very establishment.

I knew he'd let her down.

"What did you say this party was called again, Han?"

Her jaw continued to dance. "Whore night. Why?"

"Just wondered."

Hanna had taken part in the activity several times since joining her daddy, but this would be my first time tagging along. A simple setup, 'whore night' involved a group of the pimp's girls working the same crowd with him close by overseeing proceedings.

If anything, his lack of time keeping confirmed to me what I already suspected, that no matter how hard Hanna protested in his favour, he was just like the rest of them.

"Come on, Han, I told you pimps are a waste of time." I blew warm air into my balled fists, attempting to keep my fingers from becoming frost bitten.

"Be patient. You'll know what I mean when you see him, Jas. He's worth the wait. To-die-for."

A parting through the crowd like Moses to the red sea caught my attention. It seemed he had finally arrived and boy, did we know it.

Hanna's eyes shone with excitement. "He's here Jas, look!"

I watched with anticipation as the pimp, dressed in an expensive matt black tracksuit with the jacket unzipped and lavish gold jewellery, sauntered past the long line of at least fifty people.

He had several half-naked bikini-clad women draped over his muscular tattooed arms as he made a beeline for the entrance to the building.

Flashes of light emitting from the crowd transpired to be a couple of sneaky paparazzi hoping to get a compromising shot of him, but he was ready for anything.

Jeez—I knew this guy was famous, but Hanna downplayed just how famous he was.

But one thing was for sure: Hanna wasn't wrong when she said he was attractive. My jaw slackened, frozen by the sight of him, where my dilated pupils locked on his body, unable to break free as I devoured his image.

It wasn't until he stalked by me that the air shifted between us and my skin tingled with an electrical charge that transferred from his body to mine.

Did he feel it too?

His ocean blue eyes met with mine briefly as he passed me by, and in that moment I was hooked.

Holy shit—

Upon the pimps' arrival at the club's entrance, the bouncer lifted the twisted red rope and granted him access.

"Welcome back Boss." He hollered over the thudding music emitting from within.

The pimp was about to step foot inside when Hanna waved her arms to grab the bouncer's attention. "Wait! We're with him!"

Hanna's daddy turned leisurely on his heels and eyed her suspiciously for a moment, flitting his gaze between the two of us when eventually he nodded. "Let them in."

The silky tones of his naturally masculine baseline tingled my senses. So far, he ticked every single box.

The pimp and his female companions were ten steps ahead of us by the time Hanna peeled herself away from the entryway mirror, after checking the bounce of her shoulder length black curls at least half a dozen times.

"Come on, Han, they've left us behind!"

"Relax," she limped her wrist in the air. "Daddy will wait for us. He and I have a connection."

I was out of breath by the time we'd plodded up the steep flight of stairs in my painfully high-heeled shoes.

Hanna reached for the handles of the glass doors when a man shaped obstacle stood in our way.

"Nope, sorry Hoe's, you can't go in there." An imposing member of staff blocked our entrance to the pimps VIP lounge. His arms held out to the side, prevented us from taking another step closer.

"Excuse me, why not?" Hanna placed her hands on her hips in the sassy way she usually did to get what she wanted.

He peered down at his clipboard. "VIP is full. Better luck next time."

I took a step forward. Now was my time to shine. "Wow, your arms look really strong. I bet you lift weights?" I licked my bottom lip seductively.

His chin lifted, and he cracked a smile. "I do actually. But the answer is still no."

Fuck! "Aww, come on," I stomped my foot. "It's my birthday!"

He leant into my ear. "Listen Lady. Do yourself a favour and take your little tushy back down the stairs and enjoy coach like the rest of 'em. We're full!"

Hanna's body tensed, and I knew from experience she was about to kick off, so I grabbed her arm and pulled her back to reality. "Come on Han, let's just go."

She craned her neck as I pushed her forward. "I'll be back," she yelled. "Watch me!"

"Jeez Han, come on, leave it, please." I sighed, edging her away from her latest victim.

"I could've taken him." She mumbled as we sullenly made our way back down the stairs. "A kick in the nuts and he would have gone down."

With an exasperated eye roll, I ignored her trash talk. I wished for just once that we could have a drama free night of fun.

"Please forget about it now, Han, OK?" I pouted as she reluctantly followed me down into the slums with the rest of the riffraff. I was going to rescue this party that hadn't even started yet if it killed me.

"Sorry Babe," she preened her hair once more. "You know how I get sometimes."

My lips remained sealed to avoid an argument with her,

but if she thought we were any better than average, she had become delusional.

All was seemingly forgotten by the time we made it to the dance floor, as we became engrossed in the celebration of my twenty-first, absorbing the heady atmosphere of the intoxicated crowd and loud music.

"Did you bring any cash, Han?" I asked as we moved in synchrony to the DJ's mix of beats that got the crowd excited.

"I've got nothing Babe," she glanced up towards the VIP lounge, "I spent my last twenty dollars on gas. I thought I'd be upstairs with Daddy tonight."

My lips pursed in the knowledge that apart from my one hundred-dollar bill, I had little to flash either.

"OK," I rounded my shoulders. "Let's get to work then."

We low-fived one another, scanning the room for fresh bait to sink our teeth into.

As usual, Hanna worked her magic on a prospective client first, as she had an extra element of self-assurance that I sometimes lacked. Whereas my talents came from observing from a distance and complimenting her introduction once she'd secured the deal.

The first trick was a skinny-looking guy about six feet

tall, with hair gelled back in a style that was a little too slick for my taste. The innocence about him implied he was a virgin, but without a doubt, Hanna would have her talons into him in no time.

It wasn't long before she approached me with a grin on her face and two filled champagne flutes, signifying her success.

"Happy birthday, Jassy." She winked at me, raising her filled sloshing flute to mine as we clinked glasses. Our pink fizz was fresh, delicious, and worth every penny of the tricks money.

Off to a great start, we giggled like pre teens at a sleepover as we celebrated Hanna's victory.

"Slick paid up then?" I asked, taking another sip.

"Shit, it's so loud in here! What did you say?"

I rubbed my fingers together, and her eyes lit up when she knew I meant money.

"Yeah, he slipped me two hundred dollars just to dance with him," she smirked. "Now, let's find our next trick."

We swayed our hips in time with the music. Each one of our free hands began exploring the other's body, something we always did to attract male attention.

She took a sip of her champagne, running her hand through her hair as she moved where her wandering fingers slid down the front of my cleavage and snaked around my curvaceous waist.

After a little while, the continued alcohol top ups courtesy of Hanna travelled through my system, distorting my vision. I hadn't reached my limit yet, but I was getting close.

As we fooled around, I caught sight of the pimp's eyes on us from his royal position up in VIP, and I immediately shied away from his glare when he caught me gawking.

Shit!

An intimidating man. Not once did I see him crack a smile or show a hint of emotion, but if he gave Hanna the reassurance she needed to continue working, then I would support her journey every step of the way.

Ugh, just look at those girls draped over him. Pathetic.

"Game on Jasmin." Hanna nodded toward the direction of the dance floor spectators, whose greedy eyes were on us. Eager men honed in on our bodies looking for a no-strings-attached night of fun.

With expertise, Hanna responded to their advances by grabbing my ass as she spotted a bodybuilder type eyeing her from a short distance away. She pulled me into her hold, and we kissed.

Intimacy with Hanna was never more than a business transaction. It was something that we both enjoyed, but it never quite reached the clit.

Secure enough with our individual sexualities, we both knew what our connection was with each other, neither one of us getting it twisted or catching feelings in order to make as much money as we could.

Our tongues explored one another's mouths as I gently cupped her breast with my free hand while she groped my backside, staying entwined with each other until we successfully acquired our target.

An abrupt hand reached for Hanna's shoulder, interrupting the flow of our performance. "Boss wants you upstairs now."

Huh? Who the hell is this dude?

"Sure, Tommy." Hanna's eyes shone with excitement. "I'll be right back, Jas."

The suited man with a serious look on his face turned his attention to me. "You come too."

Wait—me? I looked over my shoulder. "Um, are you talking to me?"

"Yeah, hurry up."

Hanna's face expressed her confusion as I followed her direction, but she grabbed my hand in hers regardless, as Tommy led the way.

"Come on Jas. Hurry!" She tugged.

"Why," I stumbled through the crowd. "What's the rush?"

Hanna hooked my arm around hers. "I think Daddy probably invited you along, so you wouldn't be left on your own. He can be kind like that sometimes."

Kind wasn't a word I would have expected anyone to use in describing that man. Although, as I often preached about people not judging me by my line of work, perhaps I should extend the same courtesy to him.

With Tommy's position of power, we made it further than our first attempt at entry to the royal suite. Now at the top of the stairs, we faced the same set of glass doors with a bouncer standing in front, blocking the entrance again.

Tommy leant in towards the human blockade. "Boss wants these two."

"But we're at capacity. No room."

Tommy's shoulders bunched with agitation. "Make room!"

With a distressed exhale through filled cheeks, the bouncer shook his head and stepped back, where he opened the door for us to walk inside.

Hanna, never one to miss an opportunity, took great pleasure in pausing by the entrance. She pulled her tongue out at the bouncer. "Told you I'd be back."

The eagle eye view from the VIP lounge was in stark contrast with ground level, and opulence was the decor of choice with the entire room bathed in tones of deep reds and golds. The dance floor below, filled with drunken guests letting their hair down, was visible from all sides of the platform and as we entered the room with all eyes on us, my heart rate quickened.

"I'm shitting myself, Han." I side eyed her for reassurance.

Why am I even here?

"Relax, Jas. He'll just want to check in with me. Don't worry."

Shit. Fuck. My stomach is churning. Why do I need to fart now? Why?

I swallowed past a hard lump in my throat as I absorbed the scene before me.

The pimp was the first person I noticed sat centrally on his red velvet throne, with golden scroll arms within the ostentatious space. A dark-haired woman knelt before him. Dim lighting offered little in the way of details, but I was pretty sure she was sucking his dick.

Two naked strippers, one on either side of him, were putting on quite a show for their master, not that he was watching.

Other than the pimp and his whores, there were a couple of men that looked more like security than friends who had joined him in his lair who seemed more interested in a game of cards than the female entertainment.

When the pimp's eyes locked with mine he beckoned us towards him with a simple curl of his index finger.

"What is she doing in here?" A pretty, red head called out from behind the pimp's seat of power. "She's not one of us?"

My cheeks instantly blushed at her vicious tongue, but she was absolutely right. I was an intruder.

I can't do this.

The pimp neither listened nor cared as he awaited our arrival. "Come stand here, bitches." He pointed to the ground before him.

With my hand still grasped in Hanna's, we stepped closer, towards his order. Together.

His eyes focused on my breasts first and took their sweet time drinking in my body as we waited for our next instruction.

After a moment, he lit a cigar and blew a plume of smoke into the air above where a smokey haze descended upon him, playing Devil's advocate with my senses.

He peered at Hanna, inspecting her. "You're one of my whores, right?"

"Yes, Daddy." She nodded enthusiastically.

He raised his thumb and index finger into a gun shape, pointing at me. "And this is your friend?"

Hanna squeezed my hand, sensing me spiral when the spotlight was back on me. "Yes, Daddy."

He nodded and gripped his cigar between his teeth as he rubbed his hands together. "Bring her to an audition tomorrow."

Wait—What?

Her hold on me tightened. "Sorry Daddy, she doesn't want to join us."

Fuck! Why did she say that?

At that moment, I wanted the ground to swallow me up, and seeing the pimp's reaction had me fearing the worst. Could I outrun him? Pfft, with the way I run, not likely.

His body became rigid in response, showcasing his powerful muscles for all the wrong reasons.

"Is that right, slut? You're too good for my services?"

"Um—" Words suddenly failed me. My cheeks were a glow and my pulse rate quickened. "Can I, um, think about it?"

The pimp rose to his feet, pushing the girl off his dick to the ground with an aggressive shove, and he stalked towards me.

Oh no! No, no, no. What do I do now?

I winced, expecting he was going to hit me, but instead he remained inert when he reached me.

Our proximity was intoxicating, and his masculine scent mouth watering. He leant towards me, close enough for the tiny hairs on my face to stand to attention.

"Sure," he mumbled against my ear, "you can think about it. Now leave."

Before I had chance to blink, Hanna pulled me by the arm and out of the lounge via the same glass door we entered through.

Once clear of the blast zone, air escaped her lungs. "Shit, Jas, that was a close one! When he gives an order, you don't hesitate!"

"Really? See, now that's the reason I don't want a pimp. He's too much. And did you have to tell him I didn't want an audition? I thought he was going to kill me!"

She shrugged, "Only telling the truth, Babe."

If I'd had my whits about me, I would have given her a smart reply. But the pimp's intimidation tactics had me unnerved.

"What are *you* looking at?" Hanna sneered at the same bouncer she'd been back and forth with for the best part of the night.

He peered up at her from his newspaper with a smug expression on his face. "That's the fastest he's ever kicked a whore out. Having a bad night, are you?"

Hanna was never shy about retaliating. With an eagerness to fight her corner, she removed an earring. "Hold me back Jas. I'm going to kick his ass!"

"Wait Han," I cupped her elbow. "Remember why we came here? We've got money to make. Forget this loser. Come on, let's go."

Back on the dance floor, I sought to shake off my encounter with the overbearing pimp while Hanna continued her quest to bag a client, so we picked up where we left off.

It was unsettling to even contemplate the idea that my best friend had thrown me under the bus back there, but had she really done anything other than tell the truth? No matter how hot that man was, the unpredictability factor diluted his charm, and nothing about my interaction with him convinced me to change my mind.

Before long, the bodybuilder eyeing our earlier dance floor scene approached us to initiate phase one of the transaction.

"May I cut in?"

His voice was deep and gruff, and his pale blue eyes pierced Hanna's with fuckable intensity. As always, she was the hooker of choice.

I nodded in agreement for her. "I'll grab another drink and give you guys some privacy."

As was usual in our parting ritual, I kissed her chastely one last time and mouthed a warning through my lips to hers. "Be careful. I've got your back."

She nodded in understanding. We didn't need to say any more.

Swaying over to the bar, I perched on a wooden stool that tilted as I sat on the hard seat. Not wanting to fall flat on my ass, I caught hold of the bar top to steady myself and regain the composure I lost in the pimp's company.

The bartender was incredibly efficient, with enthusiasm

for the job. He swung the length of the bar with elegance, tending to his customers, and swiftly approached me, ready to take my order.

"What can I get you, Beautiful?" He smiled a winning grin as his eyes stole a glance at my cleavage. His perfect white teeth gleamed through the darkness of the club's strobe lighting.

"Well, it's my birthday so—"

"Double shot of whiskey." A low, grumbling male voice interrupted from behind me.

Excuse me?

I snapped my head towards the sound and my mouth instantly dried when I realised who the voice belonged to.

Instinctively, I smiled when my eyes met with the pimp's, but he didn't reciprocate, leaving the intensity of his glare forcing me to look away first, like a cowering dog.

But his alluring proximity and the electrical charge between us encouraged my body to betray me, and as my skin dampened in response, my lips parted.

Was it a weakness on my part that he did things to my body that no man had before, without even touching me? Or was this part and parcel of the pimp's charm?

His masculine scent still lingered in my nostrils from our earlier encounter and the tingling sensations sparking between us melted my core, where my vagina clenched in anticipation for more of him.

Immediately, the bartender handed him his drink, and just like that, he was gone.

"Sorry gorgeous," the bartender smiled. "He's the boss. So, anyway what can I getcha?"

My rendezvous with the pimp still had my pupils dilated, and my breathing hitched. I cleared my throat to regain some self-control. "Um, vodka and coke, please."

"Coming right up."

My drink was with me in seconds, passing my lips and slipping down my throat in one fluid motion. That was the drink that took me from fuzzy to *nicely* drunk.

Tipsy and lightheaded, I turned on my stool, scanning the room for Hanna. I needed to check on my girl to make sure her guy was behaving himself. Regardless of the pimp's presence, I still didn't trust that he would be there for her if she really needed him.

Finally, I caught a glimpse of her out of the corner of my eye where she was still moving seductively with her man on the dance floor.

Aww. There's my girl.

The body builder's tight-fitted white shirt showcased his

bunched veiny muscles as his fingers slid up and down her back while they locked lips. He was going to get lucky tonight, and she was going to get paid.

Hanna's eyes finally met mine, and I pointed to the dimly lit bathroom sign at the opposite end of the club.

We pushed our way through the throng of dancing singletons and forced open the bathroom door where, of course, there was a massive line.

"Shit, I'm desperate," I danced from foot to foot, holding myself, suddenly feeling like my bladder was the size of a marble.

"Jasmin, my guy, wants us to go back to his hotel room. He's got a friend for you." Her eyes glistened with the unspoken promise of a lucrative evening.

Finally! I was losing hope that anything would happen tonight.

"Perfect. Did you know I love you, Han?"

She nudged me with her shoulder. "You're drunk. But yeah, I know."

"I really, really do. Anyway, what's the plan with Hulk?"

Hanna had lost focus on our conversation and was checking her makeup in the mirror. "Hulk? Who's that?"

"The muscly guy you've been dance floor fucking the

last hour? Kinda looks like the incredible Hulk. Don't you think?"

Suddenly the snorting giggles took a hold of me and I was more drunk than I realised.

Hanna chuckled at the sight of my belly laughs. "How much have you had to drink?"

"Um, a couple? Maybe four. Come on, let's pee and get out of here."

Alcohol coursed through my entire body, giving me a false sense of reality as I followed Hanna back towards the dance floor to finalise the arrangements with Hulk.

"So ladies, this guy right here is my buddy Owen." Hulk introduced us to his friend, who seemed a little shy, but not a totally lost cause.

After a brief conversation between them, Hanna nodded at Hulk as they verbally shook on their deal.

"Great," she smiled. "Shall we get out of here, then?"

He gave Owen the thumbs up, and I took his clammy hand as Hanna led us towards the exit.

Just as we were about to leave the club, a figure cast a shadow over us, forcing each of us to crash into the others back.

What the—

The pimp stepped out in front of Hanna like a shield with an unmatched intensity.

"Hey Daddy." Hanna rose to her tiptoes and kissed his cheek.

"Where you goin'?" He stared at the men, settling his focus on my hand clasped around Owen's

Hulk piped up with misplaced alcohol infused confidence. "It's OK Buddy, I know a great—"

"Buddy?" The pimp growled with contempt. His muscular frame towered over us all.

Hanna tucked her hair behind her ear. "We're just going to a hotel, Daddy."

We all waited in anticipation for the pimp to respond, where finally he looked at Hanna. "Check in when you get there."

Sheesh, this guy needs to let off some steam. A spa day wouldn't go a miss.

"He's so intense!" I whispered to Hanna as we climbed into the nearest cab that had its call light illuminated.

"Who? Daddy? Yeah, he is, but he's the best pimp in L.A and I'm lucky he accepted me."

"No Han, he's the lucky one. But he definitely scared the crap out of me."

She eyed me accusatorially. "Well, as you refuse to join him, you don't need to worry."

OK, Miss sassy pants!

I knew she wanted to lecture me again, but that would have soured the already tense mood.

"Where to?" The uninterested voice called from the front of the cab as we all took our seats behind him.

Hulk grabbed onto the driver's head rest. "233 West Lane Hotel, my man."

No sooner had the wheels set in motion than Hanna wasted no time, already working Hulk into quite a frenzy opposite us. With her hand between his legs, she fondled his dick as she devoured his mouth.

Owen, on the other hand, was stiff as a board—not inside his trousers. He needed a little bump start with my capable hands and now was my time to make a move in getting him warmed up the best way I knew how.

It was common knowledge in our game that the more the client craved you, the more generous they were with their payment, and with Hanna's head start, I had some catching up to do.

With a steady, confident motion, I moved my hand up his jean-clad thigh towards his soft bulge. I leaned in close to him and muttered in his ear, "You like that?" I purred as I scraped his earlobe with my teeth.

"Sure," he chuckled nervously. "What's your name?"

Ugh. He better not be a questions type.

Our time together was already as stale as a week old bread roll and we certainly didn't need to add dry conversation to the mix.

"Jasmin," I lied. I never told a stranger my real name. The less they knew about me, the better.

"Sweet." He looked anywhere but me, mainly at the two lovebirds opposite us who were almost fucking in their seats.

Fifteen painfully silent minutes later, we arrived at our destination, a familiar-looking hotel.

I climbed out of the cab first, a successful tactic I'd learned from Hanna that ensured the client paid the fare, leaving Hulk to pick up the tab for all of us. But he seemed the type to thrive on the opportunity to flash his cash and didn't bat an eye at the fifty-three dollar total.

The four of us made our way to check-in at the main desk of the hotel lobby. Now that I was inside the place, I remembered this wasn't my first time in the establishment and likely wouldn't be my last.

It was a hot spot for married men who told their wives they were on a 'business trip' when, in reality, they were playing out their sordid fantasies with whores who were all too happy to oblige. I wondered if the two men we'd picked up tonight fell into that category.

Despite the Hotel's dated and old-fashioned decor, it was clean, at the very least. There was a faint scent in the air of wax polish mixed with bleach and I pondered how many elusive stains they had attempted to clean up that morning.

We followed Hulk's lead, who bypassed the desk towards his pre-booked room, when an elderly man yelled from his propped-up position behind his serving counter.

"Hold on! $40 each for the hour," he croaked, looking at us with disdain.

Was it that obvious?

"I already have a room, old man?" Hulk pulled out his key card as evidence.

"Not my problem, Pal. Forty dollars each or get out."

There was no way Hulk was going to walk away from the opportunity of a night with Hanna, and the old man was taking advantage of that fact.

Hulk opened his fancy designer wallet, bulging with

notes, and tutted as he counted his money animatedly, tossing $160 down in front of the conman.

The old timer slid the cash off the counter into his hand with a sly smile on his face. "Enjoy folks."

We all followed Hulk towards the carpeted staircase, taking the flight up one level to his room on the next floor.

Room number 132 had a green painted door with brass hardware decorated with a sign that warned against urinating in the hallway.

Hulk took his keycard and slid it into the reader to gain access. "Let the fun begin," he said with a grin as he stepped inside first.

The room itself had two double beds, side by side and sectioned by a small wooden table with a lamp sat on top.

Wait. What is that smell?

The colour scheme reminded me of a chest infection; green and yellow wallpaper with a green carpet and matching bedding. But the style of the room wasn't important. We could look past anything if the money was right.

I took hold of Hanna's arm. "Before we start, Hanna and I need to pee. Right Han?"

"Yeah. Sure." She nodded in agreement. "We'll be right back."

My face twisted at the sight of the bathroom. Minus the weird smell, it was in keeping with the rest of the facility, boasting an avocado four piece bathroom suite packed into the small windowless room. The only airflow coming from a worn-out extractor fan that hummed too loudly.

I blew into my cupped hand, checking my breath, and scooped up my breasts, creating heart stopping cleavage.

Peering into the small mirror that hung just above the basin, I reapplied some gloss and smiled at my reflection. A soft glow to my cheeks and blush red lips to match my outfit; I was ready.

Hanna lifted the toilet seat. "Oh, my God. Please tell me why people can't flush! There's a whole ass turd in here!"

"That explains the smell, then." I chuckled as I ran my index finger over the gloss to smooth out the application.

"And the damn flush is broken!" She groaned as she pulled the leaver repeatedly.

"Just pee over the turd. Don't stress now or you won't be in the right mindset to come for your guy."

"Ugh, I guess." She crouched over the bowl. "Wait with me while I tinkle."

"Of course I'll wait."

I chewed my lip anxiously as uninvited images crept into my mind's eye.

"I can see you over thinking Jas, what's wrong?"

Am I that obvious?

"Um, well, we don't know these boys. I don't want a repeat of you know what—"

"Relax, OK? I've messaged Daddy, and he knows we're here. All I gotta do is send S.O.S, and he'll be over in a flash."

"OK," I exhaled, shaking my hands to rid of the tension.

If Hanna was so sure about this, why was I freaking out so badly? Old wounds hadn't yet scarred.

She interrupted my reverie, sensing that I was about to spiral again, "OK, I'm finished. Let's go!" Pulling me forward, she took the lead back into the bedroom.

When we reentered the room, I found Owen sat on the edge of the bed, his hands clasped together with a strained look on his face.

Hanna leapt into Hulk's lap on the bed opposite with an excited squeal. "Come here Baby," she purred, "let's put on some music."

I turned my attention to my guy, smiling sweetly. "So, Owen, what would you like to do?"

Intense throaty vocals burst through the speaker of Hulk's phone as he pressed play on his playlist. Hardly the vibe for a relaxing evening, but we'd have to make do.

Owen looked at his watch. "Dunno really. What did you have in mind?"

Um, sex?

Eye contact was a problem for him. I found that telling of a man's character and their intentions. He was hiding something; probably his wedding ring.

I slid carefully onto the sheets next to him and crossed my legs elegantly, one leg over the other, to elongate my frame.

Something about his body language screamed regret and having made it this far, the last thing I needed was a runner. Hanna would never let me live it down.

The sobering truth was I needed the money, and I had to produce some of my best moves to seal the deal.

Hanna groaned incoherently into Hulk's mouth as they consumed each other while dollar signs rolled in her eyes like a slot machine.

Shaking off the terrible start, I rolled up my proverbial sleeves with a point to prove to myself that I was just as good at this as she was.

"Don't worry about them." I turned Owen by the chin to look at me. "This is our time."

I rose from the bed and unzipped my favourite red dress

from the back, pulling the zipper all the way down to the base of my spine.

He glanced at me briefly, but focused mainly on his expensive leather designer shoes that had probably never stepped foot in an establishment like this before.

It wasn't until I slid down the spaghetti straps to my midriff and removed my bra to expose my bosom that he stole a peek.

"Do you like?" I asked, biting my lip seductively.

"Mm-hm," he nodded.

My breasts being natural and voluptuous, with perky peach nipples, always took a client's breath away. But Owen was a difficult customer to please.

I took a hold of his hand in mine and placed it on my breast, encouraging his hand to close around the fullest part. My bare nipple puckered under the massaging pressure as my body responded quicker than his.

"Err, Jasmin, this is my first time in this sort of—"

"Shh," I put my finger to his lips. "Don't worry, I'll look after you."

As my dress pooled at my feet, I removed my red lace thong and let it fall from my hand onto the ground.

"Oops," I giggled, reaching forward where I put both my hands on his shoulders, pushing him down onto the bed beneath him.

The metal buckle protested as I unclasped his belt, tugging down his dark denim jeans and boxers in one swift motion, freeing him.

Shit.

His nerves were evident in his flaccid penis. But me being me, I never shied from a challenge and I had to work with him some more yet, to relax him into the right frame of mind.

I sat astride him with my hands by his head, where I leaned forward to kiss him. My lips locked with his as we formed a connection just strong enough to get a reaction from his body.

The heat between his legs improved when his eyes closed and I rubbed my naturally lubricated flesh over the length of his dick.

"Did you bring a condom?" I murmured in his ear, pulling his lobe into my mouth.

Safety was a top priority for me and while I was already on the pill, I still wanted all my clients to use a protection.

Bareback had the potential to earn more money, but I wasn't about to get saddled with an STI.

His eyes shot open. "Sorry, I didn't. I'm sorry."

With a tight smile, I grabbed my purse, pulling out a

standard-sized condom, tearing open the foil packet with my teeth.

I reached down and handled his soft pink length in my hand, where I pumped him with my fist before rolling on the condom down to his root.

He groaned a little in appreciation for my touch. "Jasmin, I'm not sure about—"

"Hey, it's OK Owen, I've got you."

Without further hesitation, I pushed the head of his penis inside me.

Like a corpse during rigor mortise, he lay stiff and uncooperative as expected, but with my patented hip roll, I ground into his body until finally his hands coiled my waist.

I offered him a seductive smile as I leant back on my heels to massage my own breasts for him.

When I closed my eyes, the music faded, and I was at my happy place; lay atop the golden white sands of the beach. I was making love to a nameless man who loved me back. Sand lodged in all our crevices but we didn't care as we had each other. My Prince Charming, my happy ever after. With an active imagination, my body warmed to my self-induced arousal, and it wouldn't be long before—

"Oh, wait, stop!" Owen whimpered.

My eyes shot open, catapulting me back to the reality of the musty hotel room. The intensity of the music reverberated through my chest just as he ejaculated, washing away any chance I had of an orgasm.

My lips thinned as I peered over at Hanna, who was receiving her second helping of oral sex since we entered the hotel room.

Owen remained listless beneath me. I pulled myself off him before his dick had finished pulsing.

He sat up with reddened cheeks. "Err, sorry about that."

I raised my hand to him. "Don't, it's fine." I smiled reassuringly as I gathering up my dress and underwear off the floor. "It's all good here. Thanks for the ride."

As I pulled on my thong and re-clasped my bra, Owen put himself away in a hurry and reached into his jeans pocket for his wallet. In doing so, a gold ring fell to the ground.

I crouched and collected it, placing it inside his palm.

"That's not what it looks like."

With my eyes fixed on his, I shook my head and smiled.

"You don't need to explain. It's none of my business."

His trembling hands pulled out a wad of notes and he placed them on the bed before gathering his belongings and leaving without saying goodbye.

Hulk raised his head between kisses with Hanna,

noticing Owen's departure. "Yo, Bud, where are you going?"

But Hanna wasn't one for sharing attention, so she refocused Hulk, turning his head to look at her.

"Forget him and eat my pussy." She bit his bottom lip. "Make me come again, Big Boy."

"Yes, Ma'am!" He growled, pushing her playfully back down onto the sheets.

My frown at Owen's hasty exit soon turned to a grin when I collected my earnings from the still-made bed and saw that he'd given me a tip. Perhaps a token gesture for me to not tell his wife?

After climbing back into my dress, I gathered my full purse and slipped on my shoes as I crept towards the door to make my escape, where Hanna didn't even notice me leave.

The hotel room door closed behind me when a figure appeared in the hallway.

A hooded man with a crooked smile eyed my body. "You're a hooker, yeah?" He shifted his weight, not able to keep still.

"Um, can I help you?" My heart rate increased, willing me to run.

"Yeah, you can help me." He stepped forward. "It's my

turn now."

With his heavy-set body leant into mine, he produced a keycard that unlocked the door where he pushed me back inside the room.

Ouch. Fuck—I stumbled. "I'm sorry, it doesn't work like that!"

In a fruitless attempt to gain distance, I took a step back when his blackened pupils caught my attention. He wiped the tip of his nose to rid of the remnants of white powder and licked the pads of his fingers.

My hard rule was never to accept pushy clients, especially those that were intoxicated.

"It works how I say it does, Bitch." He grabbed my forearm, pulling me towards his body.

The stench of his breath mixed with fear for my life made my stomach somersault. I tried to snatch myself away from him, but his restraint only tightened around my neck.

The music was so loud it drowned out my chances of Hanna realising my plight and after several failed escape attempts, hitting his chest and flailing my arms, he pushed me back into the centre of the room.

"Get your hands off me!" I feigned authority, but the quiver in my voice gave me away.

Hanna's eyes darted around the room when she heard my scream. "Jas? Shit!"

Her panic forced Hulk to scramble to his feet. "What's going on here, Dude?"

The stranger reached into his jacket. "Don't move," he snarled through gritted teeth as pulled out a knife. "Stay where you are. This is between me and the hooker."

My heart pounded in my ears, and my knees weakened as my vision blurred.

Hulk dived forwards, grappling the junkie to the ground, trying to disarm him. There was a fraught tussle, but the way the junkie's eyes shifted as he wielded the knife had me fearing the worst. As with what Hulk gained in muscle mass, he lacked in stamina, slowing his pace and rendering him useless.

Hanna and I remained frozen in time as we watched the men fighting with Hulk's overconfidence failing him.

"Help!" I called into the abyss. "Somebody help us!"

The sounds of their struggles and our chances of rescue drowned out by Hulk's playlist as the same song repeated.

"Ahh fuck!" Hulk dropped to the ground with a thud, clutching his side, where a pool of blood stained the carpet in an instant, flooding the floral pattern with a crimson tide.

"Oh God, no!" Hanna cried. Her face paled as our only chance of survival lay in a heap on the floor by her feet. "You stabbed him!"

My eyes darted to the exit. *Am I next? Should I chance it and run?*

The attacker stood tall over Hulk's helpless body, his chest heaving with laboured breathing. He wiped the blood from his mouth with the sleeve of his shirt and smiled.

"That's what I thought." He mumbled as he spat a blood infused ball of spit on the floor.

I made the mistake of taking a step which caught the junkie's attention. The look on his face altered when his eyes became fixed on mine.

Run! Now!

As I took another step forward, he snatched my body, enveloping me in his arms, using his body weight to overpower me.

With a feeble push against his chest, I fought to escape my captor, but he was much bigger and stronger than I was. His clammy hands manhandled my weak body onto the bed, using my wrists as an anchor, forcing me to lie down on the mattress.

At first, I flailed my legs, but my efforts were in vain;

I knew then that I couldn't escape my sealed fate and the sounds of the playlist etched into my mind as the tone of the song matched the scene I found myself in.

Hanna made a move in my peripheral vision where I caught her eyeing up the base of the lamp, but I shook my head in warning not to help me. Her getting stabbed wouldn't achieve anything other than two dead hookers.

My attacker clamped his blood stained knife between his yellow teeth, unzipped his fly, and fought with me to spread my legs.

"Open up Bitch!"

Dry from lack of arousal, my internal delicate flesh stung as he forced entry inside my unwilling body.

It was apparent then he was raping me, but with my experiences of the past, I had already become accustomed to such events, so I reverted to behaving the way I knew best. I lay motionless and quiet, staring him in the eyes, resolute, forcing him to face his decision to take my body without consent.

Struggling would only give him more enjoyment than he deserved, so I waited in silent acceptance as I took what he forced inside me. A stray tear rolling down my cheek was the only evidence of my suffering as I received his attack, with my best friend watching me.

There was a sound from the other side of the hotel door, someone in the corridor, but the music from inside our room distorted my perception of distance.

Who's there?

My skin prickled when the door swung open violently where the God-like creature in pimp form stood at the threshold of the room with his gun drawn, scanning the area to assess the threat.

Hanna, on her knees, cradled Hulk's head, rocking back and forth as she pointed toward the junkie. "Daddy, help us, please!"

Without missing a beat, the pimp came up behind my attacker and smacked him round the back of the head with his gun before the man's intoxicated body could retaliate. He fell to the floor instantaneously. He was out cold.

As I curled into a ball, the pimp holstered his weapon and followed the sound of the ear-splitting music towards the bed, where he turned down the volume. The sudden silence became deafening.

He peered at Hanna as his chest heaved with adrenaline.

"What the fuck happened in here?"

"Oh Daddy," she sobbed. "That crazy ass hole stabbed my

client and attacked my friend. I could've been next!"

As Hanna spoke of our tales of misfortune, I watched as the pimp absorbed the picture she painted.

But he seemed distracted by something as his eyes moved around the room and with a look of contempt he sniffed the air, and sniffed again before scowling.

Peering down at my attacker, he kicked him in his stomach.

"What the fuck is that smell? Did you shit yourself?"

Out like a light, not even a groan or grumble emitted from his lifeless body. *Is he dead?*

The pimp didn't rush when he turned his attention to me with tension in his jaw. "You good?" He asked in a detached tone. "You look kinda pale."

"Um, yes. I think so."

Just like that, my emotions checked out and went on vacation. I was in damage repair mode, where my only concern was that I couldn't take my eyes off the pimp and his sculpted tattooed body.

He glanced at me again as if he wanted to say something but refrained. Instead, he reached inside his jacket pocket and pulled out a slim line silver cigar case.

With a serious expression, he chose a cigar and gripped it between his teeth, offering the selection towards me.

"Here," he thrust it in my face. "Looks like you need one more than I do."

I shook my head, struggling to make eye contact with his intensity. "No thank you. I don't smoke."

He flicked the lid of his lighter, sparking a flame to heat the exposed tobacco, and took a deep inhale.

On the exhale, he extinguished the lighter flame with a snap close to the lid.

"Any other punk ass bitches need handlin' here or are we done?" He turned to Hanna as he adjusted his weapon in the waistband of his tracksuit pants.

"No. Thank you for this Daddy," she blushed with a girlish tone that I recognised instantly. She had feelings for him.

The pimp beckoned forward someone who waited at the door. "Tommy, get this piece of shit outta here."

Broadly built, with a hint of humanity behind his hard exterior; Tommy was a member of the pimps crew I recognised instantly from the club. He looked down at my attacker. "Do you want me to do the honours, Boss?"

The pimp nodded. "Yeah," he sneered. "Take your time with it, but check his pockets first. Any money he's got is mine for the inconvenience."

Tommy patted him down and produced several items

from his pockets. "There's a key card here, Boss," he said, holding up the evidence."

The pimp narrowed his eyes with a frown. "A key card to this room? Pay that old timer at the front desk a visit. He might need a meetin' with my gun."

"Yes, Boss," Tommy agreed as he dragged the junkie's limp body along the floor as the pimp turned to leave.

Hanna stumbled to her feet from the ground beside Hulk.

"Daddy, is my guy going to be alright?"

He leant over Hulk's body with arrogance, taking another puff of his cigar. "You alright there, Buddy?"

Hulk groaned in response, unable to speak.

The pimp smirked. "It's just a scratch, but take him to the emergency room and make sure he pays."

His ocean blue eyes took one last look at me with an intense glare as electricity remained charged between us. He leant towards me and for a brief second where I thought he might kiss me, but instead he pinched the torn spaghetti shoulder strap of my dress between his fingers.

"Shame," he said flatly as he let it fall.

His features gave nothing away, but I caught him glance at my cleavage.

With a closing exhale, he turned on his heels, stalking to

his exit, where the door closed firmly behind him.

My knees buckled as I released my breath, where Hanna caught a hold of me, pulling me into her body.

"I'm sorry that happened, Jassy," she stroked my hair. "Are you OK?"

I nodded. "Of course I am."

CHAPTER 2

"Get your hands off me!" I yelled into the pitch darkness. Shivering in the biting cold, I stood all alone.

The sound of the knife cutting through the air as my attacker approached me grew louder, and a warming trickle travelled down my sternum.

Wait—is that blood? *Am I dying?* Someone help me, please. Anyone?

I bolted upright in bed the next morning, breathless and with a cold sweat soaking my skin.

Wide awake; the dream I had faded into insignificance and I could no longer remember what had caused my body to react so violently, but my racing heart told me it probably involved last night.

My head was pounding from the heavy drinking, and the intense sense of being used lay prevalent in my bones.

I hadn't yet showered off the series of unfortunate events that had taken place at the hotel.

Shit—I didn't even remember getting home. Was I that drunk? Or that traumatised by it all, I couldn't decide which.

I stumbled out of bed and stretched my arms above my head to ease some of the built up tension trapped in my spine.

The events from my birthday celebration replayed unwelcome in my mind, not able to shake the image of the junkie who attacked me. Last night was an example of how girls like me wound up dead and had Hanna's pimp not saved me. God only knows where I would be now.

Gingerly, I wandered over to the shower cubicle in the far corner of my bedroom.

Along the way, I tripped over one of my discarded red heels and fell into the corner of my dressing table, banging my knee, bringing me back to the present with a thud.

"Ahh, damn it!" I mumbled with a grimace as the pain shot up my thigh to my stomach. Instinctively, I rubbed at the invisible wound that matched my feelings about last night while my scattered makeup and perfumes littered the floor like a representation of my thoughts.

On my knees, I scooped up what I could salvage, irritated, when I picked up a shard from my favourite perfume bottle smashed to pieces, mirroring my shattered soul.

With my legs crossed, like I was back at school, I'd just collected the last fragment of glass when my phone screen illuminated with a text.

< *Hanna* > *Are you OK Jasmin??*

In a defensive move, I flipped the phone over, knowing that Hanna would want to talk about what happened last night, but I wasn't ready yet, and maybe I never would be.

A gentle tap on the door snapped me out of my reverie.

"Jasmin? Can I come in, please?"

I knew it was Bob before he announced himself by the way he knocked so timidly.

Bob, my foster father, was on my safe list. Something about his voice relaxed the tension in my shoulders. But most importantly, we shared an element of trust.

The authorities placed me into the care of Bob and Nancy as a disturbed pre-teen where one of the biggest issues they faced was my hang-up about anyone using my real name, reserved only for the people I really trusted, and back then, I didn't trust anyone.

Jasmin was my mum's name and as a child who had just lost her mother, it was my way of keeping my connection with her amidst the abuse my step father forced upon me once she'd passed.

Over time, Jasmin became my powerful alter ego and nothing phased me while I embodied that character. But the sad fact was, my true self was a wilted rose within a bed of thorns that the psychologists tried and failed to bring back to life on more than one occasion.

My latest therapist, Dennis—he was number five—explained it as my 'coping mechanism', which was probably true. And we would analyse the life out of his theory at every boring session.

But really, it was simple: You either find a way to deal with your trauma or it'll consume you. I didn't have time to dwell on my past when I had clients' needs to serve.

"Hey, Jassy, I don't think you heard me knocking." Bob stepped inside my room cautiously, as if there might be an invisible trap. "Can I come in?"

"Sure." I continued to busy myself with clearing the mess on the carpet. "I already folded the laundry."

One thing I appreciated about Bob was that he respected my boundaries. With discretion, he tiptoed in and sat on my bed, where he tapped the cover to invite me to sit next to him.

He understood me well enough not to interrogate me, but I could tell he wanted information.

"This isn't about laundry, Jassy. I heard a bit of a ruckus

just now and wanted to check in on you." He looked down at my scuffed knee with a marred brow. "You were out until late last night. Nancy and I were worried."

With my chin down, I glared at him through my lashes, "Bob, don't talk shit. Nancy wants me out of here, and you know it!"

He didn't argue with me. I wasn't wrong.

"Listen, Jasmin." He adjusted his position, disturbing the mattress coils. "I'm here for you. You realise that, don't you? Whatever happens, I would like to think that after all these years, you would consider us friends."

I smiled weakly in response. *Friends?* I suppose he was the closest I'd ever had to a friend, besides Hanna.

Bob stood, as if understanding my silence was his dismissal. He turned to me and raised his fingertips to touch his lips, where he kissed them and blew the token my way.

I raised my hand and caught the kiss as we shared a smile.

Even though I played hardball with Bob, he was a decent man who'd never tried to harm me.

"Catch you later, Jassy."

As he left the room, I let out a breath my subconscious

had been holding in, trying to conceal my recurring visions of last night.

Bob couldn't find out what happened to me. It would break him, and that was the thing about him—he wasn't an evil man, but he was guilty by association of being married to his hideous wife, Nancy.

I couldn't wait for the day that I could flip her the bird one last time and leave for good.

My phone buzzed by my feet. This time, it was a call.

Please don't be Troy, please. I can't deal with weirdos today.

Thankfully, a photo of Hanna's beautiful, smiling face lit up the screen. She still wouldn't be able to convince me to talk about last night, not in a million years.

"Han—"

"Baby girl, I wanted to check you were good! I texted you?"

"Sorry about that. I was just—"

"Anyway, listen," she interjected. "My guy paid up! I got three hundred dollars in my hand right now. Can you believe it? I need to go shopping, so I'll pick you up in ten minutes, OK?"

Holy shit, she's good.

"Wait, Han—is Hulk OK?"

"Yeah, thank God. I took him to the emergency room like Daddy said. It was a deep cut but didn't catch his organs." The line fell silent as I heard her rummaging. "Anyway, girl, I'm on my way. Get dressed, because I know your ass is still in your underwear."

With very little time before Hanna arrived, I attempted to complete the initial task I'd set myself.

I turned on the shower and allowed the room to fill with steam before climbing in to cleanse my soul, washing off yesterday's tormenting memories. With hesitation, I washed between my thighs expecting to feel tenderness, but thankfully not a physical injury remained.

Resilient by nature, this was a setback for sure, but not one I wouldn't bounce back from, eventually.

In true Hanna style, she sounded her horn eight minutes after we hung up the call.

I grabbed my phone and bag, slipped on some white sneakers to complement my denim skirt and pink cropped baby tee, and ran to Hanna's car, hoping to avoid the troll on the way out.

No sooner had I closed the car door, she was ready to talk.

"Girl, I got *laid*," she rung out every syllable.

"I know," I giggled. "Pretty sure he ate you out more times than he'd had hot meals."

"He fucked so good. Shit! Shame we didn't get to finish what we started—Are you sure you're OK, by the way? I mean, I realise we're not big talkers."

"Yeah, I'm fine, Han. My thirty-second ride on Owen was *so* worth it." My sarcasm gave away my feeling of disappointment. Disappointment that my best friend was better at this than I was.

She started the car's engine successfully on the second attempt and, with a stiff turn of the wheel, she manoeuvred her way into the L.A traffic.

"Did your guy pay?" She arched a questioning brow.

"Yeah, he did. Thanks for sorting that for me."

She peered at me with a smile. "No problem. One last time, you good?"

"Yeah, I'm good. I swear."

"As long as you're sure, but if you need to talk, I'm here for you. We all need help one way or another, Chloe."

Hanna was the only person who used my real name, reserved exclusively for when we weren't working with clients. It had taken me a couple of years before I trusted her enough with the responsibility, but she understood the weight behind it and was honoured when I gave her that privilege.

What Hanna was always good at was talking about other people's feelings, dissecting and understanding them in great detail to distract from her own. But when it came to looking after herself; she was a closed book.

"We could talk about *your* feelings for once?" I teased, nudging her shoulder, trying to defuse her building second-hand rage.

"Pfft, good one," she smiled. "But seriously, though, just because we are whores doesn't mean we aren't human, and it pisses me off when men think they can't rape us."

"Mm-hm," I nodded in agreement, but just hearing that four letter word sent chills down my spine.

It was true there was an ever-present stigma that rape didn't exist in our world. I wasn't the first victim and I wouldn't be the last.

I peered over at her beautiful side profile, noticing her brows knitted together as she kept her focus straight ahead, and I wondered what part of her past she was replaying in her mind's eye. Regardless of us being best friends, we never spoke about our baggage, neither of us wanting to drag the other down with our shit, so I let her brood for a while, and we drove the rest of the way in comfortable silence.

We arrived at the mall just before lunchtime, where parking was chaos, so we ended up on the far side of the parking lot.

"Lets grab a coffee first. My hangover needs it." Hanna said as she secured the strap of her Gucci purse around her neck. "We'll go to Coffee Lounge."

The coffee shop located at the entrance to the mall was busier than I'd ever seen it, and we struggled to get a table for the best part of twenty minutes.

As this wasn't our first time, I knew Hanna's order already. A small vanilla iced latte with cream and sugar.

"What are you having, Chloe?" She asked, while clicking her fingers at the server to grab their attention.

"Ooh, let me think, um—"

"A small vanilla iced latte with cream and sugar." Hanna began reeling off her list. "My friend here will have the same, but with a cream cheese bagel."

"Gotcha. It'll be over to you in five minutes," the friendly young woman said with all American charm.

My face twisted in discomfort. "Ugh, I feel nauseous," I announced, clutching my stomach as I pushed my plate away containing a half eaten cream cheese bagel.

"You're not pregnant, are you?" Hanna smirked into her drink.

"Jeez, imagine?" My eyes widened at the prospect. "Thankfully, he didn't get a chance to come before your pimp saved me."

"Mm-hm." She eyed me speculatively as she sipped her drink with her pinkie finger extended.

My lips thinned into a line as I watched her silently judge me.

Fortunately, for the sake of our trip, she didn't pursue it further, but I knew she wanted to give me a hard time about joining her pimp again.

As she licked the cream from her top lip, Hanna rose from her seat with money on her mind. "This is my treat. I'll pay up and we'll get out of here."

Arm in arm, we strolled through the mall, looking for ways to spend Hanna's cash, and that would most definitely start with a new outfit.

Our skirts were a little too short and tops a little too tight, but the way we dressed never failed to attract male attention, so there wasn't a reason to fix something that wasn't broken.

Hanna's first destination of choice was a clothing store I often walked past but never entered. Eye watering price tags hanging from the mannequins always dissuaded me from embarrassing myself.

"What do you think?" Hanna asked as she held up a denim miniskirt and bralette top in front of her for me to scrutinise.

"Hmm, the skirt, yes, but what about a different colour in the top?" I put my index finger to my lips to contemplate the options. "That deep orange colour behind you would suit your skin tone perfectly."

"Yeah, but my tits look better in this one." She held up the original top again.

"OK yeah, good point. Go with that one then."

Boldness being Hanna's middle name, she tried on the skirt right there on the shop floor as if there wasn't another person around.

In reality, there were at least five women browsing nearby, all of whom pretended like they didn't notice, but their side eyed glares told a different story.

This was absolutely something Hanna would do. She had so much confidence in her body and she had every right to—she was unquestionably beautiful.

"So, are you going to hook up with Hulk again?" I asked, trying and failing to cover her modesty by holding up the tiny bits of fabric around her middle.

She grinned when she replayed a private memory. "He took my number, so I hope so. His dick was massive, and he knew exactly what to do with it. My clit is still throbbing now."

"Jesus, Hanna," I looked over my shoulder, "you'll get us kicked out!"

"Ahh, who cares! This place needs a bit of livening up, anyway." She waved her hand theatrically, rolling her eyes.

I shook my head and handed her the rest of her bags as we made our way to the cashier.

"You always get lucky with clients," I mused as we queued for the next assistant.

"Well, that's not true, is it?"

"Come on Han. I can't remember the last time I got laid by a decent guy who wasn't a complete weirdo or at least had some stamina."

"By weirdo, do you mean that phone sex guy?" She giggled in remembrance of the figurine story I'd told her about previously.

"You mean Troy? You know it's bad when he isn't even

the worst."

Hanna pulled me in for a side on hug. "They'll never have stamina with you, Chloe. You're way too hot."

Her words of affirmation never failed to evoke a smile from me. "You always say the right thing."

As we exited the store, Hanna pointed to a boutique with modern signage over the door. The window was stocked with gorgeous pieces of jewellery of varying kinds.

"I need some new jewellery; let's go in here," she wandered over, pulling my sleeve for me to follow.

My senses tingled in response to the uncomfortable atmosphere as eyes stalked our every move whilst we perused the place. It was a classy store, but was it really that obvious that we weren't?

"Come on Han. That assistant hasn't stopped staring at us since we walked in." I sighed as she tried on her fourth bracelet option.

"Oh yeah? Wanna give her something to look at?"

I knew exactly what she meant by the wicked glint in her eye, but I didn't want to encourage it in the shopping mall.

"Behave yourself Hanna! Hulk set you on fire, didn't he?"

"You've no idea Chloe. The way he licked my ass as he played with my clit. Oh. My. God. It paralysed me."

She was always guaranteed to provide too much information.

A tall man in uniform stood abruptly in our path. He seemed irritated and bad tempered. "Hold on a minute, ladies."

Who's he?

Hanna stepped forwards with confrontation on her mind.

"Can we help you?" She snarled as she looked him up and down with attitude.

His walkie-talkie emitted white noise in the background and he turned down the volume to berate us.

"You ladies have been on my radar since you entered this mall today. I've seen *you* in here before," he honed in on Hanna with narrowed eyes, "didn't I kick you out last time for stealing?"

"No, that was my sister," Hanna lied, fluttering her lashes.

She was an only child, and hearing that she had stolen again was a painful reminder of her living in the past, as she only reverted to that behaviour when something bothered her.

He adjusted the way his pants sat around his thick waist.

"I want you to leave quietly. Don't let me catch you in

here again."

"Yes, Sir," I said, grabbing Hanna's arm, "come on, we're out of here."

The sun was warm, and the heat kissed my skin as we exited the air-conditioned building.

As we approached the car, I seized the opportunity.

"Han, what was that back there? Is it true? Have you been stealing again?"

"You've known me long enough to understand what I'm like, Chloe. Sometimes I self sabotage. I can't help it. It's like I have the money, but there's a part of me that craves the excitement. I guess I just love fucking shit up for myself."

She unlocked the car doors, and we climbed in. We could both relate to each other in that respect. Self sabotage was a difficult trait to rid yourself of once it had taken a hold.

We drove along the freeway in contemplative silence back towards my foster parents' house.

With Hanna's latest incident on my mind, I couldn't help but replay all the shitty situations I'd gotten myself into over the years. The rape induced nausea was most prevalent, and it was clear that my subconscious was begging me to heed its warning and listen—for a change. This time I couldn't seem to shake it off.

"Hanna, I was thinking. You know what happened with that junkie last night? Well, the thought of putting myself in that situation again—I'm not sure I can."

She side eyed me, listening to my every word. "Really?"

I nodded. "I need your advice. What do you think I should do about it?"

She sighed heavily as she prepared herself for the same story. "You need a pimp, Chloe. I've told you this countless times before."

"Yeah, I know, but this time I'm listening."

"You remember what happened to me with that psycho? When was that? Like a year ago? It's been that long, yet it still bothers both of us. That fracture to my jaw was the last straw, and I'm so glad I made the right choice in joining Daddy. You've seen him in action. He's amazing."

She'd used this anecdote before—and she was right—but I habitually didn't listen to people trying to help me.

"See, that's the thing Han, had your daddy not saved me, I'd probably be dead."

I could sense within myself that I was getting emotional, and Hanna felt it, too. And as we rarely exposed ourselves deeply enough to evoke any kind of emotional response, we were in uncharted waters.

"Look Chloe, before I came to collect you today, Daddy

asked if you'd made a decision about auditioning for him."

My mouth fell open in disbelief. "He did? Why didn't you tell me?"

"Because you made it very clear already that you didn't want to."

Shit.

"Oh." I looked at my knotted fingers. "What did you say to him?"

"I was honest and said I didn't think so. Have you changed your mind?"

I ran my tongue over my teeth as I processed the simple question that had a yes or no answer. Eventually, I nodded, "I think so."

"OK, If you want to do this, then let's do it. I'll tell Daddy you want to audition."

My heart rate picked up pace, but why? Was it the prospect of gaining protection from him, or was it more to do with the fact that his face had popped into my mind at least a dozen times since I'd opened my eyes this morning.

"You will? Thanks, Hanna. I'm nervous all of a sudden."

"Not gonna lie to you, Babe. The audition process is intimidating, for sure, but he's so fucking hot. I'd do anything for that man."

The way she spoke about the pimp surprised me. He was

stunning to look at, but I imagined that was where the plus points would end, and I thought Hanna was more street smart than to fall for someone like him.

"From the little I've seen of him, I can see why. He's gorgeous. Have you got the feels?"

"Nah, I've no chance with him. He's the unobtainable kind; my favourite," she giggled.

She made a left instead of a right and instantly I wanted to vomit.

"Um, Han, where are we going?"

"His place. It's only a few blocks away."

Suddenly, the seat belt felt too tight over my chest. "Now? As in right now?"

"Yeah, it's on the way to yours, anyway."

A swell of butterflies formed in my stomach, and adrenaline took hold of me. But this seemed like the right thing to do. *Right?*

As we approached, the properties became more and more extravagant with imposing facades and gated tree lined driveways. We were most definitely in the better part of town, and this pimp was successful.

She pulled her car into the vast driveway dressed with ornate wrought-iron gates at the wide open entranceway.

There were security guards posted around the place, but

it was surprising just how accessible his home was.

I gasped in amazement. "Wow, this is beautiful."

The house itself stood within a very impressive-looking manicured garden, straight out of a celebrity magazine.

"I know, right? I'm so lucky to live here."

There were several men wandering around the grounds —that was more like a parking lot—tending to its well-stocked luxury vehicles of all colours, shapes and sizes.

We parked up in one of the few remaining spaces available where Hanna's car looked very much out of place.

My heart thumped stronger than ever. *Oh God, we're here. We're actually going to do this.*

"You ready for this?" She asked, studying my features carefully.

I stared up at the intimidating exterior white walls of the house and wondered what he might be doing on the other side.

"Not really, but we're here now."

"OK, Girl, listen up."

Hanna began preparing me for what might lie ahead. From the little information I retained from her thirty-second boot camp, I would need to pass the audition in order to become one of Daddy's girls.

OK. I can do this.

She unclipped her seatbelt. "Let me just go and check that he still wants to give you a chance. I'll be right back."

Fuck—I hadn't thought about him changing his mind! *What if he says no?*

As I watched Hanna leave for the mansion, I ran my clammy hands up and down my thighs, nervous at the thought of his reaction.

What if he rejected me? What if he was joking at the club and I was being pranked? *Are they all laughing at me now?*

My self-esteem couldn't handle that thought and the longer I waited, the more I wanted to hop in the driver's seat and haul ass.

All I could do in that moment was busy myself on my phone, scrolling through social media stories of celebrities I didn't care about. Maybe I could Google the pimp?

I was just about to send out a search party when Hanna finally emerged from within with a victorious grin on her face. The meeting with the man in question had seemingly gone well.

"He said yes. Come on!" She threw open the car door, grabbed my hand, and pulled me out. "Get into character now. You'll need your best moves, Jasmin."

She escorted me over to the house, giving me no time to mentally prepare myself.

"All you need to remember is not to freak out. Do as he asks, and it'll be cool, OK?"

"Yes," I nodded.

My hurried footsteps crunched over the golden decorative gravel beneath my sneakers as we walked fast paced along the driveway towards the house. It would be the same sound my heart would make if the pimp crushed my dreams of getting the protection I needed.

The imposing front door opened just as Hanna reached for the handle where an intoxicated female stood before us in heels and black satin underwear; nothing more.

She held a glass of pale liquid with a disorientated look marring her features. The track marks in her arms were evidence enough to suspect she'd recently injected heroin.

"Hurry your asses whores! I don't got all day!" The deep, throaty male voice coming from inside projected around his mansion.

Without a moment's hesitation, Hanna took charge over the threshold into the lion's den.

I'm gonna shit my pants. Why do I need to fart again?

Hanna was as nervous as I was, which was

disconcerting, to say the least. I could tell she was when she tucked her hair behind her ear. Pressure mounted at the idea it was likely because she had vouched for me, and, if I messed this up, she too would suffer the consequences.

But all I could do was give it my best shot.

We halted before him, side by side, within his grand living room for our next instruction where he eyed us speculatively, raising from a richly upholstered plush leather sofa to greet us.

"Welcome to my crib," he said with a shrewd smile as he held out his arms wide, gesturing towards the surrounding finery.

It was a lovely house for sure, and he made it obvious he was the reason behind its success, but we weren't here for a house tour. This was business.

I peered skyward at his handsome face as he looked down at me. What a gorgeous man; even more so in daylight. But focus wasn't an attribute I possessed under pressure and right now, my head was about to explode.

The scent of his aftershave caressed my senses when his hand remodelled his tousled, coiled black curls on top of his head. The action accentuated his biceps' muscle, uncovering a hint at his all over body tattoos.

Without question, money oozed from his pores, and a confident arrogance dripped off his tongue. "Aight, let's get straight down to business. I'm a busy man. She says you changed your mind and want a daddy? And I could use more hot bitches. Shit's been slidin' round here recently." He focused his sneer at a pale-faced woman who lounged on the sofa behind him.

Shit—do I say something? But what would I even say?

Hanna tucked her hair behind her ear again. "Thank you for giving my friend a chance."

Hmm, something like that would have been fine...

"OK bitches," he rubbed his hands together. "Let's see what you got."

Hanna and I looked at each other with wide eyes and no clue.

The worrying part was Hanna didn't seem to understand the assignment either, and it unsettled both of us. I'd hoped for more guidance than this on one of the biggest days of my life.

While he waited, the pimp took his seat next to the pale woman. Lighting a cigar, he crossed his ankle over the opposite knee and his free arm rested on the back of the couch as he took a long drag of his Cuban. "Today hoes."

We kick started events by undressing each other,

not really knowing what he preferred from his lack of direction.

It was a peculiar out-of-body experience as I watched my own shaking fingers pop open the buttons of Hanna's shirt as though they were controlling themselves.

Am I breathing too loud? Can he hear me?

But once down to our underwear, he stood up again with excitement.

"OK, so far, I like what I see. Stop there." He stalked towards us and leant into Hanna's ear, where he kissed her neck. "I wanna watch you lick your friend out."

Hanna's body responded to his lips. "Yes, Daddy," she moaned in cooperation with an air of giddiness.

Without so much as a moment to breathe, he placed his hand on top of her head and pushed her down onto her knees before me.

It was he who hooked his fingers inside my lace panties and pulled them over my rear and down my legs to fall at my feet.

He stepped back with his arms folded, his cigar between his teeth as Hanna's expert tongue circled my clitoris with my ass cheeks in the palms of her hands.

But as Hanna worked her magic, a couple of new females entered the room and sat down at Daddy's feet. Our audience was growing.

What are they, dogs?

One of the new members to join the room, a blonde with fake breasts and misplaced confidence, pulled down his pants and took his dick into her hand, where she pushed him to the back of her throat.

My eyes honed in on her uninvited intimacy with him, my mind struggling to stay focused on my scene with Hanna.

His response to her bold action didn't attract his attention away from us. He cupped her head in his hand, but his eyes remained fixed on mine.

After a minute, the pimp seemed impatient. Pushing the blonde away from him, he took his seat again, and she followed.

"Enough on the pussy." He called to Hanna. "Now lick your friend's asshole."

Wait—this is new. We haven't played this hard together before...

It was clear by the fire in his eyes that the pimp was enjoying this performance we were giving him, providing him inspiration to create an act for us to perform for him. And it was becoming a turn-on for me, too.

The girl milking his dick didn't stop when she knelt between his open legs to pick up where she left off. But irrespective of her trying, he wasn't paying her the consideration she so badly craved.

As I straddled over Hanna, who lay in waiting amidst the deep pile cream carpet, she gave me a reassuring nod. She'd prepared me for the unexpected and I realised then that she'd also done this at her own audition.

In working my way up to it mentally, I closed my eyes and, as instructed, she licked the rim of my anus.

"New girl, grab your fine ass tiddies while she rims you."

At the pimps behest, I caressed myself, pulling on my nipples to stand them to attention for the master's pleasure.

His powerful presence made me so hot for him and I desperately wanted to please him, but it didn't go unnoticed that this was a power move, pushing me to my limit to see how much control he could relinquish over me.

He turned to face the gathered crowd, where silence fell upon the room while they waited for his order. "Everybody out," he commanded with unshakable authority.

As the room cleared, leaving just the pale-faced girl on the couch, he took me by the hands and helped me to my feet, where he brought us both forward to stand before them. Who was this woman? And why was she allowed to stay?

On closer inspection, she was pretty. With long, thick, dark hair, she had soft freckles dusting her nose and apples of her cheeks, giving her a girlish charm. At some point, she was beautiful, but this girl held a world of pain in her soul.

As we waited, the pimp, whose name I'd yet to learn, clasped his hands together in conclusion of our opening act.

"OK, this is how it's gonna be. New girl, I'm gonna fuck you."

Holy shit.

It was at that moment I realised just how much I'd wanted him to say that from the start. Physical attraction never caught me off guard, but with this man, well, he'd completely disarmed me.

When the pimp stripped off his bottom half, he revealed what I had suspected earlier when the blonde gagged; he was well endowed beyond anything I could have possibly imagined. He must've had at least eight inches to work with, maybe a little more, and his prominent erection was hard to ignore.

Freckles tore open a condom packet and passed the

rubber to him. It seemed well rehearsed and completely natural between them as he silently rolled it on.

Perhaps they were a couple? *Ugh, I hope not.*

The pimps' warm hands prickled my exposed skin when he grabbed me by the waist and turned me to face away from him.

My breathing hitched as I waited in anticipation for the next move.

Starting at the nape of my neck, he ran his fingers along the length of my spine until he reached the base. There, he bent me over to part my cheeks. His finger trailed the pathway from spine to rear and he pushed the tip inside my puckered entrance, teasing the sensitive opening.

Then he withdrew, putting one hand on my waist and the other wrapped around my chest as he pulled my body towards his so his torso connected with my back. His throbbing dick slid between my thighs and burrowed through my labia as he entered my vagina.

Before I could acclimatise, his speed quickly gained pace as heat radiated from him when he took my breast in his hand, massaging the fullness. My whole body thrust forward and backward with the intense motion as he took me for his pleasure.

As I closed my eyes, I was back on the beach, only this

time, the pimp was there with me. His naked body lay in waiting for me to accept. We were happy. He wanted me.

His hand against my chest pulled my ear to his lips. "Are you on the pill, slut?" he panted.

"Yes."

He withdrew and my eyes shot open, bringing me back to reality.

"Take the condom off and suck my dick, you little whore." His eyes burned bright with an intense orgasm waiting in the wings of our orchestrated masterpiece.

Without question, I dropped to my knees, where I peeled off the condom to reveal his thick, hot cock.

He ejaculated a bead of pre come when his aroused flesh met with my warm breath. I licked the tip, tasting his offering that provoked my body to react.

As I peered up at him through my lashes, I pulled the entire length to the back of my throat when he released a soft moan of appreciation.

Before long, he took my chin between his fingers and pulled me to stand. It was then I thought he might kiss me, but he turned me to face away from him again, where he parted my cheeks and slid his dick inside my lubricated flesh once more.

As before, he started by increasing his tempo, but this

time it was different and he quickly slowed, savouring the moment with me. Our skin to skin contact no longer confined within latex only increased the intensity of our connection.

Oh, God, yes!

My insides stretched when the temperature increased, and then he released a primal groan. "Fuck!" he moaned as he leant into my back, his orgasm consuming him.

When he withdrew, yearning took a hold of him and he rubbed the head of his soaked penis against the entrance of my vagina, pushing the soft edge inside again with a need to experience more.

Fuck, this is so hot. I'm so close. Don't stop.

But then he pulled away completely.

"It's your turn now, slut. Stop playin' with your cunt and get over here on my dick."

The pimp grabbed hold of Hanna forcefully by the rear. He turned her around, so she too faced away from him, but this time he parted her cheeks with different intentions.

He held out his hand silently for Freckles to furnish him with a fresh condom.

Our eyes met, and the blackness of his pupils expanded as he thrust the foil packet against my chest.

"Roll it on for me."

Every move I made caused the swollen flesh between my legs to throb. His semen filling my insides took my threatening orgasm so close to the edge.

With a shy smile I did as instructed, and he gave me a nod of appreciation that probably meant more to me than it did him.

Hanna yelped at first when she received his relentless erection inside her anus, but knew better than to make too much of a fuss about it. Like a trooper, she bravely took the charge, and with those inches, that would have been no mean feat.

Being her best friend, I needed to help my girl out and save her some discomfort by getting him to come quicker. One of the oldest tricks in the hooker manual, it was something we girls regularly had to pull out of the bag to help a friend in need.

I crouched before him and cradled his balls in my hand. His immediate response was a slowing of his pace, where his banging rhythm on Hanna's ass dwindled as he enjoyed what I was offering him.

That's it, Baby. Come for me.

He withdrew for a few beats while I sucked on his testicles.

"Shit!" he closed his eyes. "Don't stop."

His penis throbbed in rhythm with me and his hand raked through my hair in a gesture that surprised me. He was more intimate and less rough than I was expecting.

When he slammed back into her for a final time, he came again just as hard as before.

He was breathless when he eventually gathered himself.

"OK bitches, I'm liking it. Good job bringin' me somethin' new to work with. New girl, I'll be your daddy. I want more of this when I say I want it. The way my dick feels after that, it's gonna be regular. I call, you come, got it? I don't play games and bitches better act correct or get corrected."

Inwardly, I was doing a celebratory dance with maracas.

"Thank you, Daddy." I beamed.

Hanna turned to face him, reminding us she was still there when she cupped his head in her hands as she kissed him passionately. His appreciation for her was evident in the way he kissed her back, squeezing her ass again as though he were restraining himself from going again.

Her confidence around him was enviable, and I wished then I had experienced his lips against mine. But I guess she wasn't new to this like I was.

Daddy sauntered across the room and sat back down on

his intimidating couch that matched his personality.

He re-lit his cigar and frowned as he thought, "What's that accent, new girl?" He looked at me quizzically.

"Oh, um—I'm from England originally, but I've lived here for years now. It seems I can't shake off the accent."

He shook his head. "Nah, don't shake it off. Clients will love that shit. Hey, say somethin' British."

Shit, this is embarrassing. Nervously, I rubbed my upper arm as I tried to conjure some inspiration.

"Um, would you like a cup of tea, Sir?"

"Haha, yes!" He clapped restlessly in his seat. "I love that shit!"

It was the first time I'd seen any sort of emotion from him that exposed his perfect white teeth.

He released a plume of smoke into the air. "How old are you?"

"Um, I'm twenty-one."

"Sweet. Listen whores, it's time you two step, I got other shit to do. Go make me some cash."

He put his arm around Freckles, who was withdrawn and lifeless. If I hadn't seen her moving earlier, I could've mistaken her for comatose.

With his attention focused on his couch partner, he kissed her as Hanna and I watched on awkwardly.

How is she resisting his charms like that?

"Go with the new girl on her first job. Show her how Daddy likes it done."

"Who, me Daddy?" Hanna asked, unsure who he was addressing as he consumed himself with matters that didn't concern us.

He snapped his head in Hanna's direction. "Yes, you."

It didn't take a genius to work out that our time was up and we gathered our clothes whilst simultaneously leaving the room.

The pang of jealousy in seeing him with that woman incessantly reared its ugly head the closer I made it to the exit.

"Hold up bitches!" He growled.

Shit! We turned to face him again.

"You'll get a text from the agency with client details. Perform good, make me big money and bring it back to me. 70/30 split. Anybody gives you shit, you call me."

He rubbed on the woman's thigh and nibbled on her neck. His erection was prominent in his pants, but it was a waste. She just didn't seem interested.

As we made it back into the marble tiled hallway, the imposing front door swung open, and a very attractive suited man strolled in as if he had a free pass to enter whenever he pleased.

Instinctively, I placed my arm over Hanna's chest. This guy stank of cop.

She stumbled forward from the force of my sudden, unexpected hold on her.

"Woah, Jasmin, it's cool. That's Daddy's brother." She smiled coyly when she made eye contact with him.

I'd not seen her blush solely from her physical attraction to someone before.

Not only had I just had sex with hot stuff number one, but I was now standing in front of his equally delicious brother. I could've passed out on the spot.

With chocolate brown curly hair, his features weren't too dissimilar to the pimp's, except for a loose curl that fell just over his emerald green eyes and a softness to his stance that invited warmth.

"Are you new?" He asked with kind eyes. "I haven't seen you here before. I've an excellent memory and would've remembered seeing someone as beautiful as you."

I nodded with my mouth ajar.

"I'm Daniele Giannetti. Pronounced Daniel in English." He held out his masculine hand that had a sprinkle of dark hair on the back. "But everyone calls me Dan."

"Hi, um, I'm Jasmin."

All I could think about in that moment was the potential opportunity of fucking both brothers together, but the longer we shared the space, something in his smile instantly relaxed me.

"Wait, Giannetti?" I mused out loud. "That name sounds familiar. I'm sure I've heard it somewhere before?"

"Giannetti haulage," Hanna chipped in, "Dan is the owner of that company."

"That's where I've heard it! You have a commercial on the local radio?"

I looked into his beautiful green eyes that were looking intently right back at mine.

"Yep, that's the one." He bowed playfully as though he was the main character at the encore of a theatre play. His personality was in stark contrast to the pimps.

"That you limp dick?" The pimp yelled affectionately from the living room, effectively ending our conversation.

"Yeah, it's me." Dan didn't seem to mind his brother's jibe. He came across as the more chilled of the two.

"Keep your dick out of my hoes!"

Dan rolled his eyes. "Nice to meet you Jasmin," he smiled genuinely with a curt nod as he walked by me towards the living room.

My cheeks filled like a balloon as I released the breath I was holding in.

"He's hot, right?" Hanna smirked as we walked back to the car.

"He is just everything!"

"I know! Rich as fuck, too." Her eyes glistened with the unspoken possibilities.

"Is he single?"

"Yeah," she nodded enthusiastically, "he is."

CHAPTER 3

The very next day, I received my first client text from the agency following my audition with the pimp.

Hanna and I were just finishing our ritual morning coffee and cake at our favourite bistro in downtown L.A when my phone buzzed.

< Agency > Lakeside Hotel 12:30PM

"You got a text?" She asked as she balled up her napkin, throwing it towards the trash can a few feet away.

"Yeah, why am I nervous all of a sudden?"

As I stared at the screen, I twirled a loose strand of my hair around my fingers with apprehension. Each letter that formed a word contributed to the anxious ball of anxiety in my stomach that made our arrangement official.

"Don't be, Babe. Under Daddy's orders, we got this one together. Where is it?" She narrowed her eyes as she peered at the screen.

"Hmm, Lakeside Hotel? I know that one. Let's finish up and make our way over, shall we?"

"Um, yeah, I guess."

She threw back the last few drops of her coffee. "Tell you what, I know you're nervous, so I'll call my girl Sharon from the agency and see what this client wants."

Her long acrylic nails tapped against the phone screen as she dialled the number for the agency from memory. Hanna's confidence never failed to impress me.

"Hey Sharon girl, it's Hanna. What's the deets on Jasmin's first client? For real? OK, bye."

Her face twisted as though she'd chewed a lemon and its curd, and my throat swelled in response.

"What? Is it bad?"

She shook her head, disturbing her black bouncy curls.

"Apparently, your guy just wants a new girl with no experience. That's why they picked you."

Oh. "But I do have experience, though?"

"We know that, Jas, but the girls in the office don't. Come to think of it, I'm not sure Daddy does either, so keep that to yourself, OK?"

"I mean sure, I guess."

She placed her hand in front of my face. "Stop overthinking it. Just do as I say and you can't go wrong."

"I'm not I swear! So is this how it'll work? I'll just get a text?"

"Yep," she nodded. "Never miss an appointment or

Daddy will get pissed."

I looked at my unread messages, where, ironically Troy had only just replied to my message from two days ago.

"But what about my old regulars?"

"Ditch 'em. Don't ever go with a client that hasn't come through the agency. The whole point of this is that they get vetted first."

"Of course, yeah." I chewed my lip. "Gotcha."

Blessed with another beautiful day in L.A, the sun shone brightly and the heat emitting from its flame invigorated my body, giving me some hope for what lay ahead.

We cruised to our destination a little over the speed limit in Hanna's car that didn't have air conditioning. The temperature within the cabin was stifling, making it hard to catch my breath.

As though she could read my mind, Hanna side eyed me.

"Crack a window if you're hot. We'll be there in a minute."

I wanted to tell her to take her time. There was no rush. Out of my depth and incredibly overwhelmed, the last thing I wanted this morning was to see a client. So much was riding on this performance, especially now I also had to pretend I was new to the job.

Jasmin; my alter ego was the character I relied upon to give my best performance, so when faced with the prospect of leaving her at the door, Chloe would need to take charge. But as she would have to be dragged from under the bed by her ankles, kicking and screaming, my sense of discomfort was taking its toll on me.

"You good over there?" Hanna asked, sensing my unravelling.

"Mm-hm."

"Good," she said with a smile, "because we're here."

The exterior of the ironically named Lakeside without a body of water in sight was just as I expected. Set back from a main road, with a small parking area to the front, the building was plain and uninviting, with painted cream stone-wash walls and little in the way of welcoming decor. This wasn't somewhere you would choose as a base for a family vacation, but for all intents and purposes, it just about met the criteria.

The hotel's reception desk was easy enough to find, where a pleasant young man behind the counter waited for our arrival with a winning smile.

He wore a mustard coloured uniform with a matching

cap and bowtie. His look was in stark contrast to my expectation but appreciated his effort none the less.

"Good afternoon ladies, and welcome to Lakeside, the home of affordable luxury."

"Hi Honey," Hanna purred as she leant over his desk, "my husband has booked a room for me and my sister while he's on a business trip. He'll be along shortly."

My lips thinned as I watched him nodding. As a spectator to the lie, it was obvious there was no husband, and we were most certainly not sisters, but this guy would have seen and heard it all.

"All checked in, here's your access card. Your husband has already made payment for the room. You will find the elevator is just down the corridor where you'll need the top floor. Enjoy your stay."

In high spirits, we trotted down the corridor arm in arm until we reached the elevator, where I noticed the problem immediately.

Red and white cation tape covered the entrance with a handwritten sign that confirmed my suspicion.

"Oh God, not the stairs!" I grumbled when I read the misspelt directions.

"It's not a big deal," Hanna grabbed my hand, "it can be the warm up."

"Holy fuck, that's a lot of stairs!" Hanna whistled as she peered upwards at the bank of steep steps spanning several flights. "We need the top floor, huh?"

"Yes Hanna, the very top." I took off my heels in preparation. "Now you're just realising why I'm so pissed?"

Half way up the fourth flight, my throat burned, as my breathing snagged in my chest. Hanna's heaving rib cage matched mine. "I can literally hear you spiralling, Chloe. Can you stop for a minute?"

How did she always know when I was struggling?

As we made the ultimate step onto the landing at the highest point of the building, I looked at my best friend for reassurance.

"I'm not spiralling this time but I was just thinking, what if he freaks out when he sees two of us? I mean, he did just book one girl?"

An image of the pimp flashed before my eyes. To displease him with a badly executed performance on my first attempt under his reign was not an option for me.

"Honey, please," she scoffed, "did you ever know a man to say no to a second girl?"

"Um, no, never."

"Exactly!" She quaffed her hair in the communal mirror

on the landing. "The client will fall to his knees when he sees us together. We are way too hot to handle OK?" She clicked her fingers in the sassy way she did to punctuate her point.

Once inside our room, I scanned my surrounds, piecing together what my client had chosen in order to get an insight into his personality.

This place was better in its design than the last hotel, with a king sized bed in the centre of the room made up in crisp white cotton sheets.

When I poked my head into the en suite bathroom nestled in the corner, I smiled when I saw a large bath with an overhead shower. *I'd love a hot bath right now.*

The first thing I did was lift the toilet seat to check it was clean.

"Stop messing around in there Chloe and come get ready!"

I rolled my eyes at Hanna's bossy nature and sashayed back into the bedroom.

"Sorry Han. You know I like to see what I'm dealing with."

The dark stained wood desk with matching chair at the end of the bed had a built in vanity mirror where Hanna was preening herself, again.

She peered at me through her reflection. "The more you relax, the better this will go."

I nodded my agreement as I watched her apply her war paint. This was Hanna's way of preparing for a client; affixing her mask of protection in the hopes it would save her from the unknown.

"You look great, Han. Honestly, you don't need to do any more. You're perfect as you are."

She clicked the lid of her lipstick closed. "Thanks Babe but I have a ritual to stick to."

You just yelled at me for doing mine!

Bored and anxious, there was only so much waiting I could do when, thankfully, a distraction caught my eye.

"Ooh, free cookies!"

I skipped over to the complimentary, condiments tray beside the coffee machine and tore open the packet, popping a bite sized chunk into my mouth.

"I forget you're still a baby." Hanna mumbled as she applied another layer of eye liner.

Wait—

My brows raised as I stopped chewing to mull over her comment, "what do you even mean? I'm literally a year younger than you."

"It was a *long* year." She said with an eye roll as she snapped her makeup pallet closed and smiled in appreciation at her own reflection.

"Um, sure." I frowned inwardly. "Anyway, this is nice, isn't it?" I stood in front of the flat screen TV in awe, having never seen one so big before and especially not in a hotel room.

It wasn't often rooms like this had more than a mattress, but our client had gone the extra mile and chosen the deluxe suite.

Hanna continued to play with her hair without a care in the world, moving each curl independently until she achieved the look she was aiming for. "Maybe he wants to watch porn?"

I jumped onto the bed and sighed, kicking my feet over the edge restlessly as I waited impatiently for his arrival.

"Do you think? I mean, an afternoon of watching TV sounds perfect to me." I snickered.

Hanna smacked her lips together to seal in her gloss and turned to me with a serious look on her face. "Honey, we don't get that lucky."

My hands knotted in my lap as anxious butterflies danced against the walls of my stomach, as I tried to conjure my usual confident Jasmin persona who remained nonexistent.

Why am I so damn nervous?

Under normal circumstances, this would have been a walk in the park, but as this was my first client since being raped and my first under the control of the pimp. It was a head fuck combination that extinguished all hopes of me getting it right.

No matter how much Hanna downplayed the severity, I knew if I messed this up. We were both in for a punishment.

"Last time, get out of your own head!" Hanna glared at me, bringing me back to reality.

She spritzed perfume all over her body, pumping the bottle top until she'd emptied half.

The overwhelming fragrance attacked my nostrils.

"Yeah, I know," I spluttered, fanning the scent away. "I just want this one over with now, you know?"

A light knock on the door interrupted our conversation.

Show time.

"Here he is, right on time," She smiled at me as she strutted with sexy, seductive confidence to answer the door. In that moment of uncertainty, I wanted to hide under the bed.

However, the man waiting on the other side completely took my breath away. He was attractive and as normal looking as one could expect under the circumstances.

"Hi." He frowned at seeing double.

Hanna picked up on his tense vibe. "Hi Honey. She's the new girl that you booked. I'm just here to show her the ropes. You know, with her being new and all."

Smooth Hanna. Real smooth.

"Oh OK, great." His tone didn't quite match his words. It encouraged the anxious knot in my stomach to swell further.

"What's your name, Baby?" Hanna purred as she reached for his shoulders to remove his jacket for him.

The tension in his upper body suggested discomfort against her boldness. After all, this was supposed to be a first timers booking.

"I'm Tony."

He was shy, which instantly put me at ease.

"I love the name Tony," Hanna smiled. "I'm Hanna, and this here is Jasmin."

At the call of my name, I rose to my feet and offered my hand to him. I needed to take part in this booking at some point.

Taking my hand in his, we shook like we'd just closed on

a million dollar deal. "Jasmin." He nodded.

Hanna didn't need encouragement, and like a bolted stallion, she took the reins. "So, what would you like from us today, Tony?"

"What do I want?" He mused. "Real talk, ladies. This is a first for me, which I'm sure you get told often. However, with me it's true. I don't have any expectations."

"Ahh OK," Hanna nodded in understanding, "is that why you wanted a new girl?"

The room silenced and his reluctance to answer Hanna's interrogation reduced the mood to dangerously critical levels. I needed a plan, and quick.

"Hey, Han, why don't you run us a bath?"

She clapped in agreement. "Ooh, good idea! I'll be right back!"

Once she'd left the bedroom, the apprehension in my shoulders lifted and suddenly I felt like me again.

Tony rested his hands in his pockets with a pensive look on his attractive face. When our eyes locked, he smiled at me.

"You're very pretty, Jasmin."

Am I? "Thank you." I blushed at his unexpected compliment. It wasn't often a client favoured me over Hanna.

He tentatively opened his mouth, but the bathroom door swung open, where Hanna poked her head into the room.

"Ready in here. Come on, guys!"

Hanna had filled the generously sized bath to the brim with bubbles and oils, the smell of which was heavenly. Her trusty bag of toiletries never failed to impress.

"Shall we undress you?" She asked as she removed her shoes and jewellery.

The tension in his torso returned. "Sure, I guess."

As a duo, we both got to work as we always did, knowing what each of our moves would be within our unspoken partnership.

Hanna seized her opportunity and took his zipper between her fingers and removed his jeans while I reached for his shirt, lifting it up and over his head, letting the thin, expensive fabric fall to the ceramic tiled floor beneath us. Once naked, we stripped off to join him.

Something about his offering was enticing. His soft penis was ample and his balls hung low, inferring his advanced age, but the confidence he held against his most vulnerable state only encouraged me to want more.

My pointed toe entered the water with feminine elegance. The relaxed sensation of the heat tingling my senses was so welcome and something I should have done sooner.

The three of us enjoyed the relaxation that the warm water provided and it set the tone perfectly.

"Wait—we need some alcohol!" Hanna exclaimed, diving out of the tub, sloshing water all over the floor, creating a slipping hazard. "I'll be right back!"

It was a little early for drinking, but I knew she was speaking from experience.

There was an awkward silence for a moment while we waited for Hanna to leave, where Tony and I exchanged glances and I wondered what he was thinking.

But once we were alone, he took his opportunity. "So Jasmin, is that an Australian accent?"

"All you Americans think that," I giggled. "I'm from England."

He smiled as his body relaxed backwards. "Sorry, you do have a bit of a mix of accents going on there. I couldn't help but notice."

"Yeah, I'm a hybrid for sure. In another ten years, the Brit in me will be gone."

He reached both arms out of the water and rested them on the sides of the tub. "Keep hold of it. It makes you unique."

The way in which his eyes sparkled with promises of safety had my body craving his connection.

"Um, unique as in good?" I blushed as I exposed my vulnerabilities to a stranger.

"Unique, great. I'm having a wonderful time with you."

Tony's reassuring smile was all I needed, and the longer he kept eye contact with me, the more I wanted him to kiss me. But when our eyes finally locked, I found myself smirking and looking away again.

He fidgeted his position, exposing his knee out of the water.

"Can I ask your age, Jasmin? The agency said they had a twenty-six-year-old that fitted my brief, but something tells me that's not true."

Shit, was Hanna right? Do I act like a child?

I wrinkled my nose as I shook my head. "I'm twenty-one. Does that put you off?"

"No, I guess it doesn't," he shrugged, "but I'm forty-two. Suppose I'm kind of old."

We heard Hanna before we saw her, bursting back into the suite, talking too loudly as though she'd already thrown back a couple of glasses for courage on the journey back to the room.

With self assurance, she returned to the bathroom holding three tall stemmed glasses and a bottle of cheap champagne.

"Who wants some?" Her rhetorical question answered as she poured the wine, filling all three glasses to the brim.

We each took one by the stem and sipped at the cool liquid. The taste wasn't as bad as I expected, but it left a tangy sensation in the back of my throat that made me wince and poke out my tongue.

Tony studied the bottle's label, matching my reaction. "Wow," he cleared his throat, "nothing Sauvignon Blanc about this is there?"

We all snickered as Hanna raised her glass in cheers. "Lakeside's finest."

As the alcohol did its thing, we were much more relaxed and enjoying each other's company.

Hanna joined me at my end of the bath and trailed her finger down my wet body, landing at my waiting nipple where she tweaked the soft mound, tightening the areola.

"So Tony. Do you want me to play with Jasmin?"

Tony's lips thinned, and he pushed himself into an upright position, where he finished his glass and placed it on the floor carefully. "No, thank you. I'm happy with how our time is progressing without that. But I appreciate the offer."

Well, that's never happened before.

The rejection gave Hanna a slice of humble pie, and instantly her smile morphed into a look of torment.

Even though I'd had my fair share of pie in the past, I doubted Hanna had the same level of preparation I did.

Her hand cut through the bubbled surface back into the water and, in a very unlike Hanna fashion, she didn't say another word on the subject.

"Shall we get out now? My skin is like a prune." Tony announced as he climbed out of the bath, giving me a glimpse of his penis again. His round testicles were the perfect size for my mouth.

Following his lead, Hanna and I towelled Tony down, and each of us adorned a complimentary robe, ready to watch TV in bed together.

Hanna lay on Tony's left, and I lay to his right while our hands rested on his muscular, bare stomach, with his arms propped up behind his head as we watched a car show of his choosing.

When our time was almost over, he reached for the remote and lowered the volume. "I've had a great time, ladies."

"Anytime," Hanna said with a heart-stopping smile. "This was your appointment, Jasmin, so I'll head out now and leave you guys for the last quarter. Catch you later."

It didn't take long for Hanna to pack up her things and leave the room after her abrupt announcement, and I knew then that Tony's earlier rejection had bothered her, not that she would want to talk about it, anyway.

But now that he and I were alone, I felt more like myself again. I reached for his face, running my fingers along his bearded jawline. Tony was intriguing, with long dark lashes and well-groomed eyebrows. His forty something skin, lightly weathered, was bewitching in a wonderful sort of way. His age wasn't an issue for me. I wanted him and I sensed he wanted me too.

He placed his hand on top of mine, and we paused to look at each other for a moment. My heart raced in anticipation and the dampness between my legs evidenced my craving for more, seeking his touch.

I opened my thighs, inviting him in. His eye caught the drift of my intention, and he squeezed my hand, taking a deep breath.

"Is this your first time?"

Huh?

"What, having sex?" I wrinkled my nose at the idea.

"No. I mean, doing this?"

Shit—

"Oh. Um, yes," I nodded. "Yes, it is."

He smiled, as if I might've told him the right answer.

"Would you object to me booking you again, Jasmin?"

"Not at all. I've had a wonderful time."

Before the conversation had chance to progress further, he swung his legs out of bed, taking his time as he pulled on his discarded jeans and shirt in front of me, giving me quite a show, and he knew it.

Closing the space between us, he leaned his fists onto the bed and gingerly kissed my lips. There were so many sensations loaded into the kiss that stoked the fire of my already roaring libido.

When I opened my eyes, he had gathered himself to leave.

"Until next time," he said with a handsome smile, handing me an envelope of cash where my smile fell as I took it from him.

Oh—

I waited until he left the room when I flopped myself back down on the bed with my arm covering my eyes. I'd never been in the company of a man before that didn't want to have sex with me, especially when I made it obvious that was what I wanted. Did that just make him even more desirable?

The filled brown envelope, bursting with notes, comprised twenty-dollar bills. I counted $300, which wasn't a bad earner for a relaxed morning with no fucking.

But with untamed arousal to contend with later, my time was up and I needed to force myself back to reality.

As Hanna hadn't bothered to wait in the parking lot for me, I hailed a cab. Destination: my foster parent's house, determined that today would be a good day in view of my time spent with Tony restoring my faith in humanity. God, it had been so long since I'd been in the company of a nice man like him.

I closed the car door, and the cab sped off, leaving me back where I started this morning, outside of my foster parents' home where I rummaged through my purse for my door key. The entire contents removed before finally finding it hiding at the bottom. But the key offered to the lock refused to turn. I tried again. Jammed.

What the—

The door opened from the other side to reveal Nancy stood in front of me; arms folded. The foul odour of her coffee-tainted breath overwhelmed my senses, and her unpleasant demeanour was in line with her cardigan.

"I changed the locks. Get out of my house now!"

With over-annunciation, she spat her words at me where a skin sizzling acid droplet landed on my cheek.

Reactively, I wiped my face with my sleeve. "Why are you kicking me out? What did I do?"

"Joan from church saw your arrest in the shopping mall yesterday with your harlot friend. You're an embarrassment to this family, and I've had enough. I've packed your belongings in this bag. I don't want to see you here again."

She pushed an old leather hold all into my chest, ironically the same one that I had arrived with when I entered their care.

"You're twenty-one now and no longer my responsibility. Get out!"

"What are you talking about? I didn't even get arrested!"

But my fight was futile. The look on her face informed me she'd made her mind up already.

Bob hovered helplessly behind her, as far back into the corner of the room as the space allowed. He didn't make eye contact with me when I eyeballed him for backup. With his eyeline focused towards the ground, and his hands nervously fidgeting in his pants pockets, he rocked slowly on his heels.

"'Friend's my fucking ass, you coward!" I sneered at him.

Tears pricked the corners of my eyes with an array of ambivalent emotions. But I would never give her the satisfaction of seeing me cry again. Ever! She'd induced enough tears from me as a child. *No more.*

Before she had the satisfaction of closing the door on me, I took control and closed the chapter on her as I turned my back towards her. If I'd stayed a moment longer, I would've killed her and let him watch.

When my foot hit the sidewalk, I looked over my shoulder.

"Thanks for nothing, you pair of fucking losers.

My quivering legs carried me down the block, jellifying with each step.

I collapsed against the nearest brick wall, where I struggled to catch my breath. My chest was tight, overwhelmed by so much raw emotion that charged into me like a raging bull.

What am I going to do now?

As my knees threatened to buckle beneath me, I battled to hold on to my belongings grasped tightly in my hands—the last remaining items I owned.

I sank to the ground where a swell of tears blurred my vision.

Don't fucking cry!

Destitute, my trembling hand reached into my pocket for my cell phone. The only person I could think of calling was Hanna.

"Hey Girl," Hanna answered in a rush, "I'm a little busy at the minute. I'll call you later, OK?"

She clearly had company, probably another client. Music blared in the background and she giggled as she hung up the call before giving me a chance to say more.

Great—just great.

My ever persistent anxiety forced images into my mind as I began playing out scenarios, weighing up my options.

I could go back and beg Nancy? *Absolutely not. I'd rather die.* Maybe I should call the foster care team? That idea was worse. They would only put me back into the system. What about the pimp? *Hmm.* Was he my only choice?

When you're a kid of the system from a whole different country with very few friends or family to speak of, situations such as this were a harsh reality check.

Resounding myself to the obvious, I scrambled to my feet and brushed myself down to prepare myself for something that required all the internal strength I had.

Fact was, most girls lived with their daddy anyway—Hanna did, and she seemed more than happy with that arrangement.

So I made my choice, given my predicament, and even though I'd only been with him for a matter of hours, I had no option other than to call on his mercy.

With my thumb raised at the edge of the sidewalk, I grabbed the attention of a passing cab driver. I needed to pay a visit to the mansion.

My stomach twisted at the thought of seeing the pimp again. He was the most insanely gorgeous man I had ever laid eyes on, and when his intimidating edge was stripped back; he was the image of perfection. Our physical connection during my audition replayed on a loop in the forefront of my mind, where sensations interweaved with desire.

Did he think about it, too?

But doubt crept in the closer I travelled towards the mansion. *Oh God, what if he says no?* The humiliation would be too much to bear.

I took a deep breath in through my nose and out through

my mouth and knocked timidly on the imposing door to the mansion three times.

Footsteps on the other side of the door grew closer until, eventually, it opened.

I took a dry swallow as I drank in the man before me. With a tall, muscular stature, the pimp wore bright white sneakers, socks and long shorts with a tight-fitted vest that showed off his toned arms and ripped stomach. The type of look only a gangster could pull off, especially with the over the top thick chain hung around his tattooed neck.

His deep blue eyes implied a great deal of complexity behind them but at the same time, gave nothing away. And with a cigar perched between his lips, he peered down at me where at first he waited, simply holding out his hand. But when I didn't react, he frowned.

"You here to pay my cut from your first client?"

Say something! Stop acting like an idiot!

Suddenly mute, I nodded and handed him the entire envelope.

Hanna had warned me to do that. 'Let Daddy pay you, not the other way round.'

My gesture pleased him, evidenced by his smirk as he began expertly counting the notes in front of me. This man was used to handling enormous sums of money.

Eventually, he handed me back my cut. "This is good for a first time, hoe. I gave you a little extra. Keep this up, and you'll make me a happy man."

He exhaled a thick plume from a long drag of his cigar. The ash coloured particles displaced through the air, catching the wind travelling the distance.

I figured now was as good of a time as any to call on his mercy.

"Um. Could I," the words caught in my throat, "shit, sorry." My face turned purple, and I fixed my focus on his shoes, giggling nervously.

"Spit it out."

I peered up at him through my lashes, not expecting his eyes to bore immediately into mine. "Could I come stay here for a while?"

His body language didn't alter. "Shit, why not?" A smile crept over his handsome features, revealing a diamond encrusted grill he'd not been wearing at the audition. "I can have your tight cunt whenever I want."

The lit cigar continued to produce a pungent odour as he filled his lungs, but for some reason, it only enhanced his look.

I shifted my weight from one foot to the other, feeling incredibly vulnerable in his presence. "Um, thank you.

Thanks so much."

He rubbed the stubble on his chin in thought. "Although," he began as he tapped the ash off the end of the cigar, "rooms are full, but I do got a place in my bed."

Did he mean he wanted me to share his bed? Surely not. I barely knew him.

He opened the door and took a step back. "Get your ass inside, then. I got shit to do."

Upon seeing the grand hallway for a second time, in a new light, it appeared so different from the first.

What I originally suspected to be a lion's den was now more like a rabbits warren.

Whores meandered the place in their matching underwear and silk robes. I expected at least one of them to welcome me or even offer an acknowledgement, but it seemed I would need to make the first move.

Hanna's refusal to pick up the phone only added to my crippling anxiety. Where was she when I needed her? I needed her now more than ever.

Evening fell upon the mansion, and I hadn't received a client booking since my arrival that afternoon.

Had Hanna been available, we could have talked through the possibilities as to the reasons why.

The notion I might disappoint Daddy now had my stomach churning, especially with how pleased he was with my first envelope.

That night, I stepped foot inside his master bedroom and waited by his already occupied super king-size bed, feeling all kinds of uninvited.

Of course, the pimp was nowhere to be seen to aid in formal introductions, and all I could hope for was that he had pre-warned the other girls who shared the room of the new arrangement.

The pimp's bedroom was stunning. Ornate decoration, with a mixture of neutral colours and gold accents, provided a warmth that completely contradicted the owner's personality. Aside from the huge four person bed, there was a large walk-in closet that expanded the near side wall of the room, an enormous TV set above a drinks cabinet and a hint of luxury implied through the open door of the en suite bathroom.

The window behind the bed was vast with little to no privacy, looking out onto the manicured front gardens and parking lot sized drive way.

The dark-haired girl with freckles lounging on the bed, I recognised immediately. She was the pale-faced girl who'd been sitting on the sofa with the pimp at my audition.

"Hi, I'm Jasmin." I gave her a small wave.

"You're the new pet, then?" She rolled her eyes with disdain, looking at me like a discarded tissue.

The champagne coloured satin sheets that pooled at the foot end of the bed exposed her well-cared-for naked body. A definite gym goer with a slim frame and long legs, she was enviable by anybody's standard. With thick hair that fell naturally into place, and flawless skin that grabbed attention, I could see why she was in the master's bed.

"I'm Tatiana." She said with an upturned lip, "I don't expect you to stay here long. He gets bored easily."

It was obvious in her tone that she didn't care for this arrangement and, if I was honest, my foster parents' home suddenly didn't seem so bad. Tatiana's attitude at the audition was clearly a character trait and sharing a bed with someone who despised me didn't make for the type of environment I was hoping for.

My new sleeping partner's scornful introduction had taken my full attention, and I'd not noticed another girl had entered the room until she tapped my shoulder.

As I turned, her angelic beauty washed over me. Her curved body had an air of Marilyn Monroe with long, wavy, dirty blonde hair that kissed the base of her spine. Her warming aura and soft features were just what I needed.

With an outstretched hand, she offered a tooth baring grin.

"Hi, newbie. I'm Alice."

"Um, hi. I'm Jasmin."

"Pretty," she said, blinking slowly. "This house is fucked up, but you'll get used to it. I need to grab a shower now. We'll talk some more later." She kissed my cheek playfully as she skipped her way to the bathroom.

I turned my attention back to the room, sensing that Tatiana was giving me the death stare. I wasn't wrong. She glared at me with repugnance.

"As you didn't seem to get the memo, Daddy likes his women clean, so you better shower before you get into bed."

Her icy tone cut through the atmosphere like a knife.

OK, then.

As time ticked by, I continued to rock awkwardly on my heels with knotted fingers at my front as I waited for Alice to finish. I was out of options and out of my depth, where rolling with the punches or leaving were my only choices.

Should I leave? But where would I go?

Tatiana continued to groom herself, making it clear she wasn't the talking type, especially not to new girls. In fact, she behaved as if I weren't even there.

I wanted to inform her that no matter how much cream she applied to her legs, it wouldn't improve on her inner ugliness. But I refrained. Making enemies on the first night, especially one you're about to sleep next to, didn't seem smart.

Alice finally strolled out of the bathroom thirty minutes later with a towel around her head and an expensive-looking towelling robe hugging her body.

"It's all yours, Honey." She smiled as she removed the towel, rubbing it through her long hair as she soaked up the water droplets.

Breathless and uneasy, with an elevated heart rate, I closed the bathroom door behind me, sighing heavily as I took in the moment of solace.

As expected, the en suite was gorgeous, with a hint of exorbitance. The entire room, in keeping with the rest of the mansion, featured marble tiles from floor to ceiling that extended all the way through to the walk-in shower with brushed gold hardware and expensive accessories. The shower itself could fit at least four people, which made sense. I imagined the pimp had several women in there with him at any one time.

I stripped off my clothes, feeling as physically vulnerable as I did emotionally, and turned on the faucet.

The water roared from the large shower head fixed to the ceiling, in long beads of dewy goodness. Steam filled the room immediately as the intense blast of heat sprayed against the marble floor, creating a false reality that I could lose myself in.

As the water beat down on my skin, the soothing sensation took the weight out of my shoulders, giving me a note of comfort amidst the chaotic introduction to the pimp's lifestyle.

The body wash smelt rich with a silky smooth texture, and I couldn't help but pour a generous helping into my palm, rubbing it all over my naked body. If only there were such a product that could rid my mind of my concerns.

Thoroughly sanitised, I turned off the water, but the thought of going back into the bedroom to sleep in bed with strangers was gnawing away at my refreshed mood.

I grabbed a plush robe from the back of the door, just like Alice wore, and wrapped myself up, pulling the soft belt around my middle, cinching in my waist.

With my hand paused on the door handle, I released a heavy exhale, willing myself to pull it open and face the music.

I can do this.

When I reentered the room, the girls were already in bed, looking at their phones.

As I didn't have many clothes with me, I resolved to having to sleep in the nude, but this was probably more normal at the pimp's mansion than wearing a pyjama set, anyway.

Not sure if the etiquette was to wait for instruction or climb right on in, I carefully removed my robe with an overbearing sense of self consciousness.

My career involved exposing my naked body, but in this house—in this room—my level of exposure burrowed beneath my skin through to my bones.

Tentatively, I clambered into bed next to Alice and lay motionless beside her, hoping to camouflage myself amidst the bedding, as her focus remained fixed on messaging someone.

Raised voices from the landing suggested we would have company at any moment, but neither Alice nor Tatiana reacted.

The pimp strolled in with his cell phone by his ear a short while later. His presence was completely disarming as he ended his conversation, launching the phone across the room, where it bounced off the wall.

Like a spectator on safari, I watched the predator as he raked his hand through his dark hair. Angry about something, he paced the room, but neither girl acknowledged the fact, simply remaining compliant in waiting.

Eventually, he settled, and as he prepared himself for bed, I watched him closely, absorbing every last detail of him.

Blessed with tanned skin and black, tightly curled hair professionally styled, he was naturally handsome.

His fade trim accentuated a skilfully applied tattoo on his neck that reached from one side to the other and up into his hairline. The single word in big bold letters read: **King**.

I assumed it was in reference to himself; or he was a supporter of the Royal family, but the latter didn't seem likely.

He stood tall at the foot of the bed, where I guessed he was well over six feet and when he caught me ogling him, a small smile dimpled his cheeks.

Not realising just how tightly I had been gripping the bed cover, subconsciously pulling it to my chin for protection, my hands had begun to sweat. Completely in awe, I was totally overcome because something about the pimp terrified me, yet drew me in concurrently.

He stripped off his clothing, starting with his vest. This man was giving us a show, and I wanted to be a season ticket holder. His eyes glistened with a primal need to serve his women as the sensations I experienced during our moment of intimacy at the audition came flooding back to the depths of my core.

With a flirtatious motive, he peeled off his vest with both hands crossed over at his stomach. The removal of the shirt revealed a well-sculpted, toned body that was already implied beneath the material. He left on his thick gold chain that hung proudly around his muscular neck, but the shorts and socks were next, leaving himself gloriously naked before us. He'd gone without underwear, but that shouldn't have come as a surprise. His dick was thick and long and filled with just enough blood to raise it from the root.

I peered at Alice, who lay dormant next to me, her cell phone now on the bedside table while she waited. She wasn't paying much attention to the king's show, but she must've seen it one too many times before.

The pimp pulled back the sheet and climbed into bed next to Tatiana on the opposite side of where Alice and I lay.

"Listen up, whores," he growled, "me and my first bitch, Tatiana, will make a baby in this bed tonight. You two can watch. One day, if you please me like Tat has, you might get the opportunity to have my baby, too."

Even though he'd invited us to watch, it felt odd to be confined within a scene that I wasn't taking part in.

He was surprisingly gentle with her as he kissed her body, running his large hands over her supple skin and settling on the heave of her breast. His dick responded without the need of her touch. The broad, plush head reminded me of cotton candy. *What I wouldn't give for some cotton candy right now.*

Alice turned to face me. "They will be at that for a while. Wanna play?"

Huh?

"What do you mean?" I whispered.

If she wanted to play sports, she'd bet on the wrong girl.

She bit her bottom lip and brushed her finger between my cleavage. "You know, a fun game." She smiled.

My skin recoiled in response to her advances. "Um—

Sorry, I'm not a lesbian."

"Neither am I. It's just seeing Daddy fucking like that turns me on. It's been like this for weeks, and I've not had a fuck buddy since Jody."

Jody? Who the hell is she? Another girl to add to the long list I was struggling to keep up with.

Alice clasped my hand in hers and slid it seductively down her body and between her legs to meet with her damp inner thighs.

I retreated my hand, hesitantly self-conscious of the act of intimacy I was about to share with a woman I didn't know.

Alice ignored the rigidity exuding from my body as she slid her index finger inside me without invitation.

The remnants of my unfinished business with the pimp and Tony intermingled with the present sensory overload and, unwittingly, my body responded.

I deepened the kiss she offered me against her provoking influence. Her hands were soft and caressing, and everything in between. This was nothing like I'd ever experienced before.

What am I doing? And why do I like this?

As I continued to internalise my struggle, we made out under the covers. She pushed her finger deeper inside my body, massaging my sweet spot as if it had a signpost with her name on it. My legs trembled as I stifled my moan, not wanting to admit to myself that my body was responding to something it never had done before.

Alice seemed to enjoy my touch, too, where out of my depth, I copied her moves right back at her.

"You're making me wanna come, Jasmin," Alice moaned as her eyelids fluttered closed where parting her lips, she released a soft groan.

With impatient breathlessness, she manoeuvred herself on top of me, pushing her exposed clitoris against mine. Her hand groped my breast as I did hers as we climbed the mountain together, sharing the same oxygen as her soft lips locked with mine.

And then it happened. My insides clenched while my hands gripped the bed sheets as I experienced my first true orgasm at the hands of a woman.

As the clenching subsided, bewildered, I lay breathless amidst the damp sheets, trying to unpick how I felt about what had just occurred.

Just like that, Alice pivoted her back towards me, resting her head on the pillow she left me with the view of her long blonde hair.

Oh no. What did I do wrong?

As she was my only friend in the king's bedroom, I felt an overwhelming urge to please her.

My first encounter with a woman as my true self left me feeling empty and confused, and lonelier than if I had been all alone.

The other occupants of the bed had drifted peacefully to sleep as my inner turmoil festered, eating away at me as I stared at the ceiling, wondering how I landed myself in this situation.

My ragged breathing was all I had to keep me company and with a powerful sensation of hopelessness, I screwed my eyes shut, concerned that the only hope I had of surviving this place didn't feel the connection with me she'd hoped for.

Was Alice my ticket to survival? The answer was bound to come to fruition, eventually.

CHAPTER 4

Alice and Tatiana were nowhere to be seen when my eyes flitted open the next morning. A restless night's sleep filled with unanswered questions left my life hanging in the balance with a groggy sense of impending isolation.

After much soul searching, I'd come to the conclusion that last night with Alice was a mistake. A dangerous lack of judgement that I could ill afford to repeat. If she no longer wanted to be my friend on the back of that, then so be it. I would have to make peace with her decision and perhaps find somewhere else to stay if it came to it. But allowing someone I barely knew make me feel so powerless and exposed was not something I was willing to repeat.

My assumption when I rolled over in the sheets was that I was alone in the pimp's bed, but seeing a masculine presence lay beside me took me by surprise.

Once King saw I was awake, his primal glare informed me of his intentions. Gloriously naked, he glanced at my exposed breasts and took hold of his erection, where he began masturbating.

When I peered down at his dick, he smiled. "I've been waitin' for you to wake up. The sluts have gone to the gym. Remember that 'cause I like my women fit with stamina."

I stole another glance at his ripped body. Watching him playing with himself was a massive turn-on for me, and he knew it. *Did he want me to join him?*

"Um, do you want me to go to the gym now?" My hoarse morning voice did little in the way of helping my cause.

He stopped abruptly and moved over to my side of the bed, closing the void between us.

"I've been needin' this pussy since last night," he growled as he climbed on top of me, parting my legs skilfully with one knee.

With his dick lay hot over my stomach, he ran his nose along the length of mine with parted lips. His breath smelt of cigars and coffee, with a hint of mint toothpaste, and it struck me then that I still had morning breath.

"You seem shy and innocent, but somethin' tells me that ain't true."

I smiled at him, conscious that I didn't want to put him off with my unbrushed teeth.

He reached over to the bedside table and opened the top

drawer, where he plucked out a condom wrapped in a gold foil packet. With intrigue, I watched as he tore it open and rolled the latex on efficiently.

But a twang of disappointment furrowed my brows, knowing that whilst during my audition we had unprotected sex, this time we wouldn't get that same connection.

The swollen head of his penis ran through the parting of my engorged flesh and he thrust his hips to gain entry inside my body.

"Shit!" He groaned as he gripped the bedsheets. "I forgot how tight you were."

An invisible glow surrounded his aura as I peered up at the handsome face of the man who gave me a chance, while he took pleasure from my body. This was the very least I could do to thank him. I wanted to offer everything to him, to implore him deeper inside me. This was the moment I'd been waiting for.

"Fuck," he mumbled, as his pace slowed to a grinding halt.

Before he allowed himself to climax, he withdrew, where he ripped off the condom and tossed it on the floor.

"Suck it." He ordered impatiently, as his toned chest rose and fell rhythmically.

Without a beat of hesitation, I sat up to meet with his body. With my hands around his thighs, I pushed his dick between my lips.

Gathering my hair in his hands, he cradled my head, rolling his hips as he fucked my mouth with careful consideration.

But once the excitement took hold, the pace soon quickened. The force in which he exuded drove me to gag.

"That's it slut. Choke on it."

But no sooner had he picked up speed, he slowed again, removing his dick completely as he took a deep breath and then impatiently pushed the head through my parted lips once more.

A bloom of delicious anticipation blossomed in my stomach, as I appreciated the powerful mans offering.

"I'm gonna nut in your mouth, you little slut. Do you want to taste my come?"

I nodded as I sucked the tip like a popsicle.

"You mean, yes Daddy?" He groaned as his hips thrust back and forth. His spade like hand supported the back of my head, setting the rhythm that I accepted.

"Yes Daddy. Please."

"That's it." he closed his eyes. "I'm gonna give it to you. Take all of it, whore."

He spilled his semen deep into my throat, where I instinctively swallowed his load, needing to devour him and anything he presented to me.

As he withdrew, a long bead of milky white semen dripped from the plush head. I took him back into my mouth and lapped up the remnants of his orgasm. I wanted everything he had.

He reached for my chin and adjusted my eye line to meet with his. With affection, he leaned forward and kissed me softly on the lips.

"Hmm, I can taste myself on your sweet lips." He hummed as he placed his thumb on my lower lip and ran the pad along the length. "There's just somethin' about you."

Transfixed, I stared into the depths of his ocean blue eyes, where he took in a sharp inhale at the nape of my neck. "You don't say much, huh?"

The point of his nose ran along the edge of my jawline while his hand snaked my waist.

As the air shifted between us, traces of Tatiana's presence from their night of passion entangled with his natural scent. But it didn't discourage me. I still wanted him to claim me; all of me. With a yearning to keep our connection, I wrapped my arms around his neck. I expected him to kiss me again, but his body became rigid.

A fleeting thought sullied his handsome features, and he hopped off the bed as if suddenly in a hurry.

His dick, still raised from his body, had more to give, and I wondered if his reluctance to continue was due to him saving some of himself for Tatiana again tonight.

Jealousy gnawed at me the more I thought about it, even though I had no grounds to feel that way. *He isn't mine.*

But could he and I ever work? With the way his body aligned with mine, was there a chance I could persuade him to give me a shot?

"Leave now, Hoe," he said, pulling his t-shirt on. "I got business to attend to."

King dressed himself in his expensive navy blue Gucci tracksuit with pants that hung just off his hips, showcasing the v-shaped muscles above his crotch.

I watched attentively as his tattooed hand scraped through his glossy black curls in front of the mirror, but Hanna's words of warning resurfaced.

Shit—

I scrambled out of bed without making eye contact with him, and grabbed a silk robe off the back of the bedroom door, making myself scarce before I angered him.

As I jogged down the stairs, tying the rope around my

middle, I couldn't help but dwell on a sense of loss. The loss of a man who didn't belong to me to begin with. How could I feel so connected to someone I barely knew?

Laughter emitted from the room at the far end of the hallway. I followed the sound to where I heard female voices coming from the kitchen.

Upon entering, the bright light of the grand open space mixed with the hustle and bustle startled me.

White marble tiles with grey veins running through covered the immense floor space. Kitchen cupboards span three walls with an impressive marble topped island central to the room. Enough bar stools were available to seat ten whores, and when that wasn't enough, a twenty-seater dining table awaited with a gilded throne at the head of the table reserved for the king himself.

A chef busied himself with several pans bubbling on an enormous stove. The aromatic flavours releasing from his artistry were mouth watering and suddenly I realised I was starving.

As I approached, I spotted Alice, with her long golden hair, sitting on a stool in a matching silk robe, her back towards me. Two other girls, who I had not yet met, were engaged in conversation nearby. I took a seat next to Alice, catching her attention.

"Hey, listen, last night—"

Her long lashes fluttered. "Last night was fun. Let's do it again," she said cheerfully, blowing the steam off her morning coffee mug, cupped between her hands.

What? "No—I, um, was going to say that it shouldn't happen again."

Her smile dropped as she studied my face. "It's OK Jasmin. All girls freak out the first time. It doesn't make you a *lesbian*. It just means that you appreciate the touch of a woman. Men can give us a hard ride, so to make up for it, we'll make each other come. That's it. Simple." She shrugged her shoulders, dismissing my concerns.

I tried to make sense in my mind of her words comparable to my feelings. Seeing her now, I didn't experience a physical attraction to her. The heave of her breasts were visible through her open robe, yet it didn't evoke a sexual reaction from me. But last night, she'd wrung me out like a wet cloth, my orgasm so violent I'd squirted a little.

Could we be fuck buddies with no complications? It made my head spin at just the idea of it. Was I bisexual? *I have no idea.* I was due a therapy session soon, anyway, so it would make for a nice change having a new topic of conversation to dissect.

She continued sipping coffee and reading her magazine as if I wasn't there—conversation over.

I fidgeted with my hands on the countertop, unsure of my next move. Alice and I weren't close enough for me to speak candidly to her. We'd known each other for a matter of hours. But irrespective of that, did I even know what I wanted to say?

"OK, then." I announced dramatically, standing up to leave.

She smiled at me, as if she were enjoying my agitation at her nonchalant reaction to my mini freak out, but she didn't say another word. She licked her thumb and turned the pages of her gossip mag as she pretended to read the articles.

Is this a game? Am I a toy? Was she manipulating me like others in the past? *Jody.*

As I meandered towards my exit, torn by my desire to play with Alice, my head met with a powerful chest, stopping me in my tracks.

"Ahh, hello again," the masculine tones emitting from his chest reverberated through my ear drums.

"Oh, hi Dan."

He took a step back to study me better. "You heading out?"

I frowned in confusion. "Um, well, I am, but not in my robe." I giggled. "I was just going to get dressed first. Then I thought I would go clothes shopping. I'm short on pretty much everything."

It was obvious in the amount of waffling I was doing that he made me nervous. Something about attractive men always caught me off guard.

My cheeks blushed as he peered at me with intrigue. I would've preferred to look my best before I next ran into him.

His returning bright white smile had me weak at the knees.

"Sorry, I thought that was your outfit. You look great."

There was absolutely no way that an educated man like Dan thought for even one second the robe was my outfit of choice for the day. Either that or it said a lot about his first impression of me.

I played it coy, twirling my hair between my fingers. "Thank you. You look good too."

"Wait, I've just noticed something. You have an accent?" He placed his index finger on his lips as he contemplated the options.

Here we go.

"Hmm. I'm going to hazard a guess at British?"

My mouth dropped open. "No way! You're the first person ever to get it right!"

He bowed in the chivalrous way he presented himself.

"What can I say? It's a talent."

I nodded in agreement. "You're really talented."

Our shared chuckle subsided, and he rolled up his shirtsleeves as though he was preparing for something.

"I actually need to go into town myself. Wanna carpool?"

Play-it-cool—

"Sure, great. I'll just go and get ready."

Oh my God. Don't fuck this up!

"No worries." he turned, "I'll wait for you outside."

Alice caught hold of my arm from behind, startling me.

"You wanna be careful, Honey. Daddy doesn't take kindly to sharing his women; especially with his brother."

"Oh? We're just going shopping?"

Her lips thinned, and she blinked slowly. "Just be careful, that's all I'm saying."

I met Dan in the driveway ten minutes later, who'd propped himself up against his expensive-looking Mercedes with chrome detailing. It gleamed against the late morning sun in a beautiful midnight blue colour that was almost black. Everything about the car said rich.

"Ready?" He asked as he held open the passenger door for me.

For sex? Yes, yes I am.

"Yep, all set. Thanks for this, Dan. It's weird being the new girl around here. I don't know anyone."

"My pleasure." He closed my door carefully behind me and climbed into the driver's side.

With a few button presses as if he were the pilot of a jet, he pushed a final red button to start the engine of his impressive machine. It roared into life, and we headed off the driveway and out towards the freeway.

"This is a really nice car." I reached out, touching the leather dashboard in front of me.

His hands caressed the matching leather of the steering wheel. "Thanks, she's new."

I nodded in agreement. "I can tell."

"Yeah? How?"

"Smells new. I love that," I breathed deeply in recognition of the heady scent of new car mixed with his cologne. My mouth watered.

There was an awkward silence for a moment, and I sensed he was waiting for me to set the tone of the conversation. Neither of us knew a single thing about the other except our names and a brief introduction to his occupation.

"Um, so, you're a truck guy?" I blurted out with little thought.

Idiot—

"Yeah, sort of," he smiled. "I don't drive the trucks, though, just to clarify."

Great, now he thinks I'm weird. Say something better.

"I didn't expect the owner of such a massive company to be someone so young."

His handsome face was smooth and wrinkle-free. I guessed he was in his early twenties at a push.

"Mm-hm, yeah. Dad left the haulage business to me."

His candour took me aback. He didn't owe me any sort of explanation, but for some reason, we were both so comfortable with each other, like I'd met him before.

"Wow, that's a big responsibility," I peeked over at his side profile as he drove with an assurance of his ability that rubbed off on me, too.

His lean, muscular arm was out straight in front of him, holding the wheel with confidence. His other rested casually on the centre armrest, positioned where our skin was close enough we were almost touching.

"Suppose it is."

His eyes fixed ahead, made me wonder what he was thinking.

Shit, I've offended him.

Deep in thought, he put his free hand to his lips, where he nibbled the tip. Our almost skin to skin contact disappeared.

"So you haven't been with Romero long?" Dan eventually asked.

"Sorry, who?"

"Oh, you know, whatever he calls himself these days. King, Daddy, inferior brother, etcetera," he smirked.

His joke against the pimp made me snigger. "This is actually my second day. He's helped me out a lot."

I got the sense that the two of them didn't always see eye to eye beneath the banter on the surface. Brothers so similar in look yet so different in personality were bound to clash at some point.

We pulled up in the parking lot of the shopping mall, where I thought the topic of conversation was over, but as he opened my door for me, his lips thinned in contemplation.

"How has my brother helped you out, exactly?" He

reached in for my hand like the gentleman he was.

There was a magnetic pull between us as his hand clasped around mine, evoking a response that fluttered in my chest.

"Um, well, I was in a tough spot with my family. They kicked me out, you see, and I didn't have anywhere else to go. So he took me into his home, which I am so grateful for."

"Hmm, yeah. Romero can be a bit of a dick sometimes, but his heart is usually in the right place."

Dan seemed to relax a little, as though replaying a nostalgic memory featuring King.

"It sounds weird you calling him that. All I've heard in that house so far is Daddy this or King that."

"The day I refer to my brother as Daddy, please shoot me with my own gun," he smiled. "Anyway, where to first, Ma'am?"

He followed me towards the women's clothing store off Park Avenue. As we strolled, I stole a glance at his side profile again, but he caught me looking.

"Um, you don't have to come with me if you have other things to do. I'm familiar with this place."

He shook his head. "No, honestly, I'm happy to. I only need to collect my suit from the tailor's, so if you don't mind, I'll tag along. Maybe I can give you a ride home afterwards?"

"As long as you're sure? I don't want to put you out."

"Not at all," he winked, with a drop-dead gorgeous, straight, white, all-American grin at me.

We paused outside a little independent boutique. It just so happened to be one of mine and Hanna's most visited stores. But as she didn't seem to want to return any of my messages at the moment, Mr. Giannetti was an excellent alternative shopping buddy.

"Can we go in here first?" I pointed towards the quaint signage showcasing their fifty percent off sale.

"Sure. You take the lead, Madam," he gestured for me to go first.

As I searched the clothing rail, I noticed him study the style of garments I was interested in and then start his own mission to find the perfect alternative.

"You know, I've never been shopping with a man before." I mused as I picked up a miniskirt that wasn't my size.

"I'm glad I could be the first," He grinned as he rifled the rails. "You'd look amazing in this." He held up a summer dress that was cut above the knee with a buttoned-down portion around the cleavage. I actually genuinely liked it.

"You think?" I bit my bottom lip at the way he looked at me.

"You have curves that this dress will showcase. What size?"

My cheeks turned pink when I heard the voice of a very flamboyant male assistant behind me.

The clerk eyed me with his hand out to the side. "Honey, she's a size 4 all day long."

I looked at him with admiration. "Wow yeah, that's right. How did you guess?"

He rolled his eyes and cocked his hip. "Sweetie, I don't guess. I know what I'm doing, OK?" With sass, he flicked his imaginary ponytail and sashayed towards us like a runway model.

Dan began searching for my size as the man continued to invade our space. He leant onto the clothes rack with his hand under his chin.

"So, tell me all the gossip. Are you guys together?"

I looked at Dan for his reaction, but he didn't respond.

"Oh, um, no we're not." My palms grew sweaty at the unexpected question.

"Shame. Your kids would be stun—ning."

Speechless, I peered at Dan again for back up, but he wasn't helping our cause. His focus remained on the clothing as if he didn't hear a single sound around him.

Half an hour later, we left with loaded bags and my purse $100 lighter. I had everything that I needed for now, but I would have to earn a lot more money to return my wardrobe to a respectable standard.

"So, that sales guy was a pain in the arse, wasn't he?" I chuckled as I attempted to make conversation.

"Yeah, I rarely go shopping, mainly for that reason."

"Oh, so is that why you ignored him and let me do the talking, hmm?" I nudged him in the ribs playfully.

"Haha, yeah, sorry about that. Media training. I have to be careful what I say to the public, so I tend not to say anything."

Wow—*the public*. I'd forgotten that Dan was just as famous as King, but he did such a good job of pretending like he wasn't. Everything felt so normal in his company. But when I looked beyond our bubble, there wasn't a single person who wasn't staring at us as we passed them by.

"As an apology, do you wanna grab a coffee?" He asked as he took hold of my shopping bags.

Eyes on stalks followed us as we walked the length of the sidewalk. Something about the attention gave me butterflies in my stomach and I didn't want my time with

Dan to end.

"Sure, OK, why not."

The place we'd arrived at wasn't my favourite. Their coffee usually tasted off, but I didn't have the heart or audacity to share my opinion with the person who was paying the bill. If this was Dan's favourite spot, then I'd embrace the fact.

Of course, he held the door open for me, and we stepped inside, where he pulled out a chair for me to take a seat by the window.

"What would you like Jasmin?"

"Just a white coffee, please."

He gave me a wholesome thumbs up. "I'll be right back."

In the two minutes we had parted ways, I thought about sex with him more times than I could count on my fingers. And if he fucked anything like his brother, I would be in for a real treat.

I watched him anxiously from my seat at the table as he ordered, where the woman behind the counter flirted with him in the most sickeningly obvious way. My blood boiled at the spectacle she was creating. Her laugh was too loud, and there was absolutely no reason for her to touch his arm. But I had to remind myself that we were just friends.

The warning Alice gave me was prevalent in the forefront of my mind. *Be careful.*

Fortunately for my ego, he seemed oblivious enough to her charms as he returned with two cups of steaming hot white coffee with a light dusting of cocoa powder on top.

"Sorry about that." He frowned at the powder. "She did it before I could stop her."

"It's fine, thank you" I blew the foam and took a sip too quickly.

Ouch shit! Did he notice? Ugh, this is so embarrassing.

I attempted to cover my reaction, but my eyes watered as I tried to stifle my internal screams.

"Hot?" He asked with a small smile.

"Just a bit," I sniffled as my nose dripped in response.

His forehead wrinkled as he took another sip. "Jeez, this coffee isn't great, is it?"

I stifled a smirk. "I didn't want to say just in case this was your spot, but no, this place isn't good."

He placed the mug on the table with a frown. "I don't really do this sort of thing normally. I'd no idea a bad coffee place existed. I guess I work too much."

"Are you not working today?"

"Yeah, I've got meetings this evening. It never stops. I

hate those guys who work all the time." He rolled his eyes, mocking his own work ethic.

I giggled as I watched him cradle his mug in his hands, seemingly immune to the heat radiating from the ceramic.

His eyes fixed on mine. "I love that sound."

I frowned as I glanced over my shoulder to see if I'd missed something obvious. "What sound?"

"Your giggle. It's cute."

He does like me! Don't say anything weird.

"Oh. Um, thanks Dan." I looked down at the demonic coffee in front of me, not sure whether I'd be able to muster up the courage to drink it again.

"Wait—You have meetings at night time?" The thought suddenly struck me as odd.

He nodded as he took another sip and grimaced. "Yuck, this coffee gets worse! But yeah, no rest for the wicked. I have international clients."

We sat in an awkward silence again for a minute as I wasn't the type of girl who could make conversation around business. Pretending to understand something I knew nothing about was not my forte.

I peered at my watch to find we'd been an hour already.

"We should probably head back soon. I'll need to get ready in case I get a call for work."

"Sure, no problem." He gulped down his coffee and licked off the foam moustache from his top lip. "Ready when you are."

Every inch of me wanted to hold Dan's hand on the way back to the car, but I refrained with every fibre of my being as the last thing I needed was my face all over the internet.

Our proximity was close enough to appreciate the magnetism repeating itself, encouraging my insides to clench hungrily for even the smallest exchange.

The car ride back to the mansion was quiet. It appeared Dan had questions to ask and more to say, but the unspoken understanding between us created a barrier, and instead the radio filled the silence. Did he regret spending the day with me? I most certainly didn't have any regrets. If anything, I hoped he would want to see me again.

A curt nod towards Dan from one of the pimps security team welcomed us back home, and Dan parked up near the front door.

As the car came to a rolling stop, he turned down the volume of the radio. "OK, so I guess I'll just have to drop you off here. I need to get home. Tell my jerk-off brother to take care of you."

"Thanks, Dan." I leant over and kissed his cheek. "I've had a really great time."

"Me too, Jasmin. It's been wonderful."

I watched with a pang of sadness as Dan's car left the grounds just as the front door opened.

King's tall frame towered over me with a look of contempt on his face. He removed the cigar from between his teeth and threw it on the floor by my feet. "Get in my fuckin' crib now, Bitch!"

Aghast, I stayed motionless in response to his unprovoked hostility. Like a terrified animal being preyed upon, I didn't know which foot to put forwards, and my hesitation only angered King further. He reached for my arm, gripping my skin tightly, as he pulled me towards his chest into a firefighter's carry. I hung limply within his hold, too scared to protest the awkward position he'd put me in.

Don't fight back.

Setting me down in the hallway with a thud, he forced me into a small, dark room behind a concealed door under the staircase. The room was dark and musty, with no ventilation or natural light.

What is this, some sort of torture chamber?

My heart was in my mouth with sheer terror at his undisclosed intentions. Was my time with Dan that serious?

Out of nowhere, he smacked me hard in the face, snapping my head in the opposite direction.

"You fuckin' my brother?" He yelled and then hit me a second time.

"No! Daddy, please," I wailed, "I didn't. I'm sorry!"

Raising my arms in front of my face, I waited for the next blow.

"You belong to me! I thought I made that clear to you this mornin'?" He reached between my legs and grabbed my flesh. "This cunt is mine. You understand, Bitch? You even look at him again, and you're dead!"

"I'm—I'm sorry."

King grabbed onto my hair and forced me to the ground. First to my knees and then flat on my back.

He stepped over my body, a foot on either side of me as he glared into my eyes, panting, with his fists bunched by his sides.

My bottom lip trembled as my stressed pupils expressed my fear. "Daddy please. I'm so sorry."

In a directional shift of trajectory, he suddenly broke eye contact. He took a deep breath and stepped to the side, where he looked at the wall ahead of him.

"You ain't makin' King money if you're dead. You're lucky I'm good at business. Now get the fuck up out of here and get in my bed. I'll punish you there instead."

In a struggle to catch my breath, I gasped, lying in the same position he'd put me in. Anxious torment consumed me that he might change his mind and attack me again for moving.

Do I lie here or do I run?

With his back turned towards me, he sat on the only chair in the room, where he lit a cigar and placed it between his teeth.

Once there was enough distance between us, I scrambled up onto my feet, keeping my focus on him in case he sprung another attack on me.

Run!

Like a newborn taking its first breath, I gasped for air when I made it back out into the safety of the hallway, where sweat chilled my brow as my trembling hands cocooned my body in seeking comfort.

Alice crossed my path as she left the kitchen on her way up the stairs. She did a double take and stopped when she saw the fresh wounds on my face, and without thinking of her own safety, she hugged me tightly.

"I did warn you, Jasmin. We've all been there, Honey. Just don't upset him again, and he'll forget all about it." She held me by the shoulders as she assessed the damage.

I sobbed tears of my past, present and future. "What do I do now, Alice?"

The corners of her mouth raised in a small, apologetic smile. "Go get cleaned up and keep out of his way for a while." She hugged me tightly again. "The downstairs bathroom is just over there. Listen, I have a meeting with Tatiana now. I'll see you later, OK?"

The sound of her bare feet padding along the stone floor was all I had left to hold on to until suddenly I was alone again.

A tingling sensation at the base of my spine made me spin on my heels to check if King was behind me, imagining him wielding an axe, waiting to remove my head at any further misdemeanour. But he was nowhere to be seen.

Petrified in solitude, I did as instructed, paying a visit to the downstairs bathroom to clean up the aftermath and assess the damage.

I turned on the faucet and scooped the cold, cleansing water over my face. The reflected image within the wall hung vanity mirror told a story. A sad narrative of a young woman who made the wrong choice. She didn't mean any harm by it. She never did. But somehow, here she was again, destitute and terrified, with a swollen eye and cut lip to illustrate her mistake.

Why did I get involved with a pimp again? I should've listened to my gut first, and then to Alice's warning.

But I genuinely thought King was a good guy, and our connection was so much stronger than his actions inside the punishment room suggested.

The way he was so gentle with me this morning; intimate. Not for a minute did I think he would be a complete psychopath, capable of this.

While contemplating my next move, genuinely considering leaving the mansion, I heard a familiar voice of a happy female sashaying her way through the wide open front door.

"Your daughter is home, Daddy!" Hanna squealed with exuberance. She must've scored big in her last job explaining why she had been AWOL the past two days.

Tentatively, I pushed against the bathroom door, where it creaked open, and our eyes met.

"Chloe?" Hanna stepped back in alarm. "What are you

doing here?"

If Hanna would have given me the courtesy of replying to my messages, or even reading them, she would have known exactly why I was here.

I sighed. "Nancy kicked me out."

She took a step closer, eyeing my face. "Oh my God," she whispered in a strained voice. "Wha—what the fuck happened to you?"

I sighed as my lower lip wobbled. "Long story. I'll tell you when I can. Honestly, I'm OK, though."

Despite my prayers against seeing him again, the door to the punishment room opened at the sound of Hanna's calling.

"Shit! I gotta go, Han! I'll find you later and we'll talk."

Hanna watched me with her mouth ajar as I scurried off towards the bedroom, fleeing to safety from the pimp. Bounding up the stairs like a marathon runner, I took the steps two at a time, and when I reached the top, I paused to listen in on Hanna and King's conversation below.

"So, what you got for me, Shorty?" He asked, behaving like nothing had happened.

"I won big for you, Daddy."

The telltale sound of lips smacking together gave me a

confusing, jealous knot in my stomach, wishing it was me in her place. *Why?*

By the time I'd reached the bedroom, their voices were just an echo.

Once inside the confines of the master suite, I closed the door behind me, resting my back against the wood with my eyes closed to rebalance my equilibrium. When my lids reopened, Alice was the first person to catch my attention. She leant over the bedside table with a spoon in one hand and a lighter in the other while Tatiana made preparations of her own.

"Um, what are you both doing?" I scowled at the obvious.

Alice produced a vacant smile. "It's just a little pick me up. No big deal."

It was a surprise when Tatiana acknowledged my existence as she glanced at my wounds. "You want some? Might take the hurt off your face. Girl, you need to be more careful if you don't want Daddy to punish you."

It sounded as though she was speaking from experience, and suddenly we had something in common.

I begrudgingly sat on the bed next to the two of them.

"Yeah, I guess I learned the hard way."

Alice handed me a bottle of her sleeping pills from the

bedside table, and shook it like a rattle in front of my face. "Here, take two of these and you'll be out until morning."

In a strange predicament, as though I'd found myself in the Matrix, I looked at the two white pills sitting innocently in her palm. *Take? Or don't take?* That was the question.

With resolve to starting a fresh tomorrow, I took the pills and chased them down with a gulp of water, ready to fast-forward this day in view of the next.

Before long, the girls were out like a light and as I lay down by their heavily intoxicated bodies, my mind drifted down the river with thoughts of Dan and a rescue mission involving romance, guns, and a bullet in King's head.

CHAPTER 5

When I woke with a start the next morning, the three of us were still in the bed together. This time it was King who had slipped away early.

My head pounded, and my heart was heavy. So much had taken place yesterday, I didn't even know where to start.

Groggy and uncoordinated, I rose out of the warm sheets and stumbled my way to the shower, feeling nauseated and in need of washing away the remnants of the sleeping pills from my body.

My first overwhelming task was to wash my hair using someone else's products, probably Tatiana's, and while I scrubbed my scalp, my mind drifted to thoughts of her and her hideous personality. Why was she so special? But more importantly, why was King happy to try for a baby with her knowing that she was a hard-core drug user? The poor child wouldn't stand a chance with parents like that. And yet he punished me yesterday, not her. According to whose twisted rule book was my trip with Dan any worse than Tatiana's blatant disrespect for him?

Frustration bubbled in my stomach, threatening to explode, and I had to redirect my focus onto something more productive before the dam burst.

After a much needed freshened up, I decided on an outfit from my new clothing collection, courtesy of Dan's approval.

Mindful of the whores still dozing, I quietly rummaged through my old leather bag of options.

Perfect. This'll work.

I held up the dress that Dan had handpicked for me, and as soon as I shimmied it over my matching pink bra and thong set, I thought about him. God, I missed him and his sweet nature. *What is he was doing right now?*

My reflection caught my attention, prompting a double take as I passed the floor-length mirror, where I assessed my appearance in more detail. With my bangs styled forward, and some carefully applied makeup, I successfully covered most of my eye bruise. I couldn't do much with the lip cut other than to coat my lips in plenty of red gloss to conceal best I could.

But the more I gathered myself, the heavier my legs became, and with each step I took, another part of my aching body warned me to leave this place for good.

Why am I still here?

"Your outfit is cute," Alice croaked in her sleepy, hungover morning voice, bringing me back to the present. Her wakefulness calmed me; I was no longer alone.

"Thanks. You like?" I gave her a twirl that puffed out my dress from the waist down.

"Yeah, I do," she yawned. "I'll have to borrow it sometime." With a devilish smirk on her pretty face, she meandered towards me, still lightly intoxicated. Her pupils hadn't yet returned to normal size. "We missed out on some fun last night, didn't we, Jasmin?"

Her explorative hand caught my attention as she reached for the buttons of my dress. First she popped open the top button, and then the next.

I began re-buttoning in protest. "Not now, Alice, I just got dressed."

"You should join me and Tat next time. It'll relax you, make you less—what's the word—frigid."

Affronted and already bruised, Alice's complete disregard for my feelings shouldn't have come as a surprise, but it did, and it hurt.

"Thanks for the offer, but I don't do drugs."

Alice exhaled with a small groan. "That's a shame. God, I'm starving."

She reached over my shoulder, prickling my senses, and grabbed a robe, hung on the back of the door behind me.

"Let's go eat. Follow me"

And follow I did.

Despite there being a kitchen full of people, I was the most lonely I'd ever felt. Breakfast in solitude wasn't my ideal kind, but Alice was chatting to someone I didn't know, and I'd not heard from Hanna at all since our fleeting visit when she arrived home last night.

As a result, I was shy and withdrawn, but it seemed my confidence was being knocked from all angles and what I thought I knew in life didn't seem to apply within these four walls.

The slim man dressed in his chef whites with silver grey hair looked upon me with kind eyes. "You look hungry, Darlin'," he smiled brightly.

I nodded, grateful that he read my mind, as he passed me a plate filled with scrambled egg and a side of crispy bacon.

"You should hit the gym after that," a whore piped up, looking at my plate with revulsion.

I'd not had the pleasure of meeting her before, but plain features and a pixie nose were all she had to offer, similar to most of the women living under King's roof.

"How am *I* your business?" I eyed her with an upturned lip.

In that moment, if she'd asked me for a fight, I would have given her one. But fortunately for her pixie nose, she didn't react to my challenge, finally choosing to focus her attention back on the black coffee she was using as a meal substitute.

It didn't take much, but my appetite completely vanished. Anxiety lay heavy in the pit of my stomach as my fight or flight activated, but I made a point of finishing every mouth full of the chef's plate.

As I chewed over my last bite, a distressed-looking man stormed into the kitchen and stood over the top of where I sat, creating a shadow over my meal.

"Um, hi?" I said, swallowing the remnants.

"Boss wants to see you. Now."

Oh, God no.

"Right now?" I squeaked.

He nodded. "Yes. Right now."

I scrambled out of my seat. "Oh, sure. OK."

I choked down the last shards of well-cooked bacon that had tried to exit my mouth twice already. The fragments scratched as they travelled down my gullet, and tears pricked my eyes again.

I couldn't handle another beating, especially not so soon after the last.

As I followed King's crony to find the man in question, I was relieved to see Hanna stood by the front door, emitting a similar expression that mirrored my spiralling emotions.

"Jasmin! Hey, girl." Hanna breathed a sigh of relief when she pulled me into a hug.

"Hey, Han! You're coming too?"

"Yeah. I'm scared." She put her acrylic nails to her mouth. "I hope we aren't in for a punishment. You sure as shit couldn't take another anytime soon." She slid her sunglasses down her nose to get a better view of my face. "Ooh Girl, he really did a number on you." Her index finger pushed the frames back into position as she regained her composure.

As we stepped out into the open air, she hooked my arm in the loop of hers.

"So, what did you do to piss him off?"

"Nothing." I shrugged, "except making the mistake of going shopping with Dan."

"What!? Dan as in Dan Giannetti, AKA King's brother Dan? That wasn't a smart move, Babe." She snorted restlessly.

"Well, I know that now, don't I?"

Her mouth softened. "Sorry, Chloe. I know you haven't done the pimp thing before, but they are very particular about their shit. It's all about power."

Hanna was right. It was a stupid error on my part, and I should've listened to my own instincts as well as Alice's warning. But now I paid the price via the wound on my face and the dent in my ego.

The man who collected us caught up to our meandering pace. "Hurry the fuck up whores. Don't make the boss wait."

We picked up speed along the driveway to the waiting pimp, who had probably adorned his boxing gloves for round two.

"We got this." Hanna's voice quivered. "We definitely got this."

Arm in arm, we drew closer to where King stood amongst his valet team in the parking lot-driveway. I took a deep, steadying breath, fearing that the worst was yet to come.

King smiled when he spotted us walking towards him. It was a confusing vision. "Yo, hoes," he said, as he steamed towards us, muscling his way in between us, cutting mine and Hanna's connection when he put his large tattooed hands around the back of each of our necks, urging us forward. "Come over here."

He escorted us towards the crowd of men huddled around his fleet of vehicles.

Are they gonna take it in turns?

The contact of my skin against his produced electricity that sparked between us. How is that still possible when I hate him? *But did he feel it, too?*

Upon our arrival, the crowd parted to reveal an identical twin set of vehicles in a beautiful sky blue colour with a white stripe over the hood and roof.

We halted right beside them where King let go and turned to face us.

"These right here are a present from King to his whores. Take a look and then come to bed and thank me."

Hanna leapt into the air with an expression like she'd just won the lottery and her eyes gleamed with elation. "Oh, my God Daddy, no way! Thank you!"

Say something. Do something!

But how was I supposed to react to such an extravagant gift on the back of an evil assault that we hadn't spoken about or even acknowledged?

Despite my internal mixed feelings of gratitude and

resentment, I stared at the cars with my hands bunched by my sides, wondering if a squeal or a yelp was the most appropriate sound to make.

My lack of response didn't go unnoticed and King was on me like a missile. He leant into my ear and breathed deeply against my skin. "You know, you don't say much, do you?"

I winced—I couldn't help it, misinterpreting the heat of his body against mine as another attack.

Vice like hands gripped my waist and turned me to face him. "Get this straight. I don't correct my whores if they behave. You need to learn quick that the correction I gave you yesterday is over. If you act right now, I won't do it again. Got it?"

I glanced nervously at the men shining my new car. Did we need to do this with an audience?

"Eyes off them and on me. Do you get my point?"

"Um, yes, Daddy, thank you for the car."

In a move that replicated Hanna's, I rose onto my tiptoes and kissed the corner of his mouth gently, still sensitive about the cut on my lip, leaving a red lip gloss stain within his stubble.

He reached into his pocket and pulled out the key to each of our cars, tossing one over to Hanna to catch mid air and the other he held out towards me.

As I came to receive it, he kept a firm hold. Both of us paused with the key between our fingers when, eventually, he smirked and released his grip. "You're welcome."

After a moment of intense sexual magnetism shifting between us, he addressed us both again. "OK bitches, listen up. Use these vehicles for work only. You gotta get rid of that heap of shit you've been drivin'. You'll kill someone or get killed, and it doesn't do my rep any favours, you get me?"

Hanna nodded in agreement and, for once, she found herself speechless.

Out of my depth, and out of control, I followed Hanna's lead and climbed inside my car as she hopped into hers.

Wow—

The welcome message on screen accompanied with a cheerful tune informed me this was a Mini Cooper S. Equipped with black leather seats and matching steering wheel accessorised with blue stitching that mirrored the car's exterior colour. She was stunning. And, of course, that new car scent I loved filled the cabin and tickled my nose hairs.

Naturally, I ran my hands around the steering wheel where the plushness of the expensive material caressed the palms of my hands.

Why did King do this for me now so soon after yesterday's correction? Was he expecting something more than sex from me in return? Or was his guilty conscience becoming something he couldn't ignore?

As best friends do in sync with one another, we stepped back out into the L.A heat together, with a smile spread across my cheeks and a grin on hers.

King didn't match our energy with a stony expression etched into his features. "Follow me sluts."

I glanced at Hanna and she at me as we accepted the king's order, dutifully following him inside the house and straight up the stairs towards his bedroom.

We reached the top of the stairs, and he pushed open the bedroom door, where he stopped still as his muscular back shielded my view.

"Tat, what the fuck is goin' on here?" King yelled, his tone laced with betrayal and his reaction filled me with an icy dread.

"Obviously we're getting high." She muttered with chemically induced confidence. "This latest shit you're selling really hits the spot."

It was clear now that she was used to overstepping King's boundaries without so much as a single consequence for her actions.

"I can see that, you stupid slut. Two times in two days? Do you want my kid born retarded or somethin'?"

Witnessing, an alpha male becoming visibly unnerved, was alarming, especially since this one was capable of anything.

As King stepped into the room, my view became crystal clear. Tatiana was in possession of a needle, not paying him much attention as he stormed towards her.

He leant over the bed and snatched the needle out of her hand. "Get the fuck out. I'll deal with you later," he snarled, tossing the drugs into the trash can next to his side of the bed that was filled with used condoms.

Tatiana tutted, "you ruin everything," she said as she eased out of bed in her own sweet time, in her lace underwear with see through thong, but she didn't care.

Alice followed Tatiana like a lost sheep, creeping out of the sheets in fear of King's reaction. Our eyes met during her departure, and the weird sexual chemistry between us hadn't yet abated, but I couldn't help but feel disappointed in her.

"These goddamn bitches always testin' my patience!" King yelled as he kicked the door closed behind them.

Hanna and I didn't want to complicate matters further. We understood our role, standing quietly up against the wall, waiting for our next instruction.

After a moment of pacing the room, he composed himself, and Daddy was back. He pulled his dick out of his shorts and began masturbating, as if time was of the essence and frustration was his driving force.

Still and quiet, we observed from our front row seats the vision of the handsome man unravelling before our eyes where, to my surprise, he didn't stop until he ejaculated.

His eyes, alight with emotion, bore into mine and there was no question he had a round two to share.

First, he grabbed hold of Hanna and pushed her down to her knees so she could suck him. Not needing to vocalise his command, she got to work without hesitation, licking at his climax and tasting all of him.

A knot of excited apprehension swelled in my stomach for what he might ask of me. There was no denying that our intimate encounters were something special. It was his behaviour afterwards that was debatable.

As Hanna worked her magic, she got King into a frenzy. This girl had some serious techniques that I could watch and take notes on all day long. Her impeccable skills served him as his dick grew solid again, while she pumped him with her fist and sucked the juice from him like he'd provided the straw to the juice box.

His eyes closed and his head lolled backwards as he absorbed her offering until it became too much and he pulled her by her hair, attempting to regain control.

"Slow down." He panted, "I need a minute."

His thick shaft, red and heated with arousal amidst the impendence of an orgasm, threatened to consume him imminently.

"Both of you, get on my bed. I'm going to show you sluts who the king is."

He reached for Hanna's shorts and tugged them down, along with her underwear, discarding the items on the floor.

Equally, he turned his attention to me. "Take that dress off. I wanna watch you."

As directed, I pulled the thin fabric over my head where I tossed it onto the waiting pile. Next were my summer sandals that he peeled off my feet while eye contact with him didn't wain.

Oh, please. Touch my body. Anywhere.

He turned his focus back towards Hanna. "Open your legs. Let me see that pussy."

My eyes fixed on the man before me while I watched

him drop to his knees, where he nestled his head between Hanna's legs. And the longer I lay spectating, the more insecure I became.

Was he still angry with me and this was my punishment? Did he want me to watch him treat my best friend with the compassion I lusted after?

Seeing his soft black curls moving up and down as he worked on her made my insides clench. The image of his tongue there. *Fuck*—I yearned for his head between my legs. I wanted him; needed him.

Hanna moaned, appreciating his expert tongue. Her head slumped as she experienced his lips against her most sensitive area.

"You need to come for me, slut?" He groaned into her flesh. "You want me to stop?"

"Don't stop Daddy, please," she pleaded as her legs trembled.

Abruptly, he withdrew, wiping his mouth. "I say when you come. Now ain't the time."

His hands snaked around my thighs, enjoying the softness of my skin. "Get these little panties off. Show me your tight pussy."

He hooked his thumbs into the waistband of the thin fabric. My skin tingled in response to the electrically charged influence of his heated hands against my body.

Fuck me.

With my rear raised off the sheets, I joined him in sliding them down seductively, where he snatched them from me and pushed the material to his nostrils, sniffing the crotch.

"Hmm. Your smell gets me hard."

He wrapped the pretty pink fabric around his dick and stroked himself with the material.

I blushed at his compliment. The more intimate our encounter, the easier it was to forget what he had done to me.

King was gentle when he licked the folds of my delicate sex, working my clitoris with slow sensual circles, just as I'd imagined he would. His ability provided skills that spoke to me more powerfully than words.

He does care about me.

I ran my hand through his hair as the warmth of his breath heated my flesh.

That's it. Shit. I'm so close.

A clench of delight formed in my stomach, building my orgasm as my hips thrusts forward into his mouth.

In response to my soft moan, he retreated, peering at me with a coy smile. It seemed as if he enjoyed getting me off as much as I did receiving it.

King looked at Hanna. "Go and sit in the corner until I say. Play with your pussy while you watch me fuck your friend."

"Yes, Daddy." Hanna reacted immediately. As expected, she scrambled to her feet, knowing his patience was as fine as the voile curtains that dressed the window.

King took her place. Lying next to me on the bed where the first kiss he offered my lips was gentle. He reached inside my pink lace bra and scooped out one of my breasts, revealing my nipple.

"You sexy slut," he hummed as he unclasped the bra band with one hand. "I love these tiddies."

As the bra fell and my breasts became exposed, the areola tightened, raising my nipples into stiff peaks in anticipation of his talent. He cupped the swell in his hands and caressed the teats with flawless execution.

"What's your name?" He whispered between strokes.

Fuck—Oh God. "Um, Jasmin." *Is it? I can't think straight.*

"I'm goin' to make love to you now, Jasmin, and this will mark our bond with each other. You got that? I told you King plays no games with his whores. I see potential in you, and I'm goin' to have you as mine. My brother can't give you what I can."

"Yes. Please." I nodded breathlessly as my composure

unravelled with every heart beat.

Our hands interlocked as King raised them by the sides of my head, pinning me to the mattress.

With his powerful body positioned on top of mine, he nudged his dick into my slick opening, lubricated by his tongue.

Oh. Oh—

Driving forward, he sunk himself all the way inside, where he moved back and forth with exquisite tempo, kissing my neck and chest, and then my breasts again.

Ahh. Shit. Please.

With my nipple in his mouth, King sucked the erect mound as he kept up his stroking rhythm deep within my core.

Eventually, he let go of my hands, allowing me freedom to run my fingers along the length of his back as I took every inch.

"You're on the pill, right?" He said between breaths, reaffirming a question he'd already asked at my audition.

"Yes, Daddy."

"Good girl." His dick swelled in response. That was his green light to claim what was his.

My moan evolved into a plea as my body reacted to our attachment.

"Tell me when you're ready, Jasmin."

That was all it took, and his words became my undoing as my body clenched, ready to release a mind-blowing orgasm.

Oh, shit. Fuck—

"I'm coming for you, Daddy!" My back arched and my insides quivered as my toes curled.

King kissed my neck as a primal grumble emitted from his chest. "That's it, you sexy whore. Come for the king."

His rhythm increased as he thrust himself forward once more until he emptied his load deep within me, wrapping his arms around my back, cradling me while he came hot and heavy. The wrath of his climax warmed my body, and we reunited in a way I didn't think possible.

King withdrew himself, rubbing the moisture from the tip of his penis over my sensitive clitoris as he planted soft kisses along my collarbone. His eyes filled with fire, looked down at my sex, where he'd just staked his claim. With primal urges, he pushed his finger inside me and placed the slick pad against my parted lips. He kissed my mouth, sealing in his gift for me, and I took it, all of it. I lapped up his kiss and moved my hands through his hair again as our tongues intertwined.

Unexpectedly, he broke away first, but when long dark

lashes framing ocean blue eyes looked deep into my soul, I couldn't help but smile. At that moment, it was just me and him in the room.

He watched my face with intrigue and brushed my cheek with the back of his hand as though he was trying to soften the blow he was about to deliver.

"Aight, Jasmin, your time is up. Leave me alone with—" he turned to Hanna with a frown, who was still playing with herself in the corner of the room.

"My name is Hanna."

"Yeah, exactly. Leave me with Hanna. You go and work out in the gym with the other whores. Don't forget, I like my girls with stamina. I can go for days."

"Yes, Daddy." My legs trembled from the intensity of my orgasm as I attempted to fulfil his order.

What I really wanted to do was stay put, monitoring what he might do with Hanna that he didn't want me to see. But an order was an order, and I pulled on my discarded clothing and rushed to my exit hastily, where the first thought I had was to find Alice.

A smirk formed on my blushed face when I thought about King's order. If he thought I was going straight to the gym after that explosive encounter, he was sadly mistaken, as there was no way I was in any fit state to work out now.

He wouldn't find out, or would he? Not unless a whore snitched, which was a distinct possibility in this house. But I figured I could handle the repercussions after seeing the side of him he'd just exposed me to. The side of him I had just said goodbye to that was now being privately intimate with Hanna. *Shit.*

My jealous demon reared its ugly head when I thought about him spending alone time with her in the placid, loving mood he was in. Why was she getting the special treatment? What did Hanna and Tatiana have that I didn't?

When the moment was right, I'd have to ask Hanna what had gone down between the two of them. I wanted to know and not know at the same time, concluding that not finding out was the less favourable option.

But what were they doing right now? My mind intrusively envisaged them fucking. His hands cradling her breasts as he pushed his dick inside her. Hanna's eyes closed, feeling him, loving him, him loving her. The thought practically turned my skin green with envy.

With resolve to ignore my resentment, I strolled into the kitchen where I soon realised I had company, and it soured my tense mood instantly.

Tatiana and another girl were at the far side of the room,

sipping coffee. As soon as they saw me enter, they began sniggering.

The mystery girl was a redhead that I thought might have been the girl giving me a hard time in the VIP lounge at King's club. It didn't take long to figure that they were talking about me.

"Does that new girl have disabilities? She creeps me out!" The redhead mumbled in my direction.

My eyes widened. *Disabilities? Me?*

Tatiana whispered something in response, but it was impossible to hear over the sound of the coffee machine percolating.

They snickered again, and instantly I was back in high school. But what was I supposed to do in a house full of whores who didn't like me? Hanna would know what to do. She'd help me handle this better than I could.

The red head leant into Tat and cupped her hand over her mouth as she side eyed me.

What is she saying? Did King think I was disabled too?

I jumped with surprise when delicate hands snaked around my waist.

When I snapped my head towards the sensation, I immediately relaxed when I saw her.

"You're jumpy," Alice said with an eye roll as she let me

go.

"Hey, sorry, Alice. I don't know why I did that."

"*Anyway*," she sighed sardonically. "King and Tat are baby-making again tonight. So, wanna have some fun?"

I paused in difficult thought about my options, which only exasperated the situation.

"Come on, Jas, we've been through this already! You need to stop with your lesbian struggles and just admit that when we fuck, it's amazing, OK? We don't love each other; we just know how to make each other orgasm. Simple."

Simple? It was anything but! She wasn't asking me; she was telling me we were going to spend the night together. Again.

I peered at the sniggerers, feeling a sense of isolation once more. If I didn't keep Alice happy, I'd have no one.

"OK." I said eventually, admitting defeat.

Her grin lit up the room, and she kissed my cheek. "Fab. Catch you later."

She left abruptly and floated towards Tat and the redhead before I could say anymore on the matter.

Oh. Bye then—

Just as I'd poured my coffee, my phone buzzed in my pocket, making me spill the hot liquid. I was so on edge today.

The message was from the agency with my next client.

< Agency > Threesome. 12 First Street 3:30PM

A threesome? They didn't come around often.

Careful planning was required to allow time for me to get showered and changed into something sexy before meeting my new clients.

With my fingers crossed behind my back, I hoped that by now Hanna and Daddy were at least finishing up their intimate exchange as I hovered outside King's bedroom.

With my ear pressed against the door, I listened for a clue as to what stage they were at.

Silence—*Phew.*

I hesitantly creaked open the door. *Don't be fucking her. Please—*

To my delight, Hanna was alone on the bed, napping peacefully, and Daddy was nowhere to be seen.

Feeling smug, I pushed open the door wider, and the hinge groaned louder. Hanna turned to face the sound and smiled when she saw me at the threshold.

"Hey," she said, a little gruff from what was clearly the best nap of her life.

"You look thoroughly well fucked." I giggled, pushing a

loose strand of hair behind her ear.

"It was amazing, Chloe. He said we were his best girls."

We?

My lips thinned. "Hmm, that's probably why those bitches were talking about me in the kitchen just then."

"Wait, who?" She propped herself up on one elbow, as if that would allow her to hear me better.

"Tat and a redhead were talking shit about me, saying stuff like they didn't like me or something, but I didn't catch much of it."

Omitting the disabled part was intentional. No matter our friendship status, Hanna would love nothing more than to tease me about that.

She ran her tongue over her teeth. "Jealous bitches. Don't worry, Daddy will keep you safe."

I squatted on the bed beside her. "Speaking of Daddy, how come he wanted me to leave, Han?"

I failed to keep the pang of my jealousy out of my voice that was simmering inside me.

"He said he wanted to give me some extra attention. Don't think too much about it. I made him happy yesterday; it'll probably be your turn tomorrow. Tat will be the one on his shit list after her latest fuck up."

I shook my head. "Shooting up whilst trying for a baby is

the lowest of the low."

Hanna nodded in silent agreement, and when I saw the sad look etched into her face, I remembered that her mother had done exactly the same thing when she was pregnant with Hanna.

"Sorry, Han—you know what I mean."

"Don't worry about it."

Time was of the essence, and when I peered at my watch, the dial served me a reality check and I needed to get my arse into gear. I jumped up and made my way to the bathroom.

"Sorry Han, I best get ready for my next client."

"Hold up," Hanna sat upright in bed. "What are you doing?"

"Like I said, just going to take a shower. You OK?"

The look on her face changed as she studied me in the condescending way she did when she assumed I wasn't being smart. "Chloe, this is Daddy's bedroom. You need to shower in the whore's bathroom."

"Ooh." I slapped my hands on my thighs with a smile. "I didn't get a chance to tell you yet. This is my room. I've been sleeping in Daddy's bed."

Her mouth opened, and her upper lip curled simultaneously.

"Since when!?"

"Um, since the beginning. I would've told you sooner, but you didn't return my calls. Listen, let me get that shower. I'll be right back."

When I re-entered the room ten minutes later, Hanna was nowhere to be seen. I knew I'd upset her with the drug comment. That shit always got to her when reminded of her mom and her abusive ways, but it was never that serious with my bestie. The next time we saw each other, we'd be the best of friends again.

I dressed in my grey pencil pleat skirt, blouse and matching grey button-up jacket, smoothing the fabric of the skirt down to iron out the creases. I desperately needed some wardrobe space.

As I turned, the mirror presented me with a reflection that I was happy with. Sexy enough to compliment the scene, but not too much to overshadow the woman. *Perfect.*

As I scooped up my keys on my way out of the front door, Tatiana was just leaving the kitchen after her latest bitch club meeting—still in her underwear—stirring a cup of something hot. "Nice suit," she smirked as she swayed her hips up the stairs.

What I craved to do then was karate chop her in the back

of the legs and watch her fall down the stairs to her doom in a *Death Becomes Her* sort of fashion. But what I decided on instead was not to rise to her childish ways to avoid having beef with King's best whore.

I'd just unlocked the car door when one of King's crew dressed in shabby overalls I recognised from earlier ambled over to me as I was about to climb inside.

With an unwashed hand and dirty fingernails, he caught hold of the car door where his cheeks hollowed on the final drag of his cigarette as he tossed it over his shoulder, blowing the thick smoke in my direction.

"Any free time for me, Sugar?" he asked with a crooked smile that revealed a missing front tooth.

"Not for you, I don't." I screwed up my nose, affronted as I tried to slam the door shut, but he kept hold of the frame.

"I'll give you one hundred bucks for a blow job right now."

The sleazy look on his face made my stomach wretch as he rummaged for the zip of his pants.

This is the last thing I need.

"No chance you creep, piss off!" I growled as I spat in his repugnant face.

His body recoiled as his hands reached for his eyes to

wipe away my revulsion.

That's when I took my chance and I closed the door, pressing the lock for added security as I hit the ignition.

With the ability to compartmentalise my trauma, I headed out to my next appointment like nothing had happened.

But this time, the box within my subconscious labelled 'deal with later' wouldn't quite close no matter how hard I battled with the lid.

My brows knitted together as I replayed the scene I'd driven away from, wondering who the hell was that guy back there.

I mean, sure, I was used to men trying it on inappropriately, but there was something menacing about that guy in particular that put me on edge, and I couldn't stop dwelling on it.

Fact was, he would've known I was one of King's girls, so why would he make a pass at me so openly?

The car ride to the other side of town was a dream, minus the anxiety. She handled beautifully, as expected, of a brand new car. The steering was light yet responsive, and the smell of fresh leather was to die for. It reminded me of my date with Dan.

As I turned off the engine outside of the client's home, I took a breath. Everything about the property was inviting, and the fragrant smell of the rose bushes along the carefully cultivated path made for a welcoming atmosphere by the time I arrived at the front door. I hoped the couple waiting on the other side matched the illusion they had spent so much time creating.

After straightening my suit jacket, I fixed my smile into place and used the chrome door knocker against the gloss black door three times and waited with a tangle of apprehension as to who might greet me on the other side.

There was a bit of movement before, finally, a beautiful, yet seemingly shy, woman answered.

Slim, with long, straight, dark hair down to her midriff, she exuded refinement. Her eyes were an enticing caramel brown, and she had the sweetest smile. Hovering behind her was who I assumed to be her husband. His build matched hers, but his face was plain and uninviting. With golden blond hair and grey eyes, he was average at best and his body language seemed unsure, clarifying that it must have been the wife who had instigated this arrangement.

After a beat of silence, I cleared my throat, "Hi, I'm Jasmin" I smiled a winner and offered out my hand to the woman.

"Oh. Hi, I'm Claire and this is John." She shook my proffered hand cautiously.

We exchanged awkward eye contact, and I giggled. "Is it OK if I come in?"

"Oh, I'm sorry. Yes, please do come inside, Jasmin. I'm a little out of sorts here, if you couldn't already tell." With shaking fingers, she swept her hair out of her eyes.

I stroked her upper arm for reassurance. "Don't worry. I'll look after you."

John was halfway up the stairs when he called down to the both of us. "Claire? Are we ready, or what?"

I'd been in the company of aggressive men before, and experience told me John didn't fit the criteria and for sure it was trepidation rather than hostility that tainted his tone.

As the exterior implied, they had a beautiful home with a modern warm toned colour palette, where the fresh scent of washed bedding caressed my nostrils as we made it to the landing just outside their bedroom.

John was already waiting inside with his hands in his pockets as Claire and I entered the room.

I took my position centrally and addressed them both.

"OK guys, you've booked a threesome, so what are your

expectations? I'll do whatever I can to deliver."

Claire didn't give John a chance to open his mouth.

"I booked a threesome because he can't make me come. I figured a woman could help? Maybe show him what to do?"

John blanched at his wife's candid words, rendering us all speechless.

But I didn't miss a beat and smiled in response. "Well, I'm sure I can help you fix that. How long have you guys been together?"

"Five years," John answered curtly, eyeing Claire as though it was five years too long.

"And in that time, have you managed to climax at all, Claire? With or without John?"

She peered over at John, who was staring at the back of her head. "Well, I can do it on my own, climax I mean, but —"

I raised my hand in acknowledgment. "Got it."

My inkling was that Claire felt curious about her sexuality, prompting her to book our appointment to test the water. She wouldn't be the first to question her preference when a partner couldn't deliver, so I focused my attention on her needs.

As luck would have it, I too had recently had my first

genuine encounter with a woman and this afforded me a level of confidence that I might not have previously possessed from the times I'd worked with Hanna.

I took a tentative step towards Claire and bit my lower lip as I peered at her through my lashes. A move that often worked on men. She, too, seemed to respond to my allure.

When she smiled, I kissed her lips, taking it slowly at her pace and it wasn't long before her body reacted, and she wrapped her arms around my neck, kissing my back.

Before matters progressed too far with Claire, I withdrew.

"Let's get John over here, shall we?"

Breathless and overcome, she nodded, watching me as I took his hand in mine and brought him towards us, coaxing the three of us towards the bed. I lay down beside Claire and began kissing her again as John watched on ahead.

"Do you like seeing us kiss, John?" I asked as I licked her bottom lip, taking it between my teeth.

He nodded, awestruck. "Yeah. Sure."

Using inspiration from my time with King, I took the lead.

"Take your clothes off and play with your dick while you watch me touch your wife."

My hand slid underneath Claire's shirt where I peeled it off her body and when I unclasped her bra, I revealed beautifully sculpted, perky breasts.

"Suck her nipples John." I ordered. "I'm going to play with myself while you enjoy her."

Claire kept her eyes fixed on me as she watched me push my finger between my slick folds and inside my vagina.

She copied my action and ran her hand down her own body and ran circles over her clitoris.

John's erection raised firm as he devoured her breast between his lips while he stroked his cock.

"Have you tasted her pussy, John?" I asked as I drove my moist finger into Claire's mouth.

Claire panted as her body responded to the sensory overload. "He's never gone down on me, Jasmin. Ever."

I placed my damp finger against her lips. "Shh. It's OK. Today is that day."

With my hair in my hands, I knelt before Claire's wide open legs. "Let me show you and then you copy, OK?"

John nodded enthusiastically. His erection pulsed in response as he continued to masturbate as per my instruction.

At first, I kissed her pussy and then I flicked the peak of her clit with my tongue. Claire's moans of agonising pleasure radiated throughout her rigid body.

I took hold of John's arm and pulled him down beside me.

"OK John, I'm going to suck your dick while you lick her pussy. I want you both to come together."

On his knees, he tentatively kissed Claire's inner thigh and while he familiarised himself, I pushed his cock inside my mouth. Alien to me at first was his size compared to King's, but it allowed me to take him all the way to the root as I offered him sweet pleasure of encouragement. With a twisting motion, I passed my hand along the length of his shaft as I sucked the head, bringing his body to the edge of glory.

"Holy fucking cow," he whimpered between her legs as he continued to pleasure his wife's flesh.

I sensed him build fast in my mouth where any minute he was about to blow.

"You nearly there Claire?" I asked as my lips smacked together when I pulled his dick from my mouth.

"Nearly." She cried as her body writhed around in the sheets.

She was so close, clear in her voice, but she was holding herself back from allowing John the chance to give her what she craved.

I leant into his ear with a seductive whisper. "Put a finger in her ass as you lick her clit."

No sooner had he entered her puckered opening, she convulsed. "Oh, my God! Help me!" She whimpered.

Claire's plea for salvation informed me of her earth shattering climax, as I sucked John's cock for the last time as he ejaculated in my mouth.

His body collapsed on top of hers as they lay in an orgasmic infused coma of ecstasy.

"Are you guys back in the room yet?" I giggled as I buttoned up my blouse.

John rolled off Claire's docile body laying beside her.

She sat up with messy hair and a smirk on her pretty face.

"Thank you, Jasmin. I think you just saved our marriage."

"Hey, it was nothing. You two have something good, and I loved helping you out. Thank you for inviting me."

She wrapped her arms around my neck, where her sweet smelling perfume relaxed my body into her hold. "Please come back again?"

"Sure, if I'm lucky enough to be invited back, I wouldn't hesitate. You just need to relax and give each other some time."

"I'll go and get your envelope. Thanks again so much." She kissed my cheek and strolled out of the room with a perky waltz that jiggled her breasts beneath her open robe.

When Claire was out of earshot, John stepped forward and tapped me on the shoulder. "I've been such a letdown for so long. Claire said she would leave me if this session hadn't worked. I'm grateful."

I cleared my throat, straightening out my blouse. "Like I said, just give each other some time. You'll get there."

With a triumphant internal smile, I shrugged on my jacket, where Claire met me on the landing. She passed me the envelope and hugged me tightly in an emotionally charged embrace I would never forget.

Traffic was light on my return home, which added to my already elated mood.

Who would have thought that only yesterday I was ready to leave the mansion and today could have provided a complete turnaround?

But as I thought about Claire and the way in which I handled her body and her mine, everything about the scene was as transactional as it was with a male client. Not once did I freak out in her company, and if anything, I actually enjoyed myself, feeling in control and completely at ease.

So what was my issue with Alice? And why was I so concerned about my sexuality when I was around her?

Did it have something to do with her holding all the cards? If I wasn't in control, then I was vulnerable?

Fuck, I don't know. But the more I thought about that woman, the deeper into the rabbit hole I fell.

My stomach was more than grateful that I made it home in time for dinner and without due care and attention—hot food on my mind—I parked my Mini in the only available spot near the entrance to the mansion. In my preoccupied state, my spacial awareness was a little off kilter, and when I swung open the door, it dinged against the car parked next to mine.

Idiot!

After a cautious glance over my shoulder to check for witnesses, I made a quick assessment where the damage revealed itself as just a small chip of paint. Relieved but shaken, I pulled my jacket tighter around me and rushed away from the scene of the crime, eager to disappear before someone caught me.

Once inside the warmth of the house, I dropped my

keys and bag on the table in the hallway and followed the delicious aromas coming from the kitchen. The chef's buffet style offering was mouth watering.

I chose a slice of beef, some garlic infused potatoes and salad with dressing. Delicious.

Sure, the plate was full, but I hadn't felt self conscious about my choices until I sat at the table with four other women. I was immediately uncomfortable when a whore eyed my portion as though I'd piled it high with dog shit.

With a grumbling stomach, I'd just taken my first bite when the room fell silent as Dan stormed in. I frowned as I watched him scan the room until he locked eyes on me.

"Jasmin," he said in a clipped tone, "come with me, please."

Curiosity as much as anything had me following his order, and when he grabbed my arm, he escorted me out of the room where everyone's eyes were on us as we left.

My mind raced through the back catalogue of possibilities as to why he had dragged me from a room filled with spectators, and then it dawned on me.

Oh shit.

"Listen Dan," I sloped behind him. "I'm really sorry about your car."

He led me into the dimly lit vacant living room to gain some privacy and, with a scowl, he turned to me. "What about my car?"

My eyes widened in the realisation that whatever this was, it was not vehicle related.

"Oh, um," I tucked my hair behind my ear, "the redhead dinged your car. Sorry, I thought you already knew."

He paused for a moment as he battled with his thoughts. Eventually shaking his head, he glared at my face.

"Forget about my car. What happened to your eye?" He studied my wounds that I had forgotten about.

"Nothing." I snatched my head away from his hold. There wasn't a chance I would snitch on King after we'd just reconnected.

"Did Romero do this to you?"

I shook my head. "No. Please Dan, I'm asking you to leave it."

His upper lip curled. "Bull shit he didn't and no, I will not leave it."

"Wait, how did you even know about this?"

As if summoned, King sauntered into the room with a couple of half naked females dripping off his arms. His steps faltered when he saw us alone.

Dan broadened his chest. "Romero, can I have a word in

private?"

King locked eyes on his brother. "Leave us sluts, I'll fuck you later."

The room descended into silence as we waited for footsteps to fade into the distance.

With vengeance on his mind, Dan pointed at my eye.

"You did this to her?"

Intimidation exuded from King when his chest puffed and his shoulders raised in retaliation as he stepped towards Dan with as much threat in his stance as humanly possible.

"It ain't none of your fuckin' business what I do with my whores."

My increased heart rate rattled my ribcage as the two of them squared up to each other.

"You feel threatened by me, Romero?"

Oh God. Dan's going to get us both killed!

"Pfft, when did your dick get so big?"

Dan stepped closer, visibly raging on my behalf, but King stood his ground.

"All we did was grab a coffee. I can't believe you did that to her face."

He smirked, enjoying Dan's agitation. "She ain't yours to care about. Look between her legs; I nutted in that tight cunt this mornin'."

"You're a prick!" Dan lunged forward and swung his fist through the air.

My hand shot to my mouth. "Oh God Dan, please stop!"

Of course, King dodged the blow, preempting the strike. He countered the attack by drawing his gun from its holstered location inside his waistband. Pure evil seeped from his pores when he placed the weapon against Dan's forehead.

"You might be flesh and blood, but I won't hesitate to pull the trigger if you disrespect me in my fuckin' crib, Boy."

Dan raised his hands in defeat to appease the elevated emotions that were scattering around the room like skittles.

"Chill out Romero. Calm down!"

King's voice remained low. "I'll calm down when you keep your fuckin' opinions to yourself. She ain't yours. Got it?" He released the safety, threatening to pull the trigger.

My knees trembled as I watched the two of them battle for the alpha male position.

"Please don't fight." My voice quivered. "Stop, please."

After a brief period of deep thought, King holstered his weapon and pulled out a cigar from his slim line silver case.

He lit the end and took a long therapeutic drag. "Get out

of my house, Daniele. I need a word with her."

Dan peered back at me, but didn't utter a word as he left the room. His embarrassment radiated from his body as he disappeared beyond my line of sight.

Once we were alone, King sauntered towards me. "You know, it makes my dick hard knowing that my little brother wants you. It makes me want you more."

He pressed his erection up against my stomach as he leaned in towards my neck where the testosterone pumping through his veins was tangible.

I want you too—

There was a timid knock on the living room door that interrupted us.

"What!?" King yelled.

A crew member stepped into the room with his hands rested at his lower back. "Sorry, Boss, but your brother is smashing up one of your cars."

"Son of a bitch!"

King gripped the cigar between his teeth and drew his weapon again, this time with intentions of using it. He stormed out of the room, leaving me breathless and confused.

What on earth would King do to Dan when he got his hands on him? Was this my fault?

My phone didn't buzz again all evening. Written in the stars for me to spend another night with Alice. The more I tried to remove myself from the situation, the deeper I found myself.

When she saw me enter the bedroom, she smiled brightly, as though she'd been waiting for me.

"Hop in," she said as she pulled the cover back to invite me in beside her.

King still hadn't arrived yet, and Tatiana was brooding quietly on her phone, probably messaging the red head to orchestrate my downfall.

"Wanna play?" Alice impatiently leaned in and brushed along my collarbone with her fingers. My nipples puckered immediately in response, betraying me like my body always did in her presence.

So obvious now, there was absolutely no way of preparing myself for this. Regardless of my vulnerability shield, she could disarm me with one touch.

I peered at her anxiously. "Um, but the light is still on?"

"So?" She swirled her finger around the same stiff peak. She knew exactly what she was doing, distracting and arousing me at the same time. "Tat doesn't care."

King burst open the door and strolled in before Alice had fully convinced me it was a good idea.

With hooded lids, he side eyed her, recognising immediately what her intentions were. "Save some of her for me, you greedy little slut."

He stripped off his tracksuit quickly and rolled into bed, turning out the lights where Alice pounced on me.

Her hands were in my hair, on my body, and inside me all at once as she attacked me like she had been craving me since last night.

Oh shit—

Before long, I found myself matching her urgency, fondling her breasts and nibbling her neck.

Alice moved her head under the sheets and between my legs, where she kissed my inner thigh.

Oh wow. Holy fuck.

Already primed from my threesome, I was soaking wet, and her delicate, skilful touch enhanced my arousal beyond my threshold. She knew what I liked even more than I did.

That's it. So close. Oh, oh, God!

A final flick of her tongue was all that was required and all too soon, I came violently into her mouth. Her kisses teased me until I had nothing left to give.

A giggle escaped her lips when her head reemerged out of the sheets. "If you were a man, I'd laugh at how quickly you come."

My salty arousal was present on her tongue as she offered me a sample, slipping it inside my mouth as I deepened the connection. With my hand in hers, she drove it between her legs where I urged my finger inside her as I palmed her clit, keeping up the rhythm as she groaned out my name.

A short while later, she, too, came for me. The resulting clench of orgasmic pleasure gave me a sense of united empowerment, something a man had never given to me before.

"Look who's laughing now. You came quicker than I did!" I said with a sly smile.

She chuckled. "Night Jasmin."

"Good night Alice."

CHAPTER 6

Alice and I hadn't spoken at all since last night, the idea of which was wreaking havoc with my emotions.

It seemed the more I tried to please her, the less impressed she was, but did she even care how I felt in all this? I'd hazard a guess at probably not.

Despite the humid temperatures in L.A this time of year, I decided on a denim skit, crop top and my go to roman sandals with leg ties.

I scooped up my car keys by the front door with an important errand on my mind that I couldn't delay any further.

Just as my hand brushed the handle, it swung open from the other side, revealing a tall, dark, and handsome man I'd hoped I might see again.

Suited and delicious, Dan's presence could knock the wind out of my sail anytime of the day.

"Jasmin, I've been looking for you!" His eyes glittered

with caution.

"Um, hey Dan, what's up?"

I looked over my shoulder, half expecting to see King running towards us with an axe. Dan's brazen attitude was asking for trouble.

He leaned into my body with his hands in his pockets.

"Romero made it clear he doesn't want me to see you again, but I have the advantage of being smarter than he is. I really want to see you."

"I'm not sure, Dan. I mean, you saw how he reacted the first time."

His eyes narrowed when he glanced at my lip. "That won't happen again. I can promise you that. I have an idea where we can see each other, and he'll be none the wiser."

The living room door opened and Dan darted across the room, where he began playing with the wall light fixture.

"Hey Mr. Giannetti," the redhead purred, "how are you?"

"Good, thanks. I noticed Romero had a bulb out."

She ran her hand along the length of his arm, "wow. I love powerful men who know how to fix things."

"Oh, please." I muttered under my breath with an eye roll to match. If Dan fell for that line, she was welcome to him.

Her manicured fingers hadn't finished prowling, and her

hand settled against his soft bulge within his grey tailored trousers.

"If you need a hand, you just let me know, OK?"

With my arms folded, I eyed the redhead as she sashayed her way along the hallway and into the kitchen with a hope and a prayer that she'd at least trip and fall on her way there.

Dan caught up to me where he cupped my elbow. He didn't even need to touch me, for my body to tingle against his proximity.

"Can I book you as a client tonight? We can spend the night together at my place?"

I turned on my heels in alarm. "That's your plan? Jeez, Dan I don't know. That sounds dangerous."

My mouth dried up like the desert and the lack of concern for his own welfare—let alone mine—was a gigantic red flag.

"I'm aware this isn't ideal, but from where I'm standing, it's the only way. He'll never find out, I promise."

His winning smile knocked me off balance. If I said no, the redhead would most certainly say yes.

My shoulders slumped in defeat against my unabating attraction to him. "OK, sure."

"Awesome." he winked. "I'll see you tonight."

In the wake of the brothers' fight yesterday, I struggled to comprehend how on earth Dan was still so bold as to walk right on into King's home, drop a bombshell and then leave as though nothing had happened. With the way he was handling things, perhaps we'd both end up in the punishment room together? I pictured a gladiator fight scene to the death, with King as the dictator, and suddenly my roman sandals had more than one purpose.

Eventually, the sound of Dan's car engine thundering to life was my cue to leave the house safely, free to go about my business as usual, where I really needed to go into town.

The welcome sensation of sun-warmed leather caressing my denim clad ass boosted my mood as I took a seat inside my brand new car, and as I thought about Dan's ludicrous proposal to see me again, I couldn't help but smile further.

Now it seemed it wasn't just me who missed our time together after our shopping trip. He had devised a way for us to spend more time together, proving I was worth more than I often gave myself credit for.

The familiar sound of the door chime as I strode into the pharmacy brought me an odd sense of comfort.

"Good morning Jasmin," The kind old dear with wrinkled features, called over to my direction from behind her counter when she saw me stroll in.

"Morning Annie."

As usual, I handed her my insurance card while she typed on her keyboard.

"You need a refill on your birth control pill?"

I nodded. "Please, I'll take a pack of sleeping tablets, too."

She slid my card along the counter with a small smile. "Need anything for that bruise, Jas?" She asked without judgement.

I shook my head. "No thanks, just walked into the door frame. You know how it is."

"Of course, Darling." She smiled as she loaded my order into a brown paper bag and passed me the goods. "Here are your meds. You look after yourself now."

After trekking half a mile to my next destination, my hands dropped by my sides when I saw the 'closed for maintenance' sign hanging in the doorway of the lingerie store that always carried my size.

Shit—

I really wanted to get myself some new underwear for my rendezvous with Dan tonight. Would he care if I turned up in an old set? Maybe I could borrow something from Alice?

When I returned home, less than impressed, I parked in one of the last remaining spots, which just so happened to be next to one of King's impressive vehicles within his fleet. I knew nothing about cars, but something told me this one was expensive.

With my tongue poking through my lips in concentration, I parked without incident, pretty pleased with myself as I turned off the engine and swung open the door.

"Careful Lady, this is a Maybach!" An invisible male voice called out from the other side of the car's body.

At first, his alarmed tone remained faceless until an average height man with weary brown eyes and a dark-haired buzz cut stood from his crouched position holding an old rag and a bottle of polish.

"Oops, sorry."

"Don't do what the last bitch did and scrape your bags down the side. This car is worth more than your life. Trust me," he glared, "you do not wanna know what Boss did to that whore. Sheesh."

His eyes wide replayed an image in his mind that seemed

to disturb to him.

"Thanks for the warning, but I've no clue what a Mayday is."

"Maybach." He corrected with a stern tone.

"Maybach yes." I blushed. "That's what I meant."

He dunked the rag into the polish. "Do yourself a favour and keep away from his fleet. Boss is very precious about his cars, and so he should be. There's a couple million dollars' worth on this lot."

I was curious why this man was so much kinder than any of the others I'd met before. "I'll be careful, thanks. What's your name?"

"They call me Snake. Listen, don't get it twisted, we're not friends. Boss sees us talkin', I'm dead. I just don't want another girl, well, you know."

Fact was, I didn't know. But something in the shine over his irises told me not to ask.

A banging noise distracted us both. The sound of which was coming from the workshop to the right of us, where a hive of activity surrounded a badly damaged BMW. They looked to be replacing the smashed up windshield.

Snake saw me gawking. "Keep your eyes on your own business. That shit with Boss and his brother could have gone real bad. Fortunately, Tommy stepped in before Dan got shot."

Tommy? That name was familiar.

I sighed as I watched the men work. "Yeah, I was there when the fight started."

"Woah shit. You're the girl they're fighting over?" Snake dipped his rag again, and this time crouched back down to busy himself.

I walked around the car towards him, hoping for more information where his whole body became visible, giving me a better look at the man I'd befriended.

His presentation was immaculate. Perfectly trimmed hair, a crisp white ironed t-shirt and utility trousers with shiny boots. He was a man who took himself and his role seriously.

"I don't think they were just fighting over me, were they?" I asked, hoping that was exactly the case.

Snake eyed me with scorn. "Shit, Lady, what's wrong with you? Don't come any closer! Do you want us both killed?"

My lack of awareness over the severity of the situation I was putting us both in only confirmed what he had already accused me of.

"Sorry, I'm new. I guess I need to get used to this."

"My advice? Be smart and get out now while you can.

This life ain't for girls without common sense."

"Excuse me?"

He shrugged. "Saying it how it is. Now bounce before someone sees us talking."

Something about Snake's serious tone urged me to listen to him, and I kept my head down as I created distance between us.

With nothing but a small paper bag in my hand, I strolled back towards the mansion, where I'd planned to raid Alice's underwear drawer, when King's irate voice travelled the expanse. He was barking orders at a small gathering of men by the front door that I was trying to gain access to.

A sweaty guy in dirty overalls with a buffing machine in his hand was getting the brunt end of King's assault.

"Son, I want this car gleamin'. If you do a shit job again, you're done. Got it?"

"Yes, of course Boss," he nodded, "my bad, sorry."

My hovering caused King to perform a double take when he saw me out of the corner of his eye. "Shorty, get your ass over here," he motioned with enthusiasm.

My heart sunk at the prospect of being in his company when he was in an aggressive mood, which seemed to be most of the time, from what I could tell. But with a shy smile, I stood by his side.

"Hey, Daddy," I said, reaching up on my tiptoes to kiss him on the cheek.

In an unexpected move, he pulled me into his chest, gripping me by the waist to face me towards the group.

"While she's here, I have somethin' to say because I heard through the vine that one of you was tryin' to get a piece of what's mine."

How did King find out about the creep? He must have eyes everywhere!

He let go of me and reached inside his waistband, pulling out a black gun. "Lets play a game, Homies. I ask you a question and if you get it wrong, you die."

Oh no. What is it with games in this house? First Alice, now King.

He opened up the clip and counted the rounds. "Aight, line up."

The frightened men produced a line of six terrified souls. Each of them with their hands in the air had a grey complexion that matched the tone of the game.

King's gun pressed against the first forehead of a young male who must've been no older than eighteen. His baby face and lack of facial hair gave him a childlike appearance that I instantly wanted to protect.

"Question goes to you first, Sam. Don't let me down 'cause I like you. Would be a shame to kill a friend."

Sam gulped hard. His quivering body evidenced his distress, but all any of us could do was watch matters unfold.

"How much would you pay to fuck this whore?"

"No money, Boss. I don't have the right to."

"Yes!" King thrust the gun into his waistband so he could applaud Sam's answer. "That's why I like you, Sammy boy."

The next man in the lineup I recognised immediately. It was him; the creep who asked me for a blow job.

My mouth opened to expose him, but the words wouldn't leave my lips.

"Clive, my man." King continued, "you've been one of my boys for what, five years?"

"Yes, Boss." The creep said. His arrogant demeanour was more relaxed than the rest.

King raised his gun again, this time to the creep's chest. "Do you want to fuck this bitch?"

Clive raised his chin with confidence. "No, Boss, you know I wouldn't do you like that."

King nodded in silent agreement, where he took one step to the right, putting him face to face with the next guy.

This time, it was the turn of a copper haired man with a warm-toned moustache I didn't recognise.

"Please, Boss, I'm sorry, please," he whined with quaking sweaty palms in front of his tormented gaunt face.

"You're sorry, for what exactly?" King snarled in a low, threatening tone, pushing the gun under the man's chin.

"I—don't know. I'm just sorry."

King pressed the gun deeper. "Did you try gettin' a nut from my whore?"

A stray tear rolled down the man's face. "No, Boss. I didn't, I swear."

"Yeah? Then why have you pissed yourself?"

The long dark stain down the man's over-washed coveralls illustrated how we were all feeling.

"You know what?" King turned to address the entire group. "I'm a busy man and I'm bored." He cocked his gun and pulled the trigger at the man's kneecap.

As the tissues exploded in slow motion with a fountain of blood that splattered against the gravel, blood-curdling screams of anguish filled the entire grounds of the property. A sound I'd never heard before.

"Let this be a lesson to all of y'all. Keep off my bitches!"

With fast breathing and unsure legs, I felt dizzy and gobsmacked all at once, wondering if I could keep upright for much longer.

"Get back to work!" King ordered, holstering his gun in his waistband.

Like a swarm of bees, they disbanded at once, none of them knowing what they were supposed to be doing next. Every single man with self preservation as his priority ignored the injured victim, who cradled his wounded leg, rolling on the ground, willing somebody to grow a pair and save him.

King didn't make eye contact with me when he stalked inside the house.

Had I done something wrong, other than not tell him who the real creep was? But had I mustered up the courage, would I have ended up with a bullet, too?

My phone buzzed suddenly, distracting me from the fraught activity of the turbulent crowd.

<Agency> Airole Way Bel-Air. Sleepover.

A message from the agency confirmed Dan was true to his word and had booked me for the entire night.

But after what I'd just witnessed, I stared at the screen with dread expanding inside me like a hot-air balloon.

The risk factor of our arrangement after King's latest

performance made me question my own sanity, along with Dan's.

I can't back out now, can I?

"Help me, please!" The man wailed as he reached his hand out to me in desperation. His eyes glistened with suffering.

And then the idea struck me. Surely I could do something to help him? King and I had an undeniable connection—we'd proved that in the bedroom on more than one occasion—so why wouldn't he listen to me now? After all, he just punished them to prove a point that I belonged to him. Didn't that mean something?

With determination as my driving force, I steamed inside the house, making a beeline for his majesty.

My sky high confidence convinced me I was going to tell him he'd shot the wrong guy. But the closer I got, the weaker I became.

By the time I'd found him sitting alone on the sofa in the living room, the belief I had in myself that shot a rocket up my arse, upped and left, leaving me stripped of my wings in front of the devil.

He'd just lit a cigar when he saw me enter. Without a word from his lips, he gestured for me to sit next to him.

Not knowing why I was even there anymore, I sat down as instructed. My body language tensed and he picked up on it immediately.

"S'up, Hoe?" He asked on his long exhale.

His simple question evoked panic in the back of my throat.

The last thing I should do right now was to tell him he was wrong. But why else would I be here?

The thought finally occurred to me I hadn't given him my latest earnings from the threesome yesterday.

I handed him the envelope stuffed inside my bag and he took it, placing it inside his pocket. "I'll pay you later," he murmured. "Just enjoyin' this smoke first."

I gulped past a dry swallow. "Sure, no problem."

Smiling sweetly, I was hyper aware that my intimidation often came across as disrespectful, but I never seemed to have words when I was around him.

"That British accent gets my dick hard," he said, fidgeting in his shorts. "Suck my dick. I need to release some tension."

He leant himself into the back of the sofa, offering me access to his body, where I didn't hesitate to reach for his erection that I'd become so accustomed to in such a short period.

The gun still in his waistband dug into his skin and he flinched while I froze in panic.

With the cigar gripped between his teeth, he reached into his shorts to grab the weapon, placing it on the arm of the chair with the barrel pointing in my direction. Did he do that intentionally?

I found my way inside his shorts again and pulled out his impressive length, that sprung free from the waistband with little encouragement.

He raised his rear off the chair and pulled down the shorts further to expose the leathery texture of his rose pink testicles.

With a kiss at first, I teased the soft skin, then moved my tongue up and down the shaft, lubricating him.

After sucking the tip, I moved my attention to the puckered skin of his testicles while running the length of his dick inside my clenched fist.

He let out a moan of appreciation and cupped the back of my head.

"That's it," he said with a hum of arousal. "Suck my dick, you little slut."

Footsteps entered the room, and eventually a throat clearing from a male voice attempted to gain King's attention.

I stopped dead with his ball sack in my mouth.

"Keep goin', Jasmin," he ordered impatiently.

He remembered my name.

As I continued my work, they conversed as if it was just the two of them in the room.

"Boss, it's Big Jimmy. He's in a real bad way and his leg won't stop bleeding. Something to do with his diabetes. Can I phone for an ambulance?"

King's parted lips didn't allow for a response as I sensed his orgasm brewing in my mouth.

He was close to his finish line when impatience took hold, and he grabbed my hair, pushing himself deeper where finally his orgasm entered the back of my throat.

"Shit!" he uttered, as his body flinched when he removed himself.

He let go of my head with a clearer frame of mind and tucked himself into his shorts, where he ran both his hands through his glossy black curls.

"Go on then," he flailed in his seat, "get him a God damn ambulance. Fuckin' weak ass bitch can't even take a bullet to the knee!"

"Thanks Boss, really appreciate it."

King paused a moment to relight his cigar, but when the man lingered, he glowered at him. "Fuck off then, and shut the door behind you!"

When the room finally became ours, King turned his attention to me.

"Which one is the diabetes again? Is that when your dick don't get hard anymore?"

I stifled a giggle at the sincerity on his face. "Um, I think that's impotence."

"Same thing," he muttered. "Anyway, Slut, that was some good head. I'll have me some more of that tonight."

He reached inside my top and pulled out one of my breasts from my bra.

My body responded as his lips clamped around my skin.

"I can't tonight Daddy." I panted against his teeth, scraping my nipple. "I have a client."

He paused and his jaw tensed. "A client, huh?"

"Mm-hm, yeah. It's a sleepover."

King seemed lost in his own thoughts when he peered into the distance.

When he and I found ourselves like this, I didn't want to be anywhere else but in his arms.

He rose from the sofa with urgency. "If I can't have you tonight, I'll have you now."

In awe, I watched as his powerful body moved across

the floor, but when I didn't follow, he turned to me with narrowed eyes, willing me to do something right for once.

He had little patience; that was for sure, and his level of coercion didn't seem to dwindle, no matter how many times he'd climaxed. But there wasn't an ounce in me that didn't want more.

When we reached his bedroom, sounds emitting from inside pricked both our ears like deer in a clearing.

King held out his hand against my chest, stopping me in my tracks, where he listened for a moment with his finger to his lips. His brows creased together when he heard a distinctive sound, a sound that had both of us thinking the same thing.

With aggression fuelled power, he shouldered open the door to reveal Tatiana's compromising position on the bed littered with drug paraphernalia.

"Right, that's it. I'm done with you, Tat. Get the fuck outta here!" he yelled in her direction, "I can't even look at you."

She was so high she wasn't capable of comprehending his words, let alone able to react to his order.

Filled with contempt, he closed the space between them and pulled her limp body off the side of the bed by her hair, where she thudded to the floor. Out cold, she had no fight against him.

"You can't even stand up? Pathetic fuckin' whore!"

"We're sorry, Daddy," Alice sobbed as she cowered, waiting for the same punishment she had consoled me over only days ago.

He threw himself on the bed and began massaging his temples as if to stem the biggest headache of his life.

"How am I supposed to bring a kid into this world when his mother is gonna do him wrong like that?"

I peered at Alice, and she at me. Neither of us was sure who he was talking to or whether he wanted a reply.

With unresolved rage, he swung his leg round and kicked Tatiana between her legs. "You're a dirty drugged up cunt!"

She groaned but remained motionless, and her lack of awareness only angered him further. "I'm fuckin' done with you and your bullshit!"

Alice and I remained inert. Instincts telling me I should leave, but my feet firmly anchored to the ground wouldn't budge.

"Alice!" He snarled. "Get the fuck out now!"

"I'm sorry Daddy—"

"I don't wanna hear what you gotta say." He pointed at

the door as his last instruction.

Silence fell upon the room, and he glared at me with residual anger. But as his eyes locked on mine, his demeanour resolved, and the atmosphere shifted between us.

"Come over here and sit on this," he murmured.

His primal desire and intentions were clear when he threw down his shorts to reveal his blazing hot erection. This man wasn't kidding when he said he could go for days.

An array of conflicting emotions lay heavy in my stomach as I gazed at the tempting offer before me, yet my worry for Tatiana lingered in the back of my mind. Did he not care as much for her as I assumed he did? Or had he finally reached his limit?

I climbed onto the bed beside him as he reached for a condom, where he rolled it down his length. He held me by the waist and hoisted me on top of him, hitching up my skirt, where he filled my insides with eight inches in one fluid motion.

"The way your pussy choke holds my dick is somethin' else," he groaned, kissing my collar bone.

He pulled the light fabric of my top over my head and unclipped my bra with one hand, replacing both his palms against my rear as he moved me up and down at his pace.

Once our rhythm became established, we drove in unison; staring into each other's eyes as we fucked. His irises shone, sparkling with raw emotion.

I came first. My consuming arousal clenched around his dick, squeezing him and spurring him on to ejaculate.

When my eyes opened, he raised me off and rolled me underneath him, pulling my skirt off completely.

On all fours, he shifted his body so his dick was in my face.

He tore off the condom and discarded it on the bed.

"You like it dirty?" He asked with ragged breathing.

"Um, yes, Daddy."

He paused for a moment in concentration until he began urinating on my chest. It wasn't much, but it was just enough. A move that a man makes when he's claiming his territory.

I scooped up a sample on my finger and put it to my mouth to taste the golden droplets. A few more drops came my way, and I licked the falling bead off the tip.

"You know your way around my dick, you filthy slut," he groaned as he sat back on his heels, where he stroked himself again.

He loved the feel of his own body, I could tell, and

watching him play with his penis made me yearn to encounter more.

He pumped three or four more times and then climaxed on my chest, rubbing the engorged head against my nipple as it puckered for him.

"I told you I need more of this," he mumbled, leaning into my ear to grab the lobe between his teeth. He kissed the nape of my neck while I ran my hands around his defined muscles.

With a soft moan shared between us, our tongues rolled around each other's mouths, exploring, devouring.

But all too soon, he withdrew with a heavy breath, creating a distance between us I'd become so accustomed to.

He pulled on his discarded shorts in a hurry and, as he rummaged in the pocket, he produced the envelope I'd given him earlier. "That reminds me. Take it."

I paused for a moment to read the complex scripture of his face and when I held out my hand; he gave me the entire envelope.

"All of it?"

He adjusted the thick chain around his neck and nodded at me.

"Wow. Thank you Daddy."

"You've done good today, Jasmin, you little British slut."

I couldn't contain my glee. The progress I was making with him in our brief time together confirmed what I'd thought from the first time we slept together. *He likes me.*

There was a knock on the closed bedroom door that interrupted our candid moment.

"Boss, the cops want a word with you," A timid male voice said from the other side.

"In a minute Sam!" King barked back without an ounce of patience as he threw on a fresh t-shirt. Even the cops couldn't command his attention.

He looked at me with softness in his eyes, reaching for my hair as he ran his fingers through the strands.

"Think about me with that client tonight, then come home and show me how you fucked him. You are mine. You know that, right?" Without warning, he slapped my behind to punctuate his sentence.

I yelped as I jerked forwards. "Yes, Daddy, I'm yours."

With the door ajar, he paused for a moment, drinking in my body, stealing one last look as though he were storing the image in his memory bank for later. And then, with a last nod, he left.

I sighed deeply and placed my hands over my beating

heart as I lay back down on the bed.

Without a doubt, he was the scariest man I'd ever come across, but in the most exhilarating way.

A low groan emitting from the ground beneath me reminded me that Tatiana was still in the room.

"Oh, shit, Tat!" I rushed around to where she lay in a heap on the floor.

She remained barely conscious, so I called the one person who I knew could help.

"Hello?"

"Alice it's Jasmin. Get up here and help Tat, will you? She's in a mess and I don't know what to do about it."

"Oh no, has she had a seizure?"

"No, well, I don't think so, but she doesn't look far from it. She needs help."

I peered over at the mass of entangled body parts on the floor. She'd been sick at some point and there was a concerning smell.

I didn't wait for Alice to arrive before I climbed into the shower in desperate need of washing away King's scent to prepare for my evening with Dan. Was it classed as cheating in my position?

Sure, King made it very clear I was his, but he didn't

add a definition behind his promise, so a night with Dan wouldn't change the relationship status we didn't have. *Would it?*

"Jasmin? Are you in there?" an angelic voice echoed around the tiled room.

"Um, yeah," I called over the roar of the water, "I'm in the shower. What's up?"

Alice sauntered into the bathroom with a smile on her face.

"Just letting you know Tat is awake. She just needed an upper."

I turned off the water and stepped into the cool air of the room, the hairs on my body raised to attention.

"An upper? I don't know what that means."

In a surprising move, Alice handed me my towel. "Get to know, Honey, you can't survive this place otherwise. Anyway, I'm going to spend time with Tat. She's upset. I'll see you later."

Upset? Why did Alice even care that Tat was upset? She didn't seem to give a damn when I was. If either of them had sense, they would stop doing drugs and stop pissing King off.

But no sooner had my inner monologue said those

words, I reminded myself of the perilous journey I myself was about to embark upon.

I'd just wrapped my hair in a towel when my phone rang.

"Hey, Han!"

"Jasmin girl, am I having the best luck or what?" She screeched.

"Why? What's going on?"

"You'll never guess. Daddy has only gone and invited me to stay the night in his bed!" She shrieked into the receiver.

I grimaced at the earsplitting sound, moving the phone away from my ear. "That's great Hanna. I'm at a sleepover with a client tonight, so it's a real shame I can't join you."

Envy crawled over my skin like an intrusion of cockroaches. *Why am I so bothered about this?*

She giggled. The sound grated on me like nails on a chalkboard when a noise in the background of her call grabbed my attention. Someone else was with her and for a moment, I could have sworn I heard King's voice.

"I best go Jas. See you soon, love you," She said eagerly, ending the call.

Stored in my subconscious, I replayed Hanna's words on repeat. King had chosen to spend the night with Hanna? Just typical that I wouldn't be home tonight.

Oh God, is Hanna my replacement?

I caught a glimpse of myself in the steamed up bathroom mirror and as I wiped away the condensation to get a better look. All I could see was hopelessness.

Hanna meant so much to me. Like sisters, we never allowed a man to come between us. So what was going on here?

I towelled myself down, in preparation for a night with Dan, where all I could do was hope that he had thought it through properly.

In a daze, I'd made it as far as the security booth at the entrance of Dan's gated community, not even sure whether I'd run a red light or failed to stop at a stop sign.

This plan was so reckless, yet I still found myself rolling down my window to speak with security.

"Welcome Ma'am," he tipped his cap. "Mr. Giannetti informed me you'd be arriving this evening. Go right on through. His place is the biggest on the left. You can't miss it." The guard said as he opened the heavy duty gate.

And there I was, suddenly stood at Dan's front door with my hand poised on the knocker. With a peek over my shoulder first to check for the pimp and his axe, I knocked three times for good luck, completely out of place and out of my depth.

He answered almost instantly, as if he'd been waiting for my arrival.

My smile reached my eyes when I saw him, forgetting just how handsome he was.

He wore a polo shirt with the top button open, a pair of great fitting jeans and sneakers. The chocolate curls that framed his forehead only added to his charm, especially the coil that rested over one of his emerald eyes.

A filled tumbler within his grasp held a double shot of gin with a slice of lime perched on the rim.

"Great to see you again," he grinned, his green eyes glistened with unspoken promise.

I flicked my hair back over my shoulder. "Nice to see you again, too." I smiled as a blush swept over my cheeks.

"Ma'am, can I take your keys?" A suited gentleman asked from behind me, making me jump.

Dan smiled at my concern. "He's my butler. Just wants to park your car in the garage."

"Oh, OK. Sure." I handed the stranger my keys. "Here you go."

Dan opened the door and held his arm out to welcome me inside where instantly, my eye was drawn towards a bunch of tall stemmed sunflowers in a vase on the granite-topped console table in the centre of the hallway.

I turned to him with a smile.

"For you," he said as he drew a sip from his glass. The ice clinked against the side as he took a hard swallow.

"They're lovely, thank you."

I reached in and nestled one of the yellow heads between my fingers, breathing in its fragrance. "I don't think anyone ever bought me flowers before."

"Ahh, another first. That dress looks great on you, by the way. I knew it would."

I couldn't help but smirk at the appreciation of the dress he'd chosen and that I'd intentionally worn. "Jeez, you're making me blush."

He walked past me and through the open plan living area, over to the kitchen island.

"Drink?" He called over as I followed him through.

"Yes please, my mouth is so dry." I perched on a stool in front if him, watching his every move.

Dan's house was in noticeable contrast to his brothers and I got the feeling a woman had been a part of making the place a home at some point.

His face changed as he looked me over while he poured,

"I'm sorry Romero did that to you."

"Don't be," I shrugged, taking the offered glass. I raised it to his, effectively dismissing the conversation.

He closed the space between us, where he ran his thumb gently along the cut on my lip.

I pulled his finger to my mouth and nibbled the tip to distract him from his brooding.

To match my playful mood, he drew his hand back dramatically. "Ouch," he mouthed as he shook his hand, waving away the imaginary pain. Dan knew how to have fun.

I giggled into my drink, taking a thirst quenching sip.

"I'm glad you agreed to this, Jasmin."

Insecurity dulled the sparkle in his eyes. After all, this daring arrangement wasn't too dissimilar to dousing in petrol and playing with a naked flame.

But I nodded in agreement when he smiled at me.

"Yeah, me too."

"Come on, let's sit."

Without hesitation, I followed him over to the enormous U-shape sofa that complimented the mammoth living space, and we took a seat next to each other, purposefully not leaving a distance between us.

"So," he rubbed his hands together, "I thought we'd order

pizza and watch some TV?"

My stomach rumbled on cue, and suddenly I was starving.

"Sounds great to me."

While we waited for our order to be delivered, Dan pressed play on a romantic comedy with Ryan Reynolds and Sandra Bullock. I wasn't sure just how into the film Dan was as he stifled a yawn on more than one occasion, but he soldiered on regardless.

But I soon realised when I didn't make an initiation that Chloe was the girl sitting on the couch beside him. I'd inadvertently left Jasmin back at the mansion. How was I supposed to treat Dan as a client when he was so good at making me feel like I wasn't a prostitute? If Chloe wanted to stay, would he even notice?

I leaned into his body in search of a cuddle, anything that would give me something to boost my confidence.

As he wrapped his arm around me, his wholesome response filled me with a warm glow when he kissed the top of my head and hummed a sigh of appreciation. So natural, as if we'd done it countless times before.

The movie credits rolled, and I peered up at his handsome face. "So, how was work? Did you have your late night meetings?"

He turned off the TV and placed his half-eaten slice of pepperoni back in the pizza box. "Works good. Usual really."

I rested my head on his chest again as I listened to him breathe. "How does that work? I mean, don't people know that you're King's brother? You know, with his reputation and all."

Dan's responding chuckle bobbed my head up and down.

"Romero's line of work that you're familiar with isn't what he puts down on his taxes."

"Oh, yes, of course," I sniggered. "Don't worry, I won't expect you to ask how work has been for me."

"Thank God. I honestly didn't want to know."

I playfully slapped his chest, "oi, cheeky."

He reached into his pocket and produced a business card.

"You'll be hearing from my lawyer, Miss," he smirked, enjoying his own banter.

I raised my hands in mock defence as if we were reenacting a bad porno. "I'm sorry, Mr. Businessman."

That familiar flutter returned from our shopping trip igniting the hunger in my belly for him I was dismissing just hours ago.

Once our chuckles subsided, our smiles morphed into looks of arousal.

"We haven't known each other long, Jasmin, but I hope you know that I like you and I'd really like to get to know you properly."

My hand reached for his thigh. "I'd really like that too."

He watched my wandering hand, reading my intentions.

"So, in view of getting to know each other. I have a question for you."

"OK, shoot." I smiled.

"Have you been a, erm, I mean, have you done your job long?"

The way in which he asked released a warning shot across the bow and instantly, I chewed my inner cheek. "Long enough, why?"

"Just wondering how old you were?"

Why does everyone keep asking me that?

"I'm twenty-one. You?"

His body tensed and his lips thinned. "Twenty-four."

I waited for him to expand on his question, but when he didn't, I leant back from the warmth of his body, suddenly feeling exposed. "Is my age a problem for you?"

"No, it's cool. I mean, I usually date women older than me."

"Oh," my pulse quickened, "should I go?"

I attempted to stand, but he caught hold of my hand.

"Sorry, no don't go." He coaxed me gently towards him and directly against his lips.

There was an element of innocence fortified by his passion. His seated position encouraged me to straddle him and our connection blossomed when the heat of his loin met with mine.

The tip of his tongue entered my mouth as our lips locked for the first time.

Dan was a fantastic kisser who didn't rush his exploration. I grasped his hair in my hands, the same texture as King's, and let him devour me. He broke the kiss and moved his lips to my neck, nipping gently at my collarbone when, breathless, he peered up at me.

"Not here. I want to take you to my bed."

We made it to the bottom of the stairs when a heavy thud landed on the front door.

"Let me in, Limp Dick," a menacing voice yelled from the other side. He thudded impatiently on the door again.

"Shit! It's Romero, fuck!" Dan hissed in panic. His eyes darted around the room for options. "Here, hide in that closet, quick!"

I rushed on my tiptoes towards a small coat storage closet behind the front door.

My heart pounded as strong as King's fist on the door.

"Hurry the fuck up!" He banged again.

Dan rushed to the entrance, fumbling with his keys between his shaking fingers. As soon as the lock clicked open, King burst through.

"What do you want?" Dan asked, dishevelled and alarmed as he met with King's fury.

"Is she here?" King asked, prowling the entrance way, eyeing the contents of the vast space.

Through the slit in the wooden panel doors of the closet, I could just about make out the two of them squared up to each other.

"Is who here? Mom?" Dan asked convincingly.

"Mom?" King tutted, "Fuck off Daniele. Don't play dumb with me, you know who I mean."

"I really don't." Dan stepped away from King, who in turn stepped towards him.

"Have you got my new whore here?"

"No. I haven't."

"Don't fuckin' lie to me, Daniele. I mean it. I'll kick your weak ass."

"You could try," Dan scoffed. The gin giving him misplaced courage.

Without warning, King punched Dan in the ribs, where

his face filled with air in receipt of the strike.

Hunched over, Dan cradled himself. "Ahh, you fucking prick! She's not here!" He yelled through gritted teeth, trying and failing to catch his breath.

King towered over him. "Leave her the fuck alone. I meant it."

"Why do you care, anyway? You've got Tatiana."

King straightened his stance and adjusted his gold chain.

"None of your business. All you need to know is that she is mine. Stand in my way and you'll meet with my gun. I ain't fuckin' around. I let it slide last time. No more chances."

Dan clutched his chest, his breathing ragged. "Fuck you," he spluttered, "get out!"

With no intention of listening to Dan's order, King meandered around the marble-topped table, his attention suddenly drawn in by the vase of my sunflowers.

He stopped and plucked out a tall stem with a curled upper lip. "What sort of man buys himself shit like this? The fact you even own a jar to put 'em in says it all."

Dan's panting didn't subside. "You mean a vase?"

"My fuckin' point exactly. Look at you, stand like a man, Daniele. I didn't hit you that hard."

"Get out Romero!"

In a change of pace that matched his ever shifting mood, King picked up the vase and threw it across the room where it smashed against the wall, leaving its mark along the surface that soaked the floor.

"Don't think I won't know if you put your dick inside her. She's off limits." His breathing matched Dan's as he affirmed his words.

Then, as abruptly as he entered, he stormed out of the house, slamming the door behind him.

With a sigh of relief, Dan perched himself on the arm of the decorative chair at the far side of the hallway, attempting to look less wounded than he actually was when I stepped out of the closet.

When our eyes met, I pursed my lips. "This isn't a good idea, is it?"

"He can't tell me who I spend my time with. You like me, right?"

I nodded. "Yeah, of course I do."

"We don't need to listen to him. He took my wife from me and I won't let him win again—"

"Wait. You're married?" I took a step back, my mouth fell open.

"Well, I'm divorced now." He winced again, still

clutching his chest as he rose to his feet.

"You can't tell me something like that and not say what happened?"

Dan uncoiled his back and flinched again. "I caught them fucking in my bed. He always wants what I have—Or what he thinks I want."

"Oh, OK. So I'm just a game to you both, then?"

"No! Not at all. Well, not to me, anyway. Probably to him," He shrugged his shoulders apologetically.

"Um, OK, I think I should go." I turned to exit, but Dan leant across the door.

"Please Jasmin, spend the night like we planned. Let me show you that I mean what I say. I'm nothing like him." He held out his hand for me to take. "Trust me."

In silent agreement, I followed him up the stairs to what I assumed was his bedroom. If I had to describe his mansion, it would be straight out of a 5-star hotel.

His ex wife must have been an interior designer because whoever influenced the decor knew exactly what they were doing. The centre of the room featured a wooden four-poster bed adorned with cotton sheets in elephant grey.

The accessories throughout the room were tasteful and modern, with a large window that looked out onto acres of fields that surrounded the property. *Idyllic.*

He enticed me onto his bed and knelt astride me. His lips planted soft kisses on my exposed skin in calculated locations that my body responded to.

I unbuttoned the rest of his polo shirt and eased it over his head. Dan's tanned body was in great shape, just like Kings with toned abs, but not quite as refined, where a hint of a bruise had already begun to form against the outline of his ribs.

He tugged at my dress and I leant up for him to get full access to remove it. We didn't unlock our lips, each one of us pleading for more.

Down to our underwear, he leant over to the bedside table and reached for a foil packet.

"Hopefully, I won't need these soon," he said, tearing it open with impatience and a glint in his eyes.

He handed me the condom that I rolled onto his erection.

What did that even mean? He wouldn't be needing condoms soon? Did he have a vasectomy booked in that he'd not yet declared?

"You're a beautiful woman, Jasmin," he murmured as he brushed over one of my nipples with his fingers, circling the areola.

My eyes closed when our bodies collided with one another as he removed my underwear, groaning out my name as his tongue entwined with mine.

As he slid inside me, the contact I felt with him differed to what I shared with King that I couldn't quite put my finger on.

We peered into each other's eyes as his hips rolled like waves towards my body.

Oh God, please.

"Is this OK?" He asked into my mouth as his body worked in partnership with mine.

The intensity built inside me and my arousal slicked my flesh where it wasn't long before my heart rate increased and my breathing quickened.

Oh, oh.

"Yes." I answered, clutching onto the bedsheets.

"Oh, Jasmin," Dan called into my hair, as his pace remained impervious.

My head raised off the pillow. "Fuck I'm coming!" I panted as my open legs quivered against his thighs.

"Jasmin. Fuck." My name was his plea, and I cradled him in my arms as he came inside me.

"You sure that was OK?" He asked as he ran his hand

through his hair.

"More than OK." I grinned. "It was perfect."

"Perfect, huh?" He tested the word with a raised brow. Kissing my lips, he rolled onto his back beside me.

I peered into his eyes, his green to my blue. Our focus didn't waver from one another, even for a second.

"Will you be my girlfriend?"

My instant reaction was to laugh, but when he remained straight faced, my lips pursed.

"Dan—"

"I know we can work."

"Really? We don't even know each other and not to mention you know what my line of work is."

"It's fine," he smirked. "If you don't agree, I will buy your time from the agency every night for the rest of my life."

"Don't be stupid," I sniggered, swatting his chest. "You'll be broke in a month."

He pretended to stab himself in the heart. "You wound me! I make more money in an hour than most do in a lifetime."

I looked into his eyes again, but this time with a sense of surreality.

So handsome and wholesome he was straight out of a fairytale, but there wasn't a single time in my life where fairytales ever came true.

"Dan, let's not ruin this, please? I'm loving spending time with you, but I'm mixed up with King and it's way too dangerous."

He shook his head. "You don't need to worry. I'll deal with him."

Our conversation required a reality check, and I wanted to tell Dan that he was crazy if he thought he could deal with his brother's wrath. And the redness from the blow of King's fist against his chest evidenced my concerns.

"Dan, please don't try anything stupid. King looks after me, has given me a job and a roof over my head. I owe him."

"You don't owe him shit! Don't ever think he's your only choice, Jasmin! Fuck!" He jumped out of bed gloriously naked and ran an exasperated hand through his hair.

The sight of the filled condom still attached to his body made me snicker.

He scowled, putting his hands on his hips. "What's so funny, hmm?"

I lowered my gaze, stifling my smile.

His eyes followed mine and when he saw his limp penis, housed in a used rubber; he realised that the look he was sporting didn't quite match his outrage for King.

He laughed in return, showcasing his sense of humour.

"Hold on," he said as he stalked into the en suite bathroom.

The sound of the toilet flushing preceded by rummaging had Dan strolling back into the room with a smile, where he cleared his throat into his hand. "Now as I was saying—" He smirked.

"You were saying crazy talk."

"Jasmin, you don't need a man like him to take care of you. He's already hit you and don't lie to me and say it wasn't him because I know that's bullshit."

I opened my mouth to say something, but he cut me off.

"I would give you the world if you let me."

"Jesus, Dan, why do you even care so much? I'm just a whore!"

"Don't call yourself that."

"But it's true!" I vaulted off the bed and stood in front of him.

"Look at me! I'm damaged goods. A prostitute that has done some nasty shit for money, stuff that would make your dick shrivel up and fall off."

He grabbed onto my shoulders. "I don't care about all that shit!"

"Clearly you do! You couldn't even bring yourself to talk about my job earlier. This isn't like the films, you know? It's not Pretty Woman."

He sighed and lowered his head, pressing his forehead against mine as he closed his eyes. "I need you."

"No. You need to win."

He shook his head. "No. Not true."

"King is the type to see me dead before giving me a chance to leave his mansion. He said I'm one of his girls."

"All that waffle he spouts doesn't mean shit. Romero doesn't care about you."

"What, and you do? You're insane Dan. I think you need help!"

He brought me into his reach, and the warmth of his naked torso soothed mine instantly. His muscular arms snaked around my body, holding our connection, and he kissed my hair. "If insanity is knowing what I want, then I'm guilty as charged."

Before I knew it, we were making out again. He scooped me up, wrapping my legs around his waist, where he carried me over to the bed for a second time.

He lowered me down, where he parted my legs and his lips kissed my body just as passionately between my thighs as if he were kissing my mouth.

"Do you like this?" He murmured with gratitude as he lapped at my sensitive flesh.

"Oh fuck, yes, yes."

Circles of slow, delicious promise encapsulated my spirit as he showed me just how much he cared.

I couldn't catch my breath as I teetered on the edge of climax.

Oh shit!

When my eyes screwed shut the gateway to heaven opened and I came to pieces against the velvet texture of his tongue.

Dan appeared from between my legs with a grin dimpling his cheeks as the evidence of his skills spread across my flushed skin.

Eventually, my breathing returned, and I peeked at him with one eye open where his grin made me smile.

"Do you want me to suck you off? You know, repay the favour?"

"No," he kissed my knuckles. "That was just for you."

"Oh." I frowned in thought, "I mean, only if you're sure?"

That was the first time a man had ever said no to a blow job. Did that mean my skills were no good?

He held up three fingers with a warm smile. "Scouts honour. So, have you thought anymore about my earlier question?"

I took a breath and paused. I wasn't sure what would

come out of my mouth next until I said it.

This man was so loving and compassionate towards me and my body. The temptation to agree to his offer, knowing that he would take care of me and love me in a way that no one ever had before, was overwhelming. I'd be a fool to pass up on an opportunity like this.

"OK, sure." My stomach flipped as the words tumbled out.

"You'll be my girlfriend!?" His excitement was palpable.

I nodded with a giggle. "How is this supposed to work, though? Do you expect me to quit my job? If you think your brother won't find out, then you're crazy. He knows everything."

"I have enough money to take care of you. You'll not need to work again. But I agree we need to be smart about this. We can work out the details another time. Don't worry about that for now."

We lay together peacefully, sated by our romantic exchange.

"Dan?" I said, running my fingers through his chest hair.

"Yeah?"

"Are you worried about what King will do when he finds out?"

"Don't worry about Romero, trust me."

I wanted to trust Dan more than my life, but his brother was a lunatic at his best. Were we taking on way more than we could handle?

"OK, but this is kind of awkward. I'm going to need to borrow some money from you. I'll need to pay King when I see him tomorrow or he'll know something isn't right."

He sat up, taking matters seriously. "Hmm, yeah, good point. Will ten thousand be enough?"

My mouth dropped open. "What?"

"Sorry, is that not enough? I'm not well up on this sort of thing."

"No." I rattled my head. "I mean, that's way too much. A thousand bucks is more than enough for one night together."

"Oh, right." Dan flicked on the table lamp and pulled out his wallet, where he efficiently counted one thousand dollars. There was at least another thousand in there, probably more. How rich does one need to be in order to carry around two grand casually like it was pocket change?

"There you go gorgeous." He smiled, handing me the notes.

"Thank you."

Dan turned out the light and grabbed me back into our

big spoon, little spoon position.

And without realising, we both fell to sleep peacefully. The most restful slumber of my life.

CHAPTER 7

After our evening of misguided passion, I left Dan's house early the next morning with promises of a relationship.

How either of us expected that to work, I wasn't sure.

Lost in the moment during our romantic exchange last night, it was clear now that we had made a big mistake.

It was way too quick and far too risky.

I snuck out of the house while he slept as soon as the sun rose from behind the hills, avoiding an awkward conversation laced with regrets and excuses. Unable to shake the nausea in the pit of my stomach, a nagging doubt crept in that he probably didn't even mean to take it as far as he did. After all, a relationship with a hooker—especially one you've known for five minutes—is a stupid move in anyone's book.

As efficiently as one could expect from a butler, my car was waiting for me round the front of Dan's property with the engine running and the heater on.

"Ma'am," he said with a warm smile as he opened up my door to help me inside, where he closed it behind me without a single question asked. How did he know I was going to leave so early? I'd not even planned my escape until my eyes opened this morning.

The radio hummed softly in the cab of the Mini, a steady companion on my drive back to King's mansion, filling the reflective silence. I turned up the volume where ironically the jingle of Dan's haulage company's commercial began playing.

I smiled in deep thought at the sound of his silky tones over the airwaves that evoked images of his soft lips on my body, his hands caressing me. My quivering insides as my orgasm consumed my soul—

A horn hooted loudly behind me, forcing me back to reality. With a sharp pull of the steering wheel, I corrected my drift into the next lane of traffic, completely awash with futile emotions. There were no two ways about it. Dan Giannetti lay heavy on my mind and no matter where I turned, I couldn't escape him. Had I just made a huge mistake in leaving so soon?

Plagued by the nagging worry that the brothers were using me to their own gain clouded my judgement, and every move I made since my eyes opened this morning suddenly seemed like the wrong choice.

Sure, Dan could say my suspicions were wrong, but my life experience told me otherwise. Never trust a man, or his word.

As I drew closer toward the house, my skin prickled when red flashing lights emitted from within the grounds of the mansion, illuminated the white walls with rumours of emergency.

The echo of my heart beat thumped within the confines of my skull and my pulse assaulted my ears as different scenarios rushed around my mind like a Catherine Wheel as to what was happening. Had King shot someone else? Was Dan involved? Hanna?

It was true that I hadn't seen much of my best friend since moving into King's mansion and the resentment that I had allowed to grow like vines inside my subconscious had created a distance between us that wasn't easy to ignore. My throat tightened at the prospect King had hurt her while I wasn't there to protect her. Was I as selfish as I felt?

I floored the gas pedal with urgency on my approach as I pulled into the crowded driveway.

Two idling police vehicles confirmed my suspicions, with their doors wide open as though the officers were in a hurry to disembark.

An ambulance parked near to the entrance of the mansion was the queen amidst the hive, with its beacon of light bathing the grounds in a crimson blanket of uncertainty.

Partially dressed whores littered the scene, like the aftermath of a morbid festival, along with members of King's crew that I hadn't even met yet. So many people and so many haunted silhouettes, each face telling a different version of the same event.

Without a further thought, I threw the car into the nearest parking space and ran towards the scene as fast as my quivering legs would carry me. The mass of people surrounding the rear of the ambulance was as impossible to wade through as treacle.

"Excuse me!" I called into the backs of the bystanders, obstacles in my way.

Up on my tiptoes, I scanned the sea of faces, cupping my hands around my mouth to project my voice.

"Hanna!" Unshed tears fractured the notes in my voice.

Where are you?

"No!" My knees buckled and time stood still when the

blood-curdling image of a black body bag being loaded into the back of the ambulance faltered my steps. Clear now that my fear was a reality. An out-of-body experience took hold of me as stars speckled my vision.

"Hanna!?"

With new found willpower to reach the other side, I forced myself through the final hurdles amidst the gathering, barging past anyone who refused to move.

As I met with the opening of the crowd, I stopped breathing when I saw my girl.

"Oh, Hanna! Thank God you're OK!" My lower lip trembled as my eyes met with hers.

My best friend, unscathed, huddled on the floor by the ambulance, sobbing into another whore's chest.

When I knelt down beside her, she grabbed hold of me around my neck, pulling me into an embrace. I drew her closer, my nose against her skin, absorbing our reality.

"What the hell happened!?"

"I can't believe it Jas—"

"Tell me Hanna!"

She tucked her head into the crook of my neck and squeezed me tight.

"It's Tatiana. She's dead."

My mouth dropped open as shock punched me in the

gut.

"She is?"

Denial refused my belief that the lifeless package being wheeled into the back of the ambulance was Tatiana's body.

How had King allowed this to happen to his girlfriend? Surely she would have been the most protected member of the mansion?

Something wasn't right here, and I sensed it in my gut that there was more to this than met the eye.

The door to King's castle opened, which triggered a flurry of activity as a stern looking male police officer emerged, escorting King in cuffs to the waiting cop car.

Our chemistry unwavering drew his eyes towards me, locking his gaze with mine as he sloped by. With a curt nod in my direction, his lips remained tightly sealed.

I frowned at Hanna. "Why have they arrested King?"

Her broken sobs distorted her ability to articulate.

"They think he did it," she whimpered, wiping her wet nose with the back of her hand.

Without warning, the ambulance doors slammed shut, provoking my startle at the abrupt sound that reverberated around the kingdom. The vehicle left the grounds with a solemn silence where the morgue would be Tatiana's final destination.

As Tat departed, an expensive-looking car screeched into the driveway, flicking up the gravel as the wheels span. I recognised the driver immediately.

Dan ran over to where King was being bundled into the back of the cop car.

"Romero! What the fuck!?" Dan yelled into the pane of glass that separated them, putting his hands on the sides of his head in disbelief as the door slammed closed behind King.

The cop car flashed its lights to signal its departure and edged forward through the horde, parting the tide of bodies as they made to leave.

Dan spotted me from across the driveway and made a shortcut straight for me. I pretended I hadn't noticed his approach, as I'd already convinced myself last night was a lie and self preservation was all I had left.

Before he reached me, one of the house whores stepped out in front of him, stopping him in his tracks.

"Mr. Giannetti, is it true?" She sniffled. "Did Daddy have something to do with it?"

He shook his head. "I've no idea."

It seemed we were all thinking the same thing. King

was capable of anything and with that notion came the unwelcome image of a bullet piercing through flesh only yesterday. So much blood and suffering.

A police officer hovered behind us just as Dan approached me.

"Daniele Giannetti?" The cop asked, looking at a hand written list of names.

Dan's lips thinned, showcasing his impatience. "Yes, Officer?"

"I need you at the station, please."

"Why? What has this incident got to do with me?"

The cop rocked on his heels. "Just following all leads, Sir."

"Son of a bitch." He muttered under his breath. "Give me a couple of minutes."

The officer nodded in agreement. "I'll wait right here."

Dan cupped my elbow, leading me away from prying ears. His forehead creased as he stared at me with discomfort marring his handsome face. "Why didn't you say goodbye this morning?"

My cheeks reddened at his unexpected question. Not only did that not matter under the circumstances, but I also didn't think he would care.

"Sorry." I chewed my lip. "I guess I just didn't want any awkwardness."

I peered over my shoulder, very much aware that we were in a public place and Dan was not being discreet about our relationship issues.

King's eyes are everywhere.

He pursed his lips with contemplative thoughts. "Why would it have been awkward?"

"Come on, Sir," the cop interrupted, "we need to go now."

Dan seemed distressed at the distance I had purposely created between us, reaffirmed by the impatience of the waiting cop. "I shouldn't be down there long. I'll call you, OK?"

"Um, sure, but I won't answer if I have work."

As hard as I could, I was trying to push him away and cut my emotional ties with him in order to protect my own feelings. The fact was I just didn't trust his intentions, and with what had just happened; Hanna and Alice were now my main priority.

His face twisted with anxiety as he took a step towards me.

"I promise I'll call you," he whispered, leaning in to kiss me, but turned away when he thought better of it.

"Jasmin!" Alice's melodic voice called, bringing me back to the more important matter of the present.

She broke out into a barefoot jog, draped in a bloodstained silk night gown with dishevelled hair and mascara stained cheeks. She looked terrible.

We crashed into one another as my arms enveloped her chilled body with my nose nuzzled into her hair. Her sweet scent shrouded my senses as she wept.

"Help me, Jas," she cried, "I don't know what to do with myself."

It was a plea for me to become her saviour, and I so badly wanted to rescue her.

"Hey shush," I kissed her hair. "It's OK. I'm here now."

My fingers combed through her long, tangled strands as I brought her comfort as best I could.

"She was pregnant," Alice murmured against my body, snivelling. "She did the test this morning."

My eyes almost popped out of their sockets as I attempted to hide the horror in my reaction. The news was enough to make me want to vomit my organs and their contents onto the ground in front of my feet.

Pregnant? And with King's baby? This was more than I could stomach.

After a moment of collectedness, I cleared my throat. "Come on, girls, it's freezing out here. Let's go and get a drink, shall we?" I needed something strong to take the edge off and quick.

The grand hallway was almost unrecognisable, with yellow police tape spanning the staircase that cordoned off the whole of the upstairs as a crime scene. A no nonsense cop with a wide stance stood at the foot of the stairs, his arms resting in the crook of his bullet-proof vest with a stern appearance that was enough to feed my discomfort.

I took a hold of each girl's hand. "Follow me. We'll sit in the kitchen."

"Alice, where is the wine kept?" I asked as I opened and closed several cupboards that did not contain what I was looking for.

She pointed to a well-stocked wine rack along the back wall that was so apparent, yet I hadn't spotted.

I plucked out the first bottle of white wine within reach and poured three glasses, and we all took a sip as I watched their distraught faces.

"I'm so sorry I wasn't here, you guys. What the fuck happened?"

Alice gulped down half the glass and wiped her mouth with the sleeve of her silk gown. "I guess it all started last night, after Daddy finished with the cops. He left the house in a horrible mood, but when he came home, he was even worse, and that carried through to this morning where he and Tat got into a fight over Daddy shooting Big Jimmy."

"What?" I rubbed at my forehead. "None of this is making any sense. Why would they fight over that?"

Alice shrugged. "Daddy accused her of telling the cops on him."

"Oh jeez, and she was pregnant too, huh?"

She gripped onto the stem of the glass and swirled the contents around the bowl. "Yep, she didn't even get a chance to tell him."

The green-eyed monster gnawed at my insides, trying to break free of my skin and expose me as the jealous bitch I was.

Embarrassed by my own reaction, I chastised myself inwardly. Not only had Tat died, but that sealed the baby's fate as well, and now wasn't the time for me to dwell on this like I mattered under such tragic circumstances.

Hanna sighed with sorrow as she replayed her version of this morning's events. "Jimmy had told the cops it was an accident; that he shot himself, so we don't get why Daddy was angry."

I rocked back in my chair, feeling as overwhelmed as Alice looked. "How did the cops know about the shooting then if it wasn't Tat?"

"There must be a mole." Hanna shrugged into her drink. "Daddy thought it was Tat."

Alice's second glass of wine had already passed her lips when she piped up again. "Tat has been his main whore for as long as I can remember, but it was like he was looking for an excuse to fight with her. When he dragged her off up to bed and slammed the door, we could hear screaming and shouting. When it went silent, I knew something terrible must've happened."

I followed suit and finished my glass, pouring another to settle my nerves. With shaking hands, the neck of the bottle rattled against the rim of the glass. "Who found her?"

Alice's bottom lip quivered. "It was me," she sobbed. "Oh God, it was me. I waited for him to leave first and when I opened the door, there was blood everywhere."

"I'm so sorry, Alice."

We sat there for minutes, just holding each other, where Hanna eventually joined us in a three-way embrace.

Alice's story got me thinking. The timing seemed too much of a coincidence for King's mood not to be linked with his fight at Dan's house.

Did I have something to do with this?

A man in overalls walked into the room, interrupting us.

"Miss Alice, there's a police officer here who wants to interview you."

She slammed her glass on the counter, spilling the contents.

"I already spoke to the cops. I don't want to do it again!"

"I know, but they asked me to come and get you—"

"Tell them to fuck off, Billy. I can't do this."

As she leant over the counter, she placed her head inside her arm, cocooned around her face.

Three police officers waiting in the wings barged past Billy.

"Right then," the first cop began, "there's too many of you to get you all down to the station, so officers Watts and Rodriguez will interview Alice and Hanna." He caught me by the elbow, "and I will speak with you."

The cop took his seat on King's throne, positioned at the head of the dining table, which I assumed was a power move.

"OK, what's your name for the record, please?"

"Um, Jasmin. I mean Chloe Adams."

"Jasmin Chloe Adams?" He raised his gaze to look at me before he continued writing his notes.

"No, just Chloe."

Vulnerable situations such as this would never fix my uneasiness. If the whores found out my real name, my entire identity would unravel.

"Your involvement Chloe?"

My fingers interlocked on the tabletop with unchecked anxiety. "I wasn't even here last night."

"Oh? interesting," his lips pursed, "you live here, though, right?"

"Well, yes, I do, but I was out last night."

He was straight on it like a dog with a bone. "Out? Where?"

Shit—I didn't want to say *who* I was with, but as Dan was my alibi, he'd backed me into a corner with no option other than to tell the truth.

"I was at Dan's house."

"Dan who? I need a full name, please. This is a police report."

I lowered my tone to prevent eaves droppers getting their daily dose of gossip. "Dan Giannetti."

The cop's obnoxious increase in volume was intentional when he opened his mouth again. "So, you were in the company of Mr. Daniele Giannetti last night at his home address in Bel-Air?"

With a cautious glance over my shoulder, I reduced my tone to a whisper. "Yes, I was."

"What is your relationship with Mr. Giannetti, please?"

"Right, well, um, he's kind of my boyfriend, but not really. We haven't known each other long."

Officer busy body scribbled something down and then abruptly flipped the cover on his pad, closing my case.

"You two ready, Watts? Rodriguez?" He called to his colleagues as he adjusted his police cap. "This one has an alibi. I just need to run something by the brother, but I think we're good."

Once they'd made their exit, my bunched shoulders released and I let out a long breath that I hadn't realised I was holding in.

Hanna darted over to me in double quick time. Her eavesdropping skills held no bounds. "What's this about boyfriend?"

"Kind of boyfriend," I clarified. "We only discussed it a bit last night."

I looked at her face for a clue of what she was thinking, knowing full well she was judging me hard.

"Shit for real? Girl, you've only known each other a few days and if Daddy finds out, I don't wanna think about what might happen."

My lips thinned. "Yeah, it is fast and my head is spinning, trust me. I'm really worried about Daddy finding out, too. I've not stopped thinking about it."

"Well, I suppose if a millionaire wants to whisk you away, then you should probably go for it. I would be selfish to ask you to stay just for me."

I smirked when our eyes met. "It's not about the money, Han."

"It's not, not about the money though, right?" She giggled. "Who wants to be a whore when you can have a man like him? If Prince Charming comes my way, you better know I'll take that chance."

I wiped away a stray tear from her cheek with my thumb. "I won't leave you, Hanna."

"Let's get one thing straight, Chloe. I came into this world fucked, and that's how I'll leave it. I love dick and money too much to give it up. You have always been a more romantic soul than me. You want love and I reckon you've found it."

That night played out in a peculiar fashion that made all of us unsettled, and the cops refusing us access to the upstairs of the mansion until the investigation was over only made matters worse.

Along with the imposing police cordon, an over night cop watched guard at the foot of the stairs so that none of us could tamper with potential evidence.

Hanna had an all night client, which was a disappointment, as I wanted to spend some quality time with her. But she swore to me she was fine and taking some time away from the house to ride some cock would give her the break she needed from her own thoughts. I couldn't argue with her logic. I would have liked that same opportunity, but as my cell hadn't buzzed with a single client all day, I was stuck here.

A group decision forced us into a girly sleepover in the main living room of the mansion. It was my worst nightmare, but with little in the way of choice in the matter, I resolved to spending the night with women who didn't like me.

King was still at the police station and none of us had been in contact with him since his arrest.

Would he go to prison over this? I couldn't even begin to think about that possibility.

Disappointment fuelled my sadness as I'd hoped to have heard from Dan, but as per my expectation, even he couldn't stick to his word. Not a call, nor a text. *Nothing.*

There were fifteen of us piled inside the expansive living room. The place was large enough to handle it, with room to spare.

"Right then girls, let's have some fun!" A hyper, over enthusiastic curly-haired girl in Disney pyjamas squealed.

I rolled my eyes at her lack of self awareness.

"Wait, I have an idea. Let's play a sleepover game!" A familiar voice called into the crowd: It was the redhead.

Just when I thought I had successfully avoided her, there she was again.

"Oh my God Michelle, yes!" A desperate whore in a peach lace bra and panties set screeched, jumping up and down so vigorously that her boobs fell out of the cups.

Please.

They all became visibly excited at the idea of playing a game suited to sixth graders, when all I wanted to do was wallow in my own self pity and go to sleep.

Michelle gathered us into a large circle in the middle of the room to address us all together. Taking centre stage, she cleared her throat. "Welcome to our sleepover, ladies," she beamed, "this is the first time we've ever had a girls only night. It goes without saying that we all miss Daddy terribly and we can't wait to have him back, but let's enjoy ourselves. Are you all with me?"

The room erupted into a round of applause with air head bimbos wishing to relive their high school fantasies and I found myself whisked away within the palpable atmosphere, clapping along in bemusement.

Michelle may as well have had a microphone, "First off girls, let us have one minute silence for Tatiana."

Like a church congregation, everyone bowed their heads, except me.

I watched as Michelle leaned in towards her sidekick and whispered something in her ear. It was clear then that she didn't give a shit about Tatiana and this marked the start of her takeover as queen whore.

"OK," she clapped, "let's get into two groups. We'll have Daddy's most successful girls come to my side of the room and the girls that don't fit the criteria can sit on the other side. I'll walk the circle and tap you on the head if you qualify."

I knew without following through with this game that she was referring to me as one of the girls that didn't fit, and the tragic spectacle of Michelle taking enjoyment in tapping girls' heads made me want to push her down the stairs again.

As expected, she reached the girl sat before me and tapped her head first. Then took a step towards me but walked right on by to the next girl, giving her the pat of approval. My cheeks expanded and my fists bunched when she looked back at me with a wry smile, achieving exactly what she'd set out to do; piss me off.

As it transpired, I and one other girl were the only two members of the group that weren't chosen to join Michelle's team.

I peered over at my unchosen partner. Around five feet ten, slender, with long limbs, she was lanky, and something about the way her nose sat on her face inferred an injury at some point. The hump was clear from a good distance away.

To most people, she was unattractive, but it was obvious to me why she was a whore. The reality being that men have kinks of all varieties and she must have fit someone's expectations.

"Ready to play with us, girls?" Michelle addressed our party of two, giggling to her sidekick again.

"Oh, piss off, you sad bitch." I retorted.

Michelle's smile slipped as she sashayed towards me with intensions of a fistfight. "Excuse me, Miss Thing, who do you think you're talking to?"

She had wound me up so tight I was ready for anything. But as I raised my fists, Alice stepped in front of me, cutting her off, protecting me like a shield from Michelle's approach.

"She didn't mean it Michelle, Jasmin is cool."

Michelle placed her hands on her hips with a glare.

"She thinks she's all that because Daddy had her in his bed. She's fat and ugly, facts!"

"Hold on a minute!" I wrestled my way past Alice's stone wall. "You're not going to speak to me like that!"

Alice pushed herself between us again. "Hey, stop you guys! Come on, Jasmin, let's go and get some sleep."

Michelle laughed in Alice's face, "Come on Alice, as if you'll be sleeping. You mean you'll try to fuck her? Everyone knows you're a lesbian. Jody can attest to that."

Her vicious tongue confirmed my speculations. My sensing that Alice was using me for her own sexual exploration was seemingly correct. Yet again, the name Jody echoed in my mind. I had to find out what happened to her.

Alice held her hand out to me, "Come on, Jas, ignore them. Let's take a walk."

As was usual in Alice's company, I found myself following her wherever she went, which on this occasion happened to be out into the garden, leaving me wondering why I agreed to it and what her intensions were.

It was dark out, but the manicured pathway throughout the acres was lit by stick lights dug into the ground.

Hand in hand, I followed wherever she took me.

I stole a glance at her pretty face. "Are you OK? You know with what happened to Tat?"

"Let's not talk about that now, Jasmin. Tell me about you."

There was absolutely no way I was about to divulge my private life to an unstable girl I barely knew. "There's nothing to tell."

She sighed, kicking loose gravel as we walked. "Everyone calls me a lesbian, but I'm not. You know that, right?"

I peered at her, where she was already looking at me for an answer. "Straight or gay, I really don't care." I shrugged.

Her grip on my hand tightened and her smile shone as brightly as the stars. "I like you Jasmin. I like you a lot."

Something in her demeanour told me she was holding something back, but whether she would open up to me in time remained to be seen. This side of her was somehow different when it was just the two of us. Her vulnerability allowed our connection to blossom in a way that gave me peace amongst the chaos.

Every part of me wanted to ask her about Jody. Were they lovers or friends? Was Jody prettier than me? However, the further we strolled, the more obvious it seemed that now didn't feel like the right time, so we wandered quietly for a while longer, lapping the grounds twice before making it back to the house.

Only a short walk from our starting point, Alice knelt down abruptly in front of me and at first my heart fluttered at the irrational idea she was about to propose to me. But relief washed over me when she returned to her upright position with a single red rose cupped in her hand that she had plucked from the well cared for bush beside us.

She handed it to me with a shy smile. "This rose reminds me of you."

I peered at her through my lashes as I accepted her gift. "It does?" I giggled. "How?"

"Roses are my favourite flower and you're my favourite whore," she snickered, bumping her shoulder against mine.

"Thank you Alice. I love it."

Our crooked nosed friend was waiting for us when

we arrived back at the house. "Ahh, there you guys are. Michelle told me I needed to hang with you, but you'd already left when I got out here."

Out of habit, I was going to apologise, but in all honesty, I was glad she hadn't been able to tag along. This was mine and Alice's moment to connect with each other on a deeper level than just sex.

"What should we do now, then?" Alice asked, looking at me to take the lead.

Suddenly, I became emboldened by our pathetic situation.

"Do you know what? I think it's about time we do what we want. Why are we bowing down to those bitches? Come on, we're going inside."

We made it back into the living room where I expected a showdown with Michelle, but the vision before me was the complete opposite.

The whores lay peacefully beneath their blankets with plush pillows from their beds, chatting amongst themselves, clearly sated after their secret game of lick Michelle's arsehole.

Alice beckoned for me to follow her over to the far side of the room where the whores had segregated our belongings from the rest of the group, as if we had a contagious disease.

She lifted the blanket and made it clear she wanted me to climb in beside her. Her beautiful smile was so inviting, but the obvious pain in her eyes was difficult for her to hide.

"I'm glad you're here," she said as we lay face to face, sharing her pillow.

"I know you don't want to, Alice, but if you need to talk —"

"Mm-hm, thanks Jas."

One of Michelle's whores turned out the light, and the room descended into darkness. The only light emitting came from the soft glow of the moon through the large window, looking out into the gardens.

"You know, we always seem drawn to each other," she whispered as she slipped a finger between my cleavage.

My body tensed in response to her touch and my thighs clamped shut. "I'm not sure about that tonight."

"Oh, come on! What's wrong with you, Jas? I thought we were friends?"

Her voice raised louder than I would have liked. We didn't need eyes on us, confirming Michelle's earlier accusation and I certainly didn't want to be the next Jody.

"What do you mean? We *are* friends?"

She blinked slowly over her glossy doe eyes. "Sure doesn't seem like it to me?"

Her need to seek comfort from my body was all well and good, but I wasn't sure quite how to respond. Irrespective of me not being a lesbian, how was I going to tell her I now had a boyfriend? Although was that even the case anymore?

Sure, I'd driven a wedge between Dan and me earlier to test his commitment. But why was I showing loyalty to someone who didn't even call me when he said he would?

Alice edged closer to me as if there was no one else in the room where she tilted her head and kissed at the fullest part of my breasts, humming with notes of joy as she took comfort from my body.

Almost certainly, she was using me for sex; I knew that. But she was my friend and friends sometimes have needs that we don't always feel comfortable fulfilling, right?

Regardless, I supported her wish to help her feel good after the traumatic experience she had witnessed only this morning.

Her delicate hands cupped my face when she placed feather light kisses against my lips. The saltiness of her tears that rolled down her cheeks intertwined with our tongues.

I broke away from the kiss. "Wait, are you crying?"

"Shh," she whispered. "No more questions."

Alice took my hand in hers and pushed it between her legs. I knew what her body desired, so I urged my finger within her folds and slipped in and out of her slick entrance.

"Make me come, Jas, please," she pleaded into my mouth.

I did as she asked and picked up pace against her clit as she continued to seek pleasure from my breasts, my body responding to her lure once more.

"Oh God, please!" she groaned heavily as my fingers worked inside her.

I thumbed at her clit, circling round and round when she moved between my legs and drove a finger inside me to mirror my actions. We kissed each other, possessing each other's mouths as we walked down the long road together.

The delicious heat inside her intensified as she tightened around my finger in response. Her liquid arousal warmed my hand as she ejaculated for me. Her orgasm came hard with a hushed cry of my name.

Please. Oh, oh.

I was so close to finishing, nearly there.

And then she stopped.

What—

Alice turned over onto her back, panting, and raised one arm over her eyes. "I needed that, thank you," she smiled.

"Um, no problem, I guess."

Taken aback, I was utterly speechless, but I couldn't cause a scene now in front of everyone. *Can I?*

The immediate sweet melody of Alice's snoring filled the silence in the room, interrupting my reverie. Sound asleep, Alice and the rest of the girls were peaceful, and a sense of loneliness crept over me that I just couldn't shake off.

In need of redirecting my negative focus and in search of a release of the tension that Alice had worked up inside my core, I took matters into my own hands. Easing my finger inside myself, I moved at my pace and under my control.

But as the buildup dwindled, my mind grew cloudier. Unsettled, I fidgeted uncomfortably at Alice's complete disregard for my feelings.

So why, if I wasn't a lesbian, was I getting my emotions entangled as though I cared?

The earlier arousal induced by Alice's hand had undeniably evaporated, leaving me with a sense of being used and worthless once again. Conflicting emotions extinguished my desire and no matter how hard I tried to shake it off, I couldn't reach the finish line. My frustrated attack against my own flesh only crushed my hopes further, and for the first time in as long as I could remember, I wasn't able to find my release.

CHAPTER 8

It was no surprise that I was the first of the girls awake the next morning.

Relentless whore giggling kept me awake throughout the night and paranoia eroded my self worth, wondering if they were laughing at me. The ever present feeling of not fitting in was taking its toll.

Checking my phone, I felt a wave of disappointment as I hadn't yet received a text from the agency with my first client of the day. Doubt reared its ugly head yet again, whether I was even any good at my job anymore. I used to have back-to-back clients when I worked alone, but now, I was lucky to get one client a day.

King had said there was something special about me, but I feared I was proving him wrong.

Loneliness found me again, and in need of some comfort, I opened up my photos app and scrolled through the latest snaps I'd taken. Hanna's beautiful face greeted me first, her grin conjured a sense of comfort within me. I really missed her when she wasn't around. And as I swiped, a couple of me and Alice from last night's sleepover made me smile.

The fact that Alice left me high and dry during our latest intimate exchange wasn't something I was going to dwell on. She needed support now more than ever.

It wasn't until I landed on a photo of Dan that I paused to look closer. I'd forgotten that I'd taken a picture of the two of us the evening he had asked me to be his girlfriend. At that moment, in his bed, we both seemed so happy. But if that were true, why hadn't I heard from him?

There was no denying that our time together in bed was amazing. A gentle lover, Dan knew exactly how to move around my body, and the way he responded to me; we were in sync. But if there was one thing I'd learned over the years, it was that if a man wants you, he will pursue at all costs. Well, where was Dan now? *Exactly.*

My arms reached above my head as I stretched my muscles to unstiffen from my night spent on the floor.

Alice stirred next to me and instinctively I froze, not wanting to wake her to protect myself from another sexual encounter that left my vulnerabilities exposed.

Once satisfied that she had drifted back to sleep, I peeled myself off the ground and padded through into the kitchen to make myself some breakfast. It was still early, and Chef hadn't yet arrived to kick start everyone's day, so it seemed odd to find his work space so lifeless. Not that it mattered, anyway, as I actually enjoyed cooking for myself when given the opportunity.

Well-stocked kitchen cupboards provided a variety of pots and pans for me to choose from. I fancied making eggs and with the facilities available, I could make the most extravagant type of egg I wanted, so I settled on scrambled with a side of buttered toast and a cup of coffee to wash it down.

"Oh, look what the cat dragged in—"

I paused mid chew at the sound of her voice. Michelle sauntered in as I was enjoying the peaceful silence.

With my lips curled, I eyed her suspiciously. "Morning Michelle."

As I swallowed my last bite of toast, I casually threw my plate into the sink.

"Daddy doesn't want you here, you know that, don't you?" She sat two seats away from me at the island, looking at me intensely as though she'd been up all night practising this speech.

I glared at her with folded arms. "Oh yeah? He told you

that himself, did he?" If she thought I was backing down, she was wrong.

"Daddy doesn't need to tell me. I know what he's thinking."

"Ahh, I see. So why am I in his bed and you aren't?"

Her shoulders raised as her body stiffened. "He just feels sorry for you, that's all. Now Tatiana has gone. I'm next in line to the throne."

A sardonic laugh escaped my mouth at her delusions of grandeur. "You're a pathetic whore, Michelle. Leave me alone."

She rose to her feet to gain higher ground. "I'm going nowhere, Honey. You leave."

We stood at an impasse. I was at a crossroads with two paths to choose from.

Do I retaliate or walk away?

Eventually, I made my mind up and confirmed my choice.

"Watch your back." I called over my shoulder as I strolled out of the room with a thudding chest.

Adrenaline fired on all cylinders as I made for the exit, and I waited a moment to take in some air and collect myself once out of her evil sights.

Now that I'd finished my morning spat with Michelle, I

desperately needed a change of clothes, ready to start my day.

"Can't go upstairs, Ma'am." A new cop remained in place, guarding the staircase.

"Um, but I need my clothes?"

She stood tall with her hands rested at her lower back—military style. With her tightly rolled bun resting at the nape of her neck, she was a badass. Not making cye contact, she stared straight ahead. "All clothing from upstairs is now stored in the gym until further notice."

I rolled my eyes, slapping my palm against my forehead in realisation that the dramatic exit I'd just performed for Michelle would have to be undone when I went back in there with my tail between my legs.

With a deep, steadying breath, I silently counted to three at the entrance to the kitchen. Once composed, I breezed through as if nothing happened.

In the short time I was out of the room, a couple of Michelle's side kicks had joined her at the table, eating their breakfast.

Michelle was enjoying a bowl of porridge and chuckled as she brought the loaded spoon to her mouth when she saw me. "Can you girls smell something?" She raised her nose and sniffed the air dramatically. "Oh, hi Jasmin, didn't see you there."

The pathetic whore still in last night's Disney PJs giggled.

"Good one Michelle."

"What is this? Goldilocks and the three whores?" I snarled as I steamed by them.

"Takes one to know one!" Michelle called out behind me as she watched me leave.

The door to the gym was closed, which came as no surprise this time of the morning. But when I reached for the handle, I could have sworn I heard a voice.

"Fuck me, Baby." A female called from the other side of the door.

I paused with my ear pressed against the wood, listening intently.

"Shit, I'm gonna come. Where's the rubber?"

My mouth dropped open at my discovery. Someone was taking advantage of King's absence and I had to find out who.

"Shh, did you hear someone? Fuck!"

My eyes widened in panic. I was about to be rumbled for snooping.

Michelle's heavy indiscreet footsteps could be heard

from a mile away when she plodded towards me. "Ew, what are you doing, you weirdo?" Her voice grated on my last nerve.

I snapped my head in her direction. "You're calling me weird when you're the one following me around this house. You're obsessed! Why do you care what I'm doing?"

"I care that you're listening in on my girls. That's an invasion of their privacy."

My brow raised in response. "Your girls? Ha! You really are full of yourself, Michelle." I shook my head at her audacity.

The door to the gym creaked open. When my eyes met with Clive the creep, my body tensed with rage.

He was at it again and the stupid whore that had been lured into his trap was no better than he was. She scurried off first, but he stood in front of me as though he were there to prove a point.

"Hey Clive." Michelle cooed. The twirl of her hair around her fingers told me she'd fucked him before.

Clive cocked his head in response. "S'up Shelley." He kept his eyes fixed on mine as he fastened his overalls back into position.

"I was just dealing with some garbage," she glowered at me, "but I'm free now if you want to hang out?"

Clive nodded as he fixed his collar. "Sure."

What in the soiled clothing, missing tooth, was going on there? She must be desperate, or he was blackmailing her...

Once given the privacy I so desperately yearned for in the mansion. I took a minute to find my personals amidst the piles of whore belongings. As it transpired, whoever was in charge of collecting the clothes from upstairs failed to bring down my hold all. And after sniffing the armpits of the light fabric, concluding that there was no smell, I resolved to wearing my favourite dress for another day.

My cell buzzed in my back pocket.

<Agency> Mr X. BDSM/Sadism. 85 New York Avenue. ASAP.

I peered at the screen, analysing the text message.

Not only was this my first client booking in a while, but it was *that* type of booking.

The sadism part didn't bother me, particularly as it was usually the client themselves that wanted some sort of punishment. My only issue with the arrangement now was that regardless of how prepared I was, Daddy still wasn't around to protect me.

The hallway was free of whores as I collected my bag and keys, but just as I was putting my phone inside my purse, I noticed something was missing.

Hmm.

Then it hit me. Someone had stolen my one thousand dollars from my night with Dan.

With frantic rummaging, I searched the deep depths of my bag only to conclude that the money was definitely gone. One of the whores had light fingers, and my guess was Michelle.

The driveway was pretty quiet as I made my way to the Mini, but I soon recognised Snake's noticeable buzz cut, where he was busying himself with tasks that required his full attention.

Seizing the opportunity while King was away, I approached him. His natural reaction when he saw me was to turn his back to discourage my assent upon him.

"Hi Snake."

He huffed. "Don't let anyone catch you talking to me. Boss might not be here, but he will find out."

"I was actually just going to ask you if you'd heard from him yet?"

Talking to his back was difficult and not being able to see his face didn't allow for me to read the situation better.

"No," he shook his head, "no one has."

I waited a moment for him to expand on his words. What was I supposed to do with such limited information?

"Don't just stand there," he barked, making me jump. "Leave!"

So if Snake hadn't seen King, and the whores definitely hadn't either. Who was running the mansion until he came home? Was it Clive?

As Clive and I found ourselves locked in a mutual hatred, the odds of me having protection dwindled to less than they were when I was going at this game alone.

Irrespective of this, was I still going to continue as normal? Yes, I was. Did that worry me? Absolutely.

I arrived just in time for my client booking with two minutes' to spare. Time keeping was important to me as first impressions counted.

Nothing about the man's home gave a sense of what might be lying in waiting on the other side. A worn out grey exterior and empty flower beds were the only visual available.

With nervous excitement that I was back in the game, I knocked as cheerfully as I could when a plain-looking man answered a minute later.

A bald head with slight growth around the back and

sides in an auburn colour was the first of his features, I noticed. With dull grey eyes and a slender build, he was tall, but not imposing.

"Come in." His flat tone and neutral expression made it impossible for me to read what he was thinking.

Whilst normally sadist clients were thrilling to be around, something in the eyes of this man made me uncomfortable.

"Thank you. I'm Jasmin," I offered my hand to him.

He peered down and reluctantly took my offer. "Please follow me."

An aroma of wet dog filled my nostrils as I entered the property and it struck me that the furniture in the living room was minimal if this was indeed his home. The further I walked into the building, the more anxious I became.

A wall clock ticked too loudly and the bare squeaking floorboards offered a hollow sound as my feet tread ground.

From the outside, the structure didn't seem so big, but the time it took for us to reach the location of his choosing left me concerned about the possibilities of performing a quick exit.

The client stopped at a door towards the back of his house that led down to a basement.

"Come," he ordered as he reached into his pocket,

producing a large black key. It was the type you'd usually see on an old chapel door; definitely retro fitted.

As the key turned in the lock, the metallic click made my mouth dry and my heart pick up rhythm. Who needs a heavy duty lock on their basement unless they were keeping something down there they didn't want to escape?

He opened the door to reveal pitch darkness. I'd no clue what was lying in waiting for me and my throat swelled at the prospect of following him any further.

"Wait." I croaked, "down there?"

"Yes. Follow."

Half way down the makeshift staircase, he pulled a light chord which sprung the strip light into action.

When my eyes adjusted to the dim lighting, I was relieved to see a normal looking set up in a clean and tidy space under the footprint of the house.

Under ground level, there was a chill in the air that raised the fine hairs on my arms in response, but nothing about what I'd seen so far activated the urge for me to run.

A large double bed took a central location along the back wall, and various sex toys, tools, and outfits hung along the outer edges.

Once we reached the bottom of the stairs, he turned to me.

"I would like you to wear this costume. The agency told me your size, so it should fit."

"Oh. Sure, no problem," I said as I took a black, skintight PVC all in one cat suit from him.

He pointed to a spot on the bare concrete floor marked with an X in red tape. "Please dress here."

Doing as instructed, I placed my feet on either side of the marking and he reached for his camera that was strapped to a tripod, and pressed a button. The camera's recording light illuminated, and that was my cue to undress.

I removed my clothes as seductively as I could, conscious of the fact I was being filmed with little in the way of direction.

The dress Dan had chosen lay discarded on the floor as I weighed up the best way to climb inside the plastic.

"Hurry, please." The elusive man ordered impatiently.

With as much grace as I could manage, I squeezed into the tight fitting material and yanked up the zip.

Mr. X sat at the end of the bed in front of me where he took out his genitals but didn't touch himself erotically like King would have. He sat motionless in waiting.

"Very good," he said. "Get the whip from over there."

There was an assortment of canes and whips lined up neatly along the back wall. I followed where he pointed and made my choice out of a selection of four.

The one that caught my eye the most was a black whip with a hand strap and brown leather tassels. Not sure why I liked it, I brought the item over to him and presented it like he was royalty.

"Whip me here and tell me how bad I am."

Right, OK—

If he really wanted me to whip his genitals, I was not one to disappoint. This type of activity was quite thrilling, and I was more than willing to channel all of my anger and disappointment towards men into the blow I provided him.

With a soft start to test his pain threshold, I cracked the whip at his penis and balls *hard.*

He screwed his eyes shut, but didn't make a sound.

"Do you like this freak?" I yelled.

His eyelids tightened as he absorbed the attack. "Again!"

As instructed, I cracked the whip a second time, harder this time. The force was just enough, and the area swelled and turned pink immediately.

He leant back on his hands as he focused on the pain. His penis wasn't growing yet, which had me questioning my talents. *Have I lost my skills?*

"Hit me again!"

I complied and whacked the leather down on his penis

for a third time. That one woke him up. His dick raised in response, and it seemed it would be severe pain that got him off.

"Look at this!" I pointed towards his hardening erection. "This is disgusting." I hit it again.

I wasn't sure how much more pain a normal human being could take to the genitals, but I sensed he was getting close to tapping out. With a firm flick, I cracked the whip one last time, and he climaxed a large load that shot up in front of him like a fountain.

He collapsed back onto the bed as his orgasm debilitated him, but still he didn't make a sound.

After only a matter of minutes, he propped himself up on his elbows to look at me. "I can only come like that. Why?"

I hated when clients opened up like this after they'd ejaculated. I wanted to say it's because you're a weirdo, but I refrained.

"Um, I'm not sure?" What else could I say to him? I was no therapist.

"Thank you. Not many women can hit me hard enough. I haven't climaxed in months." He offered me a tight smile. The first hint of emotion that I'd seen from him.

Suddenly sensing a connection with the authentic

version of him, I leant in to kiss his cheek.

His demeanour stiffened. "Mr. X doesn't like that," he said robotically.

His body language turned cold, confirming I'd misread the situation completely.

"OK, so I think I'll leave now. Thanks for inviting me to spend time with you," I said as I cautiously unzipped the outfit to change back into my clothes.

"Hang on!" he scowled, "I have you for another two hours yet!"

My sudden rush to leave had inadvertently infuriated him. I paused at the zip of the cat suit. "What would you like to do now, then?"

I would have done anything in that moment to take it off. My claustrophobic, sweaty skin pleaded with me beneath the plastic material.

"Take your clothes off and lie on the bed with me."

He scooted back on the bed to the head end, making room for me to join him.

Without hesitation, I did as he asked, and after removing the outfit, I lay awkwardly beside him.

After a moment of silence, I attempted to make eye contact.

"Shall I see if I can make you come another way?"

His head turned to face me as if controlled remotely. "No."

"Come on, let's give it a try. What's the worst that can happen?"

I reached for his dick, that was now a healthy shade of bright pink.

He lay frozen with his hands gripping the bed sheets for dear life as I got to work.

The whip induced climax was still evident on the tip, so I had a task on my hands to get him hard again, but I knew what I was doing. It was time to prove to myself that I hadn't lost my skills.

I pushed his short length into my mouth and sucked him gently at first. I played with his balls and consistently kept up the rhythm until we made some progress. Eventually, he grew, the sight of which made me grin inwardly.

"This is hot," I said as I played with him. "Do you have a condom?"

To my surprise, he reached over to the drawer within the bedside table and handed me a foil packet. I skilfully unwrapped it with my teeth and rolled it down onto him.

I didn't think too deeply into my next move as I climbed onboard, straddling my legs either side of his slender frame. Holding his dick in my hand, I granted access for his erection to enter me, where I immediately moved my body up and down quickly to keep him firm. After all of this effort, I couldn't afford for him to go soft now.

I clasped my hands around his and pushed them onto my breasts. Despite keeping his eyes tightly closed, I knew he was still with me.

"Come on, fuck me!" I yelled, pounding myself on top of him as hard as I could. The assault against his testicles from my ass cheeks alone would have made any other man groan.

Before realising what I was doing, I slapped him hard in the face. He moaned out a painfully excited cry.

That's it.

As my first hand stung, I swapped to the other where I raised it high and smacked him in the face again. "Come for me, you freak!"

"Ahh!" He pleaded as he ejaculated once more.

I halted immediately at the sense of his dick flinching inside me. Before climbing off, I waiting for his orgasm to finalise and flopped down next to him on the bed.

Panting and sweaty, I steadied my breathing in an attempt to slow my heart rate. That was the hardest I had worked in a long time, and my reddened palms stung from the attack on his flesh.

"Wow. I can't believe that just happened," he whispered. His hands held rigidly by his sides.

"Amazing though, wasn't it?" I grinned at my first class efforts worthy of top prize.

He handed me my money in an envelope, but in the short period it had taken him to fetch it, I noticed that the part of him I had brought to the surface had disappeared again.

Not wanting to waste time counting it in front of him, I rolled it up and tucked it into my cleavage and after dressing quickly; I made to leave.

An intrusive thought crossed my mind that he might wait for me to attempt my exit and then capture and cage me for the rest of my life, and a sensation of urgency prickled under my skin that told me to get out now while I still could.

How he moved his body around the room gave me the creeps and as his hands rummaged inside a drawer looking for something, I took that as my cue to leave.

With haste, I placed my foot on the bottom step of the staircase.

"Hold on! Where do you think you're going?"

Ahh!

An anxious tidal wave crashed through my body. Eyes wide, I gripped the banister and hoisted myself up the treacherous steps, two at a time. Not willing to give him a chance to kill me, I ran as fast as I could through the house and towards my exit.

The same floorboards from earlier offered the sound of a two beat thud at first; my feet. But then there were suddenly four.

Shit! Fuck, he was behind me. I knew it, but I was too scared to look back. *Hurry!*

As my pace quickened, my accuracy lessened. I tripped over my own foot and stumbled.

"I'm right behind you!" The tone he used was unrecognisable, evoking shock waves of adrenaline that pierced through my skin.

The door was right ahead, so close, within my reach. But the warm breath of his heavy breathing hit the back of my neck. *Shit!*

With my life flashing before my eyes, the fresh air hit me in the face like a bolder hanging from a crane as I threw open the door. I was dizzy and nauseous simultaneously, but when I peered behind me, he hadn't followed me out into the daylight.

In pursuit of safety, I ran towards my car where my adrenaline fuelled shaking hand opened the door and the slam shut behind me marked my protection.

I pulled my phone out of my bag with trembling hands and texted the agency.

<Agency> Mr. X, BDSM/Sadism. 85 New York Avenue. ASAP.

<Me> BLOCK!

When my phone rang, it interrupted my ragged breathing. At first, I thought it was the agency telling me I had to see that man again. But when I checked the caller I.D, I frowned at the unknown number.

"Hello?" I answered cautiously.

"Jasmin? It's me."

Could it be? *Am I hearing things?*

"Daddy, is that you?"

"Listen. I'm gonna text you an address. I need you to come by now."

"Um, OK, sure."

I didn't know what else to say. The sound of his voice suddenly made my legs turn to jelly.

He hung up, and within seconds, the address was in my inbox.

<UNKNOWN> 17 Santa Fe Ave, Compton

I arrived twenty-five minutes later at the address in the

rough part of town.

I pulled up to a small, rundown trailer with boarded-up windows where tall weeds that hadn't been cared for in a long time had overgrown the wrap around garden.

As I exited my car, the stench of cannabis filled my nostrils and the sound of relentless barking dogs violated my ears.

In true King style, he threw opened the trailer door before I knocked. My pupils dilated at his handsome masculinity, that never failed to render me speechless.

Not having seen him for a few days, my memory of his features had diminished. I took a moment to drink in all that he offered.

His glossy black curls styled effortlessly on top of his head had me wanting to run my fingers through the short strands. The angular lines of his perfectly defined nose sitting above his plump rose-tinted lips framed his face to perfection. And the relaxed position of his mouth afforded me a glance at his diamond encrusted platinum grill.

The fabric of his white vest—beneath his thick gold chain—clung to his muscles, showcasing every sinew. And the way he wore his sweat pants; hung low, just above the v shaped muscles provoked an urge within me to run my fingers along his warm glowing skin. An artist had unleashed their talents on his sleeve tattoos that span the full length of each arm down to his fingertips. Those same hands had encapsulated my breasts a matter of days ago, and now, in front of me, I yearned for our electrically charged interactions once more. This was our time.

King took a moment to assess the safety of our situation, and after checking over my shoulder to ensure the cops hadn't followed me, he allowed me to enter with the same arm out gesture his brother had showed at our sleepover.

Apart from their differing intensity levels and tattoos, they were similar in a lot of ways.

Upon entering the dank place, I wasn't expecting us to have company, but there was another man in the room with us I hadn't met before. To me, he looked to be of Mexican heritage, but I could have been wrong. He had just finished packing away some equipment and was busying himself with rolling up a joint, focusing all of his efforts on his cylindrical friend.

"So, what do you think?" King asked, turning to look at me with a bright eyed expression.

For a moment, I thought he was referring to our surroundings, and if that was the case, my review was not good.

The living area within the abandoned trailer was empty apart from a small, old-fashioned two-seater sofa in the centre as the only piece of furniture available.

The exposed rotten floor boards smelt damp, and the bare walls were stained. A small old school box TV, nestled in the corner, was broadcasting a foreign film I didn't understand.

"Well? What do you think!?"

"Um, about what?" I peered down at the ground, feeling intimidated by his overbearing presence.

"Got myself a new face tattoo. My guy here done it for me. So?"

As I studied his face for a moment, he turned his cheek towards me, revealing words in another language scrolled around his left eye socket. The fresh tattoo raised the delicate flesh, with a pinkish fluid build up underneath. It was clear now that the other man in the room had just tidied away his tattooing equipment when I walked in.

I screwed up my nose in response to the idea King had received a tattoo in such unsanitary conditions.

"Shorty, why you got a look on your face like you smelt shit? Did you shit your pants, Carlos?"

"No, Boss."

"So why does my hoe got a look on her face like you did?"

I sensed anger building inside him. Never having an issue with stuttering over my words before, he had that exact effect on me now.

Come on, Chloe, say something.

"Um, what does the tattoo say?"

He visibly relaxed once I'd engaged my vocal chords. "It's Italian. Veni, vidi, vici. I came, I saw, I conquered."

"Oh." I ran my eyes along each letter, studying the chosen font and trying to make sense of the reason he had chosen that phrase in particular.

"Oh? Is that all you gotta say to me?"

The atmosphere suddenly shifted and King drew his gun from the waistband of his pants, aiming it at Carlos.

"She don't like my new ink, Homie. What we gonna do about that?"

"Oh, God!" I raised my hands in alarm. "No, please Daddy, don't shoot him. I do like it. I love it!"

King glared at me for a moment, analysing my sincerity and when my gaze didn't falter, eventually he softened.

"You love it, yeah?"

"Yes, Daddy." I nodded to reaffirm my words.

King paused, distracted as he took his time to evaluate my body as he holstered his weapon.

"What's goin' on back at my crib?" He asked, taking

a step towards me. His irritation moments ago suddenly dissipated.

I didn't so much as flinch, not wanting to distract him from offering me his masculine touch.

"How do you mean Daddy?"

I wasn't sure if this was yet another game of question time with King, resulting in a blow to someone's kneecap. My stomach suddenly flipped over at the idea. *Would he shoot me?*

"I've been gone a couple of days. You missed me?" The tone of his voice sounded unsure. If I didn't know any better, I would have assumed he was looking for reassurance.

"Of course I have Daddy."

"Good. I missed you too." His long, muscular arm reached forward and his electrically charged fingers stroked my cheek. The primal look in his eyes told me he felt it too, and the notion that this man brought me here because he missed my company was difficult to comprehend. I closed my eyes, relishing in his touch.

"You were the only whore that wasn't at the house when Tatiana died and I know the cops have crossed you off their list. I need your help, Jasmin."

Oh—

Like a dagger to the heart, King had revealed that this orchestrated rendezvous was more about me doing him a favour than him actually missing my company.

My confidence left the building along with my self respect.

"What do you want me to do?"

"They've released me for now on bail, but I know the cops are snoopin' round my business tryin' to find somethin'. I've paid a guy to take the rap for Tat, so until he's jailed I'm layin' low for a few days. For now, I need you to keep things back home straight. You feel me? While I'm gone, there's gonna be all kinds of nonsense goin' on and I need a pair of eyes I can trust. I can't trust my boys. They're easily swayed by pussy when I'm not around to remind them of their place."

"Um, OK," I giggled nervously, fidgeting on the spot.

He was so intimidating and alluring, wrapped in a sculpted body of gorgeousness.

"What happened to Tat was an accident. You get me?"

King surprised me with his offering of a story time I didn't have the balls to ask for. I nodded my agreement in a state of stunned silence.

"You saw what she was like. That bitch used hard drugs every damn day and disrespected me more times than I could count. I couldn't trust her. Can I trust you to keep a watch out for me?"

I thought about my options. I could either say yes and live or no and die.

"Yes, I'll do it for you." I smiled at him and he visibly relaxed.

"That's my girl. I told you this one was a keeper," he called over to his friend, who was several smokes into being stoned.

King put his hands around my waist, setting off an intense surge through my nervous system. "You been fuckin' my brother?" He leant into my neck and took in a deep inhale, as if he could tell.

"No," I lied. This was not an AA meeting, and honesty was not the correct choice to make.

He paused in thought, assessing my words. "Good." he said finally, "he can't have you because you're mine."

Every part of my being wanted to ask King if he'd heard from Dan or at least knew where he was, but I refrained. Bringing his brother into the conversation now would result in my body bag being laid down next to Tatiana's in the morgue.

King's curious hand reached behind me and squeezed my ass, propelling my body forward as he coaxed me into his chest.

The heady masculine fragrance emitting from his skin was mouth watering. His cologne was a welcome reminder of feeling safe back at the mansion lay beside him in his bed and I suddenly missed him more than I realised, even with him standing right in front of me.

"My dick got hard by just bein' on the phone with you earlier," he said, kneading my ass like dough. "Do you know why?"

"Um, I dunno?"

Was this another game he was playing? My anxiety picked up pace again, never sure of my place around him.

"Because it needs your tight pussy, that's why. I'm gonna take you now."

His mouth was suddenly on mine. Our hands greedily making their way around one another's bodies, consuming each other. The taste of cigar smoke mixed with alcohol on his tongue made for a potent cocktail of alluring sensations.

I broke away from the kiss, panting, "What about him?" I asked, looking over at his stoned friend, who hadn't seemed to notice our entanglement.

"Let him watch me fuck my whore. See him get hard for you."

King led me over to the sofa and bent me over the back, exposing my ass to the room. He peeled off my dress like removing the skin from an orange, "No panties huh?" He said nibbling the soft skin of my cheeks.

I waited in silent anticipation for the next move and my hands clutched onto the fabric of the chair, anchoring myself into position.

King's grip tightened on me instantly. "Who did you fuck today?" His tone suddenly changed. He was mad; really mad. I sensed his position behind me solidify.

"I had a client, Daddy." My exposed rear as I lay bent over the sofa left me vulnerable to his assault.

"What client was that, then?" He pulled out his phone and scrolled as though he were looking for something.

"Just a random guy. I don't know him. The agency messaged me. Did I do something wrong?" Tears threatened to well in my eyes as my voice quivered.

Do not cry. Keep calm.

"Son of a bitch!" King yelled, thrusting his cell back into his pants pocket. But I didn't understand why. Nothing about this morning with the client had deviated from the rules. At least I hoped not anyway, for my own sake.

With unchecked fury, he pulled out his erection from his pants and began masturbating violently in my direction.

He was choosing speed over pleasure with a tense posture that meant business. His free hand gripped my ass cheek, parting the crack so he had a view of the puckered opening.

My body lay helplessly, afraid to move in case it only angered him further.

I closed my eyes and focused on my breathing and I was back on the beach. Only this time, my happy place had a shadow cast over it, blocking out the sun.

All too soon, the familiar sense of warm liquid against my skin told me he had climaxed.

"I could smell another man on you, Jasmin. Needed to get rid of that stink, taking back what's mine."

King had such a territorial nature that was a massive turn on for me. The idea that another man had been intimate with me was too much for him to handle, and I wondered if other whores had provoked the same sort of reaction from him. *Tatiana?*

King had inadvertently exposed a hidden vulnerability that he'd tried so hard to quell. The way he had to re stake his claim on me showed the depth of his feelings ran deeper than he would admit and maybe he had brought me here for more than a favour, after all?

The alluring sensation of his warm ejaculation dripping

down my skin was all I needed to confirm the depth of our emotional connection.

Anticipating King's next move, he suddenly pushed me forward back into position, leant over the sofa with my naked ass exposed to him.

"Did you use a rubber with the guy you fucked this mornin'?" He asked as he leant his body into mine. His erection rested between the crack of my cheeks.

"Yes, Daddy." I replied, sensing that I needed to be in the brace position for his next move. The tension radiating from him when speaking about the client was discernible and King's dick was inside my vagina on my last word. His hunger for my body and his need to reclaim every inch of me were tangible.

Stroke after stroke, the arousing sensation of his length expertly caressing my sensitive internal flesh brought me to the precipice of my climax.

"I can feel your cunt is ready. You wanna come like this?" He groaned through gritted teeth, continuing the deliciously sensual pace.

"Yes. Please Daddy."

"Come on Jasmin, give it to me." My master ordered, and I obeyed.

As my flesh quivered; his body responded, and we

came together in a glorious overload of electricity and magnetism. The loose connections from our absence had now reunified.

King's body fell forwards, resting his entire weight against my back as we gasped for air, seemingly not enough oxygen in the room for both of us. His powerful hands gripped my waist and spun me round to face him. "You get me comin' so hard. Shit! Carlos, ain't she somethin'?"

"Yes Boss," The stoned man slumped in the corner of the room with his eyelids half mast was barely aware of his surroundings. There wasn't a need for self-consciousness around our audience. He was practically out cold.

"Did you eat yet?" King's piercing blue eyes bore into mine, still holding onto me like a life raft.

On cue, my stomach rumbled, "No, I haven't."

"Carlos, go get us some eats."

But he had already fallen asleep.

"Carlos, you stoned fucker! Fuck!"

King finally released me and stalked over to his friend, smacking him round the head to wake him up.

"Ow shit, Boss!"

"You're lucky I just got a nut or my gun would be down your throat. Don't test me."

King thrust a wad of notes into Carlos' chest. "Take this

and get food. Now. What do you want to eat, Jasmin?"

"Anything, I really don't mind." I said as I pulled my dress back over my head.

I wasn't comfortable deciding. The idea I might pick something he didn't like was a scary concept.

"Get chicken. Hurry the fuck up, Boy."

Carlos departed in a slow motion stupor sort of way, and suddenly, we were alone in the trailer.

This was the first time we had been alone together since I'd known him. Sure, we'd spent time alone fucking in his bedroom, but as we stood now, there was no one else within the four walls. It almost felt like a date.

"Come sit." He gestured to the filthy couch. "Sorry about this. Not much choice."

"It's OK, I don't mind."

I was getting good at lying to him, but my opinions on the couch really didn't matter when I was in his company.

King lit a cigar and took a long, contemplative drag. "You remember what I asked of you?"

"Yes Daddy. You want me to keep an eye on things back home. I will. I promise."

The heat between us shifted again. "Come off the pill. You need one of my babies inside you. That's how you know you're special. Once I'm home, we will try for a baby."

What? Was this King's way of trying to secure my position of working for him while he was away?

This was too soon, and we both knew it. My subconscious detected it as another ploy to separate me from Dan, but his worry was unnecessary, since Dan had already vanished.

This sort of play must have worked for the other women, but for me, having a baby this way didn't seem right.

"You know, Jasmin, the fact you don't say much pisses me off and gets me hard at the same time."

"Sorry Daddy. I do want a baby with you."

His sly smile lit up his eyes as he perched the cigar between his teeth and rested his arms along the back of the sofa. I'd made him happy.

Carlos had finally arrived back at the trailer forty minutes later with a bucket of fried chicken and a large bottle of lemonade. The smell emitting from the meat was mouth watering.

King placed the food between us. "Carlos, go wait out front with Tommy. I don't want any interruptions."

I watched him grab the first chicken wing from the bucket, analysing how he completed the task so that I could copy the action.

"Dig in." He ordered.

With as much femininity as I could muster, I attempted to eat the slippery chicken without making a mess or dropping the fat all over me.

King's tactic was to devour as much as he could in as little time as possible, like he was a member of a pack of wild dogs who must finish first.

I peered at his side profile while he ate. "Did it hurt? Your new tattoo?"

"Nah." he licked the grease off his lips. "Only pussies feel pain."

Whilst still being fresh, the blushed colouring around the lettering had started to fade. Face tattoos weren't normally my thing, but King could pull anything off.

"What?" He asked as he wiped his mouth with the free napkin.

I hadn't realised I was staring. "Nothing."

"Nah, go on what? I got a booger?"

King pulled out his phone camera to check his nostrils, the sight of which made me giggle. The most genuine giggle I'd released in some time.

He stopped at my sound, and his eyes shone. "What now?" He asked, stifling a smile. He wasn't mad; he was joining in.

"You said booger." I giggled again.

"Yeah?"

"It's one of those words that makes me laugh, is all."

I tried to suppress my snicker, not wishing to take my internal joke too far.

"Well, when you got a booger, what do you call it?"

His body language was calm, his legs spread wide and his hands relaxed loosely. I felt safe to continue having fun with him.

"Oh, you know, bogey or something like that?"

The sound that escaped his mouth in reaction to my revelation rendered me speechless. Astonishment surged through me in discovering that someone like him possessed the ability to produce a man's chuckle.

"So you say you got a bogey? Shit, that's the funniest thing I ever heard." He laughed again, holding his stomach as though he'd got the belly laugh muscle cramps. "You're funny for a woman, Jasmin."

"I'm very funny, actually." Lost in the moment, I swatted his chest playfully.

Instantly, his mood changed, and he caught hold of my hand in a vice like grip and his soft glowing eyes morphed into daggers that pierced into my soul. Immediately, the temperature between us turned glacial, and I froze with my breath held and my heart racing.

We were on pause for a moment, where I could see him assessing the situation carefully. Then, as though he had a system reboot, he released me and focused his attention back on the chicken. Not saying another word on the subject, he scooped out a piece and chomped on it like it might be his last meal.

The bucket was empty, and our bellies were full when King rose to his feet. "Get back to the crib and keep your eyes peeled for me."

This was my cue to leave. From previous experience, I knew not to hover when receiving an order from him. I hoisted myself to my feet and made for the exit, where I sensed him following close behind me.

As I reached the door, he spun me round to face him and rested his hand against the frame. He kissed me forcefully, pushing his weight up against me so my back hit the crumbling plaster of the nicotine stained wall behind me. We got into a passionate entanglement quickly, effectively erasing the awkward moment earlier. It would've gone somewhere further had his phone not rung in his pants pocket.

"Shit," he said in an irritated tone as he frowned at the

caller I.D.

"Yo, Brother?" He said as he answered.

King's face lit up with a radiant smile as he absorbed the words being spoken to him. "So it's a go? Yes, my man. Sweet. Later," he grinned as he placed his phone back in his pocket. "Step now, shorty. You're my eyes and ears, don't forget it. I'll be home in a couple of days."

CHAPTER 9

Hours felt like days since I last had contact with King or his absent brother Dan.

The weather in L.A had taken a turn that matched my mood. Miserable.

Dressed in my skirt and short-sleeved top that offered a hint of cleavage paired with a light jacket, I stepped out of the house to my first appointment of the day with my purse over my head to shield myself from the heavy rainfall.

The only information provided by the agency regarding this client was that his name was Mr. Clinton, and his address was located ten miles away.

Once I'd made it safely inside the Mini, I sat for a moment in contemplation. *Why am I feeling so low?*

The sense of loss I was feeling for each of the men in my life pained my chest like heart burn, coupled with the fact that Alice had distanced herself choosing to spend more time alone than she did in my company.

Confliction within my mind confused my rational

thinking. I was angry—no—furious at Dan's sudden departure, with no explanation of the reasons why. How could someone behave that way and treat me like I was their everything one minute and nothing the next? I'd lost count of the amount of times I had looked at the photos I'd taken with Dan, willing him to come to life through the pixels.

Rain continued to pour in sheets onto the windshield as my bottom lip trembled. Not only was I grieving the loss of one connection, but with King also lying low, it left me vulnerable living in his home unprotected. How many more of the whores were going to attack me while I was defenceless?

Regardless of concerns for my own safety, I had been keeping to my word and holding my ear to the ground for something to report back to him when he eventually returned. When that would be, only he knew. However, so far, there wasn't much to tell. King underestimated the power that he held over the house, even in his absence.

I arrived at the appointment on time and parked in a convenient spot right outside the property.

Besides the storm soaking the ground and distorting my view through the window, the house seemed innocuous enough.

Small, but it had charm with a ruby red painted door and a tall tree in the front yard with a tree swing. Scattered kid's toys covered the lawn, creating an entirely different picture in comparison to yesterday's client.

I brushed myself down to remove the imaginary creases from my outfit and prepared for whatever lay beyond. Not knowing the client's requirements filled me with apprehension that was difficult to ignore.

With a final boost of courage, I leapt out of the car and ran along the path, hoping that the occupant would answer quickly to save my hair from getting drenched.

To my surprise, it was a middle-aged woman who opened the door. She seemed very anxious and out of sorts.

"Upstairs," she whispered with a paranoid edge.

In an attempt to read her tired expression, I searched her face for more information before I unwittingly threw myself out of the frying pan and into the fire. But her agitated demeanour was all she offered.

"Hurry, come in." She urged with shaking hands, ushering me inside and closing the door behind me. "Please go upstairs!"

Water dripped from the strands of my hair as she

pointed towards the wooden staircase without a carpet, and the idea I might slip on the way back down if in a hurry to leave had me nervous. I was cold, wet, and dishevelled. This client was not going to be pleased.

"You want me to go upstairs?"

"Yes!"

Her insistence, with no reasoning behind it, was alarming. *Is this the part where I die?*

I stood for a moment to assess my exit point. If I did as instructed, all I would need to do to escape would be to run straight back down again and through the red door. With an attitude adjustment, I pulled up my proverbial big girl pants and placed my foot on the first step. *Think of the money.*

When I reached the top, I nearly collapsed at the sight of the figure before me.

Chocolate brown curls with an angular nose and strong jawline framed his handsome smile. Dan was standing at the top, with his hands in the front pockets of his great fitted jeans.

A clap of thunder rumbled right above us that made me jump and spontaneously run towards him.

"Hey," he murmured, enveloping me in his arms.

"Why haven't I heard from you!" I grumbled into his chest.

Am I dreaming?

"Romero has got eyes all over me. He really doesn't want me seeing you, so this was the only way."

"Really?"

The idea that even whilst on the run, King was doing everything he could to keep Dan away said a lot about his intentions.

"I even tried to follow your car yesterday so I could speak to you, but one of his dick head crew cut me up. Nearly crashed my damn Mercedes!"

The thought of him being harmed hollowed my chest. "Not your new blue car?"

He nodded. "It pissed me off, to say the least."

With a sigh, he squeezed me into his chest, and I wrapped my arms around his waist, squeezing him back.

A sound travelling from the room beneath us reminded me we weren't alone. "Who was the woman that let me in?"

Images of Dan being intimate with her flooded my vision. After all, he said he preferred older women...

"Oh, that's just my Aunt Mary. She despises Romero and was more than happy to help. God, I've missed you," he hugged me a little tighter. "I have a plan."

I leant my head back to read his face. "A plan? For what?"

"For us to be together. I know what Romero is like. He's decided to mark his territory on you because he wants what's mine. But with my line of work, I can't afford to have a black eye, so we have to be careful."

The weather continued to storm outside, creating a level of intensity that matched the aura between us. The thunder roared, and a flash of lightning lit the entire room, illuminating Dan's sharp features.

"OK, what's the plan?"

"Mexico City."

"I'm going to need more than that, Dan?"

My head scrambled at the lunacy of our position. I'd not seen Dan in days, and now he wanted me to run away with him?

"We can move to Mexico City, just the two of us. All I need to do is cut him off in business. He'll soon let us go."

My hands dropped by my waist as I chewed over his chaotic reasoning. "Can't you just do that anyway, without having to move to a completely new state?"

The idea of leaving King after our secret date yesterday left me anxious. Of course, Daddy was intimidating, but the chemical reaction between us was binding, and while I had feelings for Dan, I wasn't yet ready to let King go, not until I was sure.

It wasn't until Dan presented me with a plan that would take me away from him that I realised how deeply my feelings ran.

"No, that won't work." Dan's lips pursed. "He'll try to seduce you and take you away from me as a punishment. I won't have that again. Moving is the only way."

"Oh, I see. You mean like when he took your ex wife?"

Dan ignored my comment, instead taking in a deep breath.

"Tell me you'll come with me, Jas?"

"Um, I'm not so sure about this."

His face dropped when he saw my lack of enthusiasm, and his hands nudged inside his pockets again. "Don't you dare change your mind on me now!"

Like King, his emotional tidal waves consumed him, but in stark contrast to his brother, he was capable of composure under the pressure.

"For Christ's sake, Dan, you're too much! You want me to run away with you after we've known each other for a matter of days?" I took a tentative step backwards. "I can't just run off with you, and I'm not stupid enough to piss King off for a second time!"

My chest heaved with laboured breaths as my anger took

a hold of me and the rain hammering against the window only added to our tumultuous standoff.

"I told you, Jasmin, once I stop distributing for him, he'll back off."

"Hold on." I frowned. "You move King's drugs around?"

It was all clicking into place now. How had I got myself entangled with the Kray twins?

"Well, I move his fertiliser around that he plants drugs inside." He shrugged.

"Wow."

I didn't know what else to say, and I expected so much more from Dan than this.

In an unforeseen turn of events, he was no better than King, and they clearly shared a damaged moral compass.

"Jasmin, please?" he murmured, interrupting my inner turmoil.

I huffed, shaking my head as I folded my arms. "That's not my real name."

"It isn't? Well, what is it then?"

This issue only added to the long list of reasons why I wouldn't be heading down south with him. We knew nothing about each other.

After a long pause and no eye contact, I cleared my throat.

"My name is Chloe. Not many people call me by my real name."

"OK. Can I ask why?"

Dan's face, etched with all manner of troubled emotions, forced the reality that this wasn't as simple as he'd first thought.

"Now really isn't the time to go into that."

Out of character and out of his mind, he dropped to his knees before me and I suddenly became aware we were still in his Aunt Mary's house, and our romantic assignation was well within earshot.

"Um, should we talk somewhere more private?" I looked over my shoulder at the bedroom door that was ajar with the sound of a kids' TV show broadcasting from inside.

Surveying the area, I could see him weighing up the options and on rising to his feet hastily, he dragged me into the adjacent bathroom and locked the door behind him.

The bathroom was tiny, with no window for me to escape out of if Dan's intensity levels were to reach my limit again. I'd not been in a room this small since my childhood back in England, and the closed door made the small room suffocating.

I shut the lid of the toilet seat and sat down with a

thud. My legs were losing their strength from the incessant anxiety that attacked my stomach, where the only option I could see was to break it off with him.

He crouched down again in front of me and placed his hands on my thighs, his eyes burning red hot into mine.

"I will die before I give up on you, Chloe. What don't you understand about that?"

I peered at him, but looked away again. "Be reasonable Dan. I need more time, please! This is too fast, and right now, not something I'm comfortable with."

My stab to his heart paused his breathing where for a moment I thought he might cry, but thankfully, he resisted. The only evidence of his unrest was the sparkle of his irises.

I softened the blow when I reached for his face and stroked his cheek in reassurance I wasn't yet ready to give up on him, either.

He placed his trembling hand on top of mine and closed his eyes. Reinvigorated by our proximity, he sat up on his heels and used his other hand to mimic my action and we stayed nose to nose, cradling each other's faces and breathing each other's air.

There was never any denying that our attachment was strong, but I didn't think it was strong enough for me to walk away from my new blossoming relationship with

King.

He interrupted my inner thoughts when he placed a kiss on my lips. The sparks flew instantly and before I realised it; I was kissing him back.

Dan scooped me up into his hold, and turned me around so that I was sitting astride him where his erection grew prominent in his jeans, begging me to free him.

I wanted to share this moment with him, even if it could be for the last time.

I unzipped his fly and pulled out his hard dick that I needed to reacquaint myself with, and, crouching before him, I pulled back his foreskin to reveal the swollen head of his erection. I kissed the tip and down the length greedily, sucking the heated flesh. He tried to stifle his moans, but the tension in his thighs told me I was getting under his skin.

He stroked my hair as I went to work on him and he swelled and warmed in my mouth, confirming he was ready.

Jas was back in the room, leaving timid Chloe stood in the corner, observing how it should be done.

Without hesitation, I rose to my feet and dropped my panties to the floor, straddling him again.

As the crown of his length met with the entrance of my

waiting flesh, I paused.

"Wait. Do you have a condom?"

Anguish marred his features when the realisation dawned on him.

"Fuck, no. I don't"

He kissed me again, deeper this time. Deep enough for us both to dismiss the fact we were about to have unprotected sex.

He grabbed my backside in both hands and helped guide me down on top of him.

This was not a romantic setting what so ever and fucking on a toilet in a random ladies' house was not a scene from a romance novel, but that was irrelevant when the feelings between two people were so powerful.

I moved up and down him as he held my ass, helping me keep the tempo. I threw my head back as I felt him both inside me and on my chest, kissing my sensitive skin. We moved in synchrony for a while longer until I felt the familiar ball of pleasure build inside me.

"You make me want to come for you," I whispered in his ear, running my hands through his loose curls. He groaned as he, too, was on the precipice of an intense reuniting orgasm.

"Oh God, I'm coming!" I groaned through gritted teeth.

As I climaxed, he joined me.

We both collapsed into each other, panting and reeling from the pleasure we'd just experienced. He kissed me tenderly and our tongues entwined, tasting one another and our intimate exchange.

"Why do I get the feeling that you're trying to say goodbye to me?" His glossy eyes shone with a rawness I'd not before seen.

"Give me some time, Dan. I can't leave yet."

"Sure. You can have time, but you are not leaving me. I can promise you that now."

Lifting me off him, he gathered himself and I grabbed my underwear, straightening myself up too, sensing the atmosphere between us altering for the worst.

Not wishing to sour the mood further, I kissed him one last time. "Good bye Dan."

He didn't call after me as he watched me leave.

That afternoon, I spent the time unreasonably expecting Dan to contact me. After all, it was me who had left him, yet part of me wanted to be chased.

Did unprotected sex with Dan change anything? Was that his way of proving to me that he was serious about us, no longer bothered by my line of work? Or did him rolling over and taking my rejection confirm to me what I already knew?

It made me anxious thinking about the way I left things with him. Was I too hasty in turning down his offer? My head was swimming with possibilities.

Despite everything, I had an important responsibility waiting for me back at the mansion that demanded my full attention. I needed to keep the kingdom ticking over while the king himself was absent. His persistent reminders to me yesterday told me how important this was to him, and with that in mind, my task for the rest of the day was to get some gossip that I could report back to him, deciding that Alice would be my first port of call.

Did the idea in the back of my mind that she'd want sex in return dissuade me from finding her? No, it didn't, but that was a thought to unpack another day.

I entered the hub of the home; the kitchen, in search of Alice.

Chef was being his usual flamboyant self behind the stove, creating a masterpiece for our evening meal. He smiled kindly at me when he saw me enter the room.

"Jasmin! Come sit. Do you want some eggs?"

He was frying something that produced a ceiling high

flame that radiated a lot of heat. The spectacle was impressive.

"Actually, I'm looking for someone. Have you seen Alice?"

"She strolled past a half hour ago in her swimsuit, if that helps?" He said, shrugging his shoulders.

"Perfect. Thank you."

I left the kitchen quickly and headed towards my target. The only access to the swimming pool was through the place I avoided most. The gym.

Now that the cops had departed, and upstairs was no longer a crime scene, the gym was fully operational again and filled to the rafters with whores.

Michelle was the first to notice my entrance. "Look who it isn't," she giggled whilst peddling on the exercise bike.

I wanted to pick up the nearest dumbbell and hit her round the head with it. But I refrained.

Ignoring her bitchiness with a clenched jaw, I stalked past the intimidating group of desperate women and headed towards the pool.

"Wonder why she's going in there, girls." Michelle addressed anyone that would listen. "Alice is in there. Have fun Jody."

Irritation at her incessant attacks against me forced my pause at the exit, where I turned to glare at her.

"I wondered why that bike seat stank of fish. You should get that BV looked at Michelle."

With a triumphant grin posted on my face when she gawked at me, I didn't look back again, focusing my energy towards my priorities. Something inside told me Michelle would get her comeuppance one day. Just a matter of biding my time.

As expected, I found the person I was looking for in the indoor swimming pool.

Not having the time before now, this was the first I'd stepped foot inside. It was hot and humid with a full sized pool in the middle of the room. The perimeter offered plenty of seating, but I wondered why a whore house would have much use for a space like this?

Alice was floating on her back like a starfish, staring up at the ceiling when I entered. It was obvious seeing her from this angle that she was still hurting over Tatiana's death. She needed a friend now more than ever.

I wandered over to the side of the pool and knelt down as close to her as I could get. I cupped my hands around my mouth to focus the sound towards her. "Hey, Alice!"

She shot up with a jolt when she heard a voice. "Oh. Hey," she said with a small smile when she saw it was me.

"Everything good?"

"Sure." Her eyes gave her away. It was obvious that she was lying.

Taking the opportunity, I sat down at the poolside and peeled off my pumps, dipping my toes into the cool water. The temperature change was welcome to soften the intense heat of the room. I sloshed my feet around, looking at the patterns they made on the water's surface.

Alice swam elegantly over to me with something on her mind. "Wanna join me?" She asked with a coy smile.

"I would, but I don't even have a swim suit. I really need to do some more shopping."

"You don't need one. Just get in."

"Come on, Alice, I know I'm a whore and all, but even I have standards." I sniggered. "I'm not letting King's cronies get a look at these bad boys for free!"

Jokingly, I cupped my breasts together in my hands and jiggled them up and down. We both giggled and before I knew it, she'd grabbed my ankles and yanked me into the water.

I spluttered as my head crowned the surface, coughing up the chlorinated water that burned the back of my throat.

"Alice!" I choked as the chemicals stung my nose. I scooped the water out of my eyes frantically, smearing makeup all over my face.

"Oh, lighten up," she smiled, moving closer to me where she reached for my soaking wet top and pulled it over my head.

Autonomously, like a baby to its mother, my arms raised in the air to allow her to complete the action.

Alice had ways of making me do what she wanted and as my nipples were already erect from the cold bite of the pool's contents, she smirked as she reached down and grasped one in her hand, offering the teat to her plush lips.

It always felt good when she touched me, and she knew it.

My naughty little secret.

"Make you come," she said as she licked and teased my nipple.

"Um. OK."

The awaited attack discombobulated me. I had known exactly what I was getting myself into when I began my search for Alice and my internal feud asked me why I had put myself in this position. Was it because I was lonely? Or had she evoked a sexual attraction within me I didn't realise I was capable of exploring?

She continued to suck my breast; the sensation created a surge of arousal in a straight line towards my clit, and then with her tongue in my mouth, she reached into my underwear, paying close attention to my swollen flesh.

Naturally, we drifted over to the side of the pool, my back pressed up against the wall as she continued to pleasure my body.

Her invasion of my mouth was welcome and my tongue met with hers, massaging; kneading. Alice's sweet scent differed heavily from the men in my life, of which made me crave her even more. With my guard down, I allowed her full access, where I emulated her impressive skills. My wandering hand returned the favour and went to work on her clit, rolling my fingers around the sensitive peak of her clitoral hood, and she leant into my neck as we exchanged oxygen.

"Hold on a minute!" Alice stopped abruptly and looked at me questioningly. "You've had sex, you're wet inside with come. I can tell. Only Daddy can come inside his girls, you know that, right?"

My breathing faltered as she brought her finger to her mouth to taste the evidence. "Daddy isn't here, so who does this belong to?"

The realisation that I hadn't yet showered since having

sex with Dan earlier slapped me in the face.

"Please don't tell."

She sucked her finger from root to tip and smiled at me with a wicked gleam in her eye.

"It's Dan's isn't it? Don't worry, I won't tell Daddy."

And just like that, she attempted to rekindle our tryst.

Her talented fingers tickled my flesh, but I could no longer concentrate. My breathing altered at the explosive orgasm building inside my core that wouldn't release until I knew more.

"How did you know?"

Alice sucked my nipple again, teasing my senses.

"Hanna told me about your secret relationship."

Her finger continued to spur me on, but the nagging concern within me must have transferred to my face and she could read me like a book.

"Don't let it ruin the mood. Come on, I want this Jas."

The notion that Hanna—my best friend—had told Alice about my secret was as hard to digest as a ball of wool. Alice couldn't be lying, as no one else knew about my relationship with Dan apart from Hanna.

Being smart, I needed to plough through, as not giving Alice the release she craved would leave me in an exposed position I could ill afford. One wrong move now and she would sing to King about my secret like a songbird at 5:00AM.

With my lips against hers, I teased at the puckered entrance of her butt hole with my finger to soften her for entry, and when she groaned into my mouth, I pushed my finger inside. I sucked on her breast and fingered her ass hole at a pace I knew she would respond to. Without warning, her pussy convulsed as she came out loud for me.

"Fuck!" she moaned as her climax rolled on and on.

I kept my finger inside her, caressing her flesh until she was spent, sealing our unspoken promise for her to keep her pretty mouth shut.

In true Alice style, she pushed away from me, about to end our encounter, until I grabbed hold of her by her wrist.

"Wait a minute. You left me high and dry last time. Don't do it again!"

Her angelic giggle warmed my soul, knowing exactly what I was referring to. "My bad. Come here."

She pulled me into her body and her finger moved welcomingly between my folds and back inside my body. She slid in and out as the water sloshed around us while I built up around her relentlessly delicious action, impatiently waiting to tip over the edge.

That's it. Almost there.

Finally, my orgasm tore through my body where my head collapsed forwards and our foreheads clashed as she helped me ride out the pleasurable waves.

"Better?" She asked as she kissed my lips while my pussy contracted.

I nodded, "yes."

Alice's eyes narrowed as she focused on the window.

"Oops, we have company," she stifled a smile.

I followed her eye-line to find an older looking man stood at the pane of glass that separated us from the outside world. He had an expression on his face that I couldn't decipher. With soiled overalls and a leaf rake in his hand. He must've been the gardener.

My instinctual reaction was to panic. I was supposed to be monitoring the other whores, not having sex with one of them.

The gardener held his mouth in a thin line as he observed. But once he saw we had spotted him, he gathered himself and got back to work, adjusting the peak of his cap as he left.

"I think we made the old man happy," she laughed as she splashed me in the face.

My eyes screwed shut in response as I laughed at her assault. The relaxed mood between us was something only

Alice could provide me with, and the way her eyes softened told me she felt it, too.

Now was my chance. I had to ask my burning question.

"Alice, what happened to Jody?"

Her lashes flickered as her eyes hardened. "What do you mean?"

"Well, I've heard Michelle mention Jody a lot. It seems like you two were close?"

Just like that, Alice defaulted backwards into the same star fish position she'd presented when I'd entered the room. Conversation over.

I waited for a moment before moving, hoping she would come back to me, but she didn't.

On my turn towards the edge, I scooped up my discarded top that was floating on the surface and clambered out of the pool.

As I attempted to re-dress, I gave her one last chance to say something; anything. But the continued silence encouraged me to leave.

Now that I'd gained some distance, the thought occurred to me I'd tracked Alice down in order to get gossip about the other girls, but the opposite happened when all I'd received was news about my relationship with Dan. How could

Hanna expose my secret to Alice like that?

Just as I reached the exit she called out behind me, "You won't leave me will you, Jas?"

I turned back around, relieved that she hadn't ended our friendship just yet. "I'll always have your back, Alice."

"That's good to know. I care about you. You're a great friend."

My encounter with Alice gave me yet another reason I couldn't leave L.A to be with Dan. My friend needed me now more than ever and I couldn't abandon her. I knew all too well how that felt.

I made my way back into the kitchen, knowing I'd have to see the whores in the gym again on the way through. I rolled my eyes at the prospect, but I wasn't going to let them intimidate me in my own home.

Alice's scent still resided in my nostrils as I attempted to shake off our encounter with my swollen flesh, a heady reminder of my orgasm by her hand.

Although, our latest interaction did have me worrying about her mental state, and whilst I had no problem offering her my body, I wasn't sure just how much I could give her as a bandaid to help her heal her wounds. Nothing I could provide would be enough to help her get through her pain of losing Tat.

Thankfully, the gym was empty when I stormed in, expecting a verbal assault. Michelle must have decided her BV needed attention at another location.

It was only then that I noticed several discarded bra and panty sets piled high in the corner of the room. *King must have fucked so many girls in here.*

I made it safely to the kitchen, parking my rear at the island where I spotted a copycat red head, who at first I thought was Michelle. But this girl was slimmer and shorter than my true nemesis. She sat on the opposite countertop with a man who stood in a compromising position in front of her. They were kissing passionately and fake Red's legs were around his waist and his hands were cradling her head.

As soon as they heard my entrance, they stopped immediately.

The male I recognised as one of King's valet team, who had been in the lineup on the day of the shooting, but his name didn't easily come to mind. *Sam?*

With his fly undone, he looked dishevelled, so it didn't take a genius to work out what had been going on between them.

"Keep your mouth shut!" Michelle's doppelgänger hissed while buttoning up her shirt.

"Are you talking to me?" I pointed at myself and glanced over my shoulder.

"Yeah, I am. Keep what you saw to yourself or I will have you fucked up. Sam, hand me my panties."

Not really in the mood for a fight in my post orgasm sated state, didn't change the fact that I would give her one if challenged hard enough.

I laughed in retaliation. "Only a coward would have me fucked up by someone else. Do the dirty work yourself."

I began removing my earrings, assessing how far she was willing to take our show down. She hopped off the counter and honed in on me like a missile, but I stood tall to meet with her. My shoulders tensed in waiting.

Before she could take the first swipe, I pulled her hair and dragged her to the floor.

"Hey ladies, chill!" Sam said, trying to deescalate the situation.

I stood my ground with a tight grip on her bottle-red locks. Sick and tired of being attacked from all sides, this was my retaliation.

Red sat helplessly on the ground, reaching around to free herself from my hold. "Let me go!"

I gave her a warning shot to the ribs. Not too hard, but just enough to give her something to think about.

"Ow, you fucking bitch!" She tried to grab me to release herself, but I was persistent.

Just as I was about to go in for round two, I heard a familiar voice.

"Jas? Jasmin!" Hanna shouted at the top of her lungs as she entered the room.

My head shot up to meet with her forlorn features, where she seemed horrified, and it brought me crashing back down to reality.

She ran over to us and pushed me off the redhead.

"Jas, what the fuck are you doing!?"

I stood motionless, panting, as I tried to make sense of what had just happened.

My outburst left me confused and the anger that had built from weeks of unresolved trauma was erupting from my subconscious like a volcano.

Hanna helped my enemy to her feet. "Hey, come on Tiffany. She won't hurt you now." And with a scowl at me, she escorted her out of the room.

Sam shook his head in disbelief. "You hoes are crazy."

When Hanna stormed back in, she beckoned me over to

her for a chat that would quickly turn into a reprimand. "What's going on Chloe?"

"That bitch threatened me, Hanna. I was standing up for myself!"

"Tiff isn't a bad girl."

"Oh? You're on nick-name terms, are you? She's just another Michelle. A bitch!"

I was getting irritated by her lack of support. She was supposed to be my best friend, but it didn't help that I now knew Hanna had broken girl code the first chance she got.

"She's my friend Chloe. Tiff has been good to me."

"Well, what are you wasting time with me for then, Han?" I threw my hands in the air in exasperation. "Go fuck your girl!"

"What's gotten into you, Chloe?"

Hanna was just as angry at me as I was with her, but I couldn't figure out why.

"So your girl Tiffany threatens me, but you come at me as if I have the problem?"

"I haven't seen you beat on a girl before. This isn't you." Hanna's tone was softer now; calmer. The way her body language changed quelled my raging anger, too.

My throat tightened as sadness threatened to bring tears to the surface.

"I don't know what you're expecting of me?" My lip wobbled. "Next time someone threatens me, I should take it?"

"That's not what I mean. I'm just not used to seeing you hit anyone. My Jasmin is a lover, not a fighter."

Hanna's complete u-turn made us both chuckle while a stray tear escape from the corner of my eye. She glimpsed my vulnerability and enveloped me in a hug, where we stood for a minute in an embrace.

"Come on Chloe. What's wrong?"

There wasn't a way for me to explain my troubles to Hanna.

Before our drift, I would have loved nothing more than to tell her about the love triangle I had found myself in. Or was it a square? We would have sat with a cup of tea and chatted the night away about all the possibilities available. But our relationship had split so far apart in such a short period that I didn't even recognise her anymore. We were almost strangers.

I kept the knowledge to myself that Hanna had broken the first rule of friendship—Secrets are for keeping, not sharing—She couldn't possibly talk her way out of it, and getting confirmation from her it was true would only make it real. At least this way, I could pretend Alice was lying in order to bring Hanna and me back together.

My lip quivered, and tears fell in waves. Before I knew it, we were both sobbing into each other's arms.

Sam was still in the room, drinking King's liquor, watching our theatrical performance play out in front of him.

We both noticed him when the rim of the bottle clinked the glass on his refill. When he caught our stare, he blanched as though he was next in the firing line.

"Sorry. I was waiting for you to finish. I wanted to check that you won't tell Boss. Please?"

The small child encased within the man's body was evident.

"No Babe, I won't tell." Hanna said, keeping me in her embrace.

I wanted to inform Sam that Hanna's word meant nothing, but he would find that out for himself.

After my emotional encounter with Hanna, I had spent a further hour crying in the shower. With a towel wrapped around my body, I rubbed at my wet hair as I made it back into King's bedroom. What I would have given to see him lay there, naked, waiting for me.

My phone buzzed on the side table. It was a call from the

agency.

"Hello?"

"Jasmin, there is an important client that wants to see you. Now."

"OK, sure. Is everything alright?"

The urgency in the woman's voice was alarming. What on earth did a client need to see me for so badly? Is Dan behind this?

"Just go now. I will message you the address." She hung up.

It took a lot of strength to ignore my instincts and get into the car to an address I hadn't been to before. This wasn't a previous client. This was someone new.

I arrived thirty-five minutes later to a poor area on the other side of town. Suddenly, this encounter smelled suspicious.

At the property, there was a thug looking man in a pulled up hoodie, sat on the front step of an old rundown two story chalet. He was smoking a cigarette and keeping a watchful eye on the surrounding area.

A fire had destroyed the neighbouring property at some point. Only ash and rubble remained.

As I approached, he looked at me speculatively. "Jasmin?" he asked on the exhale of his smoke.

"Yes."

He pointed with his chin to a side gate that led round to the back of the property. "Go round back."

Not wishing to spend anymore time with the stranger than I had to, I followed the order, sensing that the man I wanted to see more than anything in the world was waiting for me at the other side.

I opened up the rusted old gate that protested against its hinges and forced myself past the overgrown bushes and weeds. The thin fabric dress I'd chosen to wear caught on a thistle pulling at the fibres, and with a tug to free myself, I continued along the path, regretting my choice of footwear.

Once round the back, delight fired up all of my synapses at seeing King lay on a sun lounger looking sexy as hell. He wore a pair of black circular Ray-Ban sunglasses that framed his handsome face, and his fresh tattoo was just about visible around the dark lens. His imposing gold chain hung low around his muscular neck and the large diamond watch he wore glistened in the sunlight.

My eyes moved directly to the ample mound of his soft dick resting in his sweatpants.

With a cigar in his mouth, he smiled when he saw me, but we weren't alone. There was another man and a woman a few feet away.

The woman, dressed in a bra and denim shorts with hooker heels, was dancing provocatively for the man who looked similar to the stoner I met last time, but it wasn't him. His hand rubbed up and down her backside as she twerked scandalously for him.

King removed his glasses and hooked them over the neck of his vest. "Here's my girl."

The way his body language changed with excitement was invigorating, and it healed the pain in my chest that I hadn't realised was there.

"Hey," I smiled shyly. I'd missed him so much.

"Come here, Sexy."

He propped up the chair and opened his arms for me to fall into his hold. I was suddenly alive after feeling so miserable.

"Sit," he ordered, pulling my body onto his lap.

He stubbed out his cigar into the ashtray that sat upon a garden table with a glass top. The flakey paint disclosed how long the place had been abandoned.

"How have you been?" he asked.

I peered around the perimeter, feeling exposed at our

open position. "Um, good, thanks."

He picked up on the tension emanating from my body.

"Don't worry. Home boy out the front is keeping an eye on things."

He tucked a loose strand of hair behind my ear and the electricity in his touch set me alight again. His finger pulled my bottom lip from the grasp of my teeth.

"You didn't take the pill today, right?"

Shit—

"No Daddy," I lied, smiling innocently at him.

I really wasn't ready for a baby and if he thought making one in the abandoned garden was a good idea, then he was insane.

"That's my girl. I told you I'll put a baby in here. I keep my promises."

He placed the flat of his hand on my vacant stomach. My breathing hitched and my lower body convulsed internally at his touch, and at that moment, I changed my mind. I'd give him anything he wanted.

The couple next to us were kissing while she moved in his lap. King watched them for a minute, drinking in the show as though he was getting some inspiration for his own encounter with me.

Our eyes locked, and his pupils dilated. "Take your

panties off," he whispered in my ear.

Without hesitation, I did as I was told and slid them off, dropping them onto the ground. He gripped my thighs and brought me closer in order for me to straddle him.

His dick was hard along his stomach, and my clit rested against his hot, thick shaft. He kissed me passionately and groped my ass with a hunger that only intensified the more we connected.

Between kisses, he pulled away. "You got dirt for me?"

His starved hands claimed every inch of my body, and I was so hot and bothered by his touch that it didn't quite compute what he meant.

His question from the other day came to my mind, *'Do you like it dirty?'* Did he want me to piss on him?

"Dirt?"

"Yeah," he said. "What's going on at my crib?"

"Oh," I giggled into his mouth as the kissing resumed.

"What did you think I meant, you crazy British slut?"

King held my neck in a firm hold while he nuzzled the swell of my breasts.

"Um, for a moment, I thought you wanted me to piss on you. You know, like the other day?"

"Shorty, you are one dick teasin' little slut and I fuckin' love it."

His tongue entered my mouth as he kissed me deeper and the heat from his engorged erection swelled the flesh of my vagina.

"Before I get lost in you. Do you got dirt or not?"

"Tiffany—"

"Who?"

Clearly, King didn't know the whore's names as much as I didn't. He still didn't even know my real name.

"She's a red head? Looks like Michelle, but worse?"

He thought about it for a second. "Oh, yeah. What about her?"

I didn't want to know what image came to his mind in that moment when he remembered who she was. Her bra and panties were probably amongst the discarded pile in the gym, and she'd likely had his dick in her mouth more times than he could count.

"She's fucking one of your men."

"She is?"

He didn't seem as concerned about my revelation as I'd expected, where clearly, the idea of me pissing on him was the more pressing matter at hand.

"Other than that, everything seems normal, Daddy."

"Good." He reached between my legs and pushed a finger inside me.

"Now I'm gonna get you pregnant. But first, this greedy little cunt is gonna piss on my dick."

Our close proximity was a sensual overload. The masculine woody scent of his aftershave mixed with the remnants of the cigar on his breath lured me in.

Fuck me.

King cupped the damp flesh between my legs, and palmed my clit as he pushed his finger deeper inside me, stroking the internal walls of my vagina. His dick throbbed beneath me and the warmth that radiated from him set my libido on fire.

"Piss on my dick, Baby," he coaxed again.

I let go of the natural clench between my legs, and droplets of urine flowed where the wetness dripped over him, lubricating our connection.

He pushed his dick inside me and kept it there a beat longer until I'd finished.

"You make me so hard, Jasmin. My filthy little whore," he growled into my neck, kissing behind my ear, feeding my hunger.

Lost in the moment, King abruptly brought me back to the present when he moved me up and down his length. The pleasure painted on his face spurred me on, and he moaned as his arousal engorged his penis.

"Shit!" His hand shot into his sweat pants pocket, halting my movement immediately.

My first thought was that he couldn't orgasm from my terrible performance and he was reaching for his gun.

But out of breath, he pulled out his phone. "What?"

He listened to the caller, and I held my breath. His penis was still rock solid inside me, but I remained still.

After a moment, he ended the call and looked at me with a glisten in his eyes.

"Cops! We gotta move now!"

He practically threw me off him as he adjusted the gun in his waistband. With skilled execution, he pushed his sunglasses back into place and pulled the hood of his jacket over his head to conceal his identity.

"But I thought you got bail?" I looked at him, confused, as the men prepared themselves for an escape. The twerking whore yelled something in Spanish, but no one paid her any attention.

"Yeah, I did, but my guy on the inside says they wanna take me in for an unspent speedin' offence. But when they detain me, they'll try to plant somethin' on me; drugs or some shit. I just need one more day. But right now, we gotta go!"

The crotch of his pants was damp from my performance.

I wondered how that might look to a bystander; a gangster on the run looking like he'd pissed himself.

He grabbed my hand and raced us towards the far side of the garden to the fence that paved the way to open fields ahead of us. I could see now why he chose this location. One could easily get lost in the tall overgrown grasses that occupied the marsh lands.

King hopped over the fence with ease and waited for me to follow from the other side. His spade-like tattooed hand reached for mine and helped me climb over. The strength that exuded from his body as he hoisted me over easily was so attractive.

We ran faster than my legs could carry me, with his taller frame covering the ground at twice the distance I could.

Gasping, I could taste the same metallic sensation at the back of my throat that always happened when I'd done too much in the gym. I couldn't run any further.

"Daddy—" I panted between breaths as we continued our gruelling pace.

"What?"

"I'll stall the police, you know, be a decoy. You get out of here."

There wasn't time to think. Milliseconds passed before

he nodded in agreement, and the hand he had gripped around mine squeezed for the last time as he bolted on foot to safety.

Now a silhouette in the distance he was out of reach and out of my life. When would I see him again? God only knew.

I slowed my pace to a halt, placing my hands on my knees to catch my breath as I waited for the police to close in on me. It wasn't long before I heard them.

"Police! Hands on your head and drop to your knees!" The female officer, accompanied by another, ran towards me and pulled out a pair of handcuffs. I complied and waited with my fingers interlaced behind my head, kneeling on the ground and ready for the onslaught.

She informed me of my right to a lawyer, but I wasn't really listening. I just hoped they hadn't caught King. My feelings for him were consuming my mind, body, and my soul.

To everyone's grievance, the cops had parked the car about half-a-mile away from the arrest site. It was difficult navigating the rocky terrain without the use of my arms, and I tripped on more than one occasion.

The male cop who didn't take his eyes off me kept a firm grip on my cuffs with his female partner in proximity with her gun drawn, but they already knew I wasn't capable of outrunning them. I was still exhausted and panting from the first attempt.

"Get in." He barked as we finally arrived, pushing my head down on entry.

The inside of the car smelt like ass and fried food, and I was certain someone had shit themselves in the back seat at some point. Nevertheless, this was the plight I now faced, but self-assured that whatever they were trying to charge me with, it wouldn't stick.

As we travelled above the speed limit to the station, I peered out of the window and thought about nothing other than King. Our relationship—if that's what you could call it—had bloomed into something more than he or I could have predicted during our short time in knowing one another. I didn't want to let him slip through my fingers and I hoped with all my heart that he felt the same way for me as I did him.

"Who's checking her in?" The female who was driving asked her partner.

"No idea Smith. I'm clocking off after this, so I don't really give a shit."

I screwed my nose up at his attitude, and Smith rolling her eyes was so relatable. Her reflection in the rear-view mirror offered me an insight into her working relationship with him.

The car pulled up outside the station where a dishevelled male cop was waiting outside to greet me upon arrival.

"I knew it'd be him checking her in," Smith muttered as she unclipped her seatbelt. "He's like a fly round shit when it's the young girls."

The waiting cop's hair was unkempt under his police officer's hat and his uniform trousers hadn't seen an iron since purchase. When he saw me, he threw his half-smoked cigarette on the ground and stubbed it out with his boot.

He descended upon the vehicle with a slight limp and opened the back of the car where I was waiting in cuffs.

The smell of his pungent smoker's breath and strong coffee made me turn my head away in disgust. His nicotine tinted fingers reached into my space as he stole a glance inside my dress.

The look of self-importance on his face revealed how accustomed to this behaviour he really was. This was what Smith was referring to. She knew what he was.

I kept my lips sealed as I waited for his next move, not

wishing to spend anymore time in a cell than I had to.

"Nice tiddies," he said with a wry smile. "Let's get one out and have a look, shall we?"

"What's taking so long, Gary!?" Smith called over, distracting him from his assault. Thankful for her interruption, he wouldn't get what he wanted today.

"Alright, alright" he sneered. "We're coming!"

The pervert dragged me over to the check in station, where a bored officer waited at his untidy desk. The badge he wore informed me that his name was Baldwin, ironically matching his hairline. Unfortunately for me, he was a bad tempered son of a bitch who did not like his job.

"Name?"

"Ja—Chloe Adams."

"Hand over your personal items."

He didn't peel his eyes away from the computer screen. My money said he was watching porn.

The arresting officer had already taken my phone at the scene, so I reluctantly handed him my Casio wristwatch, hopeful I would see it again.

"Jones, take this one to holding cell five and do a final body check," Baldwin called over to a woman who was standing stock still in the corner of the room with her hands behind her back, in waiting.

At a guess Jones was mid thirties and quite attractive, but her eyes were too kind for the role she was in. They gave away her weakness. She took me by the cuffs and led me into the 'check in room'.

The place was a small cell like room with flakey paint walls and dark green woodwork. The tiny window had bars and there was a small desk with some implements laid out on a silver medical tray that made me gulp.

"OK, Miss, this is uncomfortable for both of us, but please undress."

My chosen line of work had me prepared, and being asked to strip in front of someone was not as much of an issue for me as it might be for some. Without fuss, I removed my dress, down to my underwear.

"Bra and thong too, please."

Stepping out of the lace, I was naked in front of her.

"OK, bend over and part your cheeks. I need to check for contraband."

As a compliant prostitute would, I spread what my mother blessed me with and patiently waited for her to finish examining me with a flashlight. For some reason, the scene made me think of Alice. I hoped she was safe back at the mansion, and I made it my number one priority to check on her once they released me.

"Thanks for your cooperation. Dress and follow me."

Cell number five was a short walk down a narrow corridor and I instantly felt nauseous upon entry.

"Can you stand by the bed, please, Miss?"

I complied. Jones was an amiable woman who was more suited as a primary school teacher.

As she came up behind me, I peered over my shoulder to look at her.

"You hate this job, don't you?"

She let out a small chuckle. "Is it that obvious?"

As I waited by the bed, she released my hands, and I heard the door clunk close behind me before I saw her leave. I rubbed at the red marks that the cuffs left on my skin, wondering what I was thinking when I agreed to this.

I sat down on the mattress-less metal bed frame to assess the facilities. The room was chilly, damp, and lifeless. Apart from the bed in the far corner, there was a toilet with a wash basin attached and a plastic shatter proof mirror above. The distorted reflection it offered me rendered it useless.

"An officer will be with you shortly," Jones called,

looking through the small cut out window of the locked escape proof door.

'Shortly' turned out to be four hours. Four long hours of my own thoughts were hell on earth. A tactic they often deployed to make your character weak, forcing you to confess to anything for an early release. But I'd seen too many Netflix crime documentaries to fall for their bullshit. I wasn't backing down now.

Not before time. A key turned in the big heavy duty metal door where it creaked open.

"Chloe Adams?" The male voice called before entering. "I'm coming in."

When our eyes met, I saw the same officer that had interviewed me at the mansion the day Tat had passed.

He looked down at his clipboard and then back at me in disbelief, his eyebrows raised in confusion, "Well, this is unexpected."

He took a seat on the uncomfortable bed frame beside me.

"So, Chloe, you seem to have been busy?" He flipped the pages to see if there was more to the tale of entanglement.

"I was just in the wrong place at the wrong time. I haven't done anything, I swear."

"Hmm, according to this report, the arresting officer saw you with Romero Giannetti?" Instinctively, he gripped his clipboard tightly at hearing King's name spoken out loud.

"I wasn't. But even if I was, he was bailed, right?"

"On that account, yes, but we have many other reasons to rearrest him."

My lip curled. "A speeding offence is hardly a reason to go to these lengths."

"You sure know a lot about Romero for someone who hasn't seen him?"

I blanched at his shift in questioning. *Shit!—Shut up Chloe.*

The officer sensed my retreat. "The only saving grace for you here, Sweetheart, is that your body search was clean."

"I'm innocent."

"OK, well, they are going to interview you shortly. My advice is to make sure you let that son of a bitch take the wrap. If you know anything about Romero, you must tell the officer."

"I don't know anything. I honestly don't!"

My feelings for King would never allow me to tell them what I knew. We'd come too far.

He sighed and shook his head. "Anyway, before I leave, are you OK?" He peered down at my welted wrists.

"Yeah, I'm fine." I leant forward and pressed the sides of my nose with my thumb and forefinger, feeling a whopping headache brewing.

Half an hour later, my cell door opened again, and a smartly dressed suited man entered with a briefcase.

"The name's Arthur. I'm your attorney and I've been assigned to your case."

"Oh? Hi."

He leant into my personal space, less formally, with a small smile. "Daniele sent me."

My lips parted in surprise at Dan's involvement, and the idea played with my emotions harder than I expected. How on earth did he know I was here?

Arthur flopped his brown leather briefcase onto the bed and opened the lid. "I'll have you out of here in the next few hours."

CHAPTER 10

My pounding heart woke me with a start and the reality of my surroundings knocked the wind out of me.

Dark, damp and cold, I was still in the holding cell. Not recalling that I'd even fallen asleep, I was groggy and disorientated. How long had I been here? *What time is it?*

I peered down at my naked wrist, remembering that the cops had already confiscated my watch, and I rubbed at the bare flesh, hoping to be reunited soon.

Hushed voices echoed from the other side of the cell door, and my ears pricked towards the sound. *Who's there?*

I winced as my joints protested in my attempt to move position atop the hard surface of the bed frame.

Eventually, the door opened and the light from the corridor illuminated the darkness of the cell, blinding me.

A figure in Officer Jones' form appeared at the entrance, standing rigidly next to a handcuffed female.

"Cell mate for you Adams."

"Huh?" I croaked, bewildered. "What's the time?"

"A little after midnight. The block is full, so you have a sleeping buddy."

"Wait. Why am I still here? My attorney said—"

"It'll be morning now before anything gets done. Hang tight."

The strange woman entered my cell, clutching a thin mattress under her meaty arm, and as the door closed behind her, the room descended into darkness once more.

Not being able to see her features made me apprehensive, especially as her scent was unwashed and her aura dubious.

"Um hi. I'm Jasmin." I waved into the darkness.

"The name's Frankie-Jo. Get your ass up."

"Who, me?" I asked, pointing to myself.

She tutted, and a small drop of spittle landed on my arm.

"Yes you, get up."

I did as I was told and hoisted my stiff limbs out of bed and stood by the door as though I was in one of King's scenes.

A tall woman, she towered over me but as soon as she threw herself down onto her mattress; the intimidation dwindled.

Do I stay quiet or do I say something?

"Um, can I get you anything?" I asked hesitantly.

She cackled, and the crunch of the mattress innards informed me she'd turned over.

"Come here Jasmin."

The sound of her nails scratching against her flesh sent a shudder down my spine as I took tentative steps closer towards her.

When I stood at the foot of the bed, I sensed her eyes scan my body and from what little she could see of me; she didn't seem disappointed.

"You're real pretty, huh?"

Was that rhetorical? *Am I pretty?*

As I fumbled over my response, Frankie-Jo shifted her weight again. "Are you a good girl, Jasmin?"

Hmm—

That question never failed to evoke distress within me, as that was the type of thing my step father would ask me.

I am good, aren't I?

"I mean, I think so?"

My words stuttered out of me with caution. If I didn't add conviction behind my answer, then she couldn't call me a liar.

"That's what I thought. We can share this cot if you want?"

Share?

I weighed up my options for a moment. To either stand in the corner all night or sleep on a single person mattress with a stranger was a tough choice to make, but refusing her offer didn't seem like the correct thing to do.

"OK," I shrugged, "sure. Thanks."

Frankie-Jo scooted over, and we sat together side by side. Now positioned closer to each other, I could just about make out some of her features through the light emitting from the small cell window, where shadows cast vertical lines down her ageing face.

A masculine woman, Frankie-Jo was heavyset with a shaved head and full body tattoos. Her eyes were dark and didn't afford any information as to her character or life story. When our eyes met, I felt as though I needed to fill the silence again.

"So, what are you in here for?" I asked casually, attempting to befriend my new sleeping partner.

"Nothing crazy," she belched. The smell of which flared my nostrils. "Just murdered my girlfriend, but she had it coming."

Fuck—Shit.

"Oh, really?" The sudden quiver in my voice exposed my vulnerability.

Frankie peered at me with her elusive irises. "Relax, you're safe. I don't kill pretty girls."

"Oh—"

How the fuck did I end up in this situation? This went from a kind gesture towards helping the man I wanted to form a relationship with, to now being locked in a cell with a murderous lesbian.

"Are you a dyke, Jasmin?" Frankie's intrusive question completely caught me off guard.

Instantaneously, images of Alice's body materialised in my vision. Her soft skin and the peak of her hardened pink nipples. My hands caressing her body. Her fingers inside mine.

"Simple question. It's usually a yes or no."

"Sorry. Um—"

But which way should I take this? If I am a lesbian, then do we have something in common and therefore she leaves me alone? Or would that give her the green light to try something with me?

The fact that I hadn't yet dived into and unpacked the answer to this important question until now was unsettling. Alice and I were friends with benefits, and that was it. *Wasn't it?* I really didn't know anymore.

Frankie's body language grew agitated as she waited for

an answer.

"Yes, I am. A lesbian, I mean."

"Thank God," she slapped her thigh. "I knew it, I could tell. Honestly, I fucking hate men and hate even worse bitches who simp after men. Who the fuck wants a man when you can have some pussy? You know what I mean?"

Phew. That was a close one, but what did she mean when she said she could tell? *Am I giving off a lesbian vibe?* If I was, what did that say about me?

"Oh yeah, I know exactly what you mean." I snorted involuntarily as anxiety induced sweat beads formed on my forehead. "Men are the worst."

"You wanna know why I hate men so much?"

I toyed with the inside of my cheek between my teeth. The issue was that no; I did not care to learn why this woman hated men, but as telling the truth wouldn't have been smart, I determined lying my arse off was the way to go.

"Yeah, sure. Why?"

"OK, buckle up, and I'll tell you a story of my first and only time with a man."

Frankie sat cross-legged, getting herself comfortable for story time I didn't ask for, taking up most of the space we were attempting to share.

"In college, I was seventeen and kind of a big girl. I guess I intimidated people, so I hadn't had an opportunity to fuck anyone yet. So anyways, this guy comes on to me and I'm like, yeah, OK, let's do this. Turned out it was for a bet and he posted my butt naked pictures all round the school. He was the first person I ever killed."

I gulped at Frankie's candidness. This insane woman sounded just like King in female form where it was nothing short of terrifying being in her company, but for some reason, I sensed she liked me.

"That's rough. I'm sorry he did that to you."

"What about you then, Jasmin? Why do you hate men?"

As soon as she'd finished the question, my answer was already waiting at the tip of my tongue, as her previous intrusion had inadvertently opened up the dusty old memory box.

"Well, my stepdad, he um—"

Frankie sighed and shook her head. "He touched you up, huh?"

"Mm-hm."

I naturally adopted a solemn demeanour whenever someone forced me to talk about him, but I felt as though Frankie empathised with me and perhaps we were getting somewhere.

"Forget about that dick wad," she smiled, "and tell me more about you. I need to know who I'm sleeping with tonight."

Adrenaline fired on all cylinders. Would she hurt me if I said the wrong thing? Did she want specifics?

"Well, I'm twenty-one—"

"Christ, Jasmin, this ain't kindergarten show and tell, gimme the real shit! You're in jail. Why?"

If I was quicker on my feet, I would have made up a lavish lie about how I too murdered people for fun. That way, she would think twice about killing me in my sleep. But who was I kidding? I was weak and afraid.

"I was helping out a—um, friend."

"Nice. I like a sweetheart who stands up for what's right. Your friend is real lucky, too many fake ass bitches out there. I get good vibes from you, Jasmin, real good."

"Um, thank you," I giggled. "I get good vibes from you, too."

"OK look, I'll tell you a secret if you put five hundred dollars in my commissary account. Deal?"

"By commissary, do you mean—"

"My fucking tab, so I can buy shit, yes! Jesus holy hell."

Frankie's mood swings were giving me whip lash but something told me that whatever she was bargaining with me for was worth hearing. Five hundred was doable, just about.

"Sure, I can do that for you as soon as I get out of here."

She paused, and the light through the window captured within her glossy irises.

"Don't forget, like the last bitch did. She regretted forgetting if you catch my drift."

I nodded, and my mouth dried as I rubbed my hand around my neck.

"The cops sent me in here to rough you up and get some intel for them, but there's something about you I like, so I figured I'd get to know you first, and it turned out I was right."

My shoulders softened at the idea she did like me, but the fact that the cops were playing dirty had me worrying I'd jumped in at the deep end when I agreed to help King. If this had gone any other way, she could have beaten me to a pulp.

Was he as dangerous as they were making him out to be?

"What did the cops say to you, Frankie? About me, I mean."

She lay back on the mattress and put her hands behind her head. "Well, they said you're involved with that Giannetti douche bag somehow. You know, that gangster pimp? They offered me two hundred bucks on my tab and a pack of smokes to find out what you might know about some prostitutes death, Titiana or whatever, but with you being a dyke and all, I figured there's no way you'd fuck with a guy like him, anyway. Am I right, Jasmin?"

My head nearly detached from my neck with how enthusiastic my nod was. "Absolutely. Men. Yuck!"

She chuckled to herself, causing the excess roll of her belly fat to jiggle. "I'm a real good judge of character and I know a liar when I see one, so we've got a deal? Seven hundred bucks wired over, asap?"

Wait, seven hundred? A minute ago she said five!

My tongue failed to activate, leaving me stranded with a mass of words trapped inside my mouth.

"Deal?" she growled. The tone she used came from within her chest.

"Yes, sure, definitely a deal."

"Awesome. Getting kinda late now, so you should probably get some sleep. I snore loud so I might keep you up all night, but it can't be helped if you know what I'm saying."

As I adjusted my position to lie down, a question formed in my mind that I couldn't ignore.

"So, how come you murdered your girlfriend?"

"Carrie was a thieving bitch who stole every cent I had.

I found messages on her phone with plans to have me framed for killing her cousin, so she could take my house and my dog Benji. So I got to her first."

"Wow. That must have been heartbreaking."

"Nah. I'm used to it. Listen, I like to have a little play before I sleep. Helps me drift off. Feel free to join me? Watch or whatever?"

"By play you mean—?"

"Finger my cunt, Jasmin, yes. Sheesh, you're a shy type, huh?"

Little did Frankie-Jo realise I was a prostitute with a back catalogue of crazy sexual encounters of my own. But the less she learned about me, the better. Just getting through the night alive was something I was clutching on to.

I lay down facing away from her, wishing that aliens would beam me up onto their spaceship and run experiments on me. Anything was better than this.

Frankie proceeded to strip off her clothes, because apparently naked masturbation was better than clothed and she wasted no time in pleasuring herself.

As we were sharing a single, it was cramped, to say the least, and Frankie's heavy laden breathing stroked the fine hairs on the back of my neck as she went to work on herself. I screwed my eyes shut and attempted to think of a happier place, and the first person who came to mind was King.

By the time my eyes opened again, her heavy breathing turned into light snoring.

Morning had broken when the sound of the cell door swinging open startled me.

Instinctively, I raised my hand to shield my eyes as the light of day shone brightly into our room. Now bathed in a warm glow, I peered at my sleeping cell mate who had been lying inches away from me, naked, for the last few hours. My lip curled at the sheer sight of her, thankful that our first meeting was in darkness. Otherwise, I didn't think I could have shared the tight space with her if I knew then what I did now.

As my eyes adjusted, I peered at the open doorway to see two men standing in the entryway. The most important being Arthur, my attorney, who seemed distressed.

"Frankie-Jo, come with me please," a male cop ordered into the room.

We had all grown impatient by the time she'd got her clothes back on, but no sooner was she on her feet than they cuffed her and escorted her out of the room.

"Don't forget!" she hollered to me on the way out. "Don't you forget about me!"

The cop frowned at Frankie-Jo as he watched her leave with his colleague and when he stepped inside my room; he scanned the place where finally he rested his contemplative gaze upon my unharmed features.

"OK Miss Adams," his lips thinned, "apologies on behalf of the department for keeping you here. Follow me for an interview."

"Please sit." The interviewing cop pointed to an uncomfortable looking chair opposite him at the wooden topped table inside the boxlike room.

The place was intimidating, with harsh bright lighting that stung my eyes, narrowing them against the intrusion.

With my attorney beside me, I took my seat as instructed.

The cop pressed a button on the voice recorder that was placed in front of me, and the questioning began immediately.

"Detective Saxon speaking and Officer Jones is present. We are here to interview—name for the record, please?"

"Chloe Adams."

"Let's start from the top, shall we?" He flipped open his beige loose leaf file of paperwork and frowned at the lack of pages.

The most handsome photo of King paper clipped to the top of the form captured my attention. A black and white mug shot that showcased his strong jaw and piercing eyes against a white backdrop. It felt as though he was watching me through the photo. My need to be with him kept my focus.

"OK, Chloe, why were you running yesterday?"

Arthur interjected before I could reply. "My client is free to run wherever she pleases. There's no law against that."

Saxon glared at Arthur. "Care to answer Miss Adams?"

"I, um, was taking a jog. You know, keeping fit." I looked at Arthur for reassurance, but he remained tight lipped.

The detective raised his brow speculatively. "Jogging? In Downtown L.A?"

"Yes, Sir."

He could tell I was lying. Anyone with half a brain cell could, but there wasn't proof to suggest otherwise.

"And you didn't see Mr. Romero Giannetti while you were out jogging in one of the most crime infested areas of the country?"

His pen tightly grasped between his fingers turned the tips from pink to white.

"You don't have to answer that." Arthur confirmed.

Phlegm gathered in my throat, and my legs twitched

under the table. Shit. Should I answer him?

I shook my head and lowered my gaze to a coffee stain on the tabletop. "No, I didn't see him."

Detective Saxon sighed and suddenly paused the voice recorder, "OK, Miss Adams," he steepled his fingers in front of his mouth, "I'd like to offer you a deal, one that would see all charges dropped against you if you could give us something, anything that can help us find Mr. Giannetti so we can put him in jail where he belongs."

My attorney shuffled in his seat. No doubt the conflict of interest between him and the two brothers was laying heavy on his conscience.

"A deal? With you?" I scoffed at Saxon, folding my arms over my body.

"Yes. It's your only way out of here anytime soon. What can you tell me?"

I turned to my attorney, intending to play devil's advocate.

"Did Detective Saxon tell you the woman he put in my cell last night was there to beat me up to get information out of me?"

Arthur's eyes widened as he rummaged in his briefcase, where he produced a pen and paper.

"Pardon me? Is this true, Detective?"

Saxon looked flustered as he ran a hand through his slicked back hair. "Not sure where you heard that, Miss," he snickered nervously while side eyeing his deputy.

Arthur looked to be onto something. "I need the information on Miss Adams' cell mate, please, Detective Saxon. I should have been notified of this before now."

After what seemed like a decade, a sheepish officer reentered the room with a matching beige file, but this time it contained a wad of pages that could have produced a novel. He slid it across the table and my attorney scooped it up.

He took a few minutes to read through the contents, where eventually he removed his glasses, putting the arm of the frame to his lips.

"The inmate you placed in my client's cell has multiple horrific murders on her wrap sheet." He dropped the file on the desk. "Detective, that woman beheaded her girlfriend with a kitchen knife and you placed her in my client's cell to get information from her? This contravenes so many laws I don't even know where to begin. How did you even manage to get that woman into this facility? You've really exposed yourself here."

"OK look," Saxon waved his hands as his foot tapped

under the table, "let's just say we forget about all of that, alright? And let's say we'll drop the case against Miss Adam's for obstruction of justice. I have the power to do that for you, OK? But I want to show you something in the hopes you'll still do the right thing and give me something to put that son of a bitch behind bars."

He opened his beige file again and slid a photo along the table towards me. I blanched at the image. Tatiana.

"You knew this girl, right?"

"Yes, Sir."

"Do you see her wounds?" he jabbed the photo. "The man you're protecting inflicted those wounds on her. Pregnant as well." He closed his eyes. "Sickening."

I stared at the photo for too many minutes. Her lifeless body covered in a pool of blood etched into my retinas. Eventually, I sighed and pushed it away. I knew in my heart he wasn't the monster they painted him to be.

"Stop protecting him and tell us something. Please, in the name of justice for Tatiana!"

We peered into each other's eyes for a flash, with his copper toned brown burrowing into my blue.

I considered my next move with little thought, as I already knew where my loyalties lay, and it was certainly not with the police after the little stunt they tried to pull with Frankie-Jo.

As I thought about King and his whereabouts, the erotic images of me on top of him in the garden yesterday came welcome to the forefront of my mind. Just thinking about him brought his masculine scent into my nasal passages. The warmth of his caress and the strength of his physique. My cheeks blushed at the vision that played out like a home movie before my eyes, and I bit my lip in response to the memory that warmed between my legs.

"Well, Miss Adams? Do you have anything to say?" Saxon's repeated question brought me back to reality.

Did he notice my cheeks blush? My body reacting to my self-induced arousal was challenging to hide, and now more than ever, I was determined to protect King.

I grew taller in my chair and lifted my chin. "Like I said before, Sir. I was jogging, and then I heard the police shouting. My fight or flight reflex must've kicked in, so I panicked and ran. A couple hundred yards out, the cops picked me up. That's it."

I took a breath, now with the courage to keep eye contact with him.

"Your fight or flight kicked in?" His eyes narrowed in speculation, not believing my bull shit for a second.

"That's correct Sir."

Finally, he turned off the recorder with pursed lips as he thrummed his fingers along the tabletop, but it was Arthur who broke the silence and packed away his briefcase.

"After the treatment my client has received, I suggest you stop clutching at straws and wish us both a good day."

Saxon thrummed for a final minute until he rose to his feet sharply and looked anywhere but me.

"OK, thank you Miss Adams. You're free to go. Jones, get her personals."

Arthur caught hold of my arm before I left the room. "Sorry about the way that played out, but we got the result we wanted in the end. Dan sends his warmest regards."

Jones handed me back my cell phone and watch. Thrilled yet surprised I got my personals back at all, I put my watch where it belonged. *I miss you, Mum.*

As soon as I caught sight of the exit to the building, I picked up pace, where back in the open, the warm air caressed my face, and I took a freeing breath as I inhaled fresh air. I hadn't realised just how anxious I'd been until the sensations of the outside world hit me.

To slow my ragged breathing, I leant my back against the cool bricks of the building to stabilise myself before I fell over.

What do I do now?

Even though we weren't in a good place, Hanna was the person who sprung to my mind when I needed support. She'd always been the person I called, and I needed my best friend, now more than ever.

"Chloe?"

"Hey Bestie. Kinda weird, but I'm at The CRDF, you know, in Lynwood? Don't ask! Can you come get me, please?"

"County jail? Shit OK, hang tight."

As I patiently waited, I took a seat on a vacant bench just outside the station. The view of the city with its daily hustle and bustle was a sight to behold when you stopped to take it all in.

I checked through my cell to see if anyone had contacted me during my time in jail. *Nothing*—Not a single missed call or text message. The agency hadn't sent me even one appointment. *Shit.*

Hanna finally screeched up to the curb, scraping her wheel along the sidewalk's edge. The speed demon never slowed for anything.

Matching her energy and wasting no time, I climbed into her pale blue Mini Cooper that matched mine except hers smelt strongly of perfume.

She paused; glaring at me as I took my seat.

"Well?" Her brow raised questioningly. "What's going on?"

"Will you still be my friend if I say I can't tell you?"

"What! Are you joking?"

The atmosphere between us reverted to the way it had during our fall out yesterday.

"Hanna, please, I promise you that I can't say anything. The less you know, the better. Believe me."

She turned her attention back to the windshield and pushed her foot down, accelerating harshly into the flowing traffic.

I grabbed onto the dashboard to steady myself.

"Shit Han, steady. You'll kill us both!"

She continued her way through passing obstacles at speed as though our lives suddenly didn't matter to her anymore.

"Shut up Chloe. I'm so fucking pissed at you right now."

"Well, shout at me then, but don't kill me, please!"

I didn't believe for a second that she would ever intentionally harm me; physically, anyway. But the nagging thought about her loose lips to Alice still reared its ugly head, and it played a part in our fractured relationship.

She eased off the pedal and regained some composure.

"Has this got something to do with Daddy?"

Still able to read me so well, Hanna glared at me for an answer.

I stalled. *Fuck*—"Sorry, what?"

Needing more time to come up with a lie. My brain attempted to find a viable explanation that didn't come with a multitude of implications.

"You heard me Chloe Adams. Did your night in jail have something to do with King? He's been gone for days and no one has seen him, but we all know he's still pulling strings back at the mansion."

"How do you mean?" I feigned innocence, tucking a strand of hair behind my ear.

Relax, she'll never notice.

"Tiffany overheard some of Daddy's crew talking about a mole."

Of course, Tiffany had something to do with it. *Michelle part two.*

I rolled my eyes inwardly, but I wasn't going to reopen that deep wound. "A mole?"

"Yeah. Someone might be reporting back to Daddy. Maybe one of us?" She side eyed me speculatively.

"Oh? Why does she think it's one of us?"

"Well, for a start, the guy Tiffany was fucking turned up dead last night."

The blood drained from my face, and my jaw lost strength, as I paled as white as a ghost.

Hanna's quiet demeanour evoked an eerie calmness that I'd never experienced in her company before. At least when she was shouting, I could shout back. Now it seemed sinister.

"You know what I think Chloe?"

The suspense she was creating made my skin prickle.

"What are you thinking, Hanna?"

"I think you're the mole."

I recoiled as her head snapped in my direction, affirming her accusation. Her eyes glistened with heartbreak as her upper lip curled at the sheer sight of me.

A weird involuntary noise escaped through my nose and mouth simultaneously.

Well, that couldn't have been more obvious.

"Why, Chloe?"

"Why, what?"

"Tell me why you are working for Daddy and stabbing all the girls in the back!?"

The increasing level of anger in her voice made me want to cower in a corner. I hated seeing her obvious hatred towards me.

"Hanna please—"

"No. Tell me now."

"Fine!"

I tried to compose myself, taking a breath to figure out which parts of the story I would omit.

"Come on then, fucking spit it."

Wide eyed, I stared at her in shock, not used to hearing Hanna speak to me like a piece of dirt. Never had we been in a situation like this before where we were going at each other, where there seemed to be no end. Our friendship was slipping through my fingers like sand through a sieve and I couldn't keep hold.

"As I was the only girl not there, the night Tat died, King said I'd have the best chance of keeping under the cop's radar, so we could meet without being followed. He needed to make sure everything was fine back home, so when he asked me for a report, I had to give him something. I didn't even go into details that it was Sam!" My chin tightened and my lower lip trembled at the realisation he was dead. "Do you think I would still be alive if I hadn't had anything to report back to him?"

She saw I was right and her twisted features visibly eased as she listened intently to my reasoning. With a sense that I was finally getting through to her, my tense shoulders relaxed.

"I'm sorry about Sam, Hanna I am, but when it's my life or his; you know I'm going to look out for myself. You would have done the same."

"So you're the new Tatiana then; queen bitch?"

"Huh? Why do you say that?"

I was confused. Sure, my relationship with King was thriving, but I would be naïve to believe that there wasn't an element of game playing involved with him.

"Isn't it obvious?" Her voice cracked as she attempted to conceal her unshed tears.

"I don't know what you mean, Hanna?"

"Come on Chloe! You're the one getting the special treatment! How can you not see it?"

I snorted in disbelief. "I wouldn't call spending a night in jail special treatment."

Hanna stopped talking, and the only audible sound came from the tyres rolling along the tarmac of the freeway.

Eventually, she sighed. "He was mine! Me and King, we had something special. We've been trying—"

No!

"Wait—you mean trying, trying?"

Please God, no.

"Yes, we've been trying for a baby." She was determined to finish her sentence, regardless of my interruption. Proud of her achievements, she had a repulsive smirk on her face that I wanted to wipe off.

With my head in my hands, I rubbed my temples with my thumbs. I could feel a whopper of a headache brewing.

"So, what are you saying, Hanna? Are you pregnant?"

"Yes, that's exactly what I'm saying."

She reached down to her stomach where she rested her hand on her invisible bump, using her thumb to stroke her cotton clad skin. Her grin dropped when she remembered the reason behind our fight.

"It doesn't make me happy knowing that you are now his main bitch. Where does that leave me and my baby Chloe?"

"Clearly I'm not his main bitch, am I? I just wasn't there that night. It's all circumstantial."

"Ha! Exactly. You weren't there because you were fucking Dan. Talk about cake and eat it!" The apples of her cheeks turned pink in frustration. "You're so selfish!"

Me selfish? What!? She was one to talk with her newly gained bestie.

"King doesn't want me, Han. Period."

As the words left my lips, a pain radiated within my chest cavity. The reality slapped me in the face that King didn't have feelings for me after all. It was crystal clear to me now that irrespective of my attempts to show him I cared by landing myself in jail for him; he treated all of his whores the same way.

If you do something he likes, he'll give you a baby. But do something wrong and he'll get violent. King had been playing us all.

My survival instinct kicked in, and in a complete about turn of my feelings, the plan with Dan would be my only way out of here. To think I was struggling to make my mind up when he shared his plans with me seemed so ludicrous now.

Hanna's words, spelled out in black and white, were comparable to a stab in the heart. How could I have been so pathetic? Whilst King clouded my judgement when in his vicinity, what I now knew left me with certainty. *New Mexico, here we come.*

We made our way straight back home in silence. No doubt she wanted to announce her pregnancy news to her new best friend, Tiffany.

Once we'd pulled up in front of the mansion, Hanna exited the car without a further word spoken. The slam of the car door told me everything I needed to know, and I didn't even have time to thank her for the lift.

As usual, King's men cluttered the driveway. Each of them making themselves look busy, but how true that was, remained to be seen.

"Hey fellas," I called out to the group, "can one of you collect my car, please?"

Like a flock of birds, they fled the scene when I'd got close enough to startle them. Sam's death had seemingly caused a disturbance in the house, and it looked as though everyone was blaming me. Guilt eroded my conscience that he'd lost his life amidst all of this, but I stood by what I'd said to Hanna. Self preservation was the most basic human trait.

Snake remained in place as the only crew member brave enough to stand anywhere near me.

"Please, Snake?"

"Boss already handled it," he turned away from me. "Your car is parked right over there."

"Oh. Thank you. Have you spoken to him, then?"

He wiped his sweaty brow with his polishing cloth. "Even if I had, Lady, it ain't something I'm going to discuss with you. Take your ass inside the house now. Please."

As ordered, my hand trembled as I pushed open the

front door to the mansion, where unspent adrenaline still coursed through my veins from my fight with Hanna earlier. Her upping and leaving me didn't give either of us the closure we needed to move forward.

Once inside, I felt even more alone than I had before, which I didn't think was possible until now. There was a hum of activity coming from the living room ahead of me. The laughter of which bounced around the walls and reverberated through my eardrums. Paranoia told me they were laughing at me, but they didn't know me or my story, just what they had chosen to believe. There would have been a time when Hanna would've stuck up for me under any circumstances, but now—she was probably the ringleader.

Footsteps against the tiled floor drew closer towards me before I saw who they belonged to. My shoulders raised as I expected a hoard of rampaging whores ready to wage war against me, but to my relief, it was only crooked nose; the girl that shared the same fate as me at the sleepover.

"Hey." I offered a small smile. Desperate times called for desperate measures, and she was one of only a few friends I had left.

"Jenny hi, good to see you."

Oh God, she didn't even remember my name. *I'm so pathetic.*

When taking a moment to analyse her look by daylight, there was absolutely no way King had ever slept with her. I refused to believe in the possibility he could keep an erection with her niche looks. It seemed cruel to have that opinion, but the eyes didn't lie and she was straight up ugly.

"Are you off to work?" I asked, eyeing her overnight bag.

"Yep, with a regular."

The confidence that radiated from her was enviable. It made me question how she could hold regular clients and I couldn't. Come to think of it, the last legitimate client I had was Mr. X just before my fried chicken date at the trap house with King.

"Good luck." I croaked with bitterness I attempted to quell.

As she sashayed on by, I stepped to the side to allow her access to the exit and on her way past, she gave me a conceited half smile, "Thanks, but I don't need it."

A yawn took hold of me as I watched her leave, affirming my desperate need for a good night's sleep after the torrid time I'd spent in jail with the crazed lesbian last night.

My first thought as I made my way up the stairs to King's

room was that Alice might be there. I'd not forgotten about my need to check on her, but right now rest came first.

Out of habit, I listened into the closed door before I opened it. Not wanting to disturb any extra-curricular activities that might have been taking place in there. Silence.

Surprised when I creaked open the door, the evidence of a murder scene had completely vanished and the room smelt sanitised, with not a single stain or clue what had happened only a matter of days ago.

Another yawn took control of my mouth again and I let out a cathartic release. This nap was about to be heavenly.

I climbed into the super king size bed when suddenly my cell buzzed in my pocket. The vibration pattern differed from a normal call. This was a video call.

I accepted the unknown caller out of intrigue as much as anything.

The screen illuminated with a handsome face. The face of a man I missed and despised at the same time.

King smiled a full tooth grin when he saw my face.

"Hey, Sexy. Where are you?"

"Um hi, Daddy."

His gorgeous features were contagious, and I softened in

response to him immediately.

"I asked where you were?" His tone turned more aggressive, but I'd no idea why.

"I'm at home, in your bed. I was just going to take a nap when you called."

King took a long inhale of his cigar while staring at me intensely through the lens. "You ain't with a client, then?"

"No Daddy. Just in bed."

I panned the camera around the room to show him the evidence. The intensity in his tone was making me uncomfortable.

"Listen, I don't got much time, but I wanted to see your face. Has your car been delivered back home yet?"

My irrational reaction was to scream down the phone that he was a lying, cheating prick who had the audacity to tell all of his girls the same shit to get them to work for him, and that it was complete bull shit he actually wanted to see me. But of course, I refrained and kept my accusations to myself. Once bitten, twice shy.

"Yes Daddy. I spoke to one of your men about it earlier."

His eyes narrowed. "Oh. Who?"

King's blunt reaction knocked me off kilter. Did I say the wrong thing again?

"Sorry what?" My stalling tactic was out in full force

again. *Should I lie?*

"Who did you speak to? Woman, I ain't got all day with this back-and-forth shit."

"It was, um," I paused for a moment. "Snake."

"Tell me why you're talkin' to my men when I'm not there? You fuckin' my boy Jasmin?"

"No Daddy! Of course not, I swear."

"Yeah? Show me that you swear."

This seemed like one of his games again, or a deadly trap I'd need to avoid at all costs. The prospect of his capabilities sent chills down my spine as I imagined the horrors he could unleash.

I gulped in anticipation. "How can I show you, Daddy?"

"Let me watch you play with your cunt. Take your clothes off now. Show me your body."

The unexpected demand provoked a surreal phenomenon. My blood boiled with fury, producing a rapid succession of emotions: anger to fear, then arousal. The effect King had on women was unparalleled. But not wishing to waste anymore of his time, I removed my dress, bra and panties lying naked on his bed.

"Lay on my side of the bed. I wanna smell your pussy on my sheets when I get home."

His filthy mouth made me smile with excitement, and

there wasn't a doubt in my mind he would sniff those sheets until he'd removed the scent completely.

On King's side of the bed, I lay with my legs open and the phone held between my feet in a vice like grip, waiting for the next directive. He had a full view of my vagina and seemed pleased with the fact.

"Beautiful pussy. Play with it. Show me how you tease it."

King removed his penis from his shorts, masturbating to my image and I watched him fixedly while I circled my clit with one finger and toyed with my nipple using the other.

"You want my dick inside you?" His raspy voice provoked my arousal.

"Yes Daddy."

My breathing hitched as I built up the delicious sensations inside my core.

"Not long Baby. I'll be home soon. Is your cunt wet for me?"

I pushed my finger inside, where the dampness encased the length of my digit. But my lack of response frustrated him.

"Are you wet Jasmin!? Give me somethin' to work with here."

"Yes Daddy, I'm so wet." I groaned, "are you hard for me?"

"Like stone, you little slut. If I was there now, you'd be chokin' on it. I need to come now. Are you ready?"

My insides clenched at his carnal choice of words.

"I'm ready."

"Fuck!" His penis pumped a thick spurt of ejaculate from the enlarged tip. The grip he held on the shaft tightened as the orgasm ripped through him.

I came undone at the view and climaxed against my finger. Not able to catch my breath until the clenching stopped.

King's eyes met with mine through the screen, "I don't know what it is about you, but I need it. Listen, I gotta go."

Without warning, the line went dead and suddenly I faced a black hole and a pit of loneliness in my stomach. Silence filled the room and all I could hear was my own laboured breathing.

The awareness of being exploited immediately after an orgasm was unwelcome, and his behaviour reminded me of a trick Alice liked to pull.

My head fell backwards onto the pillow while I attempted to reset my equilibrium. Psycho analysis wasn't my strong suit, but even I figured that what he had just done was fucked up by anyone's standard. What was wrong with him? One minute he's getting my best friend pregnant, the next he's having phone sex with me. Why didn't I heed the warning Snake had given me to get out now while I had the chance?

The emotional rollercoaster was too much for even the most stable character to take, and I wasn't strong enough for this. The now familiar bubbling sensation of anger formed in my chest again. Regardless of the fact I had enjoyed my phone sex encounter with the hottest man on the planet, it didn't change the issue that there was too much evidence pointing towards him having no feelings for me what so ever.

Before I knew it, I was awake and the sky out of the bedroom window had fallen into darkness. I'd slept for at least four hours, one of the longest naps of my life.

I smiled when I spotted a welcome angelic face had snuck in whilst I was sleeping. Naked, Alice was snoring softly beside me with her body completely uncovered. The soft skin of her arm lightly pressed against mine, keeping the connection between us open. It was nice to see her looking peaceful, especially when the last time I saw her, she was anything but.

Both of us underestimated the attachment we shared and her eyes blinked open as if she knew I'd awoken.

"Hey Sleeping Beauty," she said with a yawn and a smile. "You're finally awake."

"I could say the same to you." I giggled, playfully swatting her thigh.

Alice's smile dropped. "I've been so alone since Tat died, so when I saw you in here sleeping, I thought I was dreaming."

Her bottom lip trembled. The pain radiating from her body was still so palpable, transferring it to me.

"Hey, come on now. It's OK. I'm not going anywhere again, I promise."

She sat up to meet with my face. "Do you really promise, Jasmin?"

In a state of undress, both physically and mentally, we were inches from our lips touching.

"Of course I do."

I instantly regretted saying that as soon as the words left my lips. Never mind what was wrong with King, what was wrong with me? I'd already made my decision to leave with Dan, so why was I making promises to a troubled heartbroken girl I barely knew?

Alice's curious hand reached for my face. "You're really pretty, you know."

The softness in her tone complimented the texture of

her skin. Her allure captivated me, drawing me towards her every single time.

"You're prettier." I sniggered, never knowing what to do with compliments.

"I think it's time we had some fun? What do you say?"

And there it was. The wicked gleam in her eye was back. My immediate intrusive thought was that she, too, wanted to use me for sex. How many times would I allow this in one night? Was it my fault that this kept happening?

I'd not yet had chance to agree to an evening of passion, when she reached into the bedside table and produced a double-ended dildo.

When my eyes met with hers, she smiled wickedly. "Ever used one of these before?"

The fact of the matter was that, no, I hadn't. But was I going to give Alice the upper hand and tell her that? No, I wasn't.

"Sure." I lied.

The brick wall I was building around my catalogue of emotions was now several inches thick. If the people I cared about most wanted to use me for sex, then I would give them an Oscar winning performance they wouldn't forget.

She slid the length of the dildo between her fingers.

"Do you wanna do it pussy to pussy or ass to ass?"

The limited options available left me with a simple choice to make.

"Gotta be pussy, surely?" I snickered again, but she didn't match my light-hearted tone.

The intensity radiating from her was almost as strong as King's. Maybe she'd spent too many years in his bed to process emotions further than arousal.

Without another word from Alice's soft lips, she kissed me. She ran her fingers through my hair whilst the intensity of our connection developed between us and my body continued to betray me as my arousal for her grew.

"Lie down." She ordered in her angelic tone.

As usual, I'd do anything she said at that moment.

She spat on the head of the dildo that she was about to insert inside me and parted my lower lips to gain access. The colossal edge of the rubber length entered my vagina and stretched my insides and, not waiting for me to acclimatise, she moved it in and out with speed.

After my earlier climax with King, my internal flesh remained lubricated, causing the entire shaft to become slick with my arousal. Alice coaxed the other end inside her own body and swallowed every inch. She didn't stop until her pussy contacted mine.

The sensation that the dildo provided, along with the

soft caress of her swollen pink flesh against my clitoris, was passionately explosive. I watched in awe as Alice's image came undone before me, with her head back and her breasts heaving only intensified my arousal further, and the orgasm building inside me was ready to release at any moment.

Suddenly, she stopped her salacious rhythm and pulled away from me as quickly as she'd entered. Removing the dildo, she placed her damp body on top of mine and straddled me with urgency.

"I want to feel your clit against mine as we come," she groaned, placing feather soft kisses against my neck as she continued her delicate incursion against me.

Without warning, my orgasm exploded against her body and we came together in an intense, heady combination of the most pleasurable sensations I'd ever had the joy of experiencing. We both gasped, reclaiming the lost oxygen between us as she collapsed by the side of me.

"Hold me, Jas."

She pulled my arm over her waist so we spooned.

How did I end up being big spoon?

Lay in silence, the air between us saturated with emotions too big for either of us to understand. My rested hand on her stomach rose and fell in time with her heavy breathing.

After a while, Alice took my hand in hers. "Jas?"

"Yes, Alice?"

The two intense orgasms I'd received in less than six hours had me exhausted again.

"You're my best friend."

Not knowing what the right response was, I reiterated her endearment. "You're mine too."

It wasn't so long ago that I would never have dreamt of saying those words to anyone other than Hanna. The closeness I felt with Alice at that moment gave me the sense of belonging that I had been craving since the day I moved to America, and if I did leave for New Mexico with Dan, I'd never forget this moment.

"How are you feeling?" I asked, still holding her in a post coital embrace with my face rested against her long golden locks.

"I'm fine thanks Jas. How are you?"

The depths of her feelings were well hidden beneath the surface again, somewhere deep inside the lagoon of her personality.

"I've been better." I sighed, "you know me and Hanna aren't doing good, right?"

Alice nodded. "I thought so. She was talking shit about

you with a couple of girls yesterday."

"Really? What did she say?"

"I'm not sure. I just heard your name. It's OK though, because you have me. I haven't had a bestie in so long."

Jody?

"Tell me about Jody? She was your best friend, wasn't she?"

It took all my strength to keep as relaxed as possible. I didn't want to scare her off now.

"Yes, Jody was everything to me."

"So, what happened?"

I wanted to coax every drop of information from her, but I knew I had to tread carefully.

She took a deep breath and let out a long sigh before story time began.

"Jody was a new girl that didn't quite fit in. Daddy wasn't that into her, and none of the other whores were interested in being friends, so I took her under my wing. Our friendship grew, and we really connected. But at some point, about a year in, she started getting really weird. Eventually, she asked me to take out a suicide pact with her —"

"Wait really!?"

"Mm-hm. She had this crazy idea that we would be

happier together in another life than we were living under King's roof. I can't lie to you Jas, I went along with her plan, but the only difference was that she had the balls to pull the trigger and I didn't."

"Hold on a minute. You guys were going to, you know, shoot yourselves; together?"

Alice shifted with discomfort. "We sat face to face, each holding a gun. But when it came to actually doing it, I couldn't."

"But where did you even get the guns from?"

"Daddy, of course, silly." She rolled her eyes as if that was the crazy part of this conversation.

"Wait, he knew!?"

The story was getting worse. If King could facilitate this, I needed to get out right now.

"No, Jasmin, we stole the guns. I figured it wouldn't matter if he found out because, you know, we'd be dead."

"So what happened?"

"Jody pulled the trigger, and I didn't. That's it." Alice shrugged her shoulders and looked down at our interlaced fingers. It was obvious she was replaying the painful scene in her mind.

"I'm so sorry that happened to you. Honestly, I'm in shock."

The thought occurred to me then that it was likely the catalyst for Alice turning to drugs with Tat. With what she had endured in this house, I couldn't blame her.

"A lot has happened since then. I'm over it. Especially now that I have you."

Something in her eyes suddenly didn't sit right with me. The sense I got I was now officially Jody's replacement left me fearful for my safety.

"I can see you over thinking again, Jasmin. Come here."

Alice enveloped me in a hug, kissing my lips again where my body betrayed me for a second time, and I kissed her back.

There wasn't an opportunity to think straight around this woman. I was under her spell, drawn in by her witchcraft.

CHAPTER 11

Darkness through the bedroom window informed me I had no business being awake at this hour, and it was eerily quiet in what was usually a house filled with boisterous females. 4:13AM, too early by anyone's standards.

The long nap I'd taken last night hadn't helped my cause, but I would have thought the intense back-to-back orgasms I'd received would have sedated me for longer.

Alice lay next to me peacefully in slumber with her limbs entangled around mine like vines. Too hot. I needed space. Carefully, I peeled her arm from my body.

Don't wake up. Please don't wake up.

One wrong move and she would be on me in a flash and I wanted to avoid any further intimate encounters with her where possible as my judgement was never clear when we spent time together.

Alice continued to snore peacefully. Now was my chance.

I tiptoed into the bathroom and gingerly closed the door behind me, where my reflection in the bathroom mirror caught me by surprise. *Who are you?*

Whilst the physical wounds inflicted by King's hand had mostly healed, there was now an extra edge to my semblance that hadn't been there before and the emotional scars that radiated through my flesh were harder to disguise than I'd realised. But was this an improved, more resilient version of me? Or were those around me inflicting damage that would never heal?

I hopped in the shower and turned on the faucet. The giant head roared to life with hot, soothing water that cascaded down my body in a welcoming flourish, where droplets bounced off my skin, leaving behind dewy beads of welcoming hydration. First things first, the lengthy hairs on my legs needed some attention, and a tidy up of my public hair wouldn't go a miss. King's razor seemed the obvious choice as it innocently waited on the little corner shelf for someone to help themselves to.

A few strokes later and it wasn't long before overgrown clumps entangled within the blades, enough to cause me embarrassment. How had I let myself go so badly?

The thought occurred to me that a client visit would normally be the catalyst for my preening regime. *No clients;*

no shaving.

While I cautiously trimmed the delicate skin between my thighs, a mischievous grin spread across my face as I thought about King's sculptured jaw line meeting the pubic hair-covered blade during his next shave. Hopefully, a chunk would fall into his mouth and choke him to death. The selfish, manipulative bastard!

Blissfully unaware, I hadn't heard my phone buzz while I was showering, but as I climbed out, I saw the screen illuminated with an incoming message.

< Bob > I hope you're doing OK Jassy. Love Bob

I nearly choked on my tongue. As if Bob, my foster father, had messaged me? I'd not prepared myself for the way I felt about him making contact. It didn't seem real that through his action, he confirmed that he actually cared about me.

Even though I didn't owe him anything, I did the right thing and sent him a brief reply.

< Bob > I hope you're doing OK Jassy. Love Bob

< Me > Fine thanks

After dismissing the distraction Bob presented me, I

continued my mission to love myself because it seemed in this life no one else did.

I rummaged in the bathroom cabinet for any luxury creams I could apply to my body. To my surprise, there were several bottles of pills that I couldn't help but investigate further and suddenly I was Detective Adam's.

Of course, Tatiana's name was on several variations of a sleeping pill and there was something that I assumed was a diet pill. Shaking my head, I sighed at the notion that even without King's input; the same result would have ultimately occurred.

I stopped when I saw a little yellow bottle with **Romero Giannetti** written on the front. The medication had a name that I couldn't pronounce: *Buprenorphine.*

The prospect that this man had more than one layer to him piqued my interest. What were those pills for?

But there was no way I could ask him without the death penalty, not a chance in hell.

All too soon, the telltale signs of stirring coming from the bedroom pricked my ears. *Shit.* Alice was awake.

I paused with my hand still inside the cupboard and my breath held. If I didn't move a muscle, she would hopefully go back to sleep.

"Jasmin? Where are you?" She called from King's bed.

I rolled my eyes inwardly at the sound of her voice. Not wanting another sexual encounter with her so soon after the last, I was hoping to get some time to myself for a change. When I wasn't in her immediate vicinity, I had clarity and could see the games she was playing with my body were to her own advantage. But when our bodies touched and our lips connected, I was her servant once more.

"Jas!" She yelled again.

"I'm coming!"

The exasperated tone fell from my mouth, harsher than I'd intended. I hoped she didn't pick up on it, as I didn't want to hurt her any worse than she already was, but my vulnerabilities also needed protecting from the people I was closest to.

When I reentered the bedroom, the concern etched on her pretty face softened and she smiled at me brightly.

"I thought you'd left me in this bed on my own when you promised you wouldn't."

"I was just in the bathroom. But look, I'm back now."

I tried to reassure her the best I could, but I suddenly sensed like it was me in need of reassurance that I would not end up in the same condition as her last bestie. *Jody.*

Alice held open the bed cover and invited me back into bed. Never able to refuse her offer, I did exactly as I was told.

The sound of birdsong woke me again at the more reasonable hour of 7:00AM.

It was only a matter of minutes before Alice opened her eyes. Angelic features and a button nose; my new best friend was awake.

"Morning, Bestie," she beamed when she saw I was still lying next to her.

"Hey," I yawned, "morning."

As predictable as a sun rise, her craving for a connection with me took hold of her body and she placed her warm fingertips on my exposed chest.

"Not now Alice. Maybe tonight?"

Her irises sparkled. "Do you think I'm ugly, Jasmin?"

Huh? "Of course not. Why are you asking that?"

"Because you'll do anything to avoid having fun with me. Has this got something to do with your lesbian anxiety?"

I pursed my lips in reaction to her jibe. Did this have something to do with that? Yes, *and* no. My main concern was my lack of self control around her that ultimately ended with me getting my feelings hurt.

"Stop sulking, Jasmin, and play with me! What more do I have to do to get you to like me?"

Unprovoked, she pulled the bedcover over the top of both our heads where a part of me felt like a kid again, playing pretend summer camp under the sheets where the only prop missing was the torch for ghost stories. Now, as an adult, it had a very different meaning.

The cocoon we shared was humid, but the scent dispersing within the space was deliciously sweet. Alice stared into my eyes, our faces close enough I could taste her warm breath, and she tipped my chin so that our lips aligned. Then she kissed me. My insides clenched as her tongue explored my mouth. Her soft skin caressed my breasts and her long nails ran the length of my body, creating tingling sensations in their wake.

Suddenly, she broke away. "How about I make you come first and then you do me? Deal?"

Without so much as a nod of agreement from me, she pushed her finger inside my moist opening that had been ready for her since our eyes met at 7:00AM.

The heat radiating from my swollen flesh tightened my core, and her delicate touch created a plethora of heady sensations that made my toes curl in response.

That's it. There.

Her tongue circled my erect peach nipples one at a time, flicking the teat as she toyed with my clit.

So close, God. Fuck—

A bang in the hallway halted us immediately. *Shit—what was that?*

Alice whipped the cover from over us and the cool air it shielded us from washed welcomingly against my flushed cheeks. Our harsh breathing suddenly silenced as the sound of footsteps up the staircase drew closer towards us.

As destructive as a storm, the bedroom door swung open to reveal the man himself. Tall, muscular and handsome. I could never acclimatise to his striking features.

With outstretched welcoming arms, he grinned.

"The king is back, bitches!"

As he surveyed the vision before him, his hands dropped to his sides when he saw the two of us in the middle of a romantic exchange.

"The fuck's goin' on here, then?"

Without hesitation, Alice leapt out of bed and into his arms as if nothing had happened between us.

"Nothing Daddy." She kissed his lips, "welcome home."

A frown developed on his handsome face, as though he was completing an algebraic equation.

"Gimme your hand, Alice. I wanna sniff your fingers."

I stared with bated breath as she restlessly placed her petite hand into his spade like grasp and he pushed her fingers against his nostrils, taking in a deep breath.

"Hmm, I'd recognise the smell of that tight little pussy anywhere. Seems you girls have been playin' while I've been gone?"

Pheromones were causing havoc with his senses and the prominent erection he carried exuded a hunger for a connection with my body, as if he was a starving man.

The intensity of our attachment reignited in an instant, but I was struggling to look past the obvious issue.

Hanna is pregnant.

My facial expression must have revealed the ambivalence I was feeling, and he knew something was off.

"What's wrong with you?"

Don't tell him. Keep calm.

"Nothing Daddy. I'm glad you're home."

"Show it then. In fact, you can both show me how much you missed me. Alice, lie down. Jasmin, go stand over there."

King being back produced a level of tension that had dissipated in the wake of his absence and no sooner had I left the safety of the bed than demonic eyes bore into my back.

"Hold up! Turn around."

Shit—what now?

"You shaved your pussy, huh? Fuck, that's beautiful." King gripped onto his erection and stroked himself at the sight of my body. "I could look at you all day."

With inspiration as his motivating force, like an overenthusiastic labrador, he leapt on to the bed, directly on top of Alice.

"Jasmin, you're gonna watch me fuck this bitch," he growled while he planted heavy handed kisses on her mouth and neck. She responded to his offer, but I knew she preferred a more gentle approach.

"Watch me fuck her and when you can't stand it any longer, I want you to fight for me and take what's yours." The masculine figure before me hung on my seal of approval, waiting with a piercing gaze until I agreed.

Power in my hands was a novel experience, and I wasn't sure how to feel about it. Only moments ago, I could no longer entertain the idea of King and his ego. He had the audacity to try for a baby with me whilst fucking my best friend, offering her the same deal? *I don't think so, Buddy!*

But here I was, now seemingly jealous that he was on top of Alice, about to fuck her brains out.

His intense glare reminded me he'd asked a question, and I nodded in agreement. If he wanted a scene, I would give him one he'd never forget.

With fire alight in his eyes, he ripped the duvet off Alice, reminding him she was still completely naked underneath. I wondered then what King's opinion would have been if he'd seen what we were up to in his bed last night.

"Yes! I like my women ready!" He beamed.

Her body was his muse and while Alice was hot for sure, her figure lacked curves that mine offered. I was all too familiar with how King liked something to grab onto when he fucked.

They kissed like their lives depended on it, and she reached into his shorts, pulling out his ample dick where she rolled on a condom. My mouth watered seeing him grasped in her hand, but trying to process the sensory overload was near impossible. I was witnessing the man I had conflicting feelings for being jerked off by my fuck buddy. Did I have feelings for her too? *Probably*. How does one even start unpacking that box?

My body betrayed me, and I dampened in response to their entanglement.

King pulled on her nipples and sucked them with yearning. His powerful hand cupped her breast as he massaged the swell she offered him. Once she'd got him into a frenzy, he wasted no time forcefully burying himself inside her, where he pounded her balls deep. There was nothing behind King's eyes as his primal urges took over when he screwed her, and I knew for a fact that my time with him looked nothing like this. He and Alice just didn't have the same chemistry we did, and I was certain his feelings for her were as shallow as a puddle based on his performance.

Was it like this with Hanna, too? *Oh, of course not*—he'd got her pregnant.

With balled fists, and fidgeting toes, my arousal couldn't take much more as my insides warmed and clenched as I watched the man I had paradoxical desires towards having sex with the woman I was closest to. Suddenly I couldn't take any more.

Stood over them, just inches away from their damp bodies, I could smell their intertwined scent as his cologne mixed with her sweetness.

"OK, that's enough!"

"You gotta do better than that, Jasmin," he grinned as he deepened his kiss on Alice's mouth, goading me. He was enjoying this.

I feebly slapped him on his muscular back and tried to

push him off, but my failed attempt only spurred him on more.

Without warning, King grabbed my arm and pulled me down onto the bed beside Alice. He moved himself from atop her and straddled me with his penis rested at the entrance of my vagina.

"You watchin' this, Alice?" he murmured, completely overcome.

He tore off the rubber and drove his dick deep inside my slick folds. I hadn't realised just how much my body had been craving this since he'd walked through the door until our bodies collided. It was clear immediately that the rhythm in which he set with me was slower; lustful, but I tried not to read too deeply into it. *He does like me?*

King's impending orgasm left him breathless. "I wanna see you play with Jasmin's tits."

Of course, Alice had already familiarised herself with my body and knew exactly how to elicit a response from me. I doubted King had any idea just how well Alice and I knew each other.

King kissed my neck as he continued his slow, steady rhythm.

Fuck—So close.

He grabbed Alice's breast, teasing and sucking on the

nipple.

"Sit on Jasmin's face."

In double quick time, Alice scrambled up onto her knees to squat over my face where she and Daddy became nose to nose.

"Come on, Jasmin, lick her pussy, you dirty whore. I see how you bitches love this shit."

He continued to plunge his dick inside me relentlessly. His engorged length saturated me with intensity and devotion. I did as I was told and caressed her wet folds with my tongue, holding onto her thighs for support as I showed them both just how much I cared.

"I know what you two sluts get up to," he groaned. "It makes me so fuckin' hard."

I hoped in that moment he wasn't expecting me to reply with a mouth full of Alice's labia to contend with.

She deepened her kiss with him whilst receiving my tongue.

"Oh, God! Please!" she cried, her body trembling with carnal desire.

It was Alice who came first. She had a weak spot only I was privy to that made her climax every time, and the swell of her flesh heated my tongue as she convulsed into my mouth.

"Aight Alice, you're done. You can watch me now while I make love to your girl."

His words caressed my skin like cashmere. *Make love? To me?*

"She isn't mine Daddy, she's yours."

Alice had been around him long enough to learn the right thing to say. She was smart and manipulative in just the correct dose.

"You damn right she's mine. Watch me take what's mine."

Alice's words stirred him and he burrowed himself deep inside me, kissing me lovingly.

"I can taste Alice's cunt on your lips. You filthy slut."

He gritted his teeth as he experienced the satisfaction my body provided him. His penis was like a red hot poker as it relentlessly massaged my g spot. With keen desire, I folded my legs around him, drawing him closer to me, deepening his welcome assault.

Fuck me Daddy.

My climax was teetering on the edge, and I was so close, yet my body betrayed me. Again. I knew my feelings for King had changed since I found out about Hanna and the baby, and now seemingly I wasn't able to give myself to him.

He was going to be a dad.

"Come on, give it up for me," he groaned impatiently.

He was growing restless for the release of his own brewing orgasm, wanting us to climax together and complete the transaction. In a last-ditch attempt, he reached underneath me and edged his finger into the puckered opening of my ass.

Woah shit—

"Fuck!" my head raised off the pillow. "I'm coming!"

My words were his undoing, and he growled into my neck as he pumped me full of his semen. He waited on top of me, savouring the moment until his penis stopped flinching inside my delicate flesh. He didn't want it to end as much as I didn't.

With his ocean blue eyes staring into mine, he stroked my cheek. "Leave us alone, Alice."

Through years of rehearsals and not an ounce of hesitancy, Alice climbed out of bed completely naked and left the room without looking back.

When the door closed, I turned to him expectantly, sensing he had something he wanted to say. Perhaps he was going to divulge the painful news about his baby with Hanna?

His coarse finger tips caressed my cheek, tingling my

senses.

"Listen, what you did, going to jail for me. I don't forget shit like that."

Images of Frankie-Jo appeared unwelcome in my mind.

Shit! Her commissary money!

"S'up with your face?" he grimaced. "You're all grey and shit."

"Oh, nothing." I altered my gaze, as if that would help. "You just reminded me of something."

He growled and fidgeted his weight as though my forgetfulness was troubling him. "Tell me."

"Well, nothing really, just that the woman I was in jail with asked me to top up her commissary account."

He narrowed his eyes and ran his hand through his hair.

"Why you sweatin' that? I'll handle it. Done."

"Oh," my hands knotted in my lap. "Thank you."

Did he already know who she was? Why didn't he need to ask any questions? *And why is he looking at me like that?*

Now that the intimate exchange between us had fizzled out, and the distractions of his tongue expended, I was furious and hurt with him all over again.

"Anyway, listen, I want you to be my girl."

Wait, what!?

"Daddy I—"

"What!?" His body solidified, and the irritated glare in his eyes was back.

The timing on my part was off, but he left me with no choice.

"You need to talk to Hanna before you say anything more."

"Why!?" He scowled. He sat back, creating a distance between us. There was vulnerability within him I had inadvertently exposed. "Who the fuck is Hanna?"

"You know? The beautiful black-haired girl you've been spending time with? She's my best friend."

His lips thinned in response to his lack of understanding.

"Why do I need your friend's permission?"

"That's not what I mean. Please, just talk to her."

"Fine, I'll talk to her right now!"

I knew I had ruined the tender moment he was trying to create, and I hated it was playing out this way. After all, he'd just asked me to be his girl.

His cell was on the bed somewhere that he was struggling to locate. "Where the fuck is my shit!"

He patted down the sheets as he attempted to find the missing device and when he eventually found it, he held it to his ear with a glare of contempt.

"Tommy. Send Hanna up now. I don't know which one she is. Ask around. Do it now!"

He hung up the call and tossed his phone in frustration amidst the sheets.

With ragged breathing, he looked at me quizzically, as he ran an exasperated hand through his glossy black tightly wound curls, trying to decipher what I was thinking.

Something suddenly crossed his mind when he looked at my lips.

"When I corrected you," he paused, "you're the only hoe that ever made me feel kinda bad about it afterwards. I'm sorry I did that to you."

King's apology knocked the wind out of my sail and sank my boat. The weight behind his words was so immensely powerful that I never imagined would ever escape his lips.

Despite appreciating his effort, his relationship with Hanna still caused me more suffering than I could forgive. How could he trick me like that?

"It's OK," I smiled, "I'm over it."

But I could sense him staring at me, desperate for contact.

"No, it wasn't OK and I'm sorry about it. Got it?"

"Yes, Daddy."

I stole a quick glance at his chiseled features. The

instant reaction it produced in my body when our eyes met returned our electricity. He felt it too.

"Good," he leant in and kissed my lips gently. "I feel different with you."

Eventually, Hanna tentatively knocked on the door, interrupting our candid moment.

"Come in," he shouted, with too much aggression.

The additional intensity he was bringing to an already fraught situation was making matters worse.

With extreme caution, Hanna opened the creaking door, like a child would at the headteacher's office, waiting for punishment to unfold.

"Jasmin tells me I need to speak to you. Why is that?"

With the sheet pulled up to my chin, I lay still, not really believing that the cotton fabric would protect me, but it was better than being exposed. I watched him closely for any sudden movements as he fidgeted in anticipation of her reply.

Hanna's hands knotted in front of her.

"King, don't wait for nobody, hurry up, Whore!"

Her eyes met with mine as she adjusted her posture to make her announcement.

"I'm pregnant, Daddy."

The words spilled out of her mouth with ease; she'd been practising. No doubt Tiffany had been the audience at her dress rehearsal.

"You're pregnant?" He snarled. "Whose baby is it?"

The fact he even had to ask that question was confusing. This was not the way Hanna had painted the picture of their love affair at all.

"It's yours Daddy."

Her cheeks blushed and her eyes glistened as raw emotions reached the surface.

"What? No, it ain't. I never nutted inside you?"

My brows creased together at his reaction. This wasn't making any sense? Hanna told me they were trying for a baby, so if that were true then, why couldn't he remember? Either he had a severe case of amnesia or she was a lying slut.

"You did Daddy."

A stray tear rolled down her cheek where she wiped away the evidence quickly with the back of her hand, but it was too late. We saw. Was Hanna as desperate for love as I was? Could she have gotten herself pregnant by a client to pass off as King's? She'd stooped lower than I ever thought possible.

"Get rid of it," he snarled. "This is not part of the plan."

He stomped over to the dresser and produced a cigar from the top drawer. With a tight grip, he rolled it between his fingers, contemplating his next move.

"You want me to have an abortion!?"

The floodgates opened, and she began sobbing with her head in her hands, creating quite a scene that I struggled to witness.

"Damn fuckin' right, I want you to get an abortion. When did I say you were havin' my kid?"

"But Daddy—"

"You callin' me a liar, Whore!?"

King's rage consumed him and if we weren't careful, he was about to combust. This was the side of him I hated seeing. The last time I saw this vision play out was when he'd taken his hand to my face.

But not wishing to see Hanna suffer any more than she already was, I placed my hand gently against his heaving chest,

"Hey, it's OK."

His eyes softened when they met with mine, absorbing my touch and recharging his desire for intimacy with me. No longer able to focus on Hanna, his eyes moved around my body with fascination.

"Get rid of it and get out of my crib."

"Daddy, let's talk about this please, don't kick Hanna out. Please don't."

Irrespective of our strained friendship, I couldn't stand to see her in anguish and I didn't want her to lose her place in the mansion.

His eyes narrowed, and he frowned at me. "Keep out of it, Jasmin."

Reminding me of my place, I cowered back to my foetal position under the quilt, awaiting further instructions.

King fidgeted with his cigar, where he placed it between his teeth, and then removed it again.

"Get out, Whore," he glared at Hanna. "I can't stand to look at you."

Hanna yelped out an agonising sob as if a wild dog had bitten her. She left the room with urgency, leaving the door wide open, and King and I were alone once more.

"Honestly, I didn't plan on gettin' her pregnant."

The sensitivity he tried so hard to hide was unmistakable. Was he lying?

"But why does she think you did?"

The images I'd created in my mind involving King and Hanna's baby making sex sessions were now dissolving into insignificance and everything I thought I knew was suddenly wrong.

With his eyes peering into the distance, he scratched his forehead. "I don't know."

It took all of my strength to contain my emotional response to Hanna's painful situation. Being told by the father of your child to terminate your baby is a situation no mother should ever have to face, and the delivery of his order was cruel and callous.

But as Hanna and I were no longer considered friends, there wasn't much I could do to provide comfort. I just hoped Tiffany would give her the support she needed.

I needed to look out for myself for a change, and besides, the jury was out on who was actually telling the truth. Was King's word to be trusted? Or did Hanna truly believe that he wanted her as much as she wanted him?

I caught him staring at me during my inner turmoil, and I smiled in response.

He placed his hand on my stomach. "It's you I want to have a baby with."

It was such a sweet expression from such a cold-hearted man. But the two elements of his personality weren't compatible enough to complete the equation. King was a walking, talking juxtaposition of anger and violence with a sprinkle of vulnerability.

With trepidation, I placed my hand on top of his and kissed his lips to offer reassurance. I was still firm that I did not want a baby with him, but he didn't need to know that.

As soon as I sensed his body relax, I climbed out of bed to get some distance between us. I just couldn't think clearly when I was around him. This was seemingly an issue I had with two influential people in the house.

With the freshly cut cigar pinched between his teeth, he frowned at me. "Where you goin'?"

"I planned on getting some new clothes today. I'm running short on pretty much everything."

King reached into the pocket of his shorts, discarded on the bed and pulled out a roll of money.

"Here, take this."

There must've been at least five thousand in total. Lost for words at the unexpected token, I leant in to kiss his lips.

"Thank you, Daddy."

"Get somethin' sexy with it. I wanna fuck you tonight in whatever you buy."

Conscious of the fact that King was watching me dress, I attempted to adorn my clothing with sexy seduction. A summer dress and sandals were easy enough to throw on and still have the desired effect.

"Wear shit like that all the time," he smirked. "It don't get in the way if I wanna take your tight little pussy."

"Do you like this dress?" I asked as I turned to look at my reflection in the mirror. It was one of my favourites.

"I don't give a shit about the dress. It's that sexy body underneath that gets my dick solid."

As I made my way to exit the bedroom, I turned to look behind me one last time to watch him as he lay on his back with the cigar between his teeth, staring up at the ceiling. Thoughts of Hanna and the baby troubled him. The same thoughts that troubled me.

Hanna. That poor girl. There was no way I could ignore what happened and let her go through with the order to abort her baby without at least supporting her. I pulled out my phone to give her a quick call, but it went straight to answerphone.

"Hanna, honey, please call me back. I'm sorry about everything. Tell me you're OK. I love you."

I waited ten long minutes, but my phone didn't ring and there were no new messages. The intense interlude was driving me crazy. I needed a distraction, and I knew exactly what would help.

With money in my pocket and a need to get away from everything, I grabbed my purse by the front door.

"Where are you off to?" An angelic voice called from

behind me.

"Shopping. Wanna come with?"

Alice beamed at my impromptu invite. "Oh my God, yes!"

The traffic on the way into town was too heavy for my already stretched tolerance.

"Move ass hole!" I yelled through my windshield, beeping my horn at a cab driver who was driving too slow.

"Yikes, you're not very good at driving, Jas." Alice's doe eyes projected her nervousness onto me.

"I'm not?"

"It's like when we have fun, you're all, you know, fingers and thumbs."

Speechless at her comment, with no idea what she meant, I replayed our time together. I'd never used my thumb when we had sex? What the fuck did she mean?

"You do realise, Jas, that when you're over thinking your eyebrows crease deeply at the bridge of your nose. Try not to do that, you'll get wrinkles."

Oh. "Um, OK."

I stared through the windshield, completely dazed. So I was bad in bed with wrinkly skin, and to finish, she thought I was a shit driver. Were there any positive elements to my skill set she was into?

"You're sensitive, you know? Jody was kinda delicate, too."

Oh, great Jody again. Maybe she used her thumbs more effectively? The conversation was not going in the direction I needed it to. *Think of something to say.*

"So, is there anything you wanna buy while we're there?"

She thought for a moment, and a mischievous grin lit up her features.

"Maybe some toys for us to use? Perhaps a bigger dildo?"

My eyes bulged from their sockets. "What!?"

"Relax I'm kidding. Jeez! Why are you so tense?"

Alice's teasing had knocked my already fractured confidence.

A lot had happened in the last twenty-four hours that I hadn't yet digested and her curve balls weren't helping.

"Um, I guess just with King coming home—"

"Don't worry, we can still sleep together. He doesn't mind."

Of course, that was Alice's first thought, but what I was actually referring to was that my feelings for him seemed crystal clear when he wasn't around but bring him into the mix and my body would betray me at any given opportunity. He made everything more complicated.

"So, what did you guys talk about when he asked me to

leave?"

My brow furrowed involuntarily at her probing question. The fact was that it was Hanna and King's business that I had no right being a part of in the first place. But then again, Hanna was quite happy to spill my secrets to Alice without a second thought.

"You're frowning again. Wrinkles, Honey."

My hands tensed around the steering wheel. "OK, but promise you won't tell?"

"On your life."

I wasn't sure if Alice swearing on my life was a good thing or not. The fact that I was lacklustre in bed would probably have her betting my life on a game of cards if the opportunity arose.

"OK so, Hanna is pregnant, and she told me it was King's. He says it's not his, and she needs to terminate."

"Woah that's crazy! Do you think she's lying?"

"Well, I didn't until I saw his reaction."

I wondered why this situation and the way he handled it hadn't abated my sexual attraction to King. Did it tell me something about myself that I didn't want to admit? Was I in love with him? Never having been in love before, all I could go off was what I'd seen in the movies.

Would the main character still fall in love with the

handsome lead regardless of his questionable behaviour? I'd have to rewatch a chick flick to find out that answer.

Alice interrupted my reverie. "Personally, I don't think Daddy got her pregnant if he said he didn't. He doesn't lie about stuff like that."

Was that true? Now that I was away from him, I was feeling sick about the whole thing.

We made it into town a short while later, finding a parking spot right outside my favourite store. The tip of my tongue was back out in the open while I navigated the tight space.

"Wow, that took a while." Alice giggled as she removed her seat belt.

Her constant nit picking was getting under my skin.

"In here first?" I asked as we made it to the entrance of the underwear store.

The shop clerk eyed us speculatively when we entered.

"So, what are we looking for?" Alice asked obliviously as she ran her fingers along a rail of thong panties.

"This will do, right?" I held up a matching bra and Brazilian thong set in baby blue.

"I guess it could be cute, but I'm not really into

underwear, though."

"I'm not buying it for you." I giggled, "this is for Daddy."

She crossed her arms over her chest in defence. "Oh, I see."

I rolled my eyes inwardly. Not realising until now that Alice and I hadn't really spent any time with each other outside of the confines of the bedroom. She was high maintenance, for sure, with a sassy attitude to match.

"Try it on then, Jas. I'll come with you."

I found myself inside a cramped cubicle with Alice's critical gaze on me as I undressed and stepped into the full set.

"You're a little bloated. Do you need a bigger size in the panties?"

I peered at myself in the mirror. Hmm, she was right. My stomach wasn't as flat as normal. I mean, all the stress I'd been under had given me constipation, but maybe Chef's calorific meals were to blame also?

Without warning, Alice hooked her thumbs into the waistband of my panties, peeling them down my legs slowly.

"Ever had an orgasm in a changing room before?" She whispered salaciously.

My throat became dry. This was playing out nothing like a shopping trip with Hanna, and I had no control what so ever.

Alice knelt before me and parted my labia with her thumbs, exposing my sensitive clitoris.

She blew softly on the skin, and the delicate flesh contracted in response, exposing the small pink pleasurable mound beneath the hood.

The tip of her tongue teased me. Flicking; licking.

"Oh, shit." I groaned in appreciation of her masterful skills.

I pressed my hands against the wall to support my buckling knees, and with continued sensual circles; she hardened my clit as it engorged with arousal. Then, as quickly as ever, I climaxed into her mouth with a squirt of pleasure.

"Fuck!"

As she rose to her feet before me, she wiped her mouth with the back of her hand.

"You're welcome. Come on, I'm bored now. Let's get out of here."

With my first successful purchase in hand and a surprise orgasm I wasn't counting on, we made our way back out into the L.A heat to continue my mission to spend King's money.

The weather was gorgeous, with a slight breeze mixed with a warmth that gave the same effect as a soothing bath.

"So, where next?" Alice asked, linking her arm inside the loop of mine.

Hanna was still prevalent within my mind as we moved toward our next destination.

"Hold on, let me just try calling Hanna. After what happened, I want to check she's alright."

I rummaged through my bag and disappointment crinkled my eyes when I pulled out my phone to find that she still hadn't responded. So I tried to call her again.

Her voicemail played for a second time, and the radio silence made my stomach churn. This was not my Hanna at all. We would have squashed any squabble we'd ever had in the past on the same day, but this was turning into something way more. I feared it was the end of our friendship for good. Had she given up on me?

As we strolled along the sidewalk, I grew aware of a sense that prickled my survival instinct. Were we being followed?

A black SUV a few hundred yards away was curb

crawling. Did they realise we were hookers?

Alice seemed oblivious and with everything she had going on recently, I didn't want to add stress to her load.

"Wait, Jas," she halted us, "look at this poster. The tattoo parlour does walk in appointments. Shall we take a peek inside?"

"Um sure, but why? I don't really—"

She grabbed my hand and propelled me forward, inside a clinical room with a vast array of tattoo designs spread across the four walls. There was an alternatively dressed female with facial piercings and lime green hair concentrating hard on tattooing a man's back. Her work was impressive.

Alice's eyes were alight with excitement. "Ooh, look at this! Wait, we could totally get matching!"

Shit—This was not a good idea, and I really didn't want to. Tattoos on men were my absolute favourite, but on me? *No.*

"Excuse me Sir, can you fit me and my bestie in for matching?"

Wait what? "Woah, hold on a minute, Alice—"

"Do you not want to match with me?"

Her heavenly features twisted with inner conflict. A master of manipulation, she had backed me into a corner.

I sighed in defeat. "OK, fine, something small. Don't ask for more than that."

"Yippee! Thanks Jas. This one?"

She pointed to a small heart shape split in half down the middle where the two halves would make a whole when re joined back together. It was inoffensive and actually quite cute.

"Sure," I shrugged in defeat, "why not?"

Alice leant into my ear, her voice a whisper. "Which finger do you use on my pussy?"

In bewilderment at the presence of hurricane Alice, I held up my digit of choice.

"OK Sir, she'll have the heart on that finger, and I'll have it on this one."

As I watched Alice have her turn first, my mind drifted to thoughts of Hanna and her baby. I envisaged Hanna and a little dark-haired baby boy cradled in her arms, but in an unwelcome twist, her vision morphed into me. As if watching my future life play out, I pictured a hollow version of myself holding a baby that had King's features. I was crying; distraught. If I stayed under King's roof, would I eventually have to follow through with having his baby? Was this a premonition? It was only a matter of time before he found out I was still on the pill.

If I allowed myself to conjure up images of raising a family, the father would absolutely not be King. His brother Dan, however, had a nurturing side that our child could thrive off, and with respect for women that King didn't possess, he was special.

Had I made a mistake dismissing Dan again as soon as King made an appearance? Yesterday I was sure; today I wasn't. Dan was the safest choice.

Alice seemed in discomfort. Her soft features had hardened under the pressure.

"How much longer?" she asked.

The tattooist pursed his lips. "I only just got started, Ma'am."

I shook my head and chuckled at her performance. So high maintenance yet so loveable.

As I would have to wait a little while for my turn, force of habit had me checking my phone again, but my lips pouted when I saw there was still nothing from Hanna.

While I had my cell still in my hand, I flicked through my social media. Had Hanna posted anything?

A news article popped up that caught my attention.

It read:

Tatiana Cummings found dead at prestigious playboy style mansion.
Local man Sandeano, "Fat Dean" Castello, arrested on suspicion of murder.

"Jeez, that's sad," I mumbled.

I hadn't realised Alice was listening to me.

"What's sad?" she asked, craning her neck to see.

Shit. The last thing she needed now was a reminder of Tatiana.

"Oh—just an article I was reading about, um, abandoned dogs."

I hadn't allowed myself to analyse my feelings about Tat's death before now, but the fact King had paid his way out of a murder charge was nauseating. Irrespective of my lack of feelings for Tat, her family must be in so much pain and have so many unanswered questions. King was a very dangerous man.

Tattooed hands entwined, Alice and I strolled back to the car with matching declarations permanently etched into our skin. What the declaration meant, I wasn't sure. But what I did know was that it made her happy, and that side of her was infectious.

For a second time, the sense of being followed raised the hairs on the back of my neck. This time I turned to look behind me to find a male in the distance who was looking in our direction. Part of me felt like I knew him, but he was too far away to be sure.

Not wanting to risk being kidnapped, I picked up our pace back to the parking lot.

"What's the rush, Jas." Alice stuttered as her fast-paced heels against the concrete distorted her voice.

"Um, nothing really. Just wanted to get back home."

She side eyed me, a little irritated at a thought that troubled her. "Oh yeah, so you can fuck Daddy in your new undies?"

"No." I chewed my lip in thought. "I just—have cramps."

"Oh my God, wait, me too! We are true besties, Jas. I actually need to grab some tampons."

There was no way I was traipsing back to Walgreens now.

"OK, you go. I'll wait in the car."

Within the confines of my vehicle, in a quiet moment of contemplation, I thought about Hanna for the millionth time today. I pulled out my cell and dialled her one last time. The phone rang and rang, but to my relief, she eventually picked up.

"Hey Han." The relief in my voice was obvious, but I didn't care.

"Hey."

"Please let me explain to you what happened?"

"It's fine, no need."

Her voice was lifeless and filled with bitterness.

"Listen Han, please, I was trying to do the right thing. You see, King had asked me to take things further with him. I wanted him to speak to you first because I figured if he knew you were pregnant, then he would back off me."

"I'm sure he'll change his mind when he finds out about you and Dan."

"You wouldn't?"

My heart thudded in my chest and my skin prickled with the sudden fear of my secret being revealed.

"Wouldn't I?"

"The Hanna I know wouldn't do me like that."

"The Chloe I know wouldn't steal my man off of me and humiliate me."

This was spiralling out of control rapidly.

"I swear to you it's not what it looks like."

"Oh, so you aren't fucking two brothers *and* Alice, messing with all of their hearts?"

"What?"

I knew exactly what she was referring to, but I needed to know how well informed she actually was.

"You have been sleeping with Alice, Daddy and Dan. Alice told me that you two are more than friends."

I peered down at the redness of my freshly applied tattoo. *Fuck—*

"How can we be more than friends when I've never had that conversation with her? Yes, we have had sex a few times, but that's it."

I was suddenly so angry with Alice. Why did no one seem to be able to keep their damn mouths shut? She had no business telling Hanna about our time together, and this was only making things worse with the best friend I was trying to keep hold of.

Hanna cackled down the phone. "You don't get it, do you? She's in love with you Chloe."

"No, she's not." *Is she?* "If that's true, this is the first I'm hearing about it!"

Hanna's disclosure completely knocked the wind out of me. *Why didn't I see this coming?*

"Little Chloe Adams. Four times a heartbreaker."

"What do you mean, four?"

"You've broken my heart, too. I thought we were best friends and had each other's backs. You've killed me a thousand times today, Chloe."

She hung up the call.

"Fuck!" I tossed my phone on the car seat beside me in frustration. It felt as though my subconscious was eating me alive.

Back at the mansion, we'd just made it through the front door when I heard a familiar voice. Hanna was in the living room, talking to someone.

"Hey, let's show Hanna the tattoos! She'll die!" Alice squealed, grabbing my hand as she pulled me along with her. She was the steam train, and I was the cart load of horseshit behind.

"Hey Hanna look! Me and Jas got matching tats!" She forced our fingers out in front of us to showcase the completed heart when pressed together.

Hanna peered over her shoulder and when she saw me stood next to Alice, she glared at us both.

"Wow. How—committed."

The chill in her tone reminded me of winter, but with a murderous twist, and Alice's behaviour didn't help acting like a puppy with over excitement that was pissing everyone off.

Michelle couldn't help herself when she saw an opportunity. She pinched her nose, "Ew, there's suddenly a smell in here. I think it's you." She pointed her elongated finger in my direction.

Violence, rage and revengeful thoughts came to the forefront of my mind. *Relax Chloe. Don't rise to it.*

"OK," I said eventually, "I'm gonna leave. Alice, I'll see you later."

"Bye Jody!" Michelle giggled as I turned my back.

Deep breaths. Don't break now.

In a state of unconsciousness, I found myself parked outside Dan's house without knowing how or why I was there.

Security still allowed me access, and I'd sailed straight through as though it was meant to be.

Dan wasn't even home, as his car wasn't in the driveway, but that didn't matter. It was a safe place for me to be away from King, the whores and everything else in between.

As though I'd hit pause on my life, I waited for hours just staring into space with a blank expression on my face. There weren't many ways to articulate how I was feeling. But to put it simply, I despised the way King treated Hanna. I loathed the way Hanna treated me and above all, the whores of the mansion had broken through my pain barrier and were now eating on the internal fragile flesh of my organs. I couldn't handle any of it anymore.

Eventually, evening had drawn in when the headlights of a car shone straight into my windshield, forcing me to squint at the brightness. A Mercedes had pulled into the driveway.

I watched closely as Dan exited his car like I was on a police stakeout. My watch told me it was 10:00PM, and it made me question where he'd been all this time. Was he with another woman?

Dan didn't spot me as he went inside his house, carrying what looked like bags of groceries.

My eager hand was on the door knocker and tapping it three times before I could stop myself, where I waited for what felt like a lifetime for him to answer.

When he opened the door with surprise in his eyes at my forlorn face standing in front of him, he stepped back with his arm out to the side to let me straight in.

"You've been crying," he said. "What's wrong Chloe?"

My eyes met with his, and the tears welled again.

"I needed to see you."

He embraced me in an encompassing Dan hug, and I wept into his chest as he tightened his hold on me.

"Romero's back home, isn't he?" Dan wasn't able to keep the disdain from his voice.

It was easier when King wasn't around, that was for sure.

"Yeah, he's back." I managed between sobs, wiping my running nose on the palm of my hand.

"He hurt you again!?" Dan pushed me back from his hug to check my face for additional damage, not letting go of me for a second.

"This isn't really about him. Well, it is—but it isn't. Mainly, it's my friend Hanna. She's so mad at me."

Dan's shoulders relaxed. "Oh OK. Why is she mad? Did you tell her you've decided we're leaving?"

His thumb ran along the length of my back to comfort me the best he could.

"No, not yet."

"What happened then?"

Holding my hand, he led me over to the sofa in the living room to take a seat, not once letting go of me, keeping our contact.

"King—"

"Please call him dick wad or ass hat in front of me, anything other than that word. I can't handle it."

"Oh, I'm sorry," I cleared my throat, "well, he said he wanted me to be his girl, so—"

"He said what!?"

Dan shot up out of his chair. I'd never seen him visibly raging before.

"Please sit down." I tugged at his arm, which took less effort than I expected. He was so much more responsive than his brother.

"As I was saying. He asked me, you know, but I had just found out that he'd gotten my friend pregnant. He told her to abort the baby. She's barely speaking to me. I don't know what to do."

"Sorry Chloe, I can't think past him wanting a relationship with you. He can't keep his fucking dick to himself, can he?"

"Dan, come on. That's not the important bit."

"You're wrong. You know the type of person Romero is? We've been through this before."

I clasped my hand around his to connect with him again.

"It'll never happen."

"It won't? Have you slept with him since you became my girlfriend?"

The blunt, unexpected question derailed me off the track and sent me hurtling into a ravine.

Shit. What can I say?

"Um, no."

I was suddenly looking anywhere but at Dan.

"You're lying, aren't you?"

Heat radiated from my cheeks, exposing my lie. I'd been rumbled. I sighed heavily, knowing that this conversation might end badly if not handled thoughtfully.

"OK, yes, I've slept with him. You know, while I'm living there, I have to give him anything he asks for."

Dan was back on his feet again and pacing about the room agitatedly.

"You can say no to him, Chloe!"

I looked down at my knotted fingers, feeling conflicted. The possibility that I might not have wanted to refuse King was evident in my continued compliance in sleeping with him whenever the offer was there. The way King made me feel in the bedroom was sensational, without a doubt, and since becoming Dan's girlfriend, I'd continued to sleep with King whenever the moment arose.

"I'm sorry I lied. If you're upset about me sleeping with King—I mean, ass hat—do you think I wanted him? No, I didn't. All I thought of was that it wasn't you touching me. I hated it."

Liar.

Dan was silent in contemplation where he fixed his gaze straight ahead, as if engrossed in an action packed film, but the TV wasn't on.

"Please Dan, he means nothing to me."

I reached for his shoulder to spark something between us. He flinched, but allowed me to place my hand there.

"Come on, please look at me."

I wasn't used to pleading with a man, but here I was doing exactly that.

When he eventually locked his eyes with mine, they shone with unshed tears. Not a single stray tear dropped, but I knew he was restraining himself as hard as he could.

"Take me Dan, please. I'm yours."

I kissed his neck to entice him in the only way I knew how.

"Sorry Chloe," he tensed, "I can't. Not now." His body recoiled away from my touch, completely rejecting me.

Air escaped my lungs. This had never happened to me before. "So that's it then? You're never going to fuck me again?"

I hadn't intended on yelling, but the blow to the chest he'd just delivered me hurt more than I could handle.

He scoffed, "when have I ever fucked you, Chloe?"

"You know what I mean,"

"No actually, I don't. It's killing me knowing that the woman I love is fucking my idiot brother."

Huh? "Wait. You love me?"

I couldn't quite believe my ears. For my own sanity, I wouldn't allow myself to believe it was true. People didn't love me. They used me.

"Isn't it obvious? I'm willing to move my whole life for you, because I love you."

Did he really love me? It didn't seem likely in such a short amount of time. No one had ever said those words to me before. *Do I say it back?*

The hopeful glint in his eyes forced my decision.

"I love you too," I whispered.

We both gawked at each other for a moment. The atmosphere suddenly changed, and I was shy.

Dan couldn't restrain himself any longer and enticed me to lie down on the length of the sofa. We kissed softy and sensually like we'd become accustomed to, and my hands ran through his hair as we claimed each other. Our tongues intertwined as we enjoyed tasting what each of us was offering.

This was my baby's daddy for sure and when the time was right, he would be the one. Not King.

I removed my underwear as he tore open the packet and rolled on the condom. With a gentle approach, he eased me down to the base of his welcoming erection.

We made love on the sofa so tenderly.

"Chloe. I love you," he called out with his climax, panting softly from the physical exertion.

I stroked his handsome stubbled face and kissed his lips as my body met with his and the welcome clenching of my release overwhelmed my senses.

Relaxed and happy, Dan emerged from the kitchen and handed me a glass of post coital chardonnay, with a boyish grin on his face.

"So, New Mexico?" I asked as I took a sip of crisp white wine from his extensive collection.

Now I was embracing the idea. I was excited to know more.

"It's as far away from Romero as possible, while allowing me to continue working," he shrugged his shoulders as if he'd already practised his response. "My attorney is looking into ways to protect my business from him."

"Oh, that reminds me. Thank you for sending him to help me. You're my knight in shining armour," I giggled into my wine. I was more tipsy than I realised.

"I wasn't going to leave you in jail." He took a cathartic gulp of the golden liquid himself.

"How did you know I was in jail?"

The burning question in the back of my mind was finally

going to be answered.

"Romero is under the impression that his men are not susceptible to bribery. He's wrong. A couple of dollars and they squeal like pigs."

"Oh? Which one of them told you?" Options ran through my mind. Was it Snake? No way. Clive?

"No idea who it was. Does it matter?"

I could sense in his tone that my probing was no longer welcome, but he never made me feel like I was unsafe around him.

"No, it doesn't matter. I haven't had much luck with men, but you have been so good to me, so thank you again."

"You don't need to thank me, Chloe."

"I do. If you knew my past, you'd get it."

"Tell me then."

He took his seat next to me and listened to every note I played.

"Um. Well, my stepdad was a son of a bitch."

I drank down my final swig of wine for courage.

Dan's grip on the stem of his glass tightened. "What did he do to you?"

"You don't want to know." I snorted, not wishing to open up pandora's box just yet. Thankfully, he didn't press me further.

"Where is your stepdad now?"

Dan's level of interest in the topic left me wondering whether he was digging for information in the name of revenge or just asking out of curiosity.

"No idea. Last I heard, they locked him up, but that was years after I was already in foster care. I don't care too much about the judicial system. They took way too long."

"Hmm, I'm so sorry Chloe," he gently stroked my thigh. "I know how hard it is to get scum bags locked up."

I hadn't really spoken to anyone about my stepdad, but having confidence in speaking with Dan confirmed I was making the right choice in being here. Not even social services got the entire story from me as a child. Just enough of the terrible stuff that got him sent down. But here I was, telling Dan my real name, sharing my life stories and feeling content. *He's the one.*

Suddenly, I felt the urge to say more. "He used to wait until night time and sneak into my room and would tell me I'd been bad that day even though I tried my hardest to be the best kid I could—"

"Chloe, don't put yourself through it." His face twisted tightly, as though he had the potential to vomit at the next word. "If it's too painful, please don't say anymore."

My mouth continued to engage, and the words tumbled

out.

"He raped me most nights and I would pray he would die a horrible death, but it went on for years."

Dan picked up my hand and kissed my knuckle.

"No man will ever harm you again, I promise, and that includes Romero. I mean it, Chloe. If he touches you again, I will not be held accountable for my actions."

I appreciated Dan's words of comfort, but he knew as well as I did that there was no way he would beat King in a battle to the top. That man was far too dangerous and terrified everybody; myself included.

CHAPTER 12

My eyes blinked open early the next morning to the sound of my cell phone dancing next to me on the bedside table right by my head.

Dan stirred and turned over to face me, but his smile soon fell when he saw the look of reflection on my face.

"Everything alright Chloe?"

I wanted to tell Dan that no, everything wasn't alright and that I'd awoken this morning with anxiety laden regret having made a decision that could see one or both of us six feet under, but instead, I gave him a small smile.

"Everything's fine."

What am I doing?

Naked and in Dan's bed, with no plausible reason to give King why I didn't go home last night, was the puzzle that I couldn't find the missing piece to.

How am I going to get out of this one?

My phone vibrated with a follow up alert and I reached over to find a message from Hanna.

< Hanna > Tats funeral is today. Thought you'd want to know. St Michaels Church 11:00AM

Tatiana's funeral was today! How was I only hearing about this now? Perhaps if I'd gone back home last night, someone would have furnished me with the knowledge. Hanna was right. I had become selfish.

Dan nudged me. "Hey, what's wrong?" His forehead creased with unease, and Alice's wrinkle warning came to mind.

I sat up and swung my legs over the side of the bed, facing away from Dan intentionally. For some reason, when we spoke about a topic involving King, I struggled to make eye contact with him.

"It's the girls' funeral today." I sighed, "you know, the girl who died at the house."

"Oh. You mean murdered?"

I gave him a stiff nod of confirmation. "I think I should go."

With my phone in my hand, I stared at the screen, reading between the lines of Hanna's message. The lack of content from a woman normally so chatty spoke a thousand words. In fact, the message alone was probably more than I deserved.

"Hmm Chloe, that's a bad idea."

Dan kissed my shoulder and rubbed his thumb over the spot to seal in the kiss, trying to get my attention back on him, but it wasn't working. I was too distracted.

"Why shouldn't I go?"

He sat up to add conviction behind his reasoning.

"It's best you start distancing yourself from them now."

"But Hanna needs me." My voice cracked, and unshed tears threatened to fall with the idea that maybe she didn't need me anymore.

He glanced over at my phone screen and his nostrils flared.

"Doesn't seem like it from the message she's sent you."

I knew he was right. He was too smart to be wrong, but my stubbornness wouldn't allow him to be. I had to keep hope that Hanna wanted me there so we could hug it out and fix our friendship.

"You don't know my Hanna. She wants me to go or she wouldn't have messaged me at all."

"OK then," he raised his hands, "go if you think it's the right thing to do, but please keep under the radar. I don't want that ass hole putting his hands on you again."

"Come on, Dan, what's he going to do? Fuck me during the service?"

I was getting agitated by his lack of support, but in fairness, I was being distant with him, which only inferred my regret in staying the night even further.

"You know that's not what I meant, although I wouldn't put it past him!"

"Look, I'm sorry, I need to go."

My voice crackled again with affliction, but it was a refreshing notion that Dan and I could have a civil, non-violent disagreement, and no one got hurt.

Don't let Hanna down.

My feet hit the ground, and I was up and out of bed before he could convince me otherwise. I needed to get space between us before he lured me back in with his wholesome boy next door charm.

"Where are you going, Sweetheart? Come back."

My steps faltered when I heard that term of endearment. No one had called me that in a genuine sense since my Grandmother had back home in England. The power behind those words made my bottom lip tremble. I kept my back towards him, not allowing him to break me down with his emerald eyes.

"I'm going to get ready for a funeral and support my best friend. Nothing you can say will change my mind. OK?"

He clambered out of bed, gloriously naked and insanely

fuckable. His hair was a mass of messy chocolate curls, with a loose tendril that had fallen in front of his eyes. His enticing olive skin was silky smooth to the touch that I wanted to feel against my lips.

With a sigh, he closed the distance I'd created and cupped the tops of my shoulders, where he placed a gentle kiss on my forehead.

"I don't want to fight with you, Chloe. I'm sorry," he said with his mouth in my hair.

Huh? "You think that was a fight?" A giggle escaped my mouth as I buried my head into the hairs on his powerful chest, where I listened to the steady beating of his heart.

He didn't question my remark, already knowing that I was referring to King and his punishment tactics, but he gave me a reassuring squeeze, letting me know we were OK.

After a moment, he released me and climbed back into bed.

My brows raised as I watched him leave.

"You're not getting up?"

I couldn't hide my surprise. It seemed unlikely that a high-flying business owner such as Dan would lie around in bed instead of working.

He propped his hands behind his head and smiled at me.

"I've given myself the day off. There are things to do and

people to see, but that's later on tonight. Today I'm just going to relax here, looking at your side of the bed that'll be empty and cold."

He exhaled wistfully with an animated pout as he rubbed the still warm bedsheets laid bare from my recent departure. The vision he was creating made me snicker.

"Oh dear, my heart bleeds," I chuckled, rolling my eyes at him as I headed for the shower.

When I entered his en suite, the lavishness that rained upon my aura gave me delusions of grandeur. I felt like a princess.

There wasn't a single piece of evidence to suggest that a whore had been here in my absence. Not a hairbrush, or body butter within view that could provoke the jealous demon that lay dormant within me. Just Dan's manly products, in Dan's modern bathroom, that sat within the walls of Dan's impressive mansion. I couldn't help but notice the irony that such an ordinary setup felt so extraordinary compared with King's lifestyle.

I'd just turned on the shower when the man of the house peaked his head around the doorjamb.

"May I join you?" He asked with a charming smile that spread his full lips.

"Be my guest, Sir."

He made it impossible for me to refuse him, and I was enjoying the playful mood we shared. I had not experienced feeling like I was home for such a long time.

Without hesitancy, he stepped in behind me and cradled me close to him as the water cascaded down our bodies, where I sensed his arousal growing against my back.

I turned around to meet with his fiery gaze, and we shared a flirtatious grin. My eyes followed the flow of water that trickled along the pathway of defined muscle down his torso until I met with the evidence of his physical sexual attraction to me.

"Sorry Dan, I don't have time for that now."

I continued to wash my body, dismissing his unspoken question.

He raised his hands innocently at my accusation. "Who said I wanted anything?"

I peered over my shoulder, giving him the look of bullshit, which made us both laugh again.

"OK, you got me," he smirked, "but I wasn't going to try anything, I swear. I guess I just can't help it when I'm in the shower with my beautiful girlfriend."

Just hearing the word girlfriend leave the lips of a man who didn't try to have sex with me restored my faith in men. Could we form a relationship that didn't rely on sex? *Does that even exist?*

Dan's cleanliness routine was thorough, and I watched with interest as he started from the top and worked his way down, but why on earth when I saw him retract his foreskin was I only just acknowledging that he hadn't had a circumcision, but King had? Was it weird that I even cared? Probably. *Is it inappropriate to ask?*

As he soaped up his genitals, he attempted to make eye contact with me.

"You OK there gorgeous, you seem distracted."

My eyes blinked as I refocused my efforts on cleaning my body. "Sorry, I was just thinking about *your cock* the funeral."

"Dan, I need to go now. Stop!" I squealed when Dan attempted to keep me in his bed with him. Somehow, he'd enticed me back under the covers for a cuddle longer than I'd agreed.

"Just five more minutes?" He asked with a pouted bottom lip. He captured my arm and pulled me back down to lie next to him.

"No, no, no!" I flailed my legs. "I'm going right now!" I fought against his encompassing hold and jumped off the bed where I ran to the door, grinning as I placed my hand on the doorknob, threatening my exit. Dan was over to me as quick as a vampire to a damsel's neck.

"You're not leaving without giving me some sugar!"

He put one hand against the door and I allowed him to close it, anticipating his next move. With a glint in his eyes, he seized me around my middle and tickled me with just the right amount of pressure, making me wriggle like a captured fish.

"Ahh!" I shrieked, "I'm gonna pee my pants, stop!"

The laughter between us was bewitching.

As soon as he ceased his onslaught, his back straightened and his eyes hardened.

"I love you Chloe, don't forget that. I'll be waiting for you."

Up on my tiptoes, I gave him a chaste kiss on the lips.

"I love you too, Handsome. I'll see you later."

While rushing towards my car the butler had already prepared for me—conscious of being late to Tatiana's funeral—I caught sight of a black SUV idling down the road, not too far from Dan's house.

The silhouettes of two men sat in the front, staring towards me evoked the prickling sensation of being followed again. Were these men watching me, or was it a coincidence?

Once inside the confines of my car, I adjusted the rear-view mirror to monitor the illusive figures behind me.

When my car set off, the van moved in my direction.

Shit! I'm definitely being followed.

With my sweaty palms losing grip around the steering wheel and my heart thudding in my chest, I panicked. Should I go back to Dan's house? Would he be able to protect me if I did?

The final decision I made was out of selflessness for my friends, and so I continued my journey towards the Church. I needed to prove to myself just as much as them I wasn't a self-centred whore.

I glanced in the rear-view again and the van was still two cars behind me. My forehead was damp, and I felt faint against my over breathing. *Surely I'm being paranoid?* Why would anyone be following me?

An announcement rang through the car speakers, making me jolt, where my cell phone maps informed me I had five minutes left of my journey before I would make it to the Church, just in time. If the men wanted to capture me when I arrived there, they would have to make their peace with God.

With a hope and a prayer, I peered into the rear-view a final time.

Wait—

I rose out of my seat to survey the entire visual within the mirror to find the SUV had disappeared.

The relief that washed over me in that moment was substantial. *Thank you, God. Thank you.*

A heavy exhale escaped my lips, and I relaxed back into my seat. I was so paranoid recently.

I reached the venue just in time and parked in the little parking lot where several other blue Minis were all lined up. That was confirmation enough that I was in the right place.

Before I left the safety net of the car to meet with whores I didn't want to associate with, I pulled down the sun visor to make sure I looked at least presentable. No makeup, with my hair slicked back in a ponytail. I'd looked better. But what was a girl to do when she ran away with nothing but herself and her anxiety?

It occurred to me then that whilst in Dan's company, I felt the safest I had since I could remember. He gave me no reason to feel anxious around him, giving me the opportunity to speak my mind.

A warm flood of welcoming images took hold of my

vision and his handsome face popped into my mind as he tickled me by the door as I was leaving. Pure elation filled my soul. We were bound by his love for me. All I'd ever wanted was to be loved, and I'd finally found it.

But did he truly genuinely love me? A nagging thought had me doubtful.

The Church's grand open doors were at the far end of a shrub lined pathway. I'd only travelled a short distance from my car when a casually dressed man leapt out from behind a bush.

"Are you a member of the Giannetti mansion?" he clicked his camera. "Do you have any comments in relation to the suspicious circumstances surrounding Tatiana Cummings' death?"

Oh great. A news reporter. Just what I didn't need.

"No comment."

He pushed his microphone towards my mouth.

"Do you think the right man has been convicted?"

"No comment!"

Pulling my jacket around me, I picked up pace, desperate to get distance from the pushy journalist who wanted an exclusive. I'd be damned if I was that girl to give him one. The faster I walked, the more distance I created as he fell back behind enemy lines.

It wasn't until I spotted Tatiana lay in rest within the hearse parked at the entrance that my footsteps faltered. There was a large gathering of people surrounding her, weeping into tissues held against their noses.

Some of King's men were amongst the crowd, wearing blue denim jeans and a smart shirt with a tie. They looked as awkward and out of place as I was.

"Oh. My. God. Girls—look what she's wearing!"

I knew it was Michelle before I turned to see her glaring at me with flared nostrils and a curled upper lip.

Shit!

On this occasion, Michelle was within her rights to say something. My summer dress was so inappropriate for the event.

"Imagine being fat, ugly and still having confidence to show up dressed like that."

With my hands bunched by my waist, I took a deep breath.

"Back off Michelle, please. Today isn't about you."

To my surprise, she eyed me with pursed lips but didn't continue her attack. Perhaps my words had resonated with her. Tatiana was dead.

I spotted a heaven-sent angel before she noticed me.

Alice looked beautiful, dressed in a classy black number that hugged her figure in all the right places, but her twisted facial expression didn't match her celestial image.

She appeared forlorn and completely overwhelmed, staring into the abyss. When she eventually saw me, she beckoned me over to her and I did exactly as instructed.

As I muscled my way through a flock of people surrounding her, I reached my hand to her shoulder to regain our connection.

"Hey Alice."

We both smiled in unison as our skin connected.

"Hi Jas."

Her demeanour was of sorrow, with gaunt features and black circles under her eyes and no sooner was she with me, she suddenly zoned out again, and I'd lost her attention.

"You haven't slept, have you?"

To make eye contact with her again, I moved my head to her eye line, forcing her to acknowledge I was still there.

Tears rolled down her cheeks with unspoken words of internal suffering.

"You left me again when you promised me you wouldn't."

Oh no!

A collider scope of images swirled in front of my vision.

Entangled snapshots of yesterday played out in my mind, but there wasn't a single element I could use as an excuse for why I didn't go home last night.

"Alice, I'm so—"

Her anguished, glistening eyes pierced into mine briefly.

"No, you're not Jas."

My stomach released flames that radiated into my throat. Was I going to be sick? How did I allow this to happen? I wanted to unzip my skin and leave my own body.

My being there suddenly felt like I was making things worse. I didn't know what to say to offer comfort, and I had no excuse why I let her down so badly.

I snaked my hand around her waist and drew her closer to me, kissing her temple, fuelling it with as much love as I could, but the anxiety emanating through her cool, damp skin was infectious, and it made my stomach hurt more.

"I'm here now," I whispered.

Her body responded to our connection, and she pulled me into a bear hug where we stood there for a moment until we both sensed his presence.

The cat was amongst the pigeons and the birds flocked at the sound of King's voice.

"Where is she?" He yelled into the crowd, his eyes darting around in search of someone. Was he looking for

Tatiana's coffin?

Snake appeared behind me and gripped hold of my forearm.

"Boss wants you. Now!" His panicked voice mirrored the rest of the unsettled horde.

In understanding Snake's assignment, I followed him through the parted crowd as he led me towards him.

King tensed when he saw Snake's hand on my arm, but visibly relaxed when he released me.

"There's my girl," he said with a glint in his eyes, reserved just for me.

"Is something wrong Daddy?"

I tried to read the tortuous expression on his face.

"Yeah, there's somethin' wrong when my girl sees me and don't kiss me."

He removed the unlit cigar from his mouth, waiting for me to make the first move. The timing in which he'd chosen to express his affections towards me seemed so inappropriate and disrespectful. We were at the funeral of his dead girlfriend, yet that didn't seem to concern him.

With my intention to kiss the man I'd already decided wasn't right for me locked into place, I questioned my sanity.

He was so handsome in all ways, but that didn't take

away from the fact that he was an arrogant, self righteous prick. So why did I want to please him? How had my body bypassed my brain and lead me straight into his alluring trap?

Just as I was about to raise onto my tiptoes, a bolshy female made her presence known. King frowned at the interruption, glaring at the intruder. "Yes, Patricia?"

I'd never seen this woman before. She was tall and overly slim with brown wiry hair that was greying at the roots. Her skin looked weathered before its time, painting a picture of her hard life.

"I need a hit of something good, King," Patricia slurred from intoxication. I could smell her breath from a mile away. "I can't bury my daughter with a clear head. Please." With a swaying stance, her jittering hand swept her damp fringe from her forehead.

Bury her daughter? She was Tatiana's mother? *Like mother, like daughter.*

"Snake will sort you out, but you owe me Pat. No more freebies."

He gave her his rigid look that would put chills down anyone's spine.

"Yeah, yeah I know."

The redness of her skin showed how deep the addiction

was as she scratched her forearm from withdrawals.

A reactive lump formed in my throat as I observed. That poor woman must have been going through hell and back at the sudden loss of her young daughter, regardless of her addictions.

I highly doubted she was aware of who Tat's killer was, but if she did, would it have altered the supplier of her habit?

In retaking control as he liked to do, King shoulder barged Patricia out of the way and, with a sharp grip of my hand, he pulled me towards him with an eagerness unsuitable for our public position. He spread the fingers of his large palm and interlocked them with mine and without saying a word; he took me over to a quiet corner, away from prying eyes.

"Listen," he said with a stoney gaze, "once the door is closed on Tat today, I wanna make it official with you."

The atmosphere between us was a mixture of intensity and electricity as he awaited my response.

But my mind was reeling, and I'd no idea what to say. The location he'd chosen and timing of his declaration were in such poor taste that it was almost a practical joke. The glint in his eyes as they burrowed into mine pierced through my psyche.

"Don't keep me waiting, Jasmin."

My automatic response kicked in again, and I smiled brightly, kissing his soft lips where, without warning, he grabbed the back of my head to keep me in place as he deepened our connection.

The ever present spark between us was there, firing on all four cylinders as I allowed his tongue to explore my mouth. As always, his flint ignited my flame, but unfortunately for King, the vision of Dan and our love making played on repeat in the forefront of my mind. But the deeper the kiss dove, King's proximity lured me into his trap again, and I was finding it hard to fight.

The smell of his skin and the gleam in his eyes with his handsome features and masculine presence. He was so fucking attractive. The strength of his hold on me and the commandment from his voice left me weak.

As he pulled away, catapulting me back to reality, I became aware of our surroundings again. *Tat's funeral.*

I hoped with all my heart that no one, especially Hanna or Alice, had seen us kiss and it was a relief to find that, other than a few of his security team, no one else was around.

King's harsh breathing became a visual of his unravelling.

"You belong to me," he said, squeezing my hand tightly where he impatiently forced it down onto his growing erection. "Ain't no girl ever made me as hard as you do. I wanna fuck you every chance I get. Me and you will have the best life. The queen of my castle."

My mouth dropped open at his outlandish speech. In a way, it felt like a twisted marriage proposal, or at the very least he was telling me he cared for me in a way he'd not been capable of before, but I would be naïve to think he hadn't spun that line with Tatiana when he'd first laid his eyes on her. So why was I falling for it? If he was selling; I was buying.

The incessant erection in his pants was still visible while I analysed and categorised my thoughts over his actions. I couldn't ignore how my body responded to him and the dampness between my legs from our proximity told me how attracted to him I was. But the harrowing notion we were at his ex lovers' funeral poured cold water on my libido that diluted my desire. My already fractured moral compass was being tested in more ways than one, and I'd still not proven to myself or anyone else that I was more than a selfish whore.

King suddenly grew agitated at himself. "Shit, I really wanna fuck you now, but I guess it'll have to wait."

With my hand still in his, he stormed towards the chaos, leading the way into the Church for the service to begin.

We all took our seats in the beautifully ornate Catholic Church where wall to ceiling tapestries decorated the space and stunning stained glass windows created a mosaic of biblical imagery.

King and I were sitting in the front row, just the two of us with hundreds of pairs of eyes glaring into the back of my head, making me feel as though the target was on my back.

We waited patiently for Tatiana to grace us with her presence for one last goodbye as her coffin made its way down the aisle, carried by six of King's men, where she finally came to rest in front of us at the altar.

King had the decency to go all out with no expenses spared at this funeral. Tatiana's coffin, made from a quality oak with gold trim, was a spectacle in itself. There was an array of fragrant lilies placed on top of the casket and a matching theme presented throughout the open space of the Church.

King's twisted features stared at the coffin as though he could see straight through it, keeping his fingers interlaced with mine, but never looking in my direction. I wondered what he was thinking as the Priest began his speech.

"Today, my friends, we say goodbye to one of God's children."

The traditionally dressed Priest had a kind face and a soft voice that suited the role perfectly and the words he spoke did Tat justice.

Half way through the service, a sound of sobbing coming from directly behind us echoed around the open space. I couldn't ignore it and curiosity got the better of me as I peeked around to find Tatiana's mother in a drug infused state high on something King had provided her. But the pain she was suffering internally had forced its way through the artificial high, and my stomach was still aflame with hurt for her and for Tatiana. It was true that I cared little for the girl when she was alive, but nobody deserved this.

King's heated flesh encompassed around mine was making me sweaty and restless. What must everyone else in the room think about me? About us? If I'd had the balls, I would've said something to him, but as usual, I remained subdued.

The Priest came to his conclusion with a warm smile, and his hands clasped together.

"A close friend of Tatiana would now like to say a few words."

All eyes focused on the elegantly dressed woman in a fitted, knee length black dress. Hanna approached the microphone and tapped it with her finger as though she'd done this before, and with Hanna like confidence; she cleared her throat and took a deep steadying breath.

"I didn't know Tat for long, but what I did know was that many people loved her. Her best friend Alice asked me to help her say a few words, as the pain was too much for her to do this herself."

Hanna's harrowing words stabbed me like a knife and the realisation that it should've been me up there helping to support Alice was a bitter pill to swallow. She was right when she'd called me a selfish bitch, too consumed in my own life, as here I was, undecided between two men whilst breaking the hearts of two women as everyone else mourned the loss of their friend. What a piece of shit I'd become. I deserved to be with someone like King.

Hanna continued to voice Alice's words to the ears that listened intently where eventually the eulogy concluded with Hanna raising an imaginary glass to cheers Tatiana with the rest of the congregation. "Here's to Tat."

Hanna left the pew with nobility and made her way back to her seat next to Alice as the fair well music played.

"You may now rise," the Priest announced, concluding

the ceremony.

Like a herd of animals, the guests all departed at once.

King still hadn't released his grip on me as though he was holding onto me as life support.

"That was some heavy shit," he whispered.

When I looked at him in agreement, a stray tear fell from the corner of his eye. As soon as he felt it, he swiped it away, snapping back into character and regaining his composure as though nothing had happened. I doubted I'd ever see that from him again.

While the masses made to leave, they parted like the red sea when King led me up the centre of the aisle towards the exit of the Church building with a mission on his mind.

But as we travelled at speed, something caught my attention. It was a man, familiar to me with piercing, copper toned brown eyes who was glaring at me from the back of the room. Was he the cop who interviewed me? What was he doing here?

In plain clothes with tight features, he was out for blood and I suspected it was now mine he was after when his eyes followed my hand rested in Kings.

King tugged me forward to catch up to his speed.

"I want to take you somewhere," he said with an air of determination.

His crew of men followed behind us while I trotted beside him with a frown.

"You do?"

"Yeah, come with me now?"

It was a question, but one that had only one correct answer. King had a habit of keeping it rhetorical.

I shrugged, "sure, can I just speak to the girls first?"

I attempted to remove myself from his hold, but he gripped tighter.

"Plenty of time for that later. For now, you're comin' with me."

My knitted brow expressed my concern as I agreed in silence to follow the man I didn't trust to an undisclosed location.

There was a black Rolls Royce phantom waiting for us just outside the Church doors. King's foot was the first to step out into the open and immediately triggered strobing lights that attacked my eyes. Instinctively, I shielded my pupils with my hand. What was that?

Paparazzi clicked their imposing cameras one hundred times a second, shoving the lens directly in my face.

"Mr. Giannetti, do you have anything to say?"

"Yeah, I do. Fuck off." King wasn't a man to mince his

words, and with me following closely behind, he steamed through them all like a bowling ball.

I caught Hanna's scowl as she watched me walk hand in hand with King to our waiting chauffeur driven vehicle. When our eyes met, I smiled, but her beautiful features twisted into a look of contempt when she saw me, where she raised her middle finger and turned her back to comfort Alice.

The guilt I suffered knowing it should have been me consoling Alice was hard to live with, but I had no choice when under King's spell. There was no way out.

"You didn't really kick Hanna out, did you?" I asked King as we took our places on the extravagant leather seats of the Rolls Royce. No sooner had we taken a seat, than the driver set off to our destination.

"No why, do you want me to?" He cracked open his window and produced a cigar from his pocket.

"Absolutely not! I'm thrilled you didn't. Hanna is my best friend."

He blew out a plume of smoke, directing it out of the window.

"I figured as much. That's the only reason she's still at the crib. My abortion guy came over to the house last night and sorted her out."

What!?

"You have a guy who comes to the house to abort babies!?" I snapped at him with a tone that matched exactly how I was feeling. But this was not a safe space for me to share my emotions and I needed to rein myself in and the alarming idea his driver was in earshot of our entire conversation added an element of discomfort I couldn't ignore.

To my surprise, he didn't react the way I expected and the tonality of his voice was softer than usual.

"Whores be raw doggin' for more cash every damn day. Shit happens." He shrugged his shoulders, as if he was dismissing an internal struggle.

"Jesus Christ." I flung my hand up to my forehead and rubbed at the headache that was yet again forming. I only seemed to get migraines around King.

He threw the barely smoked Cuban out of the window. "This type of talk is ruinin' the vibe. Forget her and come here."

He reached over for me to sit in his lap, but sensed my hesitation when I looked at the driver. Reading my thoughts, he offered his version of reassurance, "don't sweat him, he doesn't listen, do you, Tommy?"

"No, Boss."

I rolled my eyes at the contradiction. King offered his hand again and this time I accepted, allowing him to pull me into his lap. There was so much room in the back of the car that I straddled him with space to spare.

"I don't know what it is about you Jasmin, I've asked myself a thousand times, but you get me all in knots and shit. You fuck me like your life depends on it and you're so fuckin' sexy it gets me hard all the time. When you're not with me, I jack off and come hard when I imagine you ridin' my dick."

My body responded instantly to the way he spoke about me and I loved primal talk like this. It was something Dan wasn't capable of. He didn't share King's edge.

The conversation suddenly changed direction as quickly as his temper when a troubling thought crossed his mind.

"Anyway, where were you last night?" His voice was low and hoarse, and the conflicting emotions emanating from him were substantial. His thumb skimmed my jaw as he pulled my lip from between my clenched teeth. It was inevitable he was going to ask me that question. After all, he'd given me money to buy something for him to fuck me in and I'd ditched without explanation.

He didn't wait long before he answered for me.

"You were at my brother's house, weren't you?"

My face displayed the horror that his words provoked and the blood drained from my skin, leaving me pale. I was dizzy.

How on earth did he know?

"That was the last time you'll see him. Got it?"

The continued lack of aggression emitting from him was disconcerting. I half expected there would be a silent attack at any moment with an axe or a meat clever.

I gulped past a hard lump in my throat. "Yes, Daddy."

"You're mine and I don't share. Did he let you meet his other bitch?"

King's confirmation that my nagging thoughts were correct made my head spin. Dan had a secret mistress, after all? He was no better than the rest of them. *Why can't men keep their dicks to themselves?*

My gut had told me there was another woman on the side, so why did I ignore it? At least with the way King operated, he laid it all out on the table. The good, the bad and the insane. He may crave to fuck any of the whores at any given time, but at least he was honest about it.

Dan is a liar and a cheat.

With new found knowledge on my side, I wanted to

please King again like my life depended on it. The memory of our fried chicken date back at the trap house roused an emotion inside me I welcomed with open arms.

I can't forgive Dan for doing this to me. He said he loved me.

I ran my hand through his tightly curled, glossy black hair.

"My pussy is so wet for you, Daddy."

I wasn't lying. I grabbed his curls between my fingers and leant in for a sensual kiss. He lifted yesterday's dress, revealing the new underwear set I'd purchased for King's pleasure.

"Shit! you little slut, I fuckin' love this."

Appreciating the way my breasts presented in my flattering bra made him grin. His ravenous hands gripped my ass to anchor my position.

"You like?" I asked with a dazzling grin.

"This is what I'm talking about. I need this."

He lowered down his pants and pulled out his thick erection. He masturbated for a moment while we kissed. God, I loved watching him play with himself. I rubbed my clit along his length as he stroked his cock. Now that it was just me and him, his presence made it so difficult to think about anybody else but the man in front of me.

Hanna, who had been at the forefront of my mind for so long, was now a distant whisper in my thoughts. Dan, who I'd agreed to be in a relationship with, turned out to be a lying cheater I couldn't stand to see again. As for Alice, well, she had Hanna to fight her corner now. None of them truly wanted me, anyway. Each of them using me to their advantage.

All I could think about now was King's massive cock filling my insides and repairing the damage that the people around me had created. He had let me down less than the rest. Despite him hitting me, King was there for me at my lowest and he'd provided me with a place to stay and food in my belly. Where were they when I needed them?

I was dripping wet when he reached in to touch my sensitive flesh, and when he raised the moistened tip of his finger to his mouth, he tasted me.

"Your pussy is better than drugs," he said as he licked off the salty moisture.

I couldn't wait any longer and made the move to push his dick inside me, impatiently in need of him claiming me so I was at least somebodies.

He held my ass cheeks firmly and spread them wide as he filled my core from root to tip. I got to work immediately, bouncing and grinding my hips on top of him as we consumed our heady reconnection. Sparks flew between us as the atoms collided. He freed one of my breasts and sucked on the nipple. It was so tender yet arousing, and I was greedy for more. My back arched in the hopes I could cajole him into sucking hungrier on the proud teat. He continued to nibble and suck on my breast as his dick massaged my insides. With King's expertise, I was guaranteed to come quickly.

"You're going to feel my come pour into your little cunt. I love nuttin' inside you," he groaned as his cock throbbed, hot and hard for me.

"Ahh, fuck!"

I came first, exploding around the swollen head of his penis like a detonated bomb and he followed shortly after, slamming my body down to meet with his upward thrust as he spilled his load heavy inside me.

Our foreheads crashed together as we breathed each other in. Sweating and panting, we attempted to draw in the limited air from the surrounding space.

After a minute, he pulled a tissue out of his pocket and wiped between my legs for me. I kissed him in appreciation of the gesture as I moved myself back over to my seat, feeling sated and satisfied.

Unintentionally, my eyes met with the driver's through the rear-view mirror. He had just seen quite a show but as was usual with all King's men; he kept his focus on the road ahead as if nothing had happened.

My orgasm induced haze dissipated and the burning question from earlier left my lips.

"So, where are you taking me?"

He tapped his finger on the side of his nose. "A surprise."

The playful side of King was something I could get used to.

A short drive later, we pulled up to an apartment building in the expensive part of town. The structure was set back, just off the seafront, where only celebrities and high fliers could afford the expensive price point. I guessed King fitted that remit.

I looked at him, confused by the lack of an explanation. *Why are we here?*

"Follow me," he said as he exited the car first.

Tommy opened my door for me and I followed King to the foyer of the very expansive architecture. The rental on one of the suites would have cost me more than a year of work could earn me.

The entrance way was stunning and in stark contrast

to any building I'd stepped foot inside before. Granite clad walls and floors gave the place opulence, fit for a king, and there he was now, walking just ahead of me, with a masculine aura about him that people admired and respected.

We headed straight for the gold plated lift doors with no need to visit the check-in desk. The double doors pinged open, and we climbed inside the carriage, just the two of us. I watched intently as he pushed a key into a slot in the wall and pressed the button for the penthouse on the control panel. This was going to be fancy.

As we rode the lift, our hands connected, and I peered up at him, but he remained indifferent. He twirled a ringed key round his pointer finger with a look of contemplation. What was he thinking? And why had he brought me to a penthouse, of all places?

The lift pinged to announce we had arrived out at our final destination, and the doors glided open with grace.

He opened the door of the apartment where we were immediately situated in the living area with a panoramic sea view ahead of us. It was a stunning sight.

The vast room itself lay bare. There wasn't a scrap of furniture within the four walls, but the open plan fitted kitchen was to die for.

Instinctively, I walked forward towards the window and peered out at the view. Buildings and trees paved the way for miles of skyline. I could spend hours by the window watching the sun rise and set. Such beauty had never blessed my eyes before.

"This is where we will raise our baby," he said as he closed the space between us. He enveloped his arms around my waist as we both drank in the scenery.

"Huh?" I looked at him completely dumb founded.

King wanted me to live in this palace? With him? I wasn't worthy.

The serious look in his eyes gave away the emotional turmoil he was attempting to quell.

"Listen Jasmin. I've seen and done some shit in my time. If I could change some of it, I probably would. Tatiana was a big fuckin' mistake. Had I got her off the drugs, she might still be here today. I regret how things ended with her, but it actually taught me somethin'. I wanna do it right with you. This place is ours. I bought it for us and it's where I will look after you and my boy. The hoes can still live at the house and the business will carry on, but I will spend as much time with you here as I can."

"Sorry, I'm struggling to understand what you're saying.

This is all so sudden."

"Nothing to be confused about. You belong to me now and I'm gonna make sure I look after you. Living here will keep you away from the drugs and shit back at the house. A perfect place to raise our family."

He wandered off for a moment, over to the kitchen, and returned holding a wrapped box with a bow on top.

"Here, open it."

Bemused, I took it from him and carefully peeled back the wrapping paper. I didn't know what I was expecting, but when I saw the contents, I swallowed hard.

My eyes met with his. "A gun?"

This wasn't my idea of a housewarming gift.

"What? You don't like it?"

"I mean. Yeah, I guess."

I tried to decipher my thoughts on his offering. A new purse would have been better.

King snatched the box out of my hand. "Well, don't fuckin' have it then!"

He burst into a fit of rage at my lack of enthusiasm for his gift. I rolled my eyes in frustration at his inability to control himself.

"I just wasn't expecting it, OK? Thank you!"

I snatched the box back from him and pulled out the gun

from the velvet lined interior. Cupped between my hands, I held it awkwardly, having no actual experience with firearms before.

His shoulders relaxed as he grappled with his internal struggle. "When I can't keep you safe; that will."

"This is too much for me to take in. I'm just a working girl."

He shook his head. "Not anymore. You don't need to do that shit now. I take care of what's mine."

Anxiety loomed in the pit of my stomach when an obvious thought reached the surface.

"But what if I'm not ready for something like this?"

"You're turning me down!?" His voiced raised too loudly again, and it made me jump almost out of my skin. But I stood my ground. I would not let him derail me this time.

"Well, for one, you scare the shit out of me, and the thought of living here alone with you is terrifying. And two, I worry that you're just doing this to piss off Dan."

My overconfident outburst took me completely by surprise, but it occurred to me in that moment, it was I who was holding the gun. The power that the black metal object provided me was striking.

My body automatically entered brace mode. If he hit me, I'd be ready.

"I scare the shit out of you?" He said quieter this time, hearing the words as if trying to decode them.

"No. Yes. A little."

I tried to soften the blow, but the anxiety we both emitted into the room was clouding even the clearest of skies.

He sat down on one of the cardboard moving boxes and absorbed the stunning view in front of us, where he rubbed his hands together as if to displace some of the anger raging inside of him. I cautiously took a seat next to him. There was a story inside him he was conjuring to the surface and I wanted to hear it.

"All that king shit is left at the door to this place. When I'm in here with you, like right now—I'm the real me."

The honest words he delivered provoked further questions.

"What are you saying?" I needed clarification. Had I not yet met the real him?

"Out there to everyone else, I'm the meanest fuckin' pimp America has ever known. I'll go down In the history books as the best. But when I'm in here, I'm a husband and a father."

Woah, hold on. "A husband?"

The Giannetti intensity ran strong through their veins.

Both brothers had the urgency to claim their prize and urinate on their belongings.

"We will get married before the baby is born, of course. I'm a Catholic man, gotta do it right."

King showing his devotion as a Catholic produced irony to the highest degree. I was in grave doubt the Bible mentioned pimps, drugs and hoes, but I'm sure he was about to prove me wrong.

"Daddy, we don't even know if I'm pregnant yet!"

Knowing that it wasn't possible for me to be pregnant left me with a guilty conscience. There was no way I could tell him I'd lied and that I was still on the pill. It didn't sit right with me to cause him anymore unnecessary pain.

"Maybe not yet, but if we keep fuckin' like we did in the Rolls, it won't be long.

I laughed in puzzlement at the surreal nature of the scene King was presenting me with.

"You haven't even proposed. Can't marry someone you aren't engaged to." I giggled at the idea of how crazy the conversation had turned.

I'd declared my love to his brother this morning. Now I was discussing marriage with King?

"Marry me."

Stunned for words, I opened my mouth, but sounds

failed to materialise. "Daddy—"

"None of that daddy shit here. That word is reserved for my son. Call me by my real name."

I froze, and at that moment, I couldn't even remember his name. *Why can't I recall?*

King, daddy and pimp were the only labels that came to mind. *Shit. What if he asks again?*

I needed to distract him before he noticed.

"This is a real head fuck," I exclaimed, overcome with dizziness. "I need to lie down."

"There's a mattress in the master bedroom, but the bed ain't built yet. Come with me."

He reached for my hand and I took his as we made our way to what would eventually be our bedroom.

The potential of the room was awe-inspiring. Blank now with beige walls and carpets, but there were so many ideas I had from being there for so little time. There were views out into the city from two sides through floor to ceiling wide panelled glass windows. I frowned at an idea relating to our privacy when King answered my unspoken question.

"There's a button here," he provided a demonstration as though he were the realtor.

One push of the button on the wall panel seamlessly frosted the glass on both sides. With his body pressed up against my back and his arms around my waist, he whispered into my ear. "When I'm balls deep in your pussy, we can do it in private or with an audience. It's up to you, Baby."

The feel of his skin in contact with mine made the hairs on the back of my neck stand on end.

"Well?" he asked.

"Well, what?"

Was he asking me if I liked the view? Or was he offering me to have a play with the privacy button? I hated his games.

"You haven't answered me. Are you gonna marry me or what?"

Holy shit, he's serious.

"Is that your best proposal?" I giggled, and when he thought for a second, he smiled back at me.

A small chuckle escaped his mouth, too. Not something I was used to hearing from him.

"Yeah, Shorty, that's the best you're gonna get from me. You've got until the end of the week to say yes. This type of shit makes me uncomfortable. The fact is, if you were any other hoe you would've said yes straight off and then sucked my dick. You're different, though, and it gets me hard. I love it."

We climbed onto the mattress together and King rested his arm over my stomach as we enjoyed the idyllic view ahead of us.

"I can make you happy," he said with a rhythmic movement of his thumb caressing my skin that provided more comfort than I could have imagined. Did I believe him?

What about Dan? The man that I thought was heaven sent and who treated me so respectfully but yet had been cheating on me the entire time.

Right now, in this room, the man I lay next to held the key to my heart. The delivery of his proposal needed work, but with what he could offer me, there wasn't a chance I could turn him down.

Life would be in the fast lane with him for sure, but it wasn't something I couldn't handle. King confirmed he wanted me, and I needed him. The baby making and marriage would come in time, but for right now in this moment, the man who I thought I loved initially was the man I was now opening my heart to. I felt scared to show my vulnerabilities to him, but I sensed he felt the same way, and his actions today displayed immense bravery, putting himself out there, allowing my admiration for him to grow beyond comprehension.

King took his hand gently to my face and turned me to make eye contact with him. He kissed me and I welcomed his tongue into my mouth as we showed each other with our bodies that we both meant business.

CHAPTER 13

Too hot. I couldn't breathe from the intense heat that radiated from inside my core like molten lava. Where am I? In hell? A figure stood before me, draped in a black cloak; a woman. She was sobbing. I tried to speak, but the words wouldn't form. The figure came into focus. Tatiana.

I shot up in bed with my breathing ragged. Confusion shrouded me in a veil of fear. Where was I again?

My surroundings came into focus, and I realised I was still in the apartment with King. He lay sleeping peacefully next to me with his arm rested over my stomach and the heat radiating from him was comparable to a furnace.

The black night sky with twinkling stars beyond the window pane informed me it was still early, but I felt so unsettled, not able to shake off my nightmare.

"What are you doin'?" King mumbled in a sleepy haze. His eyes were still closed, but he was aware I was fidgeting.

I stroked his arm to comfort him. "Nothing, go back to

sleep."

He mumbled something unintelligible, "I ain't sleepin'," and produced a soft snore from his flared nostrils. Just like that, he was out like a light again.

With a gentle manoeuvre, I unfolded myself from his grasp. A move similar to one I'd performed with Alice. *God, I hope she's OK.*

When I couldn't sleep, it usually meant I had something on my mind, and on this occasion, there was plenty going on in my head that I'd not brought to the surface and processed, and I needed to get out of bed and clear my head. With having slept in the nude, I shrugged on King's t-shirt that was way too big for me and made my way into the empty living room.

My cell phone was still on the countertop in the kitchen where I'd left it last night. Had Hanna messaged me or Alice? *No, nothing.*

The lack of communication from anyone left me with a strong sense of abandonment. I hadn't even received a scam email wanting my bank details. This was an all-time low.

After the time I'd spent with Dan yesterday, why hadn't he tried to communicate with me somehow? He wasn't yet aware I knew about his mistress, so he'd have no reason to hide from me. Was he too busy entertaining her with his tickling? Well, if that was the case, I hoped he'd tickled her to death, and he also died during the process. Not that I wanted to hear from him, anyway...

Once a cheater, always a cheater.

I stood in quiet contemplation with my phone in one hand and the other rested on my hip, staring out of the window, studying the peaceful view through the large panes. It was so tranquil out there at this time of night with just the sound of the waves crashing against the rocks filling the void of silence.

Why was I even thinking so deeply into other people's opinions of me when I was standing within the footprint of King's new apartment that he'd bought for me?

But my issue was that I did think deeply, and often. And my thoughts were like a runaway train focusing on the way I left things with Hanna and Alice. If I could just get Hanna to forgive me, I was sure Alice would follow suit. Hanna was always a night owl, so I figured calling her at two in the morning shouldn't be a problem for her. When I dialled her number, it went straight to voicemail.

Frustration prickled my skin, induced by my lack of control over the situation. With a heavy sigh, I tossed my phone down on the counter, resting my elbows on the hard surface where I cradled my head in my hands. There was a buildup of pressure behind my eyes as a few tears threatened to escape.

Why was I so emotional? Sure, a lot had happened recently, but I was stronger than this.

As I peered around the dark and empty space King had offered to me as my new home, I bit my bottom lip with overwhelming concern. There was a very slim chance that I would be happy alone in the apartment with him as my only source of company, but regardless of its beauty, wouldn't I feel lonely? Could I talk to King about my concerns? If I did, would he even listen? Maybe I'd have to broach the subject with him another time. He really did scare the shit out of me, so the timing would need to be perfect.

The back and forth in my mind between all of the main characters in my story continued to feed my migraine. I absent-mindedly span my phone around on the counter with my finger as I thought about my true best friend. The deeper part of my brain that didn't want to lose her replayed memories of us in happier times. We would spend hours in each other's company, laughing and joking. Now it was all gone.

It made me jump when King's hands rested on my shoulders, bringing me back to my reality.

"When I wake up and my woman isn't lyin' next to me, I get irritated. What's goin' on?"

I peered at him over my shoulder.

"You talking like that confirms what I said earlier about you scaring me."

He span me around to face him and in one swift move grabbed me by the waist and raised me up to sit on the counter.

"Does this scare you?" He asked as he parted my legs and nestled his head between my thighs.

His feather soft kisses on my clit had me like putty in the palm of his hand. I grabbed onto his hair and tugged as he licked my sensitive skin, his tongue worshipping my body in slow sensual circles of delight. His sensational skills brought fire to my core, taking me to the edge of the earth exploring uncharted territory. The soft stubble of his cheeks tickled my inner thighs as his mouth performed an act of intimacy that a man of his calibre shouldn't be able to provide.

"Say my name," he groaned, "let me hear you."

His name? *Shit!*

My body grew rigid as I fought between the cloudiness of my arousal and the clarity of his order.

Oh God. *He's so good at this.*

"Fuck," I whimpered as my body flinched against his continuous heady assault.

He growled as his tempo increased.

"When you come, I want to hear my name."

Oh. Oh—

"Oh, shit Romeo!" I exclaimed as he flicked his tongue against my clenching flesh.

His head rose from between my legs as he smiled.

"Romeo?"

"It just came out. I couldn't think straight," I smiled shyly. The plumpness of my cheeks turned pink.

"I like it," he nodded. "Am I Romeo and you're that sexy slut who sucked his dick?"

"Juliet? I don't remember oral sex in the play." I sniggered. "Besides, didn't they both die in the end?"

"We can be the new version with lots of head and no dyin'. I got too much livin' to do."

He reached around into the fruit bowl and grabbed a banana, and I watched him with interest as he unzipped the skin. He took a bite and looked at me. "You good now?"

I kicked my legs back-and-forth beneath me with my

hands clasped around the edge of the counter top. "It's been a really weird few days, but thank you for that little present. You're one hell of an athlete with your tongue."

I stroked his face, drinking in every inch of him when he took another chomp down on the exposed pale fruit with his eyes locked on mine. When he swallowed, he paused.

"Marry me."

His repeated order now carried much more weight, and his eyes glistened as his pupils dilated. This meant so much to him. Was there more to this than sibling rivalry?

My lips thinned, and I sighed. "Just let me think about it a little longer, please?"

"You're one frustratin' woman!" He rose to his feet, exasperated, and held his hand out for me to take. "Come back to bed," he commanded, pulling me down off the counter.

He tossed the banana peel into the trash can and grabbed an apple. Clenching it between his teeth, he scooped me up in a bridal style carry and walked with ease back to the bedroom. It was never a question with him; always a command.

King plonked me down on the bed.

"An apple too?" I asked, taking it from between the grip of his teeth, where I took a bite with a shy smile.

"What's mine is yours," he purred with a seductive grin, taking the fruit back for himself. "Snacks stop me smokin'. I don't like doin' that shit at this time of night."

To my surprise, I watched as he climbed into bed beside me, where he didn't initiate sex. I figured he might've wanted to finish himself off after eating me out on the kitchen island; but he didn't.

"Come here." He pulled me in towards his warm, inviting body and the tension I'd been feeling earlier now evaporated, but I couldn't help worrying about the intense position he had put me in. King and I knew nothing about each other and with no attempts by him to work on that, I needed to make the first move.

"Romeo?"

The room was dark, but I sensed him smiling at his newly adopted nickname. "Yeah?"

"I was thinking, we don't know much about each other, do we?"

King's hold on me stiffened as though he felt I was drifting from him.

"I know your cunt is sweet and my dick loves it. What more do I need to know?"

My brow furrowed. "You're basing your feelings for me by what your dick says?"

"Well, yeah. That's what all men do."

His penis responded, confirming his statement by growing against my back as a reminder it was there.

Wait. "Men really do that?"

I found it hard to believe that Dan operated in that way. He never once made me feel like his dick ruled his head. King—on the other hand—was a different breed.

"Yeah. We do."

His lack of interest in bringing something of use to the conversation was irritating.

"OK, I'll start I guess. Where are you from?"

"I'm from America and you're from London. See, we know everything we need to know about each other."

"Who said I was from London?"

Had one of his previous girlfriends been from the UK also? An unwelcome image of King fucking a whore on a Union Jack bed spread dampened my spirits.

"You did," he yawned. "I got shit to do in the mornin'. Go to sleep."

"Well, that's not what I said, but sure."

If I were a child, my arms would be folded over my chest and I'd be pouting. Why was I jealous of an ex girlfriend that probably didn't exist?

His chest inflated and deflated with a deep sigh. He knew

I was pissed off, and for some reason, he cared.

"Go on then, tell me where you're from."

Had the lights been on, he would have seen my grin spread from ear to ear and knowing that he wanted to please me meant more than anything.

"I'm from Manchester, England."

"Same as what I said."

"Not really." I rolled my eyes in the safety of darkness. "Where are your family from? I mean, I know you're American, but what's your heritage?"

"I'm Italian. My parents moved here from Italy when I was a kid. No more questions. Sleep."

"Oh OK. Night then."

When I awoke at a more sensible hour, the sun was shining through the window and I was more refreshed, with a clearer head. I still had no clue how I felt about King's persistent proposal, but that was the least of my worries for now.

"Morning," I called to the handsome chunk of hot stuff lay next to me.

He was awake but dozing, so I climbed out of bed in search of my clothes that I had tossed on the floor last night.

"Where you goin'?" He said gruffly, with his eyes still half shut. The morning erection he was sporting caused me a distraction.

"I have things I'd like to do today. I need to check on Alice and hopefully see Hanna. They will probably be at the house at this time, so do you wanna take me back now?"

"OK. I need a shit first. Give me ten minutes."

He hoisted himself into a seated position where the prominence of his hard on reminded me of a game of ring toss.

"That isn't part of the revised proposal plan, is it? Taking a shit instead of getting down on bended knee?" I called to his departing silhouette as I fastened the clasp of my bra.

He turned on his heels back towards me and swatted my backside. "You wish."

With a yelp at his playful assault, I giggled as he leant in to kiss my neck, where he brushed his fingers over the swell of my breasts. There were still no attempts to fuck me. I was growing impatient.

Twenty minutes later, we were in his car, heading back to the house and for the first time since I'd known him, King was driving with his entourage following close behind us. It was then I noticed they were in a black SUV.

Hmm.

We both sat in quiet contemplation for most of the journey home where King's playlist provided some lyrical entertainment through the sound system. Ironically, a lot of the songs he played described the pair of us. Pimps and hoes were a theme that he seemed keen on and the enjoyment was obvious in the nod of his head and the tap of his finger against the steering wheel in time to the beat. He reached for the volume button and turned it down.

"I didn't realise how much I needed some alone time, you know? Last night was my favourite night in ages." He reached over and squeezed my hand.

Wow!

"It was fun, thank you. I need to be honest, though. I'm not sure I can hack living in that apartment on my own."

"Let's just see how it goes."

He had a welcoming calmness that relaxed me instantly, and the way he allowed me to express my concerns was comforting. I couldn't argue with his fair approach. I would try it for him.

We pulled up outside the mansion and he parked effortlessly in a spot reserved just for him. Before we exited the car, King put his arm across me like a seat belt, stopping me from moving.

"Hold on, let me prep."

I frowned in confusion as to what he meant, but my question became answered when he raised his backside off the seat and reached into his waistband for his gun.

He inspected the bullet chamber to ensure it was fully loaded. My instincts had me leaning away from him, my back against the car door.

"Should I be worried?" I eyed the gun speculatively.

"I'm always expectin' someone is gonna pop a cap in my ass. You always gotta be prepared, Shorty."

"Ahh, there's the King I know."

I realised then that the version I appreciated back at the apartment was now gone.

"Don't get it twisted. When we're here, act correct. I can't have anyone thinkin' I've gone soft as it's my street cred keeps me alive. This game is dangerous, you hear me?"

His dilated pupils affirmed his words. He was deadly serious.

"Yeah, I understand."

"Good. Now kiss me and let's go."

With a sudden urge to stake my claim before the whores got their greedy hands on him, I wrapped my hand around the back of his head and pushed my tongue inside his mouth. Our kiss, filled with desire, heated my loins, and I yearned for him to fuck me so badly.

His breathing was uncoordinated. "If I didn't have shit to do, you'd be on my dick. Fuck, you drive me crazy."

With a salacious smile, I exited the Rolls and headed towards the house. But my smile soon turned into a scowl when I realised I was walking alone.

King's men had halted him along the way to update him on something he'd missed while we were at the apartment last night. Whatever they were talking about seemed important.

Now that King's alluring pull had weakened by our distance, my head cleared of the arousal induced fog allowing Alice to weight heavy on my conscience.

I peered down at our shared tattoo. A reminder of a happier time only a few days ago. How things can change in an instant. With new found conviction, I needed to find her and check she was OK after Tat's funeral. If Hanna was telling the truth and Alice was indeed in love with me, then I had a duty as her friend to talk to her about it. I treasured our friendship enough to round off the square edges.

As if by pure luck, Hanna and Alice were chatting in the kitchen, the most popular hangout spot in the house. When I entered the room, they both stopped talking.

Hanna slapped her hands down dramatically on the counter and hoisted herself off the stool where she made to leave, but I grabbed her by the arm.

"Please. Don't. I need to talk to you both."

The desperation in me was evident. I needed her to give me a chance.

She rolled her eyes and sighed, but did me the courtesy of sitting back down where she rested her restless hands in her lap.

"Hanna, firstly I want to say that you're my best friend and I need you back in my life. All this shit with King is a misunderstanding."

"A misunderstanding enough for you to spend the night away with him? Do you think we're all fucking stupid, Chloe?"

It made me furious she revealed my real name in front of Alice. She was playing dirty.

"Hanna, please, it's not like that!"

I knew I had no argument. It was exactly like that, and I had no plausible excuse.

"I wonder what your other *boyfriend* would make of this?"

The hatred she held inside herself for me was unprecedented. I was in shock at her low blow.

"You're being a bitch Hanna."

"I'm a bitch? *Me*? You're fucking delusional. Get the fuck away from me. You're dead to me." She stood up for a second time but followed through with her threat and stormed out of the room. Theatrics was always her strong suit, and that was a winning performance deserved of an encore.

"Fuck!" I yelled. It was cathartic.

Tears welled in my eyes again, and there was a burning pain in the back of my throat as I tried to suppress the flood.

Alice didn't say a word. She was so pale. The girl I knew had deserted.

"Alice, I'm sorry I wasn't there for you at the funeral, and I'm sorry I've been a shit friend to you."

"It's OK," she replied, staring into the distance.

"No, it's not. I should've been the one to help you with your speech for Tatiana—not Hanna. I'm so sorry, OK?"

My voice cracked when it dawned on me just how selfish I'd been.

Alice reached for my hand, that was scrunched by my side, and she unpeeled my fingers where she kissed my tattoo, nuzzling into my hand like a kitten to its mom, and I knew she was craving comfort. There was no way I was going to have sex with her, though. In my mind that ship had sailed, and I needed to draw a clear line in the sand when it came to our friendship. I pulled my hand away carefully and sat down next to her.

"Listen. I need to talk to you," I tread cautiously, aware of her delicate state. She didn't respond, so I carried on. "Hanna told me a few home truths. She said that you had feelings for me and that I'm a piece of shit. I agree with her. I have been a complete bitch and I need to make things right with you. You know I love you as a friend, don't you? I will always be here for you, but I want you to know that I can't be in a relationship with you."

"Is Dan the other boyfriend?" Alice asked, as if she hadn't heard a word I was saying.

I tried to remain indifferent. By now, lying was something I'd become accustomed to.

"No. Look, Hanna is talking crap to stir it up." I tried in vain to move past her exposing question. "Please, Alice, do you hear what I'm saying? I want to be friends with you so badly, but I need you to understand."

"I do, crystal clear."

"You understand that we are just friends?"

I felt the need to reiterate my point. Had she even listened to a word I'd said?

"Yep."

She straightened out her rumpled skirt laid atop her slim thighs, perfecting the flow of the fabric.

I paused for a moment, anticipating more from her, but she stayed silent.

"Phew. That's a load off my mind" I breathed out a heavy sigh. "Come here, give me a hug."

I pulled her towards me and we hugged briefly until she let go of me first.

"Do you mind giving me some space, Jas?"

It was obvious to an idiot that I'd hurt her.

"Sure. Whatever you need."

I turned back to face her at my exit out of the kitchen in the hopes she'd smile at me, but she hadn't acknowledged me leave, still so consumed by grief. I closed the door behind me, feeling so relieved that I had dealt with one mess. *One down, two to go.*

My phone buzzed in my pocket, interrupting my musing.

"Um, hello?"

What did King want so soon? I really wanted to find Hanna.

"Come up to the bedroom. Now." He hung up with no further explanation. Did this man think I had nothing more important to do with my day other than follow his every command? I exhaled with frustration, but did as I was told.

When I entered the bedroom, I was surprised to find that we had company, and I highly doubted sex would be on the cards. I was relieved. If I'd got caught in that web, I wouldn't be able to climb out of it until at least tomorrow. Hanna couldn't wait that long.

Two of King's men were in the room with us, heavily armed and on edge. They had their hands rested on holstered pistols by their waist bands.

King addressed me first. "Listen, word on the street is there's a bounty on my head."

I raised my hand to my mouth, instantly in shock.

"Oh God, really?"

"Doesn't get any realer than this, Baby. First things first, where's that gun I gave you?"

"Oh um, in my bag—I think?"

I needed to check that. Not that I was capable of using it.

"Keep that piece on you at all times. When you're in the bath, it's on the side of the tub. You're ridin' my dick; it's on the bed, and when you're playin' with your cunt, it's in your other hand." His piercing eyes glared into mine. "One of my best men will be shadowing you anyway to keep you safe, but If you need to shoot, you don't hesitate to pull the trigger. Got it?"

I nodded, swallowing past a hard lump in my throat. "Got it."

So what was I supposed to do now? I'd suddenly lost all my freedom and the unfinished business with Dan, AKA cheating tickler, was no closer to being resolved. What if I'd wanted closure?

"Are we all in danger, then?" I asked, with a knot in my stomach. I sounded more feeble than I intended, but the thought that we were guilty by association was a terrifying consideration.

"Probably not, but word will be out by now that you're my girl after the fuckin' paparazzi at the funeral yesterday. I will do what it takes to keep you alive."

My throat swelled further. "What about the other girls?"

"I don't really give a shit about them and I doubt the guy huntin' my head will, either. A hoe or two might get caught up in the crossfire, but it is what it is."

He loaded up several guns laid out on the bed, pushing the bullets into the chambers and slotting in the magazines.

"We'll stay here at the house for a while. King don't run from anybody. I ain't no pussy bitch. Am I right, boys?"

He looked at his men for approval, and they nodded in response.

"Um, what should I do about clients?" I asked nervously.

His shoulders rose with immediate agitation.

"The agency better not be bookin' you out?"

"No, they haven't been but—"

"Good," he nodded. "I told them you're off the books now."

"Oh. Would've been nice to tell me that."

Oops.

King raised a finger in the air, halting everyone's breathing.

"Leave us alone a minute." His voice was abruptly menacing.

The men left quickly and shut the door behind them. King had that effect on everyone.

"Don't fuckin' speak to me like that in front of anybody!" He whispered through gritted teeth. "Play along with what I'm about to do."

I winced, expecting to be hit in the face.

"You fuckin' cunt, don't you dare disrespect me!" He yelled for the benefit the men listening on the other side of the door.

He hit the wall hard for effect, as if he was hitting me.

"Sorry Daddy." My voice cracked and my bottom lip quivered.

King leant in to my ear, "I mean it, woman, keep yourself in check when we are with other people. I fuckin' love your attitude when we're fuckin', but not in front of my men, who I control through fear. Got it?"

"I'm sorry."

He visibly relaxed when he saw my unravelling. I saw in his eyes that he was trying to keep himself calm for my benefit.

"Leave the room holding your face and don't say anythin' to anyone." He cupped my shoulders and kissed my lips. "And don't tell the whores about the bounty. Mine and your lives depend on them not knowin' we're expecting trouble."

"Got it." I kissed him in return.

Our latest interaction was the polar opposite of our time at the apartment. I left the room with haste and ran down the stairs as instructed with my best high school drama face on making it believable that he'd just hit me. Not that there was anyone around to witness it. Unusually, the ground floor of the house was empty. *Where is everyone?*

There was a tall, bulky man with a bald head waiting at the bottom of the stairs for me and I recognised him as the driver of the car at Tat's funeral. His eyes locked with mine and he nodded his head in acknowledgement of my arrival.

"Hi Boss, I'm Tommy. I'll keep a watch out for you."

He lifted his shirt to reveal a gun stashed in its holder.

"I'm Jasmin." I reached out my hand for him to shake. "So you're going to follow me around? Like all the time?"

"Sorry, Ma'am, no touching, but yeah, I'll be following you. Don't worry, you won't know I'm there. Just go about your business as normal."

The expression on Tommy's face dropped when he saw my less than enthusiastic response to King's protection detail.

"Was it you that was following me the other day while I was out shopping with Alice?"

"No, Ma'am."

Tommy pointed his gaze towards the ground, confirming the opposite.

We spent that afternoon filling time watching rubbish on the TV. King was busy doing something in his bedroom that I wasn't allowed to take part in, and I was bored and lonely.

Tommy kept himself busy on his phone at the opposite end of the living room to where I sat, and the only sound in the vast room came from the television show I wasn't paying attention to. There hadn't been a single whore in the house all day, which I found odd, but Tommy assured me it was normal for this time of year.

"Tommy?"

"Yes, Boss?"

He immediately placed his phone in his lap and hung on my every word. The power I had inherited through my relationship with King was alarming.

"I'm bored. Do you have any recommendations?"

"Boss told me to keep you here at the house. So, the gym?"

I screwed up my nose in response. "Ugh, no, I hate the gym!"

A ludicrous suggestion.

"Shit, I dunno then."

Tommy seemed alarmed at his own lack of creativity.

"Ooh, I know! Let's bake a cake!"

The sudden sense of excitement within me made me shriek. It had been so long since I'd had chance to do some baking and the thought of giving it to King as a present gave me butterflies.

"What do you mean by *we?* I ain't making no cake, Boss."

"Follow me, Tommy. I'm excited about this."

I led the way into the kitchen, sensing that he really didn't want to accompany me, but he had orders to follow.

With a clatter and bang through the cupboards, I looked for my ingredients and eventually found everything I needed, apart from a mixing bowl on the top shelf in the store room.

"Tommy, can you grab that bowl for me, please? It's too high for me to reach."

He cleared his throat as though something had lodged there that he couldn't rid of and with thinned lips, he passed me the bowl and took his military style rested position a few feet away from me.

I placed my carefully weighed butter and four eggs into my bowl and plugged in the electric whisk. Of course, it was a fancy contraption with copious buttons that I'd no clue of their operational use. With a hazarded guess, I pressed the biggest button available, and the blades sprung to life, flicking the contents of the bowl all over my face. The raw egg blinded me.

"Shit Tommy, help!" I called out in blind panic with my eyes screwed shut.

I felt Tommy's hands on mine before I saw him. He wrestled the machine out of my hold and brought it to a standstill.

In a thoughtful gesture, he passed me a towel, and when I wiped my face, our eyes met and we both burst into a fit of laughter at the chaos I'd created. He was just as covered in butter and egg as I was.

The atmosphere changed in an instant when the door nearly ripped off its hinges as King stormed into the room.

"Have I missed somethin' here? You been fuckin' my girl, Tommy?"

Tommy blanched, his skin paled as white as a sheet.

"No Boss. Nothing like that."

"It's OK Romeo, he just rescued me from this out-of-control whisk."

I raised up the offending item so he could slot together the missing pieces.

"Looks to me like you were doin' some kinky shit with butter. You got butter on your dick, Tommy? Did she suck it off for you?"

"No Boss. I swear."

He didn't need to look at Tommy with his next order. He kept his glare fixed on me. "I need a word with Jasmin. In private."

Had I overstepped the mark? I just wanted to make a

cake.

Tommy closed the door behind him, and King descended upon me.

"What the fuck are you doin'? I leave you with my best home boy for five minutes and you're suckin' his dick?"

"That's not what I was doing. I was making a cake for you."

King's eyes softened when he'd taken a moment to think rationally. "You were makin' *me* a cake?"

"Well, I was trying to until I fucked it up."

A nervous giggle escaped my mouth as I looked at the mess I'd made. I wasn't trying to piss him off, but I had the uncanny ability to do it often.

"I don't think anyone ever made me a cake before."

There was an edge to his tone that was almost innocent and I'd unwittingly exposed a side of him he kept hidden at all costs.

"Do you want to make it together now?"

"Nah, I'll fuck you first and then you can make me the cake."

Verbal consent wasn't on his mind when he bent me over the counter top and drove his erection between my labial folds and inside my vagina from behind. I got the feeling this was his way of staking his claim over me instead of the traditional declaration of love.

"I gotta nut in you every God damn minute to keep men off you. They ain't havin' what's mine."

His penis stretched me open and stroked my sensitive internal flesh as I received him gladly. Since we shared a bed last night and he hadn't attempted to fuck me, my body had been longing for this contact. He slapped my ass, leaving a red imprint behind.

"Don't make me jealous again, I mean it. I don't want to be mad at you all the time."

"I won't, I promise." I panted, "take me Romeo please."

With one last thrust, he pumped his semen inside me while pulling my body towards him, giving me everything he had.

"Keep that fuckin' nut in there. Let it drip out. I don't care as long as everyone knows who you belong to. You ain't got my ring on your finger yet, so this will have to do."

I put both arms around his neck and drew him into my hold. "Shall I make Sir's cake now?" I asked with a smirk.

King nodded with a hint of excitement.

I clasped my hands together, "right, come on then, you can help me. Get me some flour, eggs and more butter."

To my surprise, King sprung to action and searched the kitchen for the ingredients I'd requested. I got the feeling he'd never stepped foot behind the counter before.

"Where are the eggs kept?" He asked as he opened the door to the microwave.

"You won't find them in there, Champ," I giggled. "Try the fridge."

"Shit, where's that?" The confused look on his face was concerning.

As I weighed out the butter, I lifted my chin to point behind him, "behind that cupboard door."

"Why is it hidden like that?" he growled, slamming doors. "You can't find shit in this place."

"This is your kitchen Romeo, ask yourself that."

I smirked at him, and he offered a tight smile back. He was no longer having fun.

I wiped the hair from my eyes with my arm.

"How about you take a seat and pour yourself a drink? I'll take care of this."

He hummed in appreciation. "That's why I'm gonna marry you. Look at my dick." He gestured towards the sudden tent he was pitching in his shorts. "My dick has always been hard, but when it's around you, it just doesn't stop."

My cheeks reddened at his compliment, always making me blush.

I'd just begun pouring out the mixed ingredients into a baking pan when a flurry of activity arrived at the threshold of the kitchen. Several of the whores were back from their appointments, and Michelle was in the lead.

"Daddy," she announced into the room for all to hear, "I've made you proud today."

She slithered into the centre of the room and draped her flabby arms around his neck, kissing his cheek.

My grip tightened on the wooden mixing spoon I was holding and every part of me wanted to hit her round the head with it, but I refrained.

He addressed all the whores as one.

"Nice work bitches. Come, show me my money in the living room."

As he was leaving, a thought crossed his mind that showed on his face. He turned on his heels back towards me.

"I can't wait for this cake," he whispered. "Bring me a slice later."

Just like that, I came crashing back down to reality with a thud, and now it was just me and Tommy alone again.

Our eyes made contact, and he gave me a look of understanding at my sudden bereavement as the demon inside me tore open the box and was now in my head rent free, causing chaos.

"Don't overthink it, Boss," Tommy said, reading my internal struggle.

"Too late."

I forced myself to continue with my task and placed the cake mixture into the oven and set the timer. An idea of placing King's head in there instead was tempting.

Once it was ready, I left it on the side to cool and took myself to bed, feeling deflated, hurt and everything in between.

Sounds emitting from the living room forced my pause at the foot of the stairs, when I heard laughing. King was having the time of his life with his whores and I wondered how many of them he'd already had sex with this evening. Is this the life I'd hoped for? Absolutely not. I was not the sharing type just as much as he wasn't, but the only difference being I stuck to my end of the deal.

The marriage proposal suddenly felt stupid. Why would I knowingly agree to marry a pimp? I shook my head at my idiocy and climbed the stairs to wallow in self pity under the duvet.

Relief washed over me when I opened the bedroom door to find the room was empty. I figured Alice must have been amongst the crowd that was entertaining King downstairs. I rolled my eyes at the painful image etched into my mind.

With a powerful urge to turn murderous, I peeled off my clothes and threw myself onto the bed. Sleep was the only cure for this headache.

CHAPTER 14

Several bangs and an enormous crash the next morning woke me from the dream I was having.

When my eyelids parted, King was the first image I saw, pacing around the room dressed in sweats and clutching a silver-plated pistol in his hand.

"What's wrong?" I asked, rubbing my sockets to rid of the sleepy haze.

"Just tense with all this shit. I took a pill and now I'm wired."

I propped myself up on my elbows to get a better view of him where, instantly, I needed to know more.

"Oh? What pill did you take?"

The thought crossed my mind that it might've been one of his mystery pills from the bathroom cabinet. *Benzo something?*

"Dunno," he shrugged, swiping the tip of his nose, "a whore gave 'em to me."

Oh, we were there again. The ever present threat of a whore being brought into the equation was always just around the corner. He likely kept one waiting under the bed to entertain himself with when he got bored with me. In fact, while I was sleeping, he probably fucked a couple of them at the foot of the bed.

The anguish must have been radiating from me without me realising. He came to sit beside me, eyeing me suspiciously.

"What's up with you?"

I shied away from his glare, as his proximity always had the potential to intimidate me.

"Um, nothing."

"I ain't dumb. Spit it."

He placed the gun down on the bedside table next to my phone, which relaxed me instantly. Was he worried he might pull the trigger if I pissed him off again?

"I guess it's just the whores, that's all."

My palms grew sweaty in response to my elevated heart rate as I dared to expose my concerns. Last night's living room giggling gala he shared with them still played on my mind.

Clear now that he wasn't paying much attention, his eyes burned bright with desire as he stole a glance at my cleavage, hooking his finger over the blanket to inspect closer.

"What's your problem with the whores then?" he mumbled.

I turned my head away from him, feeling defenceless and needy. "Doesn't matter."

He looked at my breasts again, but this time had the decency to keep his hands to himself.

"You know they're part of the package, right? The bitches are half of my business."

Oh.

That was not the answer I wanted to hear. In my mind, I wanted him to declare his love for me, perhaps playing one of those small guitars where he would declare to me via sonnet that if I wanted them gone, he would see to it in a heartbeat. The more I thought about his actual response, the harder I needed to vomit.

King didn't notice my internal struggle when he took the corner of the blanket and peeled it off my skin, revealing my naked body underneath.

"Look at that shit!" He licked his lips. "I wanna take my dick out and pump my load on your big tiddies."

Footsteps on the landing, followed by a welcome knock on the door, interrupted King from his futile mission.

"What!?" He yelled to the poor unidentified soul on the

other side.

When the door opened with caution, Snake stood in the frame. With wary eyes and a pale complexion, he seemed more than flustered.

"Sorry to interrupt, Boss, but when would you like to leave?"

King threw his arm out in front of him to scrutinise the dial of his diamond encrusted watch.

"Give me fifteen minutes. I have some business to attend to with Jasmin."

Business? With me? Hah!

If King thought I was in the mood after the way he made me feel last night, he had another thing coming.

"Right Boss sure, but it's just—"

King snarled like a dog. "It's just what?"

I knew his aggression was because of the threatening release waiting impatiently at the tip of his penis, but did he have to shout at everyone all the time?

"Well, Boss," Snake cleared his throat, "It's just that Tommy said now was a good time. You know, with our situation and all."

"Fuck!" King exclaimed, flailing his arms as though he didn't know what to do with himself.

He reached over me to collect his gun from the bedside

table and holstered it inside his waistband, where he rose to his feet and stared at me. "Get up Jasmin, you're comin' too. Bring that gun I gave you."

Meeting His Royal Highness's expectations, I dressed myself and brushed my teeth in less than five minutes. My outfit of choice was a simple pair of black leggings and a cropped t-shirt and I finished the look with my white sneakers. After having no idea where we were going or what we were doing, it seemed like the safest choice.

Downstairs in the grand hallway and by the front door, we were all gathered around Tommy, who was giving the team a briefing. As Tommy spoke about the rules and regulations of the secret trip, King handed me a rough textured grey blanket.

"Here, put this over your head."

Without understanding, I took the blanket and looked at him quizzically, hoping for more information.

"We're hidin' from anybody that might be watchin'. All it takes is for someone with a drone to spot me and I'm sniped, so we hide our identity when we leave the house. Got it?"

I nodded my head.

"Let me hear it."

"Yes Romeo, I got it."

He turned his attention back to Tommy who, like a flight attendant was demonstrating a piece of equipment I'd no idea of its use, and I pulled the blanket over me as instructed, propping open the section around my face so I could see where I was going.

Snake opened the front door with a stern look. "Follow me," he commanded with his hand hovering behind me as he ushered me into the back of the black SUV that idled by the entrance.

My backside instantly sweated between the lycra of my leggings against the heat of the leather as I waited with restless sensations in my stomach for King to climb inside the back of the van with me. He seemed to take a lot longer than I did.

Eventually, he dived in and the door slid closed behind him, where he pulled a similar blanket off his head and tossed it in the footwell. His intentionally tousled curls were unscathed by the scratchy fabric.

I smiled at his handsome face when he looked at me.

"Um, so are you going to tell me where we're going yet?"

He looked out of the window, watching the van manoeuvre around his expensive cars within the driveway.

"Shootin' range. Figured you needed some practice."

"What?" I gulped, "Oh, jeez."

Suddenly I needed an in flight sick bag. There wasn't a single other thought I could have conjured up that would have been worse than this.

He turned to face me with a pensive look. "Is there a problem with the shootin' range?"

"No. No problem."

He produced a cigar from his jacket pocket where his dextrous fingers rolled it around to prepare the contents for the heat of the flame.

I watched as flakes of tobacco fell from the end like crumbs of a cookie.

"Tell your face that, then. I'm doin' this to protect your ass. Did you bring your gun?"

Fuck.

My widened eyelids almost allowed for the eyeballs to escape. "Shit. I'm sorry, I was rushing."

As his lips tightened like a butt hole, his fingers gripped the brown cylinder, until he placed it between his teeth.

"You're lucky I ate a slice of that cake you made this mornin'. That shit put me in a good mood."

"Aww," I beamed, "you ate some? Did you like it?"

Hope filled my voice that perhaps he did like me more

than the other girls, after all. Did he smile when he took the first bite? God, I wished I'd been there to see.

He patted the seat next to him, inviting me to sit closer.

"Yeah, was real good."

With a triumphant grin, I did as I was told and scooted over, where he draped his arm around my shoulder. He took a deep inhale of his cigar and blew the by-product out of the window.

"So you gonna marry me yet?" He asked on the exhale.

Confused, I looked up at him through my lashes.

"But you said I had until the end of the week?"

"I was hopin' you'd decided by now. You either wanna or you don't."

Did I want to, or not? Last night I'd made my mind up that I didn't want this life with King, but here I was with his arm around me. Realistically my options were to either choose Dan, who was a secret cheater—the worst kind—Or, I could choose King, who cheated, but out in the open with no qualms and nothing to hide.

But what about Alice? Hmm, Alice who? With the way Hanna had driven a wedge between us, choosing her friendship wasn't an option either.

As I mused, the sudden notion occurred to me that perhaps I didn't have a choice in this, anyway. King, a man who never accepted the word 'no', wasn't suddenly going to do so now, was he? Had he already made the decision for us, or would he allow me to walk away from him if that was what I wanted?

My throat closed up at the prospect I might be trapped within his kingdom.

"How far to the shooting range?" I croaked in need of a glass of water.

"Just a couple minutes. You good?" He eyed me suspiciously. "You look sick."

My body was in self-destruct mode and at that moment, I wanted to slide open the door of the moving vehicle and dive out where death would have been a welcome outcome.

"I'm fine, thanks. Just nervous about shooting."

My fidgeting, clammy hands intertwined in my lap as I imagined me—of all people—firing a gun I'd no idea how to use.

"I figured as much. You have to get used to pullin' the trigger. A bullet in the head doesn't give second chances. Ain't that right Tommy?"

"Yes, Boss!"

As usual, Tommy was our chosen driver, who took the role seriously. Reminding me of a cop in his sunglasses, short-sleeved white shirt and bullet proof-vest, he played a professional part.

A short drive later, our vehicle stopped in the middle of nowhere, where tall trees spanned for miles.

Tommy and the rest of the team scoped the area with their weapons drawn first before they allowed King and me to exit.

My legs jiggled with unspent adrenaline while we waited for the all clear. It was way too early in the morning for so much anxiety. Why didn't I eat breakfast?

The door eventually slid open, and King took my hand in his. "Let's go."

We arrived at a picturesque, secluded woodland area where there wasn't a building or structure in sight for miles around.

"It's beautiful here." I said, in awe of the natural landscape. Under different circumstances, it would have been romantic.

King wasted no time in handing me a small silver handgun.

"Here. Take this."

Heavier than I expected; it differed from the gun he'd gifted me at the apartment, and I held it as though it was a purse, unaware of the correct gun holding etiquette.

"Shit, woman, not like that!" He gesticulated. "Grip it hard like it's my dick. Don't flail it around!"

He came round behind me and placed his hands on top of mine and with his arms as the guide; he raised them as he aimed the gun into the distance. His growing erection with radiating heat was a distraction, with its firm composition digging into my back. But he ignored it. This was more important to him.

"Aight listen, imagine the target is your worst enemy. Aim for the centre of the head and pull, but remember to prepare for the recoil. On a gun like this, it won't kick back much, but keep your stance strong. Bury your feet into the ground."

I screwed my nose up at his words and looked down at my white sneakers.

"I need to dig a hole before I shoot someone?"

That part was never in the films.

King, Tommy and Snake broke into a fit of laughter.

"I told you she was hilarious, boys. Shit, that got me."

He continued to belly laugh, holding his stomach. It was as though Dan was attacking him in one of his tickle fests.

"No, Jasmin," he said finally, "you don't dig a hole before they're dead. Do that after when you're burying the body."

My mouth dropped open. This was getting way more

complicated than I wanted it to be.

"I don't need to do that today, do I? It's a little warm for shovelling dirt."

Abruptly, the laughter stopped, and his body grew rigid with agitation.

"Stop makin' this more difficult than it needs to be. Follow me and we'll do some shootin'"

We arrived at a clearing a brief walk down a narrow path where Snake had taken the initiative to line up some targets for me to practice my aim by placing ten weighted cardboard mannequins two strides apart in a row across our line of sight.

King stepped up first and cocked his gun, where the sound of metal sliding against itself chilled my skin against the warmth of the sun. He placed his feet shoulder width apart and held out his gun in front of him.

A moment later, he fired three shots, one after another.

The reverberation shook the air, sending birds erupting from their nests in a frenzy, their departure leaving the glade draped in an uneasy silence.

"Nice work, Boss!" Tommy called as he walked over to the mannequin. "Head, chest and crotch."

My eyes darted from the mannequin to King and back

again. Was he expecting me to do that?

"Your turn. Come on." King coaxed me over to stand by the side of him.

My trembling hands clasped around the gun, but the sweat on my palms made my grip feel loose. I attempted to copy the stance King had taken. Feet shoulder width apart, gun stretched out in front.

"I'll help you with the first shot." He said with excitement as he came around behind me again.

With his warm breath against my ear, I screwed my eyes shut when I felt his finger resting over mine on the trigger. He pressed down, and I shot the first bullet.

"Nice work," he said when he saw the bullet had pierced a hole through the cardboard head. "Do the next one on your own."

I took a deep, steadying breath and held out the gun again, but the adrenaline coursing through my veins made it impossible to keep my aim steady. I closed my eyes again and pulled the trigger.

There was a moment of silence until there wasn't.

"Fuck! Shit!" King called out in alarm. When I opened my eyes, Snake was on the ground.

Oh my God, have I killed him?

King ran over to Snake's limp body. "You stupid fuckin'

whore! Shit!"

Tears pricked my eyes, and I sobbed at the chaos I'd created within a scenario I didn't even want to be involved in. I blanched when King stormed back towards me.

"What the fuck is wrong with you? Snake is part of our protection detail. Without him I'm dead!"

"I'm sorry. It was an accident."

The tears continued to fall, and I dropped the gun on the ground.

"Pick that up," he snarled, "and hand it to me. Now!"

Like an errant child, his command left me reeling, but with a dry gulp, I did what he asked and handed him the offending weapon, where he snatched it.

"Get in the van and wait there until I'm done here. You stupid fuckin' bitch. Shit!"

I sat in the SUV with my hands knotted in my lap. This was bad. *Really bad.*

An eternity condensed into minutes when suddenly a fresh van pulled up to the clearing and two fully black clothed men exited in a rush like a SWAT team. No sooner had they arrived than Snake—who was wincing—was being stretchered into the back of the vehicle, where I assumed he was being whisked off to the hospital.

I felt so damn guilty about what had happened, but King had asked so much more of me than I was capable. The fact that he'd gotten so mad at me was justified, but speaking to me like he did was unforgivable. No matter how hard he tried to be a nice person, the bottom line was that he just wasn't.

Dan wouldn't have yelled at me like that. In fact, Dan wouldn't have put me in that position in the first place.

The SUV door slid open and Mr. Angry climbed inside, slamming it closed behind him where he was still raging beyond comprehension. Tommy clambered into the front seat, and we set off back to the reality of the mansion.

Other than the radio playing quietly in the background, not another sound could be heard from within the cabin, apart from King's heavy breathing.

Finally, he pulled out a cigar from inside his jacket pocket and lit it with haste, where plumes of smoke filled the space, making me splutter.

His inherent decency surprised me when he cracked open the window upon seeing my reaction.

"What you did back there could have given me a death sentence. You do get that?"

I sensed his glare, but I couldn't look him in the eye.

"Yes. I'm sorry. It was an accident."

"Who closes their fuckin' eyes when they shoot? Dumb slut man."

With a slug to the gut, air evacuated my lungs. "Don't speak to me like that!"

I immediately snapped my mouth closed when the reality of what I'd just said hit me.

Am I insane?

King inserted almost the entire length of the cigar into his mouth, as though it had the power to prevent him from doing something terrible to me. He sucked on it harshly enough that it hollowed his cheeks as a bead of sweat formed on his brow while his internal fury consumed his entire body.

"Suck my dick now!"

His aggressive command sent chills down my spine when he pulled his erection out of his pants, impatiently waiting for my response.

I collected my hair in one hand and threw it over my shoulder and with not a hint of hesitation; I leant in to receive his firm length, pushing it between my lips into the heat of my mouth. The hot tip had just made contact with the back of my throat when King's hand encased the crown of my head and forced his entire penis into my gullet.

Naturally, I gagged at the assault, as he was too big to take him all the way without warming up to the idea first and he knew it.

"You're gonna take every inch, you stupid whore."

He gritted his teeth and tensed his jaw as he continued pushing himself against me.

My head bobbed up and down to his rhythm and his hips thrust upward with my downward movement, deepening the relentless invasion.

Thankful that I had some luck on my side, it didn't take him long to come and the warm liquid fired to the back of my throat, where I instinctively swallowed, even though I resented the fact.

Once he'd ridden out his climax, he released my head, allowing me to retake my seat at the opposite end of the rear cabin where I sat as far away from him as the space allowed. King put himself away and continued to smoke his cigar, looking out of the window in deep thought.

We remained silent for the rest of the ride home, and all I wanted to do was cry, but I stemmed the flow. I didn't want to give him anymore satisfaction.

I'd not seen or heard anything from King all afternoon and it wasn't until the evening when he gathered all the whores together in the living room to make an announcement that I laid eyes on him again.

My inclusion was a relief, but when both Hanna and Alice did everything in their power to ignore me, my heart broke further still.

"As you all know, Snake took a bullet today." King glared at me. "It was friendly fire. But as we're a man down, I want you all in your own rooms tonight. No fuckin' about. My men can't keep you safe if they don't know where you are. Got it?" He paused for a beat. "Now fuck off."

The group dispersed at his order, like aerosol out of a can, but I stood stock still to watch his next move.

Will he smile at me? Nod at me? Anything?

But with one last scowl in my direction, he left the room.

Hanna and Alice were stuck to each other like shit to a blanket and as they too left the room with their arms interlocked, they acted like I didn't exist to either of them.

How could there be so many people in the mansion that didn't like me? I was beginning to not even like myself.

With a heavy heart, I kept my head down and left for the safety of the confines of the bedroom, feeling the same hollow pit in my stomach that never seemed to abate in King's castle.

When I made it to the bedroom door, the light was already on, which could only mean someone was already occupying the space. As the door creaked open, announcing my entrance to the occupant, he looked at me.

"What are you doin'?" King asked with contempt as he paced around the bed that was strewn with guns.

He looked to be alone, but I could have sworn I heard someone in the bathroom.

I peered towards the sound of the running shower.

"Um, I was coming to bed?"

"Nah," he curled his lip, "I told you, no whores in here. You got your own room."

My heart nearly stopped. First, he shouts at me and then I'm just another whore?

"Oh, sorry."

He filled his lungs with air like an inflated balloon, as if he wanted to reel off all the ways he wanted to kill me, but he let the oxygen escape again.

"Just until Snake is back," he calmed his tone. "If I'm assassinated in my sleep, I don't want you gettin' a bullet, too."

The sentiment behind the idea was almost sweet, but I sensed the real reason was more to do with the fact that he just couldn't bear to be around me any longer.

"Um, well, you never gave me my own room before, so where should I go?"

The distress consuming me was apparent in my body language as I fidgeted, and I simply couldn't hide it, not that he noticed as he was busy counting bullets.

"Ask Tommy. He's still assigned to you. Step now, I got shit to do."

I closed the door behind me as though I was closing the book on our relationship to find Tommy hovering down the hall where the look on his face told me he'd listened to mine and King's conversation.

"Follow me, Boss."

I'd never actually been past King's bedroom before on the second floor of the mansion. There were at least eight bedroom doors I'd walked by before Tommy halted us at the door that would allow entrance to my room.

I placed my hand on the handle when a thought occurred to me. "I don't have to share, right?"

Tommy rocked on his heels with discomfort at engaging in conversation with me.

"What do you mean?"

"When I moved here, King said there were no spare

rooms, so I wanted to check I'm not sharing with anyone?"

His lips thinned as he checked his watch. "Women come and go in this place. All I know is this room is free. I'll be sitting right out here if you need me."

I glanced at what I suspected to be Tommy's sleeping arrangement, which comprised a small wooden three-legged stool and a pillow with no pillow case.

"But where will you sleep?"

"Don't worry about me Boss, I got a military background so I can sleep on a washing line. I'll pop a squat right here and take a few minutes when I need to."

"Really?" I frowned. "I mean, you could always sleep on my floor?"

A little company right now wouldn't have gone a miss. But we weren't on the same page when Tommy gave me a death stare, followed by ample squirming.

"We've already got one man down. We don't need me laid out, too."

Jeez, don't remind me.

I doubted I'd ever be able to look Snake in the eye again after my idiocy at the shooting range.

"Is Snake going to be OK?"

Tommy opened the door to my bedroom, ushering me

inside. "Go in. You never know who's listening in this place."

I got the feeling he was referring to King over anyone else, but even the whores played games of their own.

"I've seen Snake take way worse than a bullet to the leg. He'll be fine don't sweat it."

Curiosity suddenly got the better of me and I took my chance, sensing that Tommy's vulnerability was making him more chatty than usual.

"Why do you guys call him Snake?"

Tommy looked behind him as though he was expecting King and his axe. He seemingly had that effect on everyone.

When he saw the coast was clear, he sighed.

"Listen, I'm only talking to you because I know you won't stop until I answer. If I tell you this, can you please stop asking me questions?"

I nodded eagerly. "Yeah, sure."

"OK, well, at the time we were serving in Afghanistan together. One particular day we were on a stakeout and he was the shooter, got the best aim I ever saw. Anyway, we waited out in the heat for hours for this Taliban guy that we'd got intel on and we had nothing to do but wait. It was deadly silent when suddenly he starts screaming like a girl. Turns out, a snake crawled up the leg of his pants and bit his nut almost clean off. He's been Snake ever since."

A giggle escaped my mouth. It was infectious, and the sight of which made Tommy smile too.

"Wow. I won't be able to look at him the same now. Did his nut survive?"

"Nah," he shook his head solemnly, "it got infected and had to be removed."

Another giggle bubbled at the surfaced as I envisaged what that might've looked like, but I attempted to suppress it for Tommy's benefit.

"I'm sorry to hear that."

My eyes shone as I clamped my lips between my teeth. *Don't laugh now.*

"Look, you didn't hear it from me! You already got me in trouble with Boss. Strike two and I'm out. You know how things roll around here. You get one chance."

"Sorry Tommy, I get it. Thanks for being here for me. I feel so alone."

"Just doing my job," he stepped backwards, "holler if you need me."

Tommy closed the door behind him, and I was completely and utterly desolate, both mentally and physically.

My giggles only moments prior now morphed into

sadness, and with a heavy sigh and a tight chin, I peered around the dimly lit yet perfectly acceptable room that made me feel anything but comfort.

How had I gone from having a spot in King's bed to now being locked away in a place that smelt of someone else's perfume?

Apart from plain beige walls, a bed and vanity table, there was a small window that looked out onto the manicured gardens, but that was it. No TV and no form of entertainment to occupy my train wreck of a mind.

Without a second thought, I sloped over to the vanity and perched on the stool where the first idea I had was to check the drawers for clues as to the previous occupant. Had he ever stepped foot in this room before and fucked the girl who occupied it? Just knowing that I was now so far away from him had my mind reeling.

Did he hate me that much I needed to be at the opposite end of the house?

I slid open the last drawer after having opened two that were empty. Nothing. Not even an old condom wrapper.

As each minute passed, the walls closed in around me and every sinew within my body wanted to escape. But could I leave King with the looming marriage proposal?

Well, if he thought that after today's performance, I was going to say yes; he was a madman. Although, was this even relevant anymore?

Had kicking me out of his bedroom meant he had rescinded his offer, anyway? Was he about to propose to whoever was currently hiding in his shower? My gut instinct told me he was having sex with one of the other girls, maybe even two.

God, I want to leave.

Suddenly, Dan's original offer to run away together felt more appealing than ever. But of course, he and I hadn't spoken since the morning of Tat's funeral, and clearly his new love interest was his top priority.

It was then I began obsessing over the idea of contacting him.

Could he be my ticket out of here?

What I needed to quiet my thoughts was confirmation that he was still interested in me and I had to know that our plan could still go ahead, otherwise how would I cope with the lockdown? With as much patience as I could muster, I waited for nightfall.

An hour had gone by when I crept over to the bedroom door and cracked it ajar to check Tommy's position. It pleased me to see him perched on his small stool, snoring heavily. He was right about his ability to sleep on a washing line. Now was my chance.

I called Dan's cell, knowing that the chance of someone hearing me at this time was slim, but it wasn't as if anyone cared, anyway.

"Hi Dan." I whispered cautiously.

He mirrored my quiet tone. "Chloe?"

His voice sounded as though I'd woken him. It was still early in the evening for me, but I guess not for everyone.

"Can you meet me now?"

He cleared his throat to rid of his grogginess.

"Sure, of course. Where?"

"Come over to the house, by the fountain in the gardens."

Dan let out a snort into the receiver. "The house? As in Romero's place? That's not a good idea."

Not a good idea because he had his other woman over? Or just because he didn't care? If he didn't pass this test, then I knew it was truly over.

"Yes, his place, as I can't leave the grounds. I'll explain when I see you. Can you come over or not?"

The irritation building up inside me was evident in my icy tone, and he picked up on it immediately.

"OK, I'll come over, but this is risky Chloe."

I hung up the call before he could make anymore excuses. There wasn't time for that when I needed a lifeline.

Anxious and nauseated, it was time for me to ready myself for my rendezvous with Dan after what seemed like so long. Butterflies released in my stomach that I couldn't catch. Had he totally given up the fight for me?

I slid open my bedroom window carefully, where my heart pounded in my ears with each movement I made as adrenaline spiked my nerve endings. I couldn't even begin to think of the ramifications of getting caught doing something as reckless as this.

As I slowly edged the window up its tracks, it squeaked in the frame.

Shit!

I stood stock still and held my breath, hoping that no one heard, especially Tommy. The house was completely silent, but I knew there were security guards around the perimeter of the mansion, too.

An ice age went by as I waited, but no one came to investigate the sound. I let out my breath and carried on opening the window for my exit.

With carefully placed movements, I climbed out and onto the tiled roof just below, where beams of light from torches shone in the distance from a couple of guards.

The intricate footwork required meant I had to discard my shoes before my continued descent down the mansion's wall via a trellis that supported a growing climbing plant.

When my bare feet touched the gravel, a wave of relief restored my breath. I'd made it this far.

I can do this.

Regardless of my lack of footwear, I took my chance and ran across the acres of lawn as quickly as my legs could carry me. If I got caught now, it would be game over for me, but with the way I was feeling about King, that was the better option.

As I ran, the cool wind whipped my hair around my face where I tread ground with as much pace as my untrained body would allow. But self doubt reared its ugly head the further away from the mansion I became. Would Dan even show up? If he went through with this test, it would tell me everything I needed to know that I was still his number one priority.

My feet blackened in the wet grass, hindering my progress, when a flood of light washed over my body. *A flashlight!*

Intuitively, I froze on the spot, my eyes darting around

the open expanse, searching for shelter. But with no viable options, I dropped to the ground and waited.

My chest expanded as I drew in oxygen, raising my body from the ground as I lay as still and quiet as I could.

Did they see me?

Masculine voices encroached upon me, but by the luck of the Gods, they changed direction at the last second.

Both men were engaging in pointless conversation.

"Let's go check on the whores," the first said. "I need some pussy."

The other huffed. "Are you stupid, Bother? You saw what Boss did to Jimmy."

"Well, I nailed Michelle last week and didn't get caught."

Michelle? Ugh! Who hasn't slept with her? Was King sleeping with her right now?

His friend laughed, "you got bigger balls than me, Dude."

Their voices became an echo as they moved further away from where I lay. Their direction headed towards the house.

God, that was close.

I hoisted myself to my feet, and I picked up pace again in need of hurrying. My life depended on it.

When I arrived at our secret meeting spot, I was relieved to find Dan stood in exactly the place I'd asked him to meet me at.

My presence startled him in the pitch black of the night and he drew his gun, pointing it in my direction, not able to make out who I was until I got close enough.

Out of breath, I was panting hard from my barefoot excursion across the estate.

"Dan it's me!" I gasped for air, "put that away!"

Seeking comfort, I hugged my jacket closer to me for protection against his weapon. After this morning's incident, I didn't care to see another gun again.

"Sorry Chloe, I wasn't expecting you to dive in front of me like that. I've just had to crawl through a bush to get here. I'm a little jumpy."

He holstered the gun once my face was in full view, where the intense adrenaline rush overwhelmed me with dizziness. The thumping of my heart almost became a melody.

"There's a bounty on King's head," I wheezed. "Apparently I'm a target too, so that's why I asked you to meet here, as we're in lockdown."

Dan leant against the water fountain for support, trying in vain to act casual when it was clear he was anything but.

"Why would you be a target?"

What could I say other than the truth?

"Because—"

"Go on?" He coaxed, agitated by my lack of forthcoming.

"Because paparazzi saw us holding hands at the funeral."

I blanched at the sound of my own voice.

"What!? Are you kidding me?"

His eyes filled with resentment where the passionate glisten over his irises shone in the moonlight.

"Believe me, that none of it was my idea. You know he would kill me if I refused him."

He kicked the fountain, which would have hurt his foot way more than it would've damaged the stone, but he didn't make a sound.

"How am I supposed to feel about this Chloe? Fuck! I'm so fucking mad!"

"I'm sorry, I really am. I still want to leave with you to New Mexico. Can we go soon?"

"Sorry, what?" he murmured. "I was just thinking about you living here with your boyfriend."

Tears threatened to fall again, although now was not the time for getting emotional. But could I help it when he was being a prick? I wanted to ask him why he hadn't tried to make contact with me, but I didn't want to hear his confession confirming that King was right, and he was sleeping with someone else. I just couldn't digest those painful words right now.

It couldn't be true that there was another woman involved when Dan was my escape route out of this place.

"Dan, please don't be mad at me."

"Mad is all I've got Chloe! The woman I'd planned to move away with has fallen for my brother, who just uses women to get back at me. He's declared that you're his girlfriend now, when you were supposed to be mine?"

I snivelled, wiping my nose on the back of my hand.

Eventually he signed, running his hand through his hair, completely lost in the darkness.

My breathing caught in my throat as my emotions took hold of me. "I know you're upset with me, but I'm stuck in this place with armed guards, watching my every move, and there's a good chance they're out looking for me now. Until the bounty is off King's head, I have no choice other than to stay here, but I need to know that we are still going to run away together?"

His shoulders slumped, and he looked beaten.

"I'm sorry Chloe, I didn't mean to yell. It's just Romero is a game player always out to get back at me."

"Get back at you? Why, what did you do to him?"

"I guess it started when Dad gave me the family business, as he said Romero wasn't smart enough. As you can gather, he didn't take it well."

So King was using me in his games with Dan after all, and the harsh reality that he just wanted to get back at his younger brother because of his Father issues now had it all making sense.

The rushing to propose to me, trying to conceive, it was all about King coming out on top to prove his father wrong. He so desperately needed to be alpha male and ultimately the superior Son.

Dan ran both hands through his hair. "OK, look, I'm going to do some digging and see if I can find out who wants Romero dead, so hopefully you can leave this place sooner rather than later."

In his own way, he was trying to offer me something, telling me what he thought I wanted to hear, but we both knew he was powerless. There wasn't a chance, as things were currently with the lockdown, that we could run away together, but I wanted more from him; reassurance that he just couldn't deliver. In hoping Dan could save me, I'd just learned the opposite. He wasn't capable of getting me out of this place anymore than I was.

"OK," I sighed, "I need to go."

Bile burned my chest cavity as it travelled into my throat, and suddenly the idea of being caught out in the dark with

King's real enemy in life—his brother—seemed like a death sentence I wasn't ready to accept. I needed to get back to the house before we were both captured.

Dan didn't argue with my decision when he leant in and kissed my lips chastely. But when I returned the kiss, I wasn't sure exactly how I felt.

I raced as fast as I could back towards the house, running across the same uneven terrain I'd already travelled.

I'd just made it to the footing of the trellis when I heard a deep, husky voice behind me.

"What're you doing hoe?" The male called over my shoulder, making me jump out of my skin.

I snapped my head around to look at him, horrified to discover that it was the Clive the creep who had attempted to hit on me, causing poor Jimmy to take the bullet to the knee.

"I'm, um, just out for a stroll," I lied unconvincingly.

"Bull shit" he retorted as he took a drag of his cheap branded cigarette. The end glowed amber as he sucked on the filter.

"Wanna keep this our little secret?" He blew the smoke in my face.

"Yes," I replied with a fake smile, knowing full well he

wanted something in return.

"Suck this," he pointed at his soft bulge as he held his cigarette between his teeth.

I straightened myself up, puffing out my chest. I didn't need to take this crap from him.

"You know I'm King's girlfriend, right?"

"You want me to tell King that his girl was escaping?"

Oh God, did he see me with Dan? Surely if that were the case, he would have accosted us together.

I raised my eyebrow and folded my arms over my chest, calling his bluff. "Your word against mine."

He paused and took another carefully considered drag as he contemplated his next move.

"Go on then, fuck off," he murmured as he flung his arm in the air while he turned to face the other direction.

I wasted no time as I hastily clambered back up onto the tiled roof, just below my window.

Once back in my room, I slid the window closed and leapt into bed where my head span, and I thought I might throw up. That was the most terrifying experience of my life.

Without warning, I heaved, and heaved again, as the contents of my stomach made its way into my oesophagus, where it threatened to exit my mouth.

Just in time, I made it to the small trashcan by the door, where I emptied the entirety of my stomach, bile, and all. My head pounded, and a cold sweat formed on my brow.

Before I could react, Tommy, like a raging bull, shoulder barged open the door, almost pulling it off its hinges. His action was a little overboard, as he could have just used the handle.

As if he'd run up two flights of stairs, completed a half marathon and finished with a long jump, he gasped for breath at the entrance to the room where he assessed the picture before him.

"Everything OK Boss?" He asked eventually, looking with concern at the trash can cupped in my hands.

"Yes, I'm fine, but I need privacy. Thanks for checking on me."

I wretched again on the last word, gesturing for him to leave. Tommy wasn't one for overstaying his welcome and he nodded his confirmation, not wishing to be dragged into anymore of my drama than he already had.

Once my stomach had settled, I rolled back into bed and closed my eyes, feeling as bad internally as I looked.

My head was racing, as though my muddy feet were still covering loose ground, and seeing Dan hadn't helped my situation at all. In fact, it made everything worse.

The mansion and the people who lived within its walls were making me miserable and the man I'd hoped could be my ticket to freedom turned out to me a fraud. And, with no reassurance that New Mexico was still an option and no security of our future, only confirmed to me what I feared was the truth. He didn't even tell me he loved me.

King was right. Dan clearly had another woman waiting for him back home, and she probably had a bubble bath standing by for him upon his return. But why did he even bother to come and see me? Was his plan to keep the side chick in case it didn't work out with me? Or was it the other way around?

As if this day couldn't get any worse, all I'd done was confirm that I was still the chess piece in the brother's sordid game to win first prize, and no matter what happened now, I could only rely on myself to set me free.

CHAPTER 15

The sensation of being rocked like a ship in the night awoke me from my deep sleep. It had been the soundest I'd slept since I moved into the mansion despite my hopeless situation.

My eyes flitted open where I was met with darkness, but I soon realised someone was in my room and they were kneeling over me, pinning me to the mattress by their knees.

"Hello? Who's there?" I whispered as my pulse quickened.

"Shh. It's me."

I knew that voice immediately.

"Um, hi?"

King fumbled about in the dark. "Where's the light in here? Turn it on."

I reached for the bedside lamp and with the flick of a switch; the room illuminated where we both squinted at the sudden assault against our dilated pupils.

When our eyes adjusted and I saw his handsome face, he

had a look of mild disgust that caught me off guard.

"What's that smell?" He frowned, holding his nose.

At first I thought I might've released gas in my sleep. We weren't close enough for that sort of confession, so I played it coy. "Um, what smell?"

He sniffed the air like a dog on a scent trail.

"Did you puke in here?"

My eyes widened at the reminder that I'd left yesterday's meals—or lack of—in the trash can and fallen straight to sleep. There was no point in denying it.

"Yes, I did."

King's face was so tightly screwed up it distorted his features. "What are you in preschool?"

"I've just not been feeling well, is all. Jeez."

I rolled my eyes inwardly. *A woman can't catch a break in this place.*

After a moment of thought, his face softened, and he looked at me with kinder eyes.

"Listen, shit got outta hand before. My rage just gets me twisted sometimes."

A snort escaped my nose. "You're not wrong there."

Fortunately for me, King ignored my misplaced attitude.

"I said some things I shouldn't have. It won't happen again."

I waited a moment, wondering if he'd offer a deeper apology, but I soon realised that was the best I was going to get from him.

"OK." I accepted, knowing that apart from his weak atonement, I had no other option available.

With having no friends and no longer able to rely on Dan, an admission of wrongdoing from King was the best outcome I could have hoped for.

King's ever roaming finger slid down my cleavage and rested on my perky nipple.

"OK, as in, we're good?"

My thoughts jumbled at the heady sensation of his finger swirling my hardened peak.

My breath hitched, "Yes."

At my confirmation, his lips clashed against mine, and we kissed with passion and longing where the lack of intimacy we'd shared was evident in our hunger for one another. My hands grasped at his curls as he devoured my mouth. We both needed this.

King had easy access to my body as I habitually slept in the nude these days, and one look at my curves had him instantly erect.

"Forget what I said about you not bein' in my bed. I can't miss this body any longer than I already have."

His hands explored the lengths of my torso with hunger and with an ardent desire of my own, I reached into his boxers and freed him. I could have sworn he was bigger than usual and my mouth watered instantly at his arousal—that was as desperate as mine—evident when his penis pulsed as his heated skin met with the open air.

I grabbed the shaft and pushed the tip into my soft damp entrance, teasing the head before allowing him to thrust all the way in.

"Shit, you're gonna make me come too quick doin' that. I don't have stamina with you."

My salacious grin exposed my intentions, and I wanted him to re-stake his claim on me again. I needed to be his girl and get my status back in the mansion, otherwise I was done for.

I was so grateful he'd come into my room to make things right between us, and pleasing him was my most critical task.

King set a slow sensual rhythm, fucking me just how I liked it. I savoured his touch, and feeling him stretching my insides had me desiring more.

I craved to make him happy and giving him my body was something that always got me what I wanted.

"Let me ride you, Romeo."

He didn't need to respond, instead he rolled himself underneath me and I was on top of him in an instant.

I rested my hands on his firm chest while I closed my eyes, rocking my hips back and forth with King's hands rested on my curves, helping me keep momentum.

Before I knew what was happening, I climaxed for him.

"Shit." I called out into the silence of the room when the intensity ripped through my body, leaving stars in my vision.

The sensation of my warm, wet pussy was too much for King's naked penis to bear and he came too, offering me his soul.

I collapsed on the bed next to him, where we were both breathless.

"That's why I wanna marry you," he smiled, completely sated.

I stroked the soft skin of his taut biceps. "You still want to marry me, then?"

"Of course. Why you askin' that?"

"Do I need to remind you of what happened yesterday?"

He took hold of my hand and kissed my fingertips. "Snake will be home tomorrow. That's done."

"Well, you sure punished me hard for it."

King's forehead creased as his eyebrows raised in

disbelief.

"You call a blow job a hard punishment?"

"It was more the way you spoke to me and the fact you didn't want me near you was the hard part."

He thought for a moment, staring at my exposed breasts as though they were the answer.

"When I get mad, I act up. I kept you away from me to protect you."

The desperation of my situation shone through at the surreal fact that his words comforted me.

"You're not mad now then?"

"No. I want you back in my bed. No, our bed. Come with me."

The sudden realisation that I was naked caught me off guard as King led me down the hall and to our bedroom. Tommy was still awake but focusing his eyes anywhere other than us.

King's bedroom was dark upon entering and I assumed we'd have company as was usual. But to my surprise, the bed was empty and it would just be the two of us sleeping in here tonight.

"Where's Alice?" I asked in the hopes I might get a chance to speak to her away from Hanna.

"She's sharin' with one of the other whores."

I rolled my eyes. "Oh, I see. Hanna, by any chance?"

"How the fuck do I know? I don't care. Get in bed and sleep."

Not wanting to ruin our moment, I did as I was told and climbed under the cold sheets that hadn't seen a body in hours. My curious mind wanted to discover what King had been doing to fill his time since I'd last seen him in this room. The potential woman in the shower popped unwelcome into my mind, but I refrained from probing. Another argument could wait.

"Good night Romeo."

"Night, you sexy slut."

Morning had broken, and the sun shone through the vast window of King's bedroom. He needed to invest in some new black out drapes.

When I glanced over to where King should have been sleeping, I found an empty space and my heart sank at the derelict sight. *Had I dreamt last night?*

My circadian rhythm was out of whack and I needed to check the time, so I reached over for my cell.

Shit, where is it?

I sat up and scanned the room. Had I left it in the other

bedroom? I distinctly remembered bringing it with me last night.

Just as I was about to move, the door swung open in haste, interrupting my contemplation, and King sauntered in, holding something in his hand. His body and face were tense, but when he saw me smile at him, he softened.

"Morning." I grinned, biting my bottom lip.

Why was I feeling so shy?

The drama of yesterday was still so fresh and I wasn't sure if he'd changed his mind on whether we were fine.

"Here." He tossed me my cell. "It's got a tracker on it now and it's tapped. Anyone contacts you and I'll know about it." He sat on the edge of the bed next to me. "That includes my brother. Don't think I didn't see that call log."

Fuck! He's probably really mad.

I picked up the phone, willing an excuse to come to my mind that explained the call to Dan. He had an urgent secret to tell me? *No.* I wanted to drive one of his trucks? *Don't be stupid.* There wasn't a single valid reason.

"OK, that's fine."

It was all I could come up with and, to my surprise, he didn't pursue the matter further.

A void of silence descended upon the room, which prompted me to peer up at him where I was met with a scowl.

"Um, what's wrong?" I asked, as my heart responded to the glare of an intimidating man.

"What the fuck is wrong with your feet?"

Huh?

Filthy with dirt, my feet were a mess and it only just occurred to me that when I should have been cleaning off the evidence of my escape last night, I was vomiting into the trash can instead. My throat dried, and I swallowed past a lump in my throat.

"Oh, well. You see." I tucked my hair behind my ear. "The issue was that because you kicked me out of your room, I had no access to a shower, so I didn't get to, you know, clean my feet."

Shit, fuck. Fuck. The worst excuse award goes to me.

His mouth tensed as his eyes narrowed when eventually he adjusted his erection and hummed.

"Nothin' sweeter than a naked woman in my shower," he paused and shook his head. "Anyway, word on the streets is that the bounty for my head in a box is one million dollars."

Grateful for his one track mind, I'd dodged a bullet, but my eyes widened in alarm at the prospect someone really wanted him dead that badly, they were willing to pay all that money.

"Shit, that's bad."

"Yeah, real bad. Snake's back now anyway, so we got a full crew again. I've told the whores this morning that things can go back to normal. I can't let anyone think I'm worried about this."

"Are you? Worried I mean."

I huddled myself, stroking my own arms for comfort.

"I'd be insane if I wasn't. I want you by my side from now on. Where I go, you go, got it?"

His honesty surprised me, but I figured it was because we were alone.

I nodded my head. "Got it."

"Listen, I've got shit to do here today, so you'll need to entertain yourself. Stay in the house. I mean it." He rose to his feet, leant in, and kissed my forehead. "I mean it," he repeated and stalked out of the room.

I sat at the breakfast bar, tucking into Chef's famous fried egg and buttered toast, when Alice walked by. Finally, she was alone.

"Alice, hi!" I said between mouthfuls. I was starving.

Her stride shifted when she heard my voice, but she didn't acknowledge me and carried on walking.

I picked up my plate and followed her out of the room.

"Hey!" I called again, "are you ignoring me?"

Alice was dead behind the eyes and I almost didn't recognise her. "Sorry Jas. I have an appointment. I'll catch you later."

"Oh OK, sure."

As I watched Alice leave, my thoughts switched to Hanna. I hadn't spoken to her properly since our latest spat. I sensed she was in the house somewhere, but I wasn't about to go looking for her and get my head bitten off again. My resolve was to make contact with her if we bumped into each other naturally.

My phone buzzed in my hand.

Before I could say a word, King spoke into the receiver. "Upstairs, Shorty." He hung up the call.

I rolled my eyes. A call at this time of day was usually an invitation for one thing, and I really wasn't in the mood for sex. With everything that had happened recently, I just felt nauseous and irritated all the time.

When I entered the bedroom, I stumbled inside when I saw an eye full of King's ass whilst he fucked Michelle from behind on our bed.

What the fuck!?

Violence consumed me and I slammed the door closed

to announce my arrival, where adrenaline pumped through my veins, and right then I was more than ready for a fight.

Why Michelle, of all people?

I watched in disgust as the man I had ambiguous feelings for leant over her back as he climaxed. When he withdrew, he was at the very least wearing a condom.

King panted with a hint of sweat covering his body. The poor baby had been going hard. *Aww.*

"Come sit with us," he ordered, pulling on his shorts and immediately lighting his post fuck cigar.

Michelle sat there like a fat pig in shit, feeling like she was finally the superior whore. The jubilant look on her face was pitiful.

Don't cry. Suck it up!

Internally, I was ripping off my clothes in anguish and emptying a magazine clip into both of their chests, but on the outside, I smiled tightly with clenched fists and strolled over to the lovely, sated couple and took a seat on the edge of the bed next to them.

To think I used to find it attractive that he slept with the whores now seemed pathetic and to acknowledge that I once became giddy that I was one of his special girls made me want to hurl. *Again.*

But since the day he proposed to me, I wished with all my

heart that he would stay loyal to me only. I didn't think that was much to ask? But it was the exact reason I still couldn't commit to him. In the back of my mind, I was still hoping I had options with Dan that I could fall back on during times like this. After last night's secret meeting, though, that plan was defunct.

At some point in the near future, I would have to make my choice whether I stayed with King, tried harder with Dan, or left the mansion alone. But right now sat on King's bed next to Michelle's naked smelly cunt and in view of King's post orgasm blush. I wanted to be anywhere but here.

"You two kiss," he instructed as he put his hands in his shorts to rub himself.

WHAT!?

Michelle didn't hesitate and moved towards me, but I pulled back. Her willingness to please King over her distaste for me demonstrated how weak she actually was.

The rage in my chest had my breathing hitched, and I folded my arms in defence. "No thanks. I'm not in the mood."

I moved away from her, creating a distance between us.

King's jaw clenched at my defiance.

"Since when does your mood count? You better correct

yourself before I do it for you!"

I knew he was acting to save face and the last thing I wanted to do was dent his reputation, but what did he honestly expect from me?

After I didn't respond, he rose to his feet aggressively and Michelle ducked her head, looking away like a cowering dog. The assault was brewing inside him, visible in his clenched fists.

"Leave us alone," he growled at Michelle with his eyes burning into mine.

Bravery came over me, and I locked my eyes with his, giving him my best scowl. I wasn't backing down this time.

Game on ass hat.

When she'd left the room, he softened.

"What's the fuckin' problem?"

"You're really asking me what the problem is? Can you not see it for yourself?"

He looked around the room as if searching for the answer that might be written on the wall.

"No?" He eventually replied.

"So you ask me to marry you one minute and the next you're fucking a woman that hates me and who stole money from me and you invite me to watch you both have sex?"

He took a seat beside me. "But I thought you liked it hot?" He scratched his head, sounding confused, as if I was being unreasonable. "And how was I supposed to know she stole from you?"

My shoulders relaxed at his reasoning, and I sighed.

"I do like it hot, but I don't want to see you with other girls anymore."

With my arms crossed over my chest again, I looked like a child having a tantrum.

"But that's what I do? It's what I've always done. These hoes need to get somethin' from me. How else they gonna respect me?"

His tone was gentle, and it allowed me to hear his words. And it seemed like we had an understanding of each other's perspective.

"Honestly, I don't know how I feel about any of this. I've been really emotional since I found out about the bounty. You ask me to marry you, yet you continue to sleep with other women. I don't want that life. I want to be with a man who wants only me."

"But you know it can't work like that, Jasmin."

I scoffed at hearing that name. "You don't even know my real name!"

I slapped my hands on my thighs in disbelief and a giggle

escaped my lips at our impasse.

"Jasmin ain't your real name? What the fuck is it, then?"

"Chloe Adams."

"See," he shrugged, "now I know your name. Simple fix."

"Nothing is ever that simple, Romeo."

"Listen, stop with the Romeo in front of everyone. Makes it sound like I got a soft dick. King or Daddy at this house. When I move you into the apartment full time, you'll have me to yourself and you can call me what you want. I'll come home to you every night. I can promise you that."

"Hold on," I pinched the bridge of my nose. "Let me get this straight. You want me stuck in that place on my own, knowing you're back here fucking whores all day? Then you come home to me at night with another girl's stink on your dick?"

He thought for a moment, and a smile crept across his face.

"That about sums it up, yeah."

His wandering hand tucked a loose strand of hair behind my ear, and his handsome grin made my mood soften a little. I nudged him with my shoulder.

"I know you're emotional and shit, Jas—I mean Chloe, but my men got this all under control. We are getting close to finding the man behind the order. Once he's dead, it's done. Then we can get back to normal. We will get married and you'll have six of my babies."

He spoke as if he'd planned out an idyllic fairy tale romance. Except this version had guns, drugs and whores to contend with.

He leant in closer to me. His cologne made my mouth water and my skin tingle.

"You're so fuckin' hot when you're pissed," he nibbled on my earlobe and nipped my neck.

The roaming fingers I'd become so accustomed to reached into my bra and took hold of my nipple between them. His touch always could set my soul on fire and peach mound puckered in response to the feel of his skin against mine. The electricity between us was back with a vengeance.

"You like that?" He asked as he cradled my breast in his palm.

My breathing hitched. "Yes."

He lay me down on the bed and lifted my dress, peeling down my underwear he paused.

"Oh, you're bleedin'," he said as he looked between my legs. "You're not pregnant."

The disappointment on his face was tangible, and he sat back on his heels, the wind knocked out of him.

The news was no surprise to me. In fact, I was elated that I wasn't pregnant, but the period had taken me by surprise as I wasn't due on yet.

King's reaction came as a shock, confirming just how much he really wanted to be a father.

"I'm sorry Romeo." I rubbed my fingers through his soft chest hair.

Just like that, he seemed to shake himself out of his mood, and his stone mask was back in place.

"Um, do you want to carry on?" I opened my legs, offering myself to him. He was a filthy son of a bitch, and a bit of blood wouldn't put him off.

He smiled at me with a wicked glint in his eyes. I knew that look. He was about to give me some of his best moves.

King leant over my body, between my open legs and kissed my mouth.

"We're goin' to try again for a baby," he said between kisses.

"Yes. God yes."

I was becoming such a good liar that it bothered me. But in that moment, I wanted him; I needed him. The extra warmth and lubrication my period provided intensified the mood, and his dick slipped inside me without friction, and my body responded immediately.

King's expert movement was deliciously slow and sensual as he pushed one of my erect nipples into his mouth and the familiar pinch of pleasure that came from his suckle made my pussy clench around him. The tempo of his welcome invasion remained consistent until my insides swelled in response. He continued until I reached my climax, and then he came inside me with a primal growl.

"You're mine," he groaned as he finished, resting his clammy forehead against mine.

When he flopped himself down next to me on the bed while we both caught our breath, I noticed my blood on his genitals and the mess that was all over the sheets.

His eyes followed mine to understand my frown.

"The housekeeper will clean it, no biggy."

"Oh yeah? That too?"

I pointed to the smattering of blood tangled in his public hair at the base of his penis.

He looked down and chuckled, "yeah, sure if I tell her to."

The notion suddenly alarmed me, "you don't sleep with the housekeeper as well do you?"

I wasn't sure If I wanted to know the answer.

"Hell no," he wrinkled his nose. "She's old as shit. I couldn't get it hard for her even if I my life depended on it."

The side of King available to me now was the part

that I adored. He was funny, gorgeous, and fuckable. Our eyesights collided, and I blushed.

"Marry me," he said again. It was becoming a tradition.

"Romeo please not now."

"Jesus Christ Chloe. When is the right time? You just got some of my best shit and it's still not good enough!?"

"I told you before. You sleeping around with other girls bothers me. I want a husband that wants just me."

The confusion on his face was unmistakable. "But I do only want you."

"Michelle doesn't think so."

I raised my brow at him to remind him of the earlier spectacle he'd forced upon me.

King rolled his eyes at me. "I told you before that I thought you liked that shit. In my head I was goin' to fuck her and it would get you so hot for me that we would have the best raw sex you've ever had. When I think about the first day I saw you and the way you performed for me with your friend. I came in my pants watching you, not even kiddin'. No girl has ever made me come like you do."

"I get your idea behind it, but Michelle was the worst whore you could have chosen."

His jaw tensed. "How much did she steal from you?"

"A thousand bucks from the um, sleepover client I had."

I chose to omit the fact that I hadn't actually confirmed my suspicion yet that Michelle was indeed the culprit.

"Aight, bet. She'll be dead by the end of the day."

"What? No!" I screeched. "I don't want you to kill anybody. I just—ugh, I don't know what I want. Making friends with Hanna would be a good start to getting what I want, I guess."

"Who the fuck is Hanna?"

"Romeo, please, surely you aren't being serious? You went through a phase of spending more time with Hanna than you did me."

I tried not to sound bitter, but I couldn't help it.

He leant into the bedside draw for a cigar and perched it between his teeth. "I only did that to make you jealous."

"You thought sleeping with my best friend would make me jealous?"

"Yes," he said bluntly. "It worked, right?"

My mouth dropped open at his revelation when the picture I'd crocheted of King in my mind was unravelling thread by thread. I closed my mouth again when I realised he was spot on.

"You slept with Hanna to make me jealous?"

He nodded as he ran his thumb over my bottom lip to release it from the vice like grip of my teeth.

Flashing images of Hanna and King assaulted my vision as I conjured all available positions they had fucked in. Bent over our bed, against the shower wall and probably missionary on the couch. Was there a place they hadn't been intimate?

"She got pregnant, though Romeo, and that hurts."

My voice broke as I felt myself welling up again. I was so damn emotional.

His muscles bunched at the idea, and his eyes closed while he composed himself.

"I already said that was a mistake. All my whores are on the pill, unless I say otherwise."

My new found confidence spurred me on as he seemed to be in a reasonable mood.

"While we're on the subject, how many other girls are you trying to get pregnant?"

"None. Don't disrespect me by askin' a question like that."

I propped myself up on my forearm to get slightly higher ground than his flat position. "Is that the truth?"

"Yes, that's the truth," he rose to match my level. "Don't call me a fuckin' liar!"

I knew I'd overstepped the mark, but the more I fought back, the less he attacked me and if this was my only game plan, I had enough stored indignation that I could unleash upon him at the drop of a hat.

I took a deep exhale. "OK, fine."

I dropped back down onto the bed and we lay side by side again.

"So what now?" He asked with the cigar still between his teeth that he'd not yet attempted to light.

I placed my hand on my chest. "You're asking me?"

"You seem to be holding all the cards here. What's the next move?"

"Ask me again once all this shit is over."

King didn't need to ask what I was referring to. We were both worried about the bounty on his head, whether he openly admitted it to the rest of the house or not.

He held out his hand to shake mine. "Deal," he said with a grin.

The firmness in his grip took me by surprise. That was his business deal hand shake—I could tell.

There was a timid tap on the bedroom door and King responded in the only way he knew how.

"What?" He yelled.

"Boss, we got your brother down here. Wants to see you and says it's urgent."

King's eyes lit up with menacing intentions. "Perfect," he

muttered. "Get that robe on and come with me."

"Wait, hold on!" I stopped at the threshold. "I need to put a tampon in."

King stole a glance between my legs and smirked. "Let me put it in for you. I can do it, for real."

A hideous image of King lining up his whores to insert tampons filled my throat with bile. But he seemed so excited to do it for me. I couldn't say no.

"I mean, sure if you want. There's a box in the top drawer of the nightstand."

King didn't need telling twice as he slid open the drawer. But instead of locating the tampon box, instead he pulled out something else. An object that instantly turned my cheeks purple.

The double-ended dildo was of considerable length, enough that he needed two hands to hold it. When he saw my reaction, he raised his eyebrow and my hands knotted in front of me. Did he already know about my moment with Alice? Did she tell him?

He put the tip of the dildo to his nose and sniffed. My eyes widened as I watched him adjust his position to sniff the other end.

"I can smell your cunt on this. Let me guess, Alice fucked you with it?"

Do I tell him the truth? Fuck, what does he already know?

"You don't even need to answer me, Chloe. It's written all over your face. I fuckin' love lesbian shit. Gets my dick like stone. But I don't like it when I ain't here to watch. I get jealous and that gets me pissed."

"Um. OK." Was all I could manage. What else could I say? The evidence was right there in his hands.

"Anyway, I don't want Limp Dick here any longer than he needs to be. Come here."

With a dry swallow, I walked forward and stood beside him as he tore open the tampon pack.

"Leg up on the bed," he ordered.

Just exactly how he knew all the tips and tricks to inserting one chilled my skin, but I did as I was told and with expert precision, he inserted the tampon and left enough string hanging down to allow for safe removal afterwards.

"Thanks," I said with a small smile.

"Anytime Sexy. Now come on, let's go."

My heart thudded the closer we got, knowing that Dan was downstairs waiting for King. Why was he here? Had he come to rescue me, after all?

The sense that I'd completely misread Dan slapped me

hard in the face. There I was assuming he had no backbone, but he had the balls to walk into King's home from where he had been banished. What if he told King the truth? Would either of us survive if he did?

Dan was waiting for us in the hallway with his hands rested in his pockets and he straightened his stance when he saw King and me emerge, holding hands on the way down the stairs, where the look in his eyes changed.

"You're interruptin' me fuckin' my girl. What do you want, Limp Dick?"

"I came here to talk to you Romero." Dan looked at me and back at his brother. "In private."

What could he possibly want to say to King without me present? My knees knocked as the cortisol engorged every cell in my body.

King scoffed. "You can say what you gotta say in front of my woman."

Dan rolled up his sleeves. "OK sure. We'll talk fertiliser right here then."

King let go of my hand at hearing Dan's threat. "Give me ten minutes Chloe."

I turned on my heels and walked away, leaving them to talk business.

I wasn't feeling well, anyway.

CHAPTER 16

Since King had announced the lockdown of the mansion, days passed by painfully slowly and the tension amongst the cooped up residents was palpable.

He flat out refused to tell me what he and Dan discussed, the day that he'd dropped by for their private meeting. But what I did know was that I'd not heard from Dan in the time since.

The weather was awful in L.A, and the rain battered hard against the expansive bedroom window, the sound of which brought comfort to ease our tension.

Even though it was the middle of the afternoon, King and I lay in bed together with the blanket wrapped around us and the TV on in the background. For the first time in a while, I felt content.

"What is this you've put on the TV?" I asked with my ear rested against his chest where the sounds on my voice echoed within the hollow of his ribcage.

"You ain't seen American Dad before?"

"No," I frowned. "Should I have?"

The look of disbelief on his face was humorous.

"Everyone watched it as a kid. Where were you?"

But his words cut deeper than he realised, and the sad fact was that my stepfather took my childhood away from me soon after my mother had passed.

Whenever I thought about him, the image of him sitting in his reclined chair watching sports and drinking beer was so clear to me against such a hazy background, and I didn't recall ever being given the opportunity to watch TV while he was around. But I didn't want to bring that up now and ruin the mood.

He filled my brooding silence. "I guess it was more popular in my time. I know you're younger than me."

He stretched his arms out wide and yawned as he began stroking my back again.

I sat up to look at him with my chin rested on his chest.

"How old are you?"

"Me? I'm twenty eight, Love," he said in the worst British accent I'd ever heard.

Aside from his bad impersonation of me, his answer surprised me.

"Really? I would have said twenty six at most."

He reached under the blanket to rearrange his genitals as

if that was helping him think. "Why? How old are you?"

"Do you have to play with your nuts while we're having a moment?" I rolled my eyes. "And I'm sure you asked me this before, when we first met. I'm twenty one."

"Sorry, Ma'am, does my itchy sack offend you?"

He made me giggle. "Yes, it does." I kissed his chest hair and breathed in his cologne. "This is nice, isn't it?" I hummed, nestling into his hold again.

"Yeah," he smiled, "I like it."

I ran my digits through the wiry, dark hair sprouting from his jawline. "You could probably do with a shave, you know. This is getting kinda long."

"Yes, Ma'am. I'll do it when I take a shower later."

Hmm, in the shower? He'd probably want to complete that arduous task in at least an hour from now and I really wanted him to do it imminently. Just the thought of the sharp hairs rubbing against my lips one more time made me want to scream.

"OK," I said finally.

His body became rigid at my curt reply. "What?"

"Nothing, just I thought you could do it now as the hair prickles me when we kiss."

I wrinkled my nose to add an element of production to my performance. It was nice to feel like these days I could speak to him without him biting my head off.

He threw the cover off himself with a groan to prepare for a theatrical exit. "Guess I'm doin' it now then!"

"Oh, don't be so bloody dramatic!" I playfully swatted his chest, but I instantly paused, remembering what happened at our fried chicken date at the trap house.

Shit—Fuck.

After a note, he grabbed my hand and kissed my knuckles in a carefree gesture so alien in our relationship.

"You're a brave woman."

I avoided eye contact, hoping I'd not roused the beast that remained within him.

"I am?" I swallowed hard.

"No one's ever hit the king and lived to tell the tale."

"Except for the queen?"

Our relationship had come so far from where we first met, and this right here was everything I'd hoped for.

He narrowed his eyes and smirked at me, "tell her she ain't the queen until she says yes. Remember that."

With playful intent, he leaned in for a soft kiss on the lips and his hand cupped the back of my head to deepen the connection.

I grimaced and retreated as the sharp hairs tickled my lips, and he growled in frustration. "Aight, wait here!"

Not that I had anywhere else to go, but I watched in appreciation as King sauntered into the bathroom, completely naked where his perky peach bottom mesmerised me during his departure.

There were a few noises at first. A flick of a switch, a squirt from a can, when suddenly the air turned cold as a mist of anger descended upon the bedroom.

"Who the fuck has used my fuckin' razor!?" He yelled from the confinements of the bathroom. "There's fuckin' pubes all snagged up in my shit! Now this is what gets me fuckin' pissed. God damn it!"

I flinched at his onslaught against the bathroom furniture, remembering that the pube culprit was me! My devilish misdemeanour from a time when I was furious with him was now coming back to haunt me. Had it been that long since his last shave?

Instinctively, I pulled the cover up to my chin and waited.

Please don't hurt me.

"Did you hear me in there!?"

I gulped in response. "Um, yeah?"

He poked his head into the bedroom with shaving cream applied to his face. "You get what I mean? You can't have fuckin' nothin' in this place without someone takin' it for themselves."

My shoulders relaxed. *Thank God.*

"Oh yeah," I rolled my eyes playfully, "I hear you on that one."

He disappeared again, and the drama continued to unfold.

"I can't fuckin' work with this shit!" he growled. "It's blunt as fuck! If your mitherin' ass didn't get on my dick, I would have waited for my barber to sort it out."

The amount of moaning and groaning coming from the bathroom was worthy of an award show nomination. King sure knew how to rage at himself when no one else was around to listen.

He strolled back into the bedroom a short time later with a fresh face and a calmer demeanour when, all at once, a loud noise on the landing outside our bedroom had us both turning towards the sound. Raised voices on the other side of the door prompted King to straighten his back and broaden his shoulders, radiating hostility.

"You can't go in there!"

"Fuck you Tommy, you fat cunt, I'll do what I want!"

King and I looked at each other as he reached for his discarded boxers, pulling them on swiftly. It wouldn't have been right to face conflict in the nude, and whoever was on the other side seemed like they wanted trouble.

The door burst open and to my astonishment it was Clive the creep who I'd had the run in with during my secret meet with Dan. The same man who had tried it on with me twice since I'd moved into the mansion.

I sat motionless as he stalked into the room and around our bed to meet with King, who was more than ready for a fist exchange.

"What the fuck, Son?" King growled, "when did your balls get big enough for you to walk in here uninvited?"

A picture of masculinity, King stood before him in just his underwear with his shoulders tensed and his chest puffed, showcasing just how much taller and more muscular he was than Clive.

I looked over at my escape route to find our security team standing in the entryway with their weapons drawn.

"What do you want us to do, Boss?" Snake called to King as he clicked down the hammer of his revolver.

It was then that I caught sight of the bandage still wrapped around his lower leg.

"It's cool boys," King cocked his head. "Leave us alone. I'm sure we can get to the bottom of this like men."

He kept his eyes firmly fixed on Clive, watching his every

move.

All too soon, the door closed behind them, leaving me wondering what on earth Clive was doing here and why he was sweating so hard.

With my knees tucked to my chest, my heart thudded, evoking a terrible suspicion in my gut that King mirrored within his stance.

The crackling sound of the relentless weather against the window added to the tension within the room.

It was King who made the first move. "So, do we got a problem, Clive?"

"Yes," he muttered as he took a cigarette from his pack and pinched it between his teeth, where he cupped the tip to light it with his Clipper. After a long drag, he said again, "yes, I do."

King took a step forward with his arms spread wide, ready for anything.

"Lets deal with it then, Son. Man to man."

Clive took another drag, taking his time as he prepared himself for battle.

"I've known you a long time, Boss," he exhaled a plume, "but shit just don't sit right with me no more. You got hoes running the joint and you don't treat the team players right these days. You used to get the whores sucking our dicks.

Now that's stopped, we got nothing, and I'm tired of it."

"What the fuck you talkin' about? You get all the fuckin' snow you want. Don't think I don't know you pricks are cuttin' my shit and resellin' it and keepin' the profit. I let shit slide when I trust you. You sayin' I can't trust you, Clive?"

Clive fidgeted as he pushed his free hand inside his dirty denim jacket pocket, where he froze for a beat as he continued to smoke his cigarette. Eventually, he stubbed it out into King's ashtray on top of the drinks cabinet. "It's about time I made some real money. I'm gonna cash in and get my million."

King laughed, a demonic sound that chilled my bones, and instantly my Romeo was gone.

"You're gonna do what, Son!?" He roared again. "You wanna cash in on the bounty, yeah? You think you're man enough to take my head?"

Alarm bells clanged in my mind, warning me that for the first time, King was unarmed during conflict and had he not been shaving his damn beard to please me, he'd have been prepared for this moment.

This is my fault.

Now was my turn to do something right for once, so while they eyeballed each other, I took my chance and reached under King's pillow for the gun he always kept there for situations such as this.

I grasped the cold heavy metal and carefully slid it under the cover with me, my finger nestled on the trigger.

From what little training I had at the shooting range, I'd need to put into practice now to protect my man. I couldn't fuck this up.

"Oi Bitch, don't you fucking move!" Clive yelled when he saw my movement in his peripheral vision. He pulled out the gun he'd been threatening to draw from his pocket and aimed it directly at me.

"Leave her out of this, you piece of shit." King snarled as he moved his body in front of Clive's aim, blocking his shot.

The creep turned his focus back to King, where his brows knitted together in confusion. "She's just a whore. What's the big deal?"

King remained silent as this wasn't the time for romantic gestures or declarations of feelings. He didn't plead for his or my life, nor did he hold up his hands in defeat. He showed me the type of man he was when faced with danger, with alpha male pride and courage emanating from his body like a flare illuminating under the darkest of skies.

As King continued to hold himself strong, he

unwittingly created an obstacle that didn't allow me a clear aim at my target.

Clive pulled down the hammer with a click, loading the round into the chamber, and at our moment of impasse, King stepped to the side to encourage Clive's focus away from my direction.

I had one chance to get it right.

My sweaty hand gripped the gun under the cover as I waited, where finally, I counted to three inwardly and reacted as swiftly as my adrenaline allowed. Pulling out the gun, I racked the slide to chamber the round. Eyes wide open this time, I pulled the trigger with the only shot I could take and the bullet skimmed past King's shoulder and hit Clive in the neck.

In reaction to receiving the bullet, his gun fired up into the ceiling as he dropped to the ground like a sack of potatoes where blood spurted from his artery as he bled out on the carpet.

When they heard shots being fired, security barged their way back inside, where it took them a moment to assess the series of events that had unfolded.

King stood over Clive, glaring at him while blood sprayed out of his body in thick pulsing squirts as he took his final breath.

As for me? Well, of course, I sat frozen in shock, with my eyes wide and the gun still clutched inside my shaking, outstretched hand, with no idea what to do next.

King glanced at Snake. "Get that Glock off her before she shoots you in the other fuckin' leg. And while you're at it, move this prick's body. This fucker was after my head."

"I'm sorry, Boss," Snake mumbled. "With him being one of us, we just didn't figure."

King kicked Clive's lifeless body in frustration. "Just get him outta here."

As his blood-soaked body was being hauled out of the room, King blustered towards me like a tornado, where concern etched into his features with just a hint of excitement.

"You good?" He asked as he grasped my chin to raise my eye line to meet with his.

"Um. I think so." My voice cracked from the anxiety induced dryness in my throat.

He smiled as his eyes studied my face. "You just saved my life."

The passion infused within his words was unmistakable, and his irises shimmered with unrestrained emotion that seldom appeared on his handsome face.

I shrugged my shoulders. "It was nothing."

With a smirk, he placed his hand inside his boxers and adjusted himself.

"Is it weird that it got my dick hard?"

"A little bit yeah," I giggled.

"Come on," he smiled as he pulled on his sweat pants. "Put one of your sexy dresses on and let's get out of here."

He reached for my hand and hoisted me off the bed.

Another murder had taken place in the mansion, except this time I was the killer. How did I feel about it? I guess the same way I felt about everything else; *numb.*

Would I ever be able to talk to someone about what happened? Certainly not Hanna, but maybe I could speak to King?

Hmm, he'd likely change the subject—like he always did—and try to have sex with me instead. Maybe I needed to book that therapy session I'd been meaning to for so long…

That afternoon, we got the news we were hoping for. Clive's cell phone held the key to finding the man who'd put the hit out on King.

Once the crew had collated their evidence, King informed me that his best shooter took out the man with one bullet while he was pumping gas at the station, and the heat died off immediately.

The animated hand gestures from King explaining the bullet's trajectory, coupled with the body movements to demonstrate how the man collapsed, was quite a performance, but none of it helped the way I felt deep inside underneath the layers.

As it transpired, the guy who placed the hit on King was a rival gang member and someone who he'd had contention with for many years over drugs, whores and area codes.

Did his death help my worries? No. But had I tried to find an opportunity to speak to King about it? Not really.

He, of course, was busy with matters that didn't concern me, and all I could do was trust that he was making the right decisions to protect us all.

Once the chaos had calmed, King gathered the crew in the usual meeting spot; our bedroom where he had something important to share with us all.

For the very first time, the crew allowed me to join a proper team briefing, which apparently I earned because of my improved shooting skills.

As soon as I stepped inside the room, I turned my back towards the blood stained carpet by the window. I just couldn't look at it without wanting to throw up.

King addressed the gathering with authority. "Listen up.

Just because this is over now doesn't mean we get sloppy. I want security on everyone and everythin'. My shit, don't hit the bowl without one of you fuckers checkin' in on it. Got it?"

The huddle of men around him agreed. "Yes, Boss!"

"Good. Now get back out there and protect what's mine!"

While the crew made to leave, King caught hold of my arm.

"You sure you're good? You look pale."

I bit my bottom lip as I assessed my feelings.

"He was a real bad guy, you know, Clive."

King cocked his head in confusion. "What do you mean?"

"Remember when you shot Big Jimmy for coming onto me? Well, it wasn't him, it was Clive."

King looked at his watch and then narrowed his eyes at me.

"And you're only just tellin' me this now, because?"

I thought back to the day that King shot Jimmy and the traumatic events that took place that I'd tried to bury deep in my subconscious ever since.

"Well, I did try to tell you at the time, but you scared me."

King caught a lung full of air in his cheeks, inflating them. On the release, he ran his hand through his hair.

"Well, I guess he got what was comin' to him in the end, huh?"

I nodded. I didn't know what else to say.

"So anyway," he fidgeted. "What you gonna do today while I'm cleanin' up all this mess?"

I glanced at the blood stain I had been avoiding looking at.

"*You* are cleaning that up?"

He smirked. "Do I look like a housekeeper to you?"

"Um, no?"

"Dead bodies don't just disappear, you know. I gotta take care of it and get the cleaners in to sort the fuckin' carpet again."

"Again meaning Tatiana?"

His jaw tightened. "Sure. Look, have you decided what you're gonna do?"

With my fingers interlaced in front of me, I looked at my feet, wondering what adventure I could take them on.

"Um, shopping, I guess?"

He nodded his confirmation. "Tommy goes with you."

I watched as he squirmed with pressing matters on his mind.

"Um. OK."

"Aight, sweet," he glanced at his phone screen, distracted

again. "I'll catch you later."

On his way out of the room, he turned and tossed a roll of cash through the air for me to catch where he winked as he left.

As per King's order, I decided that actually, a bit of retail therapy was exactly what I needed, and with his cash in my possession, I was more than equipped to enjoy myself.

Just knowing that King was there to pick up the pieces while I decompressed was worth its weight in gold and what he lacked in empathy, he sure made up for in usefulness.

The longer I'd been away from Dan, the further I was falling for his brother and, as King was trying to keep me happy to the best of his abilities, I was at the deepest depths of his ocean with no way of swimming to the surface.

My new found confidence in my relationship gave me energy in my stride as I departed through the main door and over to my Mini, where finally the sun was shining again.

Tommy was waiting for me as I walked across the lot, where he gave me a curt nod.

"Boss says I'm taking you shopping?" He asked as he

twirled his car key around his finger.

"No, I'll drive. I've missed my car."

My Mini and I hadn't been in each other's company for some time now, but she was still glistening, despite the earlier storms. The boys had kept her looking well.

"Hey, she's looking fabulous," I called over to the valet team, who dispersed quickly upon my arrival.

The news of Clives' demise had spread amongst the men fast, like high school gossip on the playground, and suddenly they treated me like I was King.

Tommy placed his hand over the car door and shook his head. "Sorry Boss, I got orders to follow. I'll drive."

With a pouted bottom lip, I sat in the back of Tommy's SUV as we cruised down the road with no real destination in mind.

"Did you decide where we're going yet, Boss? I can make a left here to go to the mall?"

All it took was for me to look out of the window at the passing objects for me to feel completely overcome with nausea.

Ugh.

"Is it hot in here?" I fanned my face. "Turn the heat down, please, Tommy."

He glanced at me through the rear-view with concern. "I

already got the AC on. You good?"

Like a bolt of lightning straight through my core, a wave of sickness hit me where the magnitude launched this morning's breakfast up my gullet and into the back of my throat.

Oh no.

My hand shot to my mouth as I heaved. Convulsions arched my back as the contents filled my mouth.

"Pull over!"

I wretched again.

No sooner had Tommy reacted than I threw open the car door just in time to spew all over the ground. The attack took me completely aback. I did not feel well.

My first thought was that the stress of shooting Snake, coupled with killing Clive, had become too much for my body to bear. Had I pushed myself to the limit?

Tommy remained seated with his hands clamped around the steering wheel, and when our eyes met through the mirror, he turned to face me. "So, do you still wanna go to the mall?"

I wiped my mouth and closed the car door. A cold sweat formed against my brow and a chill shivered down my spine.

"No Tommy, I don't. Take me to pharmacy. I need

something for a stomach bug."

With Tommy waiting in the idling SUV, I entered the local pharmacy where the kind eyed woman in a white lab coat gave me a warm smile from behind her counter.

"Afternoon Ma'am. Welcome to Walgreens. How can I help you?"

What I wanted to do was ask if she had anything that helps with the lasting effects of murdering someone, or at the very least injuring a man, but I refrained.

"Um, OK." I tucked my hair behind my ear. "So I guess I'm feeling a little nauseous. Do you have anything for that?"

"Mm-hm," she nodded in understanding. "Have you actually vomited?"

"Um, yes. Just now, actually."

"Mm-hm. Sore breasts?"

Wait—How did she know?

"Oh my God, yeah. Is there something going round?"

She chuckled as she turned her back on me to find something from her wall of pills and medicines. Eventually, she faced me again with a box.

"You'll be needing this, Ma'am. Twenty dollars please."

I frowned as I took the box, wondering what kind of stomach ache pill costs that much money, but when I read the words *pregnancy* and *test*, my eyes widened in horror.

"Um, this is a pregnancy test?" I croaked. In absolutely no way, shape or form, was I pregnant. I couldn't be. Could I?

"Yes, Ma'am."

I shook my head and placed the box on the counter. "I take the pill and I'm on my period. I'm not wasting money on this."

She picked it back up and raised her eyebrow. "Have you had unprotected sex recently?"

Suddenly images of King's naked body appeared in my vision as his declaration of our love making replayed on repeat. But as the situation revealed itself, the figure of the man before me was no longer King, but Dan.

Fact was, I'd had unprotected sex with both of the brothers and now my promiscuity was coming back to haunt me.

"Um, yeah. A little," I murmured.

"A little is all it takes, Honey. I've been doing this job for a long time. Trust me," she winked as she placed the box back into my palm. "Pill or no pill. Babies can still happen."

Bewildered, I found myself walking back to the car, twenty dollars lighter and holding something that could potentially change everything. How many times had I slept with King without protection? Too many to count. As for Dan, well, that was just one time. So with the law of averages, if I was indeed pregnant, King would be the father, right?

Let's be real. If the dad was anyone other than King, I might as well sign my own death warrant.

"Mall?" Tommy asked when I took my seat in the back of the car.

"Huh?" I stared at him in shock while I tried to piece together the words he'd just said. "Oh, um, no. Take me home, please."

I had no memory of our trip back to the mansion as we pulled into the driveway.

I left Tommy to park the car as I made my way inside. I was just about to head up to our bedroom when the sounds of voices coming from the living room caught my attention. I paused to listen where I leaned in closely to tune into their conversation.

Instantly, I recognised a few of the whore's voices and my money was on Michelle being the ringleader.

"Daddy," a faceless voice whined, "we wanna know what's going on. Why aren't you sleeping with us? Some girls are saying you are getting rid of us for a new group?"

His earthy masculine tone was blunt. "Nah, not true."

The way he addressed them was a world apart from how he spoke to me these days.

"But what did we do wrong, Daddy?"

He exhaled, and I heard him stalk the length of the room where the smell of smoke informed me he'd lit a cigar.

"Look, word was gettin' back that some clients said my whores lacked stamina. If I'm workin' you bitches too hard at home, then you can't bring me my money. No more fuckin' at home until performance improves. Got it? And that also means with each other. Don't think King doesn't know what you dirty sluts get up to."

King's words made me grin from ear to ear. He had taken the time to think of an excuse not to sleep with them for my benefit.

With how hard King was trying to keep me happy, I was really starting to fall for him and, without a doubt, we were closer than ever.

But had we become so close because he wanted *me* to provide an Heir to his throne? Could a pregnancy fix everything I'd been worrying about?

The idea rolled around my mind at one hundred miles an hour, where the answer to everything could well be inside the box in my hand.

Once behind the privacy of the closed bathroom door, I tore open the packet where, initially, I would need to familiarise myself with the instructions.

It was a long time ago since I'd last done a test, but I wouldn't dwell on the reason I'd needed to.

Hovering over the toilet bowl, I held the stick between my fingers and urinated on the textured tip.

My shaky digits tapped on the sink next to where the test lay, but I refused to look at the little window until I'd counted two minutes.

If the test is positive, how would I know who the father was? Would it be wrong for me to pretend that King was the only potential option in this? Could I live with myself if he wasn't?

So many questions made my nausea even more potent.

Finally, it was ready.

I flipped over the stick and narrowed my eyes at the little result window.

Oh—

Not pregnant.

Hmm. Wow. I was not expecting to feel so deflated.

I took a seat on the toilet lid and stared at the opposite

wall, trying to decode why I felt so upset when I didn't even want a baby in the first place.

Could a child with him have really secured my safety in the mansion? Would it've finally made me special to him, giving our relationship exclusivity?

Jeez. Was the answer to all of my problems now so blatantly obvious? I *needed* to birth his child.

In my haste to find the initial result, a thought occurred to me and I plucked out the balled up instructions from the trash to check the wording again.

Wait, hold on. Two lines mean pregnant.

Adrenaline flooded my veins as I picked up the stick to compare the result with the illustration, and as my eyes adjusted past the stars in my vision. There they were. Two blue lines.

I am pregnant.

I wasn't sure how it was possible, but the universe wanted me to do this. *I'm gonna be a Mummy?*

Was I catching the break I needed in safeguarding my future?

God, I'd been so stupid. Of course, giving the man I wanted a life with the key to his happiness would ultimately release the lock, withholding mine.

My feelings for King suddenly hit me hard. The baby that

he had longed for had become a reality for both of us. I could give him what Tatiana didn't get a chance to.

Now in the realisation that instead of counting on Alice for security she couldn't provide me, my baby could do that for me gave me a sense of certainty I didn't realise possible.

Did that make me a terrible person? A bad mother? Relying on a child to give me what I needed.

The knowledge I now possessed repaired the anxious wounds within my subconscious that never quite healed, like a scab that constantly reopened until finally someone applied the band aid.

My baby. My saviour; my very own bundle that I could love unconditionally who would protect me from the unknown. King couldn't harm me if I was carrying his child. I was immune.

It was then I solidified my plan to keep my paternity worries to myself. Our lives depended on it.

My hand reached down to my stomach and caressed the home of the baby growing inside me. The way my body had been feeling recently now seemed so obvious. My breasts were tender and swollen and my appetite was through the roof. As for my mood swings, well—that went without saying.

With a grin as wide as the Cheshire Cats, I placed the test in my bag and decided I would tell King the wonderful news tonight. Would we make love first? Or after? Would I tell him I loved him? There were so many factors to think about, but I wanted it to be right. He had to believe that there was nobody else in this apart from me and him.

First things first. I needed to tell Dan that he and I were through. With no chance of changing my mind, our relationship—if that's what you could call it—had to end now.

But why, when I thought about breaking it off with him, did the door to Dan feel like it was half open? Did I still see him as my life line? My back-up plan if King's volatile behaviour took a turn for the worst?

He was the first man to tell me he loved me. Could I easily let that go? But had he already done that, anyway? Wasn't there another woman involved?

Over half an hour went by while I agonised with myself over reasons why I should or shouldn't go and see him. I didn't know how I would find the courage to say goodbye to him, but my heart was speaking to me in a way I couldn't ignore, and I simply had to see him one last time.

In using tip toeing skills of the past, I bypassed the living room gigglers and creaked open the front door to find the usual scene. I knew getting to my car unnoticed was a conundrum, but I wasn't one for shying away from a challenge.

The men were busy, as was usual, but my main concern was evading Tommy, and he sure didn't make that task easy.

"Hey Tommy," I smiled at him, keeping eye contact to make him nervous.

"S'up Boss?"

"King said he needs a hand with something inside. Something to do with our bedroom carpet."

He adjusted his holstered gun and gave Snake a look. "Shit, OK."

As I watched my plan fall into place, I realised the obvious.

"Oh, he wants you too, Snake. A big job that carpet."

Bingo.

No sooner were the men out of sight than I was behind the wheel, ready to haul ass.

Dan's office was a few blocks away from the mansion and

shouldn't take more than ten minutes to get to if traffic was light. A quick in and out task, I would be back home before they realised my trick. I would tell Dan my news and see his reaction. Simple.

The Giannetti building was famous in its own right. The brothers became well known over the years for King's antics and Dan's familial association that hit the mainstream media, at least on a weekly basis.

So it came as no surprise that the building that housed Dan's office matched their celebrity status.

Without ever having a reason to visit before, I'd not been able to appreciate how stunning the architecture was. The front elevation was floor to ceiling with glass panes, with several floors expanding at least one hundred feet tall. Embossed black letters broadening the width read: Giannetti Haulage.

I entered through the vast door of the modern building with confidence. The foyer impressed with its enormous size, featuring a central horseshoe desk and doors opening to corridors from all angles. Stone floors echoed with an orchestral symphony as the heeled shoes of business women tapped their way along the expanse.

As expected, in any similar arrangement, there was a beautiful-looking receptionist sat at her check-in desk doing anything but a hard day's work.

I eyed her name tag: Gabby. "I need to speak to Dan Giannetti please, tell him it's Chloe, and it's urgent."

Gabby looked up at me through her lashes and blew a gum bubble. When it popped, she smiled. "Mr. Giannetti is a very busy man and doesn't see anyone without an appointment."

I showed her my best bad bitch glare and leant onto the desk into her personal space. "He'll want to see me."

She leaned away from me into the back of her chair. "Regarding what, may I ask?"

"None of your business!" I snarled, clearing my throat with my hand raised to my mouth to mask the sudden feeling of nausea. *Not now. Don't vomit here.*

Her face screwed up at the spectacle of my immediately pale complexion, and suddenly, I had the ability to make someone uncomfortable.

"One moment," she said as she picked up her desk phone and pressed a button. "Sir, there's a woman here, Chloe, who wants to see you. Are you sure? Yes, Sir."

Gabby placed the phone back into its holder but didn't make eye contact when she peered at her manicured fingernails and then pointed towards a door at the far end of the room.

"Please follow the corridor behind me and take a left to his office."

"Thank you Gabby," I offered her a triumphant grin while I held my head high as I sashayed beyond her desk to my confirmed destination.

But the closer I got to his office, the more nervous I became, and my powerful stride faltered weakly, where suddenly feeling like the smartest move I could make now would be to back out while I had the chance. What was I thinking in coming here? Did pregnancy hormones have something to do with it?

Before I could change my direction, Dan opened the door to his office, anticipating my arrival. He knew immediately that something was wrong just by me being there, and his innocuous stance and the opened collar of his shirt revealed how distressed he was.

"What's wrong Chloe?"

I looked over my shoulder, feeling insecure about a potential audience within listening range of my sensitive information.

"Um, can I come in first?"

He opened the entrance and gestured to a chair opposite his desk and once I'd made it inside; he closed the door.

Dan's office was lavish, to say the least, and the room screamed masculinity but with a soft feminine edge that allowed the visitor to relax into the space without feeling intimidated. I sensed it was intentional.

The vaulted ceiling allowed for so much light and space, and the walls were a mixture of classic creams and neutrals with a couple of personal items that gave a glimpse into Dan's personality, such as wall hangings and a shooting rifle presented centrally above his head just behind his desk.

One particular picture caught my eye. It looked to be a family photo that included Dan and King on a fishing trip. They looked so alike, almost twins, with an arm around each other and a boyish grin shared between the two of them. As a team, they carried the weight of the load, holding up a large fish out front to capture the moment. Happiness radiated from each boy, and the visual affirmed my decision.

Dan's desk was as big as a double bed, made from solid oak with metal legs. There wasn't an item out of position, from his computer monitor to the mouse and down to his pen. Everything had a place. The office was a mirror image of Dan's personality.

"What is it?" He asked again impatiently as he opened the button of his suit jacket to perch on the end of his desk before me.

"Dan—"

"No, Chloe!" He cut me off.

My forehead creased as my eyebrows raised. "Let me speak?"

Dan padded over to the far wall, where he took two short glasses from his cabinet and held out a bottle of whiskey in silent question. He poured his drink first. "I know what you're going to say. The answer is no!"

I watched him, decanting the brown liquid into the second glass, knowing full well I couldn't drink it, but he was clueless to the fact. *For now.*

"You don't know what I'm going to say."

He took a swig and winced as the liquor bit the back of his throat. "Yes, I do. You are going to say you can't leave with me because you've chosen Romero. I knew this would happen if you spent time away from me. The answer is no and I'm not giving up on us and we are sticking to the plan. Everything is in motion and I'm so close to finalising on a property in New Mexico." He passed me my filled glass, and I took it, not wanting to halt his flow. "When I came over the other week and spoke to Romero, I threatened to pull the plug on our business arrangement and he sang like the wimp that I knew he was. He said I could have you."

What? No!

My hand shook, and the contents of the glass produced waves that nearly spilled over the sides.

"I'm not a fucking play toy that the two of you can fight over! King told *you* that you could have me? yet he told *me* you have another woman? What the hell are you both playing at!?"

This can't be real. Surely Dan is lying? Isn't he?

Either way, I couldn't let this revelation derail me. I had a baby to protect, and I still had important matters I needed to discuss with him. Regardless of whether they were both still using me, I had to end this mess now.

"I don't have another woman Chloe," he scowled. "Clearly Romero is lying."

Were they both compulsive liars? Could I believe a single word out of either of their mouths?

So, Dan didn't have a woman after all? He'd simply not been in contact because of King? But would King give me away like that? Did I know either of them well enough to have any idea where the truth lay?

No.

Tears welled in my eyes. This was heartbreaking.

"Dan—"

He cut me off again before I could continue and his mouth was on mine, kissing me as if his life depended on it. I sat motionless in the chair with my hands grasped around the metal arms of the seat for grounding. I was holding on for dear life, but I knew I was getting lost in him and he could feel it, too.

My reluctance to kiss him back soon melted away when his tongue explored my mouth. The way he smelt and how his skin felt against my body encouraged me to open my mouth and accept him in. Why did this happen every single time?

With sudden clarity, I twisted my head away from him, breaking off the kiss. It was now or never.

"Dan, I'm pregnant."

His lack of response forced me to look him in the eyes for an insight into his reaction.

"You're pregnant?"

He tested the words as he flopped down on his desk and looked straight ahead with his eyes glazed over. Pain etched into his handsome face and his olive skin had paled. He didn't move an inch.

"Who's the father? I mean, shit!" He ran his hand

through his hair. "I didn't have a condom, you know—Could the baby be mine?"

Fuck—

Eye contact became a problem for me as I scrambled for a plausible reason to explain how I knew for sure that Dan wasn't the father of my baby.

"No, it's not yours. King is the father."

"How are you so sure?"

"Because I just know!" My chest tightened and my stomach flipped as my forehead dampened. Speckles clouded my vision as I blinked through the haze.

"How Chloe!?"

"Because I was on the pill when you and I had unprotected sex." I paused for a beat. "Look, I know this is hard to hear but King asked me to come off it, you know, so we could try for a baby and I couldn't refuse him. That's how I know it's his." *Liar!*

He took a dry swallow. "Oh. I see."

Telling Dan the version of events that King was aware of seemed like the safest play, and he didn't need to know the truth anymore than King did. If hurting Dan's feelings was my way out of this, then so be it. Dan didn't have the ability to harm me in the way his brother could, and whilst this was a lie, it was the type of lie that had good intentions behind it. What Dan didn't know wouldn't hurt him. Besides, it wasn't his, anyway…

"It's the reason I can't leave with you, Dan. I'm so sorry. I didn't really want to get pregnant, but it happened, so it has to be over between us."

The room silenced for way too long, so long that the sound of my breathing became too loud for me to bear.

After the quietest minute, I raised out of the chair to leave.

"So it's definitely Romero's?" He asked, halting my departure.

"Yes," the potential lie caught in my throat. "It is."

He paused with his lips parted as he mulled over his choice of words. "I still want you to come with me," he whispered.

Huh?

"Are you for real?" I took a step away from him. "I've just told you the baby isn't yours. It's over."

"It's not over in my eyes," his voice cracked with distress.

I pinched the bridge of my nose. "What I don't understand is why you continued to let me live in King's house and allowed me to forget about you?"

Dan blanched at the thought of answering my question, and he took a contemplative sip of his liquor. "Romero and

I made a deal."

Instinctively, I folded my arms over my chest. There was a strong suspicion growing inside me that I didn't want to know the answer to my next question. "You made a deal? What kind of deal?"

"Romero said I could have you if I agreed to shift ten million dollars of cocaine for his biggest client. Once the shipment had landed in Puerto Rico, he would hand you over to me, but until then, I needed to keep away from you with no contact."

My legs shook when a surge of adrenaline knocked my knees. "Are you serious?"

"That's the deal we shook on and as he told me he'd tapped your cell phone, I had no way of reaching you. In the time we've been apart, I've been planning our future together. It's all in hand Chloe."

My mind went into self preservation mode and completely shut down where the urge to leave immediately took a hold of me.

"I'm sorry, Dan, I can't do this. I've got to go."

"Chloe, wait, please—"

I left his office before he could stop me and slammed the door on the way out. With desperation, I ran for the exit of the building as quickly as I could to avoid him chasing after me. This was all too much.

Once I was back in my car, tears streamed down my face in waves as I attempted to catch my breath. There was so much emotion inside of me it was almost too much to control. I could not allow myself to believe that after how well he had treated me recently, King would have agreed to use me as tradable goods. *Could he?* Would my pregnancy undo this mess and force him to renege on his deal with Dan?

I drove back to the house with one thing on my mind. I needed to speak to King and clear everything up.

Once the house was in view through my windshield, déjà vu hit me like a tonne of bricks where emergency vehicle flashing lights in the driveway and people gathered at the entrance to an ambulance were witnessing the aftermath of a tragedy.

Not again. No! Not again!

I parked up carelessly and raced over to the gathered crowd. King this time was standing amongst the group where his tall stature saw his head and shoulders above the rest. When he saw me, he grabbed hold of me in an enveloping hug.

"What's happened?" I asked into his chest. The shock of the scene washed away my anger towards him and his deal with Dan instantly.

King cut straight to the point. "Alice man. She's killed herself."

My knees buckled, and he caught me before I hit the floor. With strength, he scooped me up and took me over to the gardens, where there was a wooden bench to sit on.

"I'm sorry Chloe, I know you two were tight." He placed a comforting arm around my shoulders.

"But—How did she do it?" I asked, not really wanting to know but needing something to make it seem real.

"Pills by the look of it. One of the other girls found her in the bathroom. It was too late already before help arrived. She probably did it last night."

"Oh, God. I really can't believe this." I peered down at my finger where the tattoo was all I had left to remind me of our time together.

"Me too. She was a decent girl. What you lookin' at?"

He took hold of my hand and glared at the mark on my finger. There was a look of discomfort on his face as he absorbed the image. "Do you wanna get out of here?"

My grief for Alice overshadowed my current ambivalence towards the man I thought I might love, who'd potentially used me in his business transaction with Dan.

"Yes," I sobbed. "I do."

He reached his hand out for me to take and as we walked towards one of King's luxury cars, a man I'd not met before jogged over to meet us.

"Boss, the cops will wanna talk to you about this," he said calmly.

"Give them my cell number. I'm going to the apartment for a few days. Come on Shorty, let's step."

With a heavy heart, I looked out of the car window at the scene we were leaving behind us. I couldn't believe Alice could do something like that to herself. The pain she must've been in, the pain I must've caused her.

King saw my silent distress. "Hey, this wasn't your fault."

I smiled a small smile at his handsome face. "Am I that easy to read?"

"Yeah, you are." He smirked to himself as a thought crossed his mind.

I took a deep, cleansing breath. *Just rip off the band aid and tell him.*

"I went to see Dan before."

King's hands bunched around the steering wheel as his

instantaneous agitation radiated from his body. It was infectious. "You did what!? Why would you do that?"

I looked out of the window again, watching objects whizz by us.

"Dan said you made a deal with him. One that involved me."

"Oh? What deal is this?"

"The deal where he transports your goods, and I'm the reward. I know all about your business, Romeo. Don't try to hide it."

"Baby Brother has a big mouth, doesn't he?"

"He's told me the truth from the start."

I could feel my voice raising with the same agitation he was emitting.

"I haven't lied to you."

"So you didn't make that deal, then?"

"Well, I did," he shrugged, "but only to secure the transportation. You already know I'd never let him have you. If I meant it, you wouldn't be in this car with me now."

I thought for a moment. What he said actually made sense.

"Do you promise you wouldn't have gone through with it?"

Was I in such a desperate situation that his explanation

was enough for me?

Whether it was evolutionary survival or plain insanity, my body urged me to accept his promise. Without him, me and my baby had nothing.

He put his hand on his crotch. "I swear on my dick."

The image of him acting a fool to lighten the mood made me giggle, releasing some of the sadness trapped inside my chest. I exhaled heavily at the predicament me and my baby faced. We deserved so much more than this, but I'd have to trust my instincts that Romeo was telling the truth. Our future depended on me making the right decision.

Tears welled my eyes again. "It hasn't hit me yet. I can't believe Alice is dead."

"I can. It was me who had to identify her body. Shit like that sticks with you."

Unwelcome images of her beautiful, lifeless body filled my vision. "Oh God. I'm glad it wasn't me that found her."

"It's always me that has to deal with the shit these bitches cause. Same thing happened with her girl, Jody."

"Oh jeez, you found Jody after she shot herself?"

King looked over at me in confusion. "Jody didn't shoot herself?"

"Huh? Alice told me that she did."

Romeo chuckled in disbelief at her tale of inaccurate

events.

"Alice has always been a crazy bitch for real."

My seatbelt suddenly felt too tight across my body and the idea that yet another person who I felt closest to had lied to me had me wanting to open the car door on the freeway again.

"Well, what happened then?"

He paused for a moment, thinking about his delivery, as he knew how much Alice meant to me.

"Shit. I'll just say it how it is. Alice shot Jody in the head."

My mouth dropped open in disbelief. "What? Why would she do that!?"

"Because Alice found out that Jody was leavin' to be with her boyfriend."

My whole body trembled as the adrenaline pumped through every sinew of tissue. Had I gotten any further into a relationship with Alice, that could have been me.

King looked at me from the side. "Why do you think you didn't see Alice in our bed anymore? I saw she'd reeled you in with her greedy cunt, and I figured I needed to protect you. Seeing that tattoo on your finger confirmed I was right."

"What do you mean?"

"She got matchin' ink with Jody, too."

Holy fuck!

"Wow. Honestly, my head is spinning."

I wiped the dampness from my forehead and the knot in my stomach had the contents climbing up my gullet again.

"This is too much. I mean, I kinda knew something wasn't right with Alice. But—"

His lips thinned into a line. "She had a tough life before she came to live with me."

"She did? Why, what happened to her?"

"A couple years back, there was this big cheese mother fucker who bought big stacks from me on the regular. He invited me over to his crib for a smokin' session, which was perfect 'cause I was tryin' to shift some of my new product."

King paused for a moment at a stop sign, and I waited on tenterhooks for him to continue his story.

When the traffic eventually cleared, the car picked up speed again.

"So yeah, my guy said he had a whore that would give me head in exchange for a bag of my new shit. You already know I love me some head, so I said hell yeah. But my dick soon went limp when he took me to her bedroom. He had Alice chained to the bed, and she looked like shit. Not my vibe at all. You know it's bad when even I can't get hard."

"Oh my God, Romeo, what did you do?"

"I bought her off him for five grand and a bag of snow and she stayed with me ever since. Until now, anyway." He suddenly looked melancholy.

"You're actually a good man. The more I learn about you, the more I like you."

I saw him smirking through his side profile. "Oh, so you like me now, then?"

I giggled. "I'm sure that'll change."

With King as the driver, it gave me the opportunity for the rest of the trip to drink in my child's father while he was at his most relaxed; driving.

His free hand rested on the centre armrest and his diamond clad bracelet hung loose on his thick wrist. The impressive tattoo sleeve he sported was like an artist's tapestry that must've been expensive and painful to apply.

My eyes tracked up his body and across to the side profile of his chiselled features with his black curly hair neatly styled on top of his head that sculptured into a fade trim down his muscular tattooed neck, and his sideburns blended into the stubble along his strong jawline. I licked my lips.

"Like what you see?" He asked, catching me ogling him.

I giggled again. "Maybe." Suddenly I was shy.

He reached over and brushed my cheek with his thumb, and his warm touch made my skin tingle.

In response to the energy exchange between us, I placed my hand over my stomach and held it there as a reminder that our baby was inside me. Right then, in that moment, I couldn't wait to tell him, but it was important to me that the timing was right. I wasn't sure if today would be ideal after what had happened to Alice. *Shit.* Was she really gone?

The valet was waiting for us at the apartment entrance when we pulled up fifteen minutes later. King hopped out first and tossed the keys to the young man, where paparazzi began taking pictures of him.

I closed the door behind me as the camera flashes bathed me in bright light while I walked over to King, who was quizzing the boy, no older than a teenager.

"Do you know how to handle a Ferrari F8 Spider Son?"

The youngster kept his eyes straight ahead of him. "Yes Sir. I've had extensive training."

"Then you'll know how much these cost. Can I trust you?"

I grabbed King's arm. We didn't need anymore drama.

"Leave the poor boy alone. Come on, I wanna get away from the camera."

King did as I asked, and I linked my arm through the loop of his as we looked ever the sophisticated couple who blended in with the other residents of the apartment building.

Upon the lift doors sliding open, I was stunned to find that King had fully furnished the apartment since my last visit.

"This is nice," I said, as I had a look around the room, running my fingers along the back of the sofa to feel the expensive fabric. "When did you do this?"

"You can change anything in here that you don't like," he said cautiously as he lit a cigar and poured out two glasses of brandy. "I have a woman that sorts out shit like this."

He held out a glass for me, and I took it automatically while the thought of the woman that had decorated the place distracted me. Did he fuck her on the new couch? On the kitchen island? In our bed?

As I was about to put the glass to my lips, I remembered the baby. *Shit.*

"That's good brandy," he said as he necked his shot back, eyeing me disapprovingly.

My smile reached my eyes as I set down the glass on the countertop. "I'm sure it is."

He mirrored my grin as if it were infectious. "We're smiling for good brandy?"

I shook my head, "not just for good brandy, no."

"Oh?" he smirked. "What else?"

My body filled with warmth as I prepared myself.

"I'm pregnant." I blurted it out with a simultaneous release of adrenaline that blushed the apples of my cheeks.

He set his glass down and his smile faded when his eyes shone. "Wait. For real?"

"Yes," I nodded. "I'm pregnant!"

The announcement had gone nothing like I'd planned in my head, but I didn't care; he was ecstatic.

Romeo came from around the kitchen island and scooped me up in his arms.

"You're really pregnant and I'm the dad?" He said again, testing the words.

Oh. Could he see right through me?

"Yes," I nodded cautiously. "The baby is yours."

He grabbed me in a powerful hug and kept me there for a moment as he smelt my hair and planted a kiss on the top of my head.

"I knew you were the one the minute I first saw you," he whispered.

I looked up at him and cupped the sides of his face in my

hands as I kissed his lips tenderly.

Romeo suddenly knelt down on his knees, resting his head against my stomach and his hands around my waist, where he placed his ear to my skin as if he were going to hear his unborn child talk to him.

"That's my son in there," he said, kissing my tummy.

I ran my fingers through his glossy curls as I felt him give me his love. "Or daughter?" I countered.

"Nah," he pursed his lips, "that's a boy in there, I know it."

He rose to meet with my face, and as his eyes narrowed when a thought crossed his mind. "But you were bleedin'?"

"It confused me, too," I shrugged. "But I went to the pharmacy and I guess she was right."

He reached into his shorts pocket for his phone and put it to his ear. "Snake? yeah, tell them to fuck off. No, not tonight. Listen, get me a pregnancy test. Drop it off at the apartment. Do it now." He hung up.

Oh.

My eyes softened as my bubble burst. "Don't you trust me?"

"I just want to be sure before I get too excited." he hugged me again. "Shit, my nerves are all over the joint," he relit his cigar that had fizzled out.

"Shouldn't you stop smoking those around me now?"

I was half joking and not really expecting him to take it seriously, but he stubbed it out into a waiting ash tray, sat upon a new accent table courtesy of the mystery woman, and he wafted the smoke away from me.

"You're right, my bad."

He strolled back into the kitchen to pour himself another drink.

We settled ourselves on the new beige sofa that faced the panoramic window, with his arm around me as we gazed out towards the skyline.

"I can't believe Alice died. My stomach hurts just thinking about it."

"Hmm, for real. Life can kick you in the cunt sometimes. Gotta rise above it."

Romeo's attempt at comfort was lackluster, but was I really expecting more from a man like him?

"It's just. I dunno," I sighed. "I guess she meant a lot to me."

"Keepin' it one hundred. I'm almost glad it happened."

With my mouth ajar, I glared at him. "You're glad!?"

"I got a feelin' she'd Jody you at some point. So, yeah. I own what I said."

There was a knock on the door that made me jump.

"It's just Snake," King said, in response to my unspoken question. He padded barefoot over to the door and opened it without letting Snake inside, where he took the goods and closed the door, locking it.

"Aight, lets go," he ordered, already assuming I would follow.

I accompanied him into the en suite bathroom and took the box from him anxiously, where I waited a second for him to leave, but he continued to stand there.

"Are you going to watch?" I asked, expecting him to take the hint and wait in the adjoining bedroom.

He smiled salaciously. "Hell yeah, I'm gonna watch."

It was awkward at first trying to pee on the stick with an audience, but I just about managed it successfully. I pushed the cap on the end and set it down on top of the closed toilet lid and we both stood over it, staring at the little results windows.

It was then that I panicked it would come back negative and my palms became clammy with sweat. I'd just ended it with Dan, but if I wasn't pregnant, would King still want me? Could we try again?

Oh no.

Eventually, the result popped up to confirm that I was indeed pregnant.

The forceful exhale through my parted lips as relief consumed me, transferred between the two of us.

"I'm one lucky son of a bitch right now." He clasped his hands around my waist and kissed me like his life was complete.

We didn't break the kiss when he pulled me up to wrap my legs around him as he carried me back into the bedroom.

"You're a sexy woman Chloe," he said between kisses as he set me down gently on the bed and leant over the top of me.

I looked over his shoulder. "Are you not frosting the windows?"

Romeo sounded surprised by my question. "Do you want me to?"

I giggled. "Not really."

He let out a primal growl at my promiscuity. "I'm so hard for you. Make me come Baby, I need it."

I pulled his erection out of his pants and toyed with him for a few strokes. He was already rock hard in response to my touch, but I knew he wasn't yet desperate. We kissed as I played with him, alternating between massaging his balls and stroking his length.

All at once, the unwelcome thought of Dan not being

circumcised popped into my head. *Stop it. Not now.*

"What?" He asked with an ability to read my thoughts.

Shit, how did he know?

"Nothing." I kissed him deeper to rid my roaming mind.

"Fuck, I can't wait any longer. I need to be inside you."

With passion, he penetrated my wet vagina and established a rhythm that could only be described as lovemaking.

The way my body responded sent surges of electricity to my core and he collapsed on top of me when my pussy clamped around him as I came for him. Our shared climax brought us back together.

As I arrived back to reality from my orgasm induced state, I smiled inwardly at the idea that thousands of people below could well have seen us make love. This was me. The type of girl that fucked her boyfriend in full view of the city below without a care in the world. He was the man I was meant to be with and we fitted each other like a hand to a glove. My saviour, and my safe haven. I was finally free.

Romeo leant over me and gently cupped my breast in his hand. "These are my favourite," he said as he delicately caressed my sensitive skin.

"Be careful, they're tender."

His touch was almost too much to bear.

He kissed my nipple and then my lips. "Why do I want you even more now that you're pregnant?"

"I'm not sure," I sniggered, "but I like it."

CHAPTER 17

The blinding radiance of the sun through the panoramic window and the commotion via the chaotic movement within our bedroom woke me early the next morning.

"Something wrong?" I asked King, who was hurriedly dressing himself.

"Snake tells me some shit is goin' down back at the house and a couple of hoes need correctin'. Somethin' to do with Alice."

Concern marred my face. "I hope you're not going to hit them."

Romeo adjusted his heavy crucifix chain around his neck as he continued to dress.

"You know that's exactly what I'm goin' to do."

"But I know how it feels to be on the receiving end of one of your corrections."

He tugged on his sneakers with a scowl. "I don't want to talk about this now."

Well, of course, he didn't want to talk about it, but that

didn't mean I wasn't ready to. If there was anything I could change about the way he operated, it would be his choice of punishments.

"Please don't kill anyone, Romeo."

He sneered, as if my comment seemed preposterous.

"I don't plan on it."

His serious eyes peered up at me as he adjusted the tongue of his footwear. "You do realise Tat pulled a knife out on me, don't you? I made a split second decision. Either let her stab me or handle it."

Woah what?

"No, I didn't know that." Romeo's unexpected admission astonished me.

"The fact she smuggled the blade into the bedroom showed weakness on my part, that's why no one knows about this apart from you. I don't kill whores for no reason. You either kill or get killed. I'm just tryin' to live."

Only he and Tatiana had the knowledge of what really happened in our bedroom that day, and there was no way of knowing if he was telling the truth or lying through his teeth. But I saw firsthand that he was trying so hard to be the man I wanted him to be and if that snippet was all I had to work with right now. It would have to be enough.

As he stalked about the place on a mission to find his watch, I smirked when he lifted the same accent cushion for the third time in a futile pursuit of the elusive item.

"When do we have to start living here full time?" I asked, handing him the watch, where he scowled as he took it from me.

Once he'd closed the clasp, he whipped the cover off me, exposing my naked body. "Get your ass up, Woman, we need to leave now!"

I reflexively covered my breasts. "Hey! OK! I'm going to, but answer the question first."

His eyes appeared wistful, as if he had already reached the conclusion that the apartment wouldn't work for us the way he'd initially planned. "Well, we don't have to if you really don't want to?"

I released a deep sigh, lost in reflection. "I'll make a final decision and let you know." Now wasn't a good time for treading on his masculinity when he had whores running wild back home.

On route back to the house, I grew restless; I just couldn't keep still and our earlier talk about Tatiana stirred up some unwelcome concerns that I didn't realise I had.

"Spit it," King said with a firm grip on the steering wheel

as he focused straight ahead of him.

I stared at him, baffled. "What do you mean?"

"You've not said a word yet since we got in the car and I know how you bitches get crazy sometimes, so what's the problem?"

His sexist remark made me chuckle, but experience served him well. He wasn't wrong.

"I was just thinking about Tatiana. You know, after what we talked about before—"

"And?"

"What's the history with you two? How did you meet?"

As soon as I asked, I regretted it. Even if he wanted to share, did I really want to find out? Was my stomach prepared for tales of sex, drugs, love, and more?

"Shit Chloe, that type of talk's gonna get my dick soft."

I puffed outwardly. "I highly doubt that, Romeo. That thing is *never* soft."

He chuckled in agreement at my backhanded compliment and smirked at me from the side, "true."

His demeanour seemed relaxed, with his elbow on the doorsill and his hands on the steering wheel presenting the perfect talking mood that afforded me the chance to really get the truth out of him.

"So, how did you both meet?"

His lips thinned as he took a minute to consider his words. It was a minute longer than I would have needed under similar circumstances, but I figured he was attempting to filter out anything distasteful.

"Tat and her Mom were street whores and Patricia used Tat to get drug money by selling pussy, you know, with her being young and beautiful. I was the guy who sold them the drugs."

As we pulled up to a red light, he looked out of the window in reverie where his rested hand raised to his mouth as he chewed on his thumbnail.

It was obvious then that he had stronger feelings for Tatiana than he let on and if I was honest with myself; it was a relief that he wasn't as cold as he led people to believe. But hearing him call her beautiful left a sour taste in my mouth that I couldn't overlook.

"How did Tat come to live with you then?"

The tension from my probing began diffusing from his pores and relaxed Romeo vanished in replacement of callous King.

"Do you really wanna talk about this shit?" He mumbled, glancing over at me with distress.

Perhaps I was playing a dangerous game, yes. But was that going to deter me? No.

As he was in nicotine withdrawal through his attempt at not smoking around me and the baby, it was sure making him antsy and he must have adjusted himself in his seat half a dozen times already.

"Yes Romeo," I smiled. "I want to know everything about you."

"Fuck," he sighed. "OK, whatever. Pat built up a long debt to me and I refused her anymore product until she settled. I ain't about to let my customers hear they could screw me over. So anyway, she gave me her daughter as payment. Tatiana came to live with me and at first I just fucked her whenever I wanted as a way to recoup my losses. After a time, she became more than that."

"Oh."

His story stunned me into complete silence. Not a single element of what he said was something I'd anticipated.

"Don't start with that 'oh' shit. You asked, and I told. Give me attitude now and I'll get pissed!"

His outrage caused a chemical reaction in my core that triggered a nuclear meltdown, and without thinking, I flailed my arms with wrath of my own. "There you go again, trying to scare me!"

Without any indication, he yanked the steering wheel where he pulled into a side road, skidding to a halt he turned his whole body to face me. "You gonna yell at me again, Woman?"

He had a satanic glare of pure evil in his piercing eyes that had me wanting to flee.

I scowled at him as my chest heaved in response, where I had a hard time taking in air as my survival instincts kicked in.

"Fuck you," I hissed as I reached for the door handle.

Tears pricked the corners of my eyes. *Don't fucking cry now!*

Romeo grabbed my arm in his firm hold. He was strong enough to pin me back into my seat with one hand. "Don't Chloe!"

"Or what exactly?" I panted. "You'll hit me again?"

My face reddened with pregnancy induced rage against him, but my outburst only further evoked his menacing side.

"Close the car door. Now!"

The shift in his tone, coupled with his body language, compelled me to do as I was told. Still terrified of him, the glare he presented showed no mercy.

As I obeyed, he shut his eyes and took a cathartic breath, as though he'd taken himself to his happy place. When he reopened the heavy lids, his tone was softer.

"I told you not to push me. I'm sorry, OK? Appreciate that I'm tryin' here, but this don't come naturally to someone like me." His shoulders relaxed, and we looked at each other intently. "Get on my dick, now."

He unbuckled his seatbelt frantically as his erection formed within the soft fabric of his shorts.

As I was the only one with a clear head, I glanced at our surroundings. Apart from the loose sand kicked up from the screeching tyres providing a veil of ignorance, we were not invisible. Paparazzi could be lurking anywhere.

"Um, Romeo, all it's going to take is for someone to walk by and see us."

With cars moving past us from all angles, and a dog walkers footpath right beside us, there wasn't an ounce of privacy that suited his celebrity status.

But Romeo, lost in himself and not listening to a word I was saying, stared at my breasts with primal intent. His erection unabating was ready and at once, I needed him as much as he did me.

I unfastened my seatbelt and climbed over and onto his lap, where he pulled his dick out from his shorts and snatched my underwear to the side as he filled me eagerly.

"I love how you wear dresses," he groaned into my neck as the length of his penis met with my insides. "Means I can have you however I want."

With a need to wash away his Tatiana love story, I rode him as hard as I could with his help to keep the tempo. He slapped me down on top of him as we fucked raw in his car where each of us used the other to relieve the stress we'd created between us. This was not about love, this was explicitly lust.

As we surrendered ourselves to one another, tyres rolling across rough terrain behind us pricked Romeo's ears as a dark- coloured car pulled up with blacked-out windows. Instantly, his grip around my waist tightened.

My pace slowed as he eyed the rear-view mirror.

"Keep goin', Baby," he whispered with encouragement, never breaking focus from the vehicle.

The length of his dick swelled inside me, stretching out my core, but his fixation on the potential threat didn't wane.

Stroke after stroke, we both rode the wave to the crest until eventually I came, and like clockwork we both struck midnight as he followed my lead, but this time his eyes remained open; focused.

When my breathing calmed and my eyes adjusted, the vehicle was gone.

"Are you OK?" I asked as I raised myself out of his lap.

"Yeah," he didn't blink. "All good."

With a groan as I manipulated my body back into my seat, I peered at the tense side aspect of his face. "Tell me Romeo, please."

He ran his hand through his hair, staring straight ahead as the battle he was having with his inner monologue surfaced.

"I was that busy arguin' with you that I didn't notice my crew weren't followin' us back home."

Oh.

This wouldn't be the first time I had exposed him to a threat and the thought of Clive the creep flooded my guilty conscience.

"So, where are your crew, then?"

As if on cue, the familiar black SUV pulled in behind our car and Romeo instantly relaxed, releasing the breath he'd held since I climbed on top of him. "Right behind us."

He restarted the engine, and I vowed to keep my trap shut for the rest of the trip back to the mansion, but something about his crew's unexplained absence bothered me, and I knew it bothered him, too.

Romeo had been upstairs in our bedroom, dealing with the issues that brought us back early from the apartment for the last hour, and we really needed to have a conversation about that. Not unreasonably, I didn't want anyone in our bedroom without me being there, and surely we'd be able to handle any business-related matters in one of the many other rooms in the house?

The unwelcome thought that the punishment room still lurked under the stairs was a topic of conversation I'd need to raise with him in the near future. If he was correcting girls today, I wouldn't allow him to take them in there. No chance.

Now being pregnant, I was armoured against his bullshit, and there was no way for him to stop me from having my say, and the power that gave me seemed to go to my head. Was I becoming more like him?

Before being consciously aware of what I was doing, the desire to confront him about my newfound passion for women's rights found me storming up the stairs towards the masculine voices coming from inside the bedroom.

I didn't bother to knock. I shouldn't need to ask permission to enter my own space.

When my eyes met with King's, he frowned. "What do you want Chloe?"

The tone he used didn't sit well with me, and if he thought it was a suitable way to address me around our guests, he was sadly mistaken.

There were five men in total, two I didn't recognise, sitting on pull out chairs playing cards around a fold-out table.

Aside from the stench of stale cigars, the room was fresh and had been thoroughly cleaned of the murder scene, where nothing but a bullet hole in the ceiling remained.

When I continued to look but not explain myself, he asked again. "You good?"

I folded my arms across my chest to dampen the vicious spirit trying to leave my body. "No, actually I'm not."

Romeo focused his eyes back onto the fanned playing cards he clutched in his hands. "Can it wait? I'm workin' here." He lifted a card, frowned and placed it back again.

"I'd hardly call a game of snap with your buddies working, Romeo."

A deathly silence fell upon the room when King's eyes shone with devilment. "Leave." He ordered the men who didn't need telling twice.

As the last man stepped over the threshold, King tossed his cards on the table in frustration. "How many times have I gotta warn you about doin' that?"

I wasn't apologetic about my behaviour as my anger towards him was doubling by the minute.

"Well, I wanted to talk to you about something important."

Romeo exhaled and flipped open his cigar holder. "Go on then!" He said as he sat back in his chair, selecting his Cuban of choice.

"What did you do to the girls that needed punishing today?"

His brow furrowed at my question. "Why is that your business?"

The cigar clenched between his teeth was waiting in anticipation to be lit, with his lighter poised at the tip ready, but not quite enough to complete the action.

I tapped my foot. "I want to know."

His cheeks hollowed as he took a puff while he coaxed the flame to ignite. "I killed them. Why?"

The release of air produced a plume of smoke that filled the room, setting an eerie scene straight out of a horror film.

"You did! What for!?"

He lifted himself out of his chair and stomped over to his drinks cabinet, where he plucked out a bottle of liquor by the neck and unscrewed the cap. "Is this an episode of crime scene investigation?"

Romeo's humorous comment broke my scowl into a

smirk when I was striving to be serious.

"Answer the question, please."

He poured himself a drink, but didn't extend the same courtesy to me. "The whores were kickin' up a fuss about Alice dyin' and sayin' they were worried they'd be next. The two ring leaders wanted me to fuck them to stop them tellin' the cops I had somethin' to do with it."

His shocking disclosure stunned me into silence. I wasn't expecting him to have been dealing with something as serious as blackmail. But all I could think of in that moment was whether or not he slept with them first.

My focus fell to the ground, unable to look him in the eye.

"And did you?"

"Fuck them? No, I didn't," he threw back his liquor, and he poured a second helping, ignoring the disapproving look on my face.

Romeo's words put my mind to rest on one pressing issue, as while murder wasn't my favourite, those whores most certainly deserved it. Blackmailing my man in order to sleep with him? *No way.*

But while I was on board with that particular correction, I'd still not yet broached the subject of the punishment room, and me never wanting to step foot in there again. As

I was on a roll, I decided to go for it. It was now or never.

"Also, something else that's bothering me. The punishment room. I want it gone."

He smiled at an opportunity that presented itself to him. "That's wife talk. As you ain't said yes yet, so no can do, Babe."

Fuck.

I rolled my eyes in exasperation, knowing that he was toying with me to downplay the severity of the situation, but I wasn't backing down. *No chance.*

"I mean it, Romeo, don't ever put me in that room again."

"Sayin' shit like that pisses me off Chloe. Watch your mouth."

"Promise me Romeo!"

"Yes! I fuckin' promise you! God damn it!" He slammed his fist down on the card table. "You make it sound like I had that storage room set up for slappin' bitches. I didn't. It just happened that I didn't want to punish you in front of everyone and it was the closest place to take you to."

He flopped down onto the bed and necked back the second glass.

My thoughts stalled at his unexpected explanation. Did I hear him right? Was I in the wrong about this?

"That isn't a punishment room, then?"

"No." His clipped tone told me he was done with me and he looked like he wanted to be anywhere else but in our bedroom.

My shoulders relaxed as the tension suddenly diffused from my body. "Oh, OK, that's settled then."

Romeo's stance loosened when he saw me smile.

"So, can I get back to work now? I had a half million bet on that card game."

"Wait, really? You weren't actually playing snap then?" I giggled in the cute way I did to get him to like me again.

"Chloe, you know how to get under my skin and test my patience in ways I didn't know possible. No, I wasn't." He walked towards me and placed his hands around my waist. "You can apologise to me in bed tonight. But right now, I need you to step."

I kissed his liquor tainted lips. "I will, but please stop smoking in here. It stinks."

He growled in irritation as he slapped my ass playfully, making me yelp. "Leave!"

I spent the rest of the afternoon entertaining myself by watching shit TV. My attempt to watch American Dad in order to find something in common with Romeo didn't go well. It didn't appeal to me in the slightest and was not even marginally funny.

I'd just finished my bowl of popcorn when there was a knock on the front door, which was odd as people just came and went as they pleased in the house normally, but as I was the only one around, I had no choice but to answer it.

Alarm bells rang instantly when two female police officers emerged from the other side of the opening.

The first officer cleared her throat. "We need to speak with Mr. Romero Giannetti."

I looked down at her badge; Officer Reed. "Sure. Come in, officers. He's just upstairs. I'll get him for you."

We had been expecting the cops to come over and see Romeo after Alice's death, but knowing they were on our property had me on edge.

Upon opening our bedroom door, I was pleased to find that only King and Tommy remained. Their card game must have ended well, as Romeo had a smile on his handsome face.

They both stopped talking when I entered. "S'up Babe?" His brows knitted together with concern or agitation. I wasn't sure which.

"Couple of cops downstairs wanna see you, Romeo."

He ran his hand through his hair. "Fuck. This will be

about Alice. I haven't got time for this shit."

Hopping off the bed, he reached inside his waist band and tossed his gun through the air to Tommy.

"Ain't about to give them a reason to take me in."

After he adjusted his thick chain, he took my outstretched hand, and I led him down to where the officers waited.

On our way down the stairs, he slid his hand up the inside of my thigh and ran it between the crack of my backside. "I'm gonna fuck this ass tonight."

His delivery was too loud. So much so that the cops heard every word evidenced in their sudden silence.

"Shush." I sniggered playfully, elbowing any part of his body I could reach behind me. But ignorant was Romeo's middle name and, with no intention of listening to me, he squeezed my ass cheek and groaned primly. I knew before I saw that his dick had gone hard.

I halted us halfway down the staircase and turned to face his erection. "Romeo, you can't meet the cops with that!" I whispered as I pointed at the hardened mound.

"This is America!" he hollered. "If a man can't have a hard on in his own crib, then there's somethin' wrong."

I rolled my eyes in exasperation and, with as much

patience as I could muster, I painted on a fake smile for the waiting officers.

As we entered the living room, the cops rose to their feet in anticipation of meeting the intimidating man they'd come here to see, and I wondered why on earth they had sent women to handle a guy like him.

"Mr. Giannetti?" Officer Reed asked in her best authoritative tone, but she was fooling nobody. Her eyes gave her anxiety away as she attempted to mask her fear. It reminded me of the way I used to feel around him back in the beginning, when everything about him frightened me.

"Ladies, I'm a busy man," King rubbed his hands together. He seemed to do that when he was trying to keep himself calm. "So, what can I do for you?"

"We need to ask you about the death of Miss Alice Wright. As this is the second death within this property in less than a month, we have opened up an investigation."

"Anyone can see she topped herself," he said matter-of-factly.

"It's that exact reason, Sir, that we are questioning you now. We also need to speak to a Miss Adams."

"Who?" He replied, clueless they were referring to me. And this man wanted me to accept his marriage proposal?

Idiot.

"Miss Chloe Adams? I believe she is your partner?"

King looked at the officer, perplexed. "She's got fuck all to do with any of this."

Habitually, he moved his hand towards his pocket in an automated response to collect his cigar case.

"Hands in the air and get on your knees!" Officer Reed ordered as she drew her gun against his chest.

Oh, no—Not again.

He raised his hands in compliance. "I was just grabbin' my smokes, damn it!"

"You can explain yourself at the station," she panted. "On your knees while I cuff you!"

King obeyed and dropped to his knees while the other officer cuffed him at his waist where she read him his rights that he'd heard one too many times before.

Romeo peered over his shoulder towards me as they ushered him forwards to their vehicle. "The boys will keep you safe while I'm gone. I won't be long."

At the last moment before he left, he gave me a reassuring wink, but I was anything but assured.

"But, wait, he hasn't done anything wrong!" I shouted in vain at the officers, who had already made their minds up before they'd even entered our home.

How could they do this to us? *I need him*, but clearly they were looking for a reason—any reason at all to arrest King, and now I understood why he went on the run after Tatiana's death.

I watched helplessly through the window as they loaded him into the back of their car, where his strong back muscles defined as he sloped into the vehicle with his arms strapped in front of him. When his gaze caught mine through the glass, he nodded at me with a small smile.

Spontaneously, I put my hand up to the pane between us, where I just wanted to touch him one last time.

As soon as he was out of sight, the sense of overwhelming vulnerability shrouded me like a cloak of darkness. I had no friends in this house anymore, and the thought of spending the night alone without him was a terrifying notion.

While I sat on the sofa alone, I wrapped a blanket around myself tightly for comfort where I sensed Alice's presence all around me. Her smell seemed to be everywhere, a painful reminder of the friend I had lost.

The cathartic sobs I should have released when I learned of her death were suddenly threatening to fall in waves.

Oh Alice.

I placed a protective hand on my stomach. "I'll keep you safe while Daddy is gone," I whispered, stroking my warm skin.

"Ha! You're pregnant then?" A voice from the open door startled me.

I snapped my head towards the sound of the female voice to find Michelle standing in the doorway with one hand holding onto the door frame. I wasn't sure how long she'd been standing there, but she's heard enough.

"What?" I asked, stalling for time.

"You're looking fat already, it's so obvious," she screwed her nose up with disgust like she'd smelt something rotten.

"Keep your fucking nose out, Michelle," I hissed back at her.

While King was away, I had to stick up for myself.

"You better watch your mouth. Daddy isn't here now to protect you."

Michelle had a sly smile and a squinty eye that I wanted to slap off her ugly face, but her words stirred anxiety within me that made me question her motives. Would she hurt me? My baby?

I rose to my feet to match her level. "You think you can threaten me!?"

But as suspected, she took a few steps closer to narrow

the void between us.

"Look at the state of you," she grimaced. "You're just another pathetic notch on his belt. He doesn't love you, you realise that, right? You're no different from the rest of us and you'll end up six feet under, just like Tat and Alice. Good luck." She flipped her hair and turned to leave.

Not capable of containing my indignation any longer, I reached for her long, tangled red strands and yanked hard, jolting her head backwards into my body.

My lips were millimetres from her ear. "Threaten me again and you're dead," I used the same menacing tone King had used against me.

After a pause to let my words sink in, I let her go, and she stumbled back to her feet. "You're gonna regret that, you fucking fat whore!"

The abhorrence built inside me as I snarled. Did she not hear the news that I was the girlfriend of one of the most powerful men in our country? She should be on her knees, begging me for forgiveness.

Harnessing my inner King, I growled, "sleep with one eye open, Michelle. Watch your back."

She didn't look at me again as she left the room, and I eyed her until she was out of sight, not allowing her to see my weaknesses as I kept my stance tall and my nerves steady. But on the inside, I was crumbling.

As an eerie calmness descended upon the room again where I took a moment to regain my composure and catch my breath. I was inhaling too heavily and my hands shook too violently. *Am I going to faint?*

I sat myself down on the sofa again, trying to relax and regroup myself for the sake of my baby as much as my own.

My anxious mind attempted to attach the firing neurons to threats I'd faced in order to make sense of it all.

Did the cops still want to speak to me in relation to Alice's death? Were they aware she and I were friends? How on earth could they assume I would be involved in the girls' murder? But suddenly Clive's dead body told a different story.

As for Michelle, did she serve empty threats, or would she go through with it and carry out an attack against me? I needed Romeo now more than ever.

Later that evening, the door knocker tapped against the wood, creating a spooky sound that echoed through the hallway. It was dark out and most of the occupants of the mansion were either in their rooms or out with clients.

I sighed and ambled to the door expecting a pizza delivery guy, but when I was met with copper toned brown eyes, my breathing hitched.

"Detective Saxon?" I choked out in dire need of a glass of water.

"Let me guess," Saxon smirked, "you went for a jog and just so happened to find yourself at Giannetti's mansion?"

Dumbfounded, I stumbled over my response. *What do I even say to that?*

"I recon your fight or flight kicked in, right? The same reflex that had you running from us and into Romero's car at Tatiana's funeral? Am I on the right track?"

"Um. Sorry, what?" I tucked my hair behind my ear and shifted my weight from one foot to the other. His surprise appearance had me completely shell-shocked.

He placed his finger to his lips in contemplation. "Hmm, but I'd say your reflexes need a little work, Chloe, as look what's happened." He raised his hands gesturing towards the mansion, "you seem to have run straight inside the gates of hell."

Saxon, out of uniform, held himself with the same level of contempt as he did at Tat's funeral and suddenly I had so many unanswered questions.

I cleared my throat, unable to stand his scrutiny a minute longer. "What are you doing here?"

His lips parted into a tight smile that didn't reach his

eyes, and he placed one foot inside. "May I come in?"

His forceful nature caught me by surprise, and I found myself stepping backwards, allowing him to enter, when in actuality, I had every right to refuse him.

"Um, I guess you can sit there," I gestured to King's usual seat cushion within the grand living room.

I perched on the arm of the opposite chair and waited awkwardly for him to say something.

Images of Frankie-Jo and the planned attack against me caught in my throat. How could he do that and then sit in front of me like nothing happened?

He took his seat dressed in jeans and a polo shirt with sneakers. Clearly, he was not here on official business, but something told me he was on the prowl for something big.

"So. Alice is dead?" He began abruptly.

"Um," I lowered my gaze. "Yes."

His powerful glare burned into my psyche, willing me to make eye contact with him.

"Have you written a Last Will And Testament yet, Chloe?"

I raised my head in puzzlement at his words with a sullen look. "Huh?"

"You're next, you know that, right?"

I rose to my feet, feeling anything but safe in his company. *What is he doing here?*

He raised his hands, sensing my retreat. "Apologies for my delivery. Please take a seat. Please."

"I'm sorry Detective, but how am I supposed to react around you when you tried to have me attacked?"

Weary behind the eyes, he looked at though he'd not slept in a week and something about his intensity informed me he took his job home with him.

"Listen Chloe, off the record, that was a call I needed to make in the hope you'd see sense. Anyway, look, you know the type of man you are dealing with here, yet you're living in his house watching women around you die, and you do nothing?"

With my lips parted in outrage, I listened to Saxon speak to me like I was dirt on his shoe. How dare he come into my home and villainize Romeo when he himself made an attempt against me?

Well, little did he know, I had a baby to defend, and he would not get away with this. Not now, or ever.

"I've nothing to say to you, Saxon. Please leave."

He hoisted himself out of King's chair and stood before me.

"These girls shouldn't have died, and I won't rest until

he's locked up and hopefully given the death penalty. Romero Giannetti is the devil reincarnated and I'm real sorry I couldn't save Tatiana—and Alice—but there won't be another death in this house on my watch. Mark my words."

I took a shaky breath and fought back the tears as I glimpsed my shared tattoo with Alice. The cop's words cut deep—no question. But self preservation would never allow me to side with him over my child's father. King and I had come too far to give up now.

"Will that be all? I wish for you to leave now."

Just as I was about to close the door on Saxon, I paused in thought. "FYI, if you want help in closing a case, don't try to have your best shot at winning attacked. That sort of plan will always backfire." I slammed the door against his nose and ran back to the living room, feeling as though I needed to be a million miles away from his location.

I'd just pulled the blanket over me when my phone rang in my pocket from a number I didn't recognise.

"Hello?"

"Chloe, it's me. They're ridin' my ass here, so I doubt I'll be released until tomorrow. Lawyer says they can't keep me long as I didn't have a piece on me. I will be home as soon as

I can. Look after my boy for me."

"OK." I stuttered.

King paused, allowing me to hear disruptive roars of aggravated men in the background, giving me an insight as to his location.

"You good?" He asked eventually, in a tone laced with concern.

"Um, I'm OK I suppose. Are you?"

He laughed down the phone like it was a stupid question.

"Yeah. Gotta go. Tell Tommy to rally the troops. He'll get what I mean." He hung up.

Frustration gnawed at me like a mouse against a block of cheese where all I wanted was Romeo back home to take care of me and our baby. I was too vulnerable to handle this alone.

Would Saxon come back again? Clearly feeling like he himself was above the law, would he make another attempt for information? While King was being held, who could I trust to keep me safe?

After a while, my internal storm stilled, and the house quietened except for the sound of female voices laughing from the kitchen next door. Were they laughing at me again?

I wrapped my arms tightly around myself in a cocoon of

security. *I can't do this.*

My phone rang again, dancing on the arm of the chair next to me, but this time I recognised the number immediately.

"Dan?" I whispered in disbelief.

He sighed into the receiver. "Romero has been arrested?"

"Wait. How did you know?"

"Does that matter? How's the baby?"

"Um, I don't think that concerns you."

"You do realise, Chloe, that it's not over between us, don't you?"

Reassurance that I wasn't completely alone was exactly what I needed to hear, but irrespective of that, I had made my choice to be with King, and I had to make it as clear to Dan as I had with Alice.

"You're a kind and caring man and you will always have a place in my heart, but my pregnancy changes everything. I'm not the one for you."

"The baby changes nothing if you don't let it," he mumbled through clenched teeth. "You are everything I need. I still love you."

"If you love me, *give up on me*. Can you please help me get King released? Please, Dan."

He sighed again. "I'm sorry Chloe, he's where he

belongs."

The line went dead as my hands dropped to my sides while tears pricked my eyes, and my throat burned from the threatening droplets that fell unceremoniously down my cheeks.

I can't do this.

Tommy cleared his throat at the entrance of the room with his hands rested at the base of his spine.

"Is everything OK Boss?" He asked cautiously, without making eye contact.

"Yes—oh wait—King said rally the troops, whatever that means."

His narrow eyes widened at my words, and he nodded his recognition where, turning on his heels, he vanished in an instant.

A tidal wave of exhaustion hit me like a tonne of bricks and I abruptly became deathly tired. Today had been one of those days I needed to forget immediately before my head exploded.

With a hollow chest, I made my way to our bedroom and climbed into our cold, empty bed where the sheets that were once warmed by several naked bodies now lay frozen and lifeless beneath me.

I lay for a while staring up at the ceiling with the cover

pulled tightly up around my neck so that the only skin exposed to the world was my face.

Every sound that I heard made me jump, and every movement made had me expecting the worst.

At that moment, I missed Alice lying next to me. God, it was painful to acknowledge she was gone. But most of all, I missed Hanna so badly. I knew it'd be unlikely that she and I would speak again, since we had said too much for either of us to go back. But that didn't mean I didn't have regrets, and that I didn't love her.

A couple of stray tears rolled down my cheeks, representing the losses I mourned, creating a chilled path in their wake as I sobbed myself to sleep with a broken heart filled with remorse.

Movement in the bedroom woke me in the middle of the night. "Who's there?" I whispered, bolting upright in alarm to find the room was pitch black.

"It's me," Romeo said calmly as he climbed in behind me, where his cologne instantly brought me comfort.

My heart thudded in my chest. "Jesus Christ Romeo, you scared me. What time is it?"

"Just before midnight, go back to sleep."

He kissed my hair and drew me closer to him, where I felt

the heat of his erection in my back. Romeo was home? Or was this a dream?

Instantly I fell back to sleep. Just the idea he was with me was enough. I was safe again.

CHAPTER 18

Two shadows huddled in cloaks as black as the night sky, beckoned me to join them. *Who are you? What is this place?* I moved closer to their distance, needing to know their names. Flames arose, flickering around their floating bodies, where finally they removed their hooded veils: Alice and Tatiana.

Sweat drenched my body as I shot upright in bed the next morning with a burning sensation in my throat. The bad dream I'd had was the second in a matter of days.

In search of comfort, I peered over to Romeo's side of the bed, but his spot was empty. I wanted to find him and hug him; needing to know that last night wasn't a dream, and he had come back home to me where he belonged.

With urgency to quell my anxiety, I peeled my damp skin from the sheets and opened our bedroom door, where I stopped in my tracks at the sound of hushed voices on the landing. *Romeo?*

Leaning towards the sound, I strained my hearing, but I

couldn't catch all the conversation.

Romeo said something in a foreign language. *Italian?*

"Got it, Boss." The identity-less male responded.

Regardless of the secrecy, I was relieved with the confirmation that Romeo had indeed returned home. But who had he been talking to, and what were they planning? Paranoia ate away at my psyche like a maggot on a corpse—Too many to choose from.

As I paced the bedroom with unease, I heard footsteps heading back towards me. *Shit.*

My heart rate picked up pace. Had he seen me eaves dropping?

King strolled in a moment later with sexy confidence and a warm smile, but he soon frowned when he caught sight of me standing in front of him.

"Are you OK? I thought you'd still be asleep."

"Yes, I'm fine." I lied.

With my confirmation, a primal growl escaped his lips.

"Look at that sexy body. Sheesh, I'm a lucky son of a bitch," he sauntered towards me with one thing on his mind.

Wait—Oh no.

Without warning, an attack of morning sickness hit me hard, and I heaved into my hand as soon as he reached me.

My eyes widened along with Kings, as I ran to the bathroom just in time, where I vomited violently into the toilet bowl.

"Shit, woman, are you alright in there?" He asked from the threshold of the room, looking anywhere but in my direction.

"Mm-hm, just morning sickness." I raised my hand for him to stand back. "Stay over there!"

Romeo ignored my request and crouched next to me, scooping up my hair out of the firing line, trying to help in any way possible. He remained reticent as I emptied the contents of my stomach.

It amazed me that someone like him possessed the ability to keep calm as he rolled off a piece of toilet tissue and gently wiped the corner of my mouth.

He eyed me carefully with an apologetic smile. "You good now?"

I nodded in agreement, receiving the tissue from his hand as I cleaned up the rest.

"It takes a lot to throw me off, but shit woman seeing you hurl like that made me go kind of sick, too. Have I got a temperature? Feel my forehead."

A snort escaped my nostrils as I sniggered while sitting down gingerly on the cold bathroom floor, overwhelmed with perspiration and unsteadiness.

"Morning sickness isn't catching Romeo. I think you're fine." I rolled my eyes at his theatrics. "If you think that was bad, just you wait until labour."

He gave a pensive look. "I think I'll wait outside for that."

With composure, he hitched his sweat pants and joined me on the floor, where he copied my knees to chest position.

I screwed up my nose at his remark. "Wait, you don't want to see your baby being born?"

"Of course I do, I was kiddin'. Not missing that day for the world."

He looked vacant for a moment, like he had something of concern on his mind, and we both sat quietly on the marbled floor, each deep in our own thoughts.

"So I guess now isn't a good time for me to get a nut?" He beamed his gorgeous smile.

I nudged my body into his with a smirk on my face. "Normally I can't resist you, but I have to say sex with you is the last thing on my mind right now."

His invisible hackles raised in response, and immediately I knew I'd offended him.

"You best mean you're off sex total and not just with me. That kind of talk makes me mad as hell!"

Unreasonable irritation formed a significant aspect of his personality not too dissimilar to Satan.

"Relax! Yes, I meant sex over all. I told you to stop scaring me."

He looked at me without smiling this time; deadly serious.

"My bad. I get protective over what's mine."

As we peered at each other in our Monk like positions, our eyes met where something about his glossy ocean irises informed me he was keeping information to himself.

"Is there something on your mind, Romeo?"

I hoped he would do a story time on his earlier secret conversation, but I couldn't directly ask and expose my snooping.

He glanced at my cleavage, and his eyebrow raised with interest. "The only thing on my mind is seein' you naked and ridin' my dick. Will I need to wait long?"

I swatted his muscular chest, an action I had no qualms about performing these days where we'd gotten to a point he didn't even tense up anymore.

"I love your romantic talk, Romeo, but I've no idea when I'll stop being sick."

In seeking comfort, I leant into his strong body, where he enveloped me in a one-armed hug.

"Crazy that I'm gonna be a dad, ain't it?"

One minute he was angry, the next he was vulnerable. So many personalities hidden beneath his hardened exterior.

But with how sure I was that I'd made the right decision that he was the father of my child, I didn't have an ounce of guilt knowing that my secret would never be revealed.

"Doesn't seem real, does it? Being a Mum is not something I imagined happening so soon."

"Have you told your Mom that you're pregnant?"

Fuck—Now isn't the time for this kind of talk.

"Um, no."

The room descended into quiet reflection again, but fortunately Romeo wasn't a questions kind of guy. My mother's passing was no secret, but her memory was sacred to me, and I only shared her with people I genuinely trusted, and while Romeo came close to my inner sanctum, he hadn't quite gained full access to the all-inclusive privileges just yet.

What was going on in his head?

"Listen," he sighed. "I've got some business to attend to which might take up a lot of my time today. Do you wanna stay here or go back to the apartment?"

Oh—

"I guess I'll stay here with you."

I looked down at the floor, feeling downhearted that this meant more time on my own.

"OK, Babe," he kissed my temple. "If you need me, call me."

He rose to his feet, keeping eye contact with me as desire clouded his thoughts where suddenly he exposed his erection.

"This is what happens when I kiss you. Imagine how you make me feel when I'm nuttin' for you."

The unholy vision of the father of my child standing before me, waving his dick, was truly remarkable. He had the ability to make me laugh without trying very hard and I must've been smiling wider than I released.

"You're not supposed to be laughin' at a man with his dick out." He snarled as he tucked his favourite toy away with a blush forming against his olive-toned cheeks.

"Hey, relax! I was laughing with you, not at your dick."

Romeo grabbed onto himself with passion, fury, and everything in between. An intense combination that often suggested he might combust at any given moment.

"This dick put a baby inside you, and now it's ready to feel your tight little pussy again. Get better quick or there will be trouble."

As he exited the room with a playful goodbye wink, I

found myself alone again.

It seemed I wasn't the only one with secrets, except the secrecy behind King's activities were driving me crazy. So many times I wanted to ask what he had been doing and where he was going, but part of me wasn't sure if I could handle the knowledge. Did he have it in him to still fuck other women? He'd already told me he'd stopped, but did I trust him implicitly? Wasn't my pregnancy now my comfort blanket and my reassurance?

Fretting over Romeo's where abouts would not do my mood any favours and, as he'd already warned me, I would be alone for most of the day, so instead of moping around, I decided to put my time to better use.

Hanna.

She had to be in the house somewhere? Just a matter of where.

I grabbed onto the sink and hoisted myself back to my feet, still sick to my stomach, but much better than earlier.

With friendship repair on my mind, I brushed my teeth to rid of the vomit taste and washed my face with a lovely fragrant foam to freshen up. It wasn't until the scent of vanilla hit my nostrils that a harrowing realisation hit me. It was Alice's.

Reactively, I ran my finger over our once shared tattoo;

our declaration. Ironically, once a symbol of being half of a whole, it was now broken, never to be put back together again. My broken heart. The reality that I wouldn't see her again hurt profoundly, and gave me even more reason to repair the relationship with my friend who was still living.

As I rifled through Romeo's closet to prepare for my mission to save my only friendship, I found my clothing options very limited.

I shrugged on one of his t-shirts; a Gucci tee with the logo down both sleeves and even though the housekeeper had freshly laundered it, Romeo's scent still lingered.

A pair of my tight fitted black cycling shorts with an elasticated waistband for comfort completed my outfit and there I was, ready to face the music.

Deliberately wearing something of Romeo's would piss off the other girls—I knew that, but I honestly didn't care. They needed to get used to the idea I was a permanent feature, as I had absolutely no intention of going anywhere.

Before I left, I studied myself in the mirror, quickly realising that I didn't yet look pregnant, but it didn't stop me turning to the side to check my invisible bump. When would I start to look pregnant? The idea of being able to show the world our creation filled me with excitement. I belonged to someone, and I meant something to him.

I meandered my way down to the kitchen, hoping to locate my bestie. Would she even speak to me? *Am I crazy? Should I have given up on her already?*

The room, usually well stocked with whores, was surprisingly quiet and the only occupants were the recently appointed twins that King swore blind he didn't sleep with. Leant against the kitchen island, they were talking over cups of coffee.

Upon closer inspection, I was relieved to find that they weren't particularly attractive. Blonde hair and over filled lips, cheeks and breasts were their offering, and I figured that wasn't really to King's taste.

"Hey, have either of you seen Hanna?" I asked as I helped myself to a mug and filled it with half coffee, half creamer.

They glanced at each other as if speaking in twin telepathy.

"Sure," Twin A smirked. "She's in the gym."

Their body language gave me a sensation in the pit of my stomach that convinced me they were up to something, but with Romeo by my side, I was impervious.

Hanna was in the gym, as expected, but unfortunately for me, she wasn't alone and it looked as if she and one of King's men had just finished having sex as I entered the room.

My timing couldn't have been any worse when I wandered in with my coffee cupped in my hands for comfort, but she saw me before I had chance to sneak back out unnoticed.

"Oh look," she said sarcastically, "it's the man stealer."

As she mocked me, she fastened the buttons on her shirt.

"Hanna—"

"Can I help you with something, Chloe? Would you like to steal this man off me too, perhaps? Maybe have his baby also?"

"Hanna, I just want to make things right, please?"

"You think I would give you the time of day after what you did to me? You back stabbing piece of shit. Who in their right mind has the audacity to get pregnant by *my* man and flaunt it in *my* face? Look at you with his t-shirt on. Pathetic. I've only just stopped bleeding from my abortion!"

"Wait please—"

"I'm constantly reminded of the child I didn't get to keep. I hope you have a miserable life with a man that doesn't give a shit about you. You deserve to experience the suffering I'm going through."

With vengeance in her eyes, she thundered towards me

and spat in my face.

Frozen solid in complete shock, I watched as she strode by me with a glare of disdain as she left.

Shaken and completely shattered by Hanna's words, the realisation hit me I had lost my best friend for good with no do overs. So obvious now, too much had happened between us for us to get back to how we used to be. I had chosen my relationship with Romeo over our friendship, and Hanna flat out refused to accept it.

But if I was honest with myself, I was glad she didn't get to keep her baby with Romeo as, let's face it; I didn't have it in me to share him with anyone else. Not even my best friend.

Hanna might eventually come around to the idea. Maybe? But I would just have to come to terms with the fact that it may never happen.

And right then, with her spit on my face, I was happy with our friendship coming to an end.

"Err, Boss?"

Shit, I'd zoned out again. The man Hanna had been fucking was still standing awkwardly by the treadmill. He was all too aware that he would get in more shit than he could handle if I told King that yet another of his men had been sleeping with one of his whores.

He clasped his hands together in a plea. "Please Boss, don't, you know—"

"Don't worry about it," I snapped. "I have more important things on my mind than this shit."

"Thanks Boss. It's just Hanna needed someone to take care of her. She's not doing good if you couldn't tell already."

I nodded my head sarcastically. "Well, I'm glad you and your dick were of a service."

"No, no," he flapped his hands in a panic, "it's not like that. She uses me, not the other way round."

"Whatever." I rolled my eyes. "Watch you back with her. She might land you in serious trouble."

After my disastrous attempt at rescuing my relationship with Hanna, I tossed my empty mug in the sink on my way through the kitchen and pushed open the patio doors at the far end where I took a stroll through the beautiful gardens to clear my head.

In a strange way, I found the scenery allowed me to connect with Alice, reminding me of our time together walking through the acres, and the same rosebush she had offered me a stem from was still producing scarlet red petals reminding me of happier times we shared. I plucked the most perfectly formed head and carried it with me as though it represented Alice, and I was holding her hand.

The birds were singing in the tall trees around me, chirping their melodic mating call, and I took a seat on the bench within the orchard, listening to their song.

"Afternoon, Ma'am," the gardener jolted me out of my reverie in what I thought might be a Texan accent. Being old school, he tipped his cap in a welcoming gesture.

I instantly recognised him. He was the guy who had seen mine and Alice's intimacy in the swimming pool.

An older gentleman, much older than any of the other males in the house, his beard was silver grey and his eyes told a story of hardship, but seeing him in person in his worn out gardening clothes made me feel differently towards him. He didn't seem like a pervert at all and with a tender kindness, sparkling in his eyes, his smile revealed his genuine nature.

"Hi" I smiled back at him, matching his warm energy.

He gestured towards the space on the bench next to me,

"Can I sit?"

I scooted over to allow him some room. "Sure."

The old timer propped up his leaf rake carefully against the wall of the toolshed, hitched his trousers at the knees and took a seat, wincing as his tired back bent forward.

"I've noticed you round here for a while but never had

the chance to say hey." He reached down into his shoe to scratch an itch.

With my upper lip curled, I glared at his tatty footwear and hoped that he wouldn't take the shoe off. With how delicate my morning sickness was making me feel, foot odour would guarantee to make me hurl and I just couldn't handle that right now.

"Oh, I don't recall seeing you before?" I pretended I didn't recognise him to save his embarrassment. "Have you worked for King long?"

He released a small reminiscing chuckle at an image he replayed fondly in his mind. "I've known that boy since he was three years old. He was a little shit then and an even bigger one now."

"Wow, you've seen it all, then?"

He stopped laughing and penetrated my soul with his gaze.

"Romero is like a son to me and I owe that kid my life, so I will do what I can to watch his back for him. The way he talks about you and that baby." He took a hold of my hand in his. "You are his weakness, and I wanted to warn you. Please be careful with his heart. He's known loss and betrayal all too many times."

I studied the old man's features, trying to read the story

behind his eyes.

"Just make him happy, darlin'."

"I will." I nodded, squeezing his hand. "I promise."

But was I making him happy? The paranoid part of me wondered if Romeo had asked the old man to say something to me. Surely not? My child's father had no mercy, speaking his unfiltered thoughts without hesitation, or an ounce of concern over the delivery or resulting injury.

The old man groaned in discomfort as he hoisted himself to his feet.

"What's your name?" I asked.

"The name's Jack, but most of these youngsters call me Old Man. I don't mind which." He collected his rake to carry on with his chores.

"See you around, Jack." I gave a small wave as I watched him leave.

"You betcha" he tipped his cap and continued his journey to tend to his masterful landscaping where the hobble in his walk exposed his advanced years.

My phone vibrated in my pocket, making me jump. I expected it to be King with demands for the sex I wasn't able to offer him earlier. That man was insatiable.

<Hanna> Sorry Chloe. Let's start again. Meet me in the

Kitchen in 10 mins? xo

    <Me > I wouldn't miss it for the world xoxo

Elated, my hand shot to my mouth as I danced on the spot. *Yes! God, yes.*

This was exactly what I was hoping for, a fresh start with my best friend. I just knew she would come around eventually.

I gathered myself together and headed back inside with a flutter of excitement in my stomach.

With impatience, I made my way straight towards the kitchen, but when I arrived, Hanna was nowhere to be seen.

I peered down at my mother's gift; my wrist watch. Hanna had said ten minutes, but it had only been four.

My stomach grumbled. Did I eat breakfast? *No, I didn't. Idiot!*

With hunger suddenly on my mind, and an extra mouth to feed, I made myself a peanut butter sandwich with the crusts cut off, just like how Grandma used to make, back home in England.

I poured out the remains of the coffee jug from earlier, taking several big gulps of the bitter liquid, as I nibbled along the edge of my nostalgic creation.

I'd just finished my last bite when Hanna strolled in and my stomach flipped with excitement.

"Hey Hanna! I really appreciated the text."

"Sure." She said as she eyed my coffee cup.

"Do you want some?" I raised the pot. "There's a little bit left."

"No, don't worry about me. You help yourself." She smiled, but it didn't reach her eyes.

"So Han, let's talk. I've got so much to say."

Hanna was not being her usual bubbly self. In fact, she was notably quiet.

"Me too Chloe. Lots to say."

The hairs on the back of my neck rose to attention. Something wasn't quite right.

"Um, is everything OK?"

Suddenly, the atmosphere shifted as it unfolded around us where the air crackled with unspoken tension.

Hanna wasn't behaving in the way I had expected from her message. Had she changed her mind again? What on earth was going on?

"I'm fine, Chloe. Are you? You're looking a little washed out."

"Um, yeah... I'm fine... I think...Ugh, wait. Jeez..."

Why do I feel so—

Woah, what was that? My eyes blurred and no matter how much I rubbed them, I couldn't focus on her face.

Hanna?

I grabbed onto the counter, attempting to sit down before I fell over as the room span and the surrounding sounds became distorted; an echo. I tried to steady my breathing. *Keep calm, it'll pass.*

Wait—has someone turned the lights out?

"Hanna?" I called into the darkness. "Hanna!?"

A silhouette strode towards me. *Help me!* But everything turned pitch black before I could react further.

Where am I? The cloaked women were back, sobbing in the darkness. I reached out to them, wanting to help their cause. Why were they crying?

The flames rose around the three of us. I wanted to ask why they were here, with me now. Alice's icy hand reached for mine, handing me a cloak. *Should I wear this?*

"Put it on Jasmin." She whispered.

Wait, what was that sound? I heard a familiar voice in the distance.

"Jasmin?"

Yes? I'm right here. Was someone calling out my name? The sound echoed in my mind, but every time I followed the voice; it moved further away.

"Jasmin?"

I'm here!

The ghosts vanished, and the flames extinguished, where suddenly I was alone in the darkness.

Then the voice became louder; clearer.

"Jasmin!" the female voice called out, now clear as day.

I jolted awake to someone shouting my name.

Startled, with a fuzzy head, I was lay on the kitchen floor.

The voices were coming from the twins.

"She's not dead then?"

"Jesus, Jess, I told you that you had put way too much of that shit in the coffee pot."

What!?

I tried to move my hands, but they were bound behind my back and my feet tied at my ankles.

As I opened my mouth to scream out for help, an anxiously chilled hand covered my face while the second twin applied duct tape.

"That'll keep you quiet," she tore off the strip. "Dumb bitch."

I struggled uselessly to free myself, tossing my body around, trying to tug my hands from the bite of the rope, but I was too weak and light-headed. *Oh God, my baby!*

The twins waited restlessly, as though standing by for

an order.

"Should we just wait here? Or—"

"Shut up Jess. No talking. Looks like she's passed out again."

A time later, footsteps that entered the room started in my dreams, but turned into my reality. I'd hoped with all my heart that it was Romeo who had come to save me, but when my blurry eyes refocused, it was Hanna.

"Thanks girls," she hugged them both. "Sit her up against that wall."

Once the twins had propped me up in position, Hanna leant in towards my face. "You realise now Chloe, having friends has its advantages, doesn't it? When you're a loner, it gets you… in this mess."

My gaze broadened as the deception engulfed me. I wanted to ask her why she was doing this, but the tape was so tight around my mouth that I couldn't make more than a muffled sound.

Hanna raised to a tall and intimidating position while she watched me struggle.

"You two can leave. Thanks for your help."

Please. My baby!

"Lets get your boyfriend in the room too, shall we? And

then we can really have some fun."

She reached into my shorts pocket and pulled out my phone. "It won't be long before Daddy comes looking for you and then I will have you both where I want you." She scrolled through my contacts. "What name is he under? Let's see. King? No. Daddy? Nope. Romeo with a heart emoji? That must be him—aww, how cute."

My eyes, as my only form of communication, glistened with doe eyed emotion in a silent plea for her forgiveness, but Hanna didn't care. She had other plans.

She began typing out a text message. "Hi Daddy. I'm in the living room if you wanna fuck?" She read aloud, chuckling to herself. "Looking forward to seeing your dick. Love Chloe. There that'll do. Send." Hanna tossed my cell on the counter. "Won't it be romantic Chloe? Lovers dying together by my hand."

My mind could not comprehend the irony of what she said where the conversation I had with King back at the apartment about Romeo and Juliet dying in the end made me violently ill. Had I manifested this?

I desperately wanted to plead for my life, but I had no power left in me other than to make feeble sounds against the tape that suffocated my mouth, wanting so badly to protect my baby; to fight for him.

Hanna grabbed the fabric of my shirt and dragged my bound body through the kitchen and into the adjacent living room. There was nothing I could do other than to allow her. *Never fight back. Don't give them satisfaction.*

She sat me in the centre of the room and strolled over to the big window, looking out into the beautiful garden.

"This place should have been mine. I deserved more from this life. You were the last person on this earth that I thought would do this to me."

I wanted to tell her I was sorry. To hug her and tell her I loved her.

Without warning, she spun around and pulled out a familiar looking gun from her back pocket. I recognised that gun. *That's mine!*

Romeo had given it to me as a gift to protect myself, that I refused to use, and the blood drained from my face in horror as Clive's lifeless body came to my mind. Was I next?

How had she found where I'd hidden that gun and why was I so stupid as to put a weapon in the bedside drawer, leaving myself unarmed? If Romeo found out, he would be so mad at me.

We stayed in position for minutes that felt like hours, with my own weapon aimed at my stomach as we waited for Romeo's arrival.

"Shouldn't be long now, Chloe. Let's find out how much he really loves you, shall we?"

The door to the living room opened casually with King looking perplexed at his phone, reading the message that Hanna had sent him, as though something didn't add up.

His face paled when he saw the scene in front of his eyes and, with lightning quick reactions, he reached into his waistband and pulled out his gun before Hanna could react.

"You fuckin' psycho, what are you doin'!?" He yelled with authority.

"I'm doing what should've already been done. She's not right for you, Daddy."

Hot, salty tears rolled down my cheeks as I squinted at King through the drug infused haze, while he focused all his attention on Hanna and her gun.

"Put the gun down Hanna," he held out a hand in front of him, his palm facing her, where he took a step forward.

"Why should I listen to you?"

"Because I am tellin' you to. Put the gun down and we will talk about this."

"The time for talking was before you forced me to abort our child," her voice cracked as her body strained against her sobs. Her hands shook with the anger that consumed her.

King took another step forward towards her.

"Keep back or I will blow your fucking head off!" Hanna screamed as she moved the aim of the gun from me to him, where she pushed down the hammer, arming the weapon.

King obliged at the sound of the bullet clicking into place and he stopped still, waiting for her next move.

They were in a standoff like in an old western, neither of them knowing what the other person's next move was.

"I fucking hate you both!" She shrieked.

King held firm with his finger securely pressed on the trigger, and I knew then he was going to shoot her when the time was right.

"What ever you wanna say, just say it now Hanna. Let's talk about this."

"OK then. Why did you choose her over me?" She wiped the well of tears from her eyes that distorted her aim.

I could tell he was struggling to find words that wouldn't offend her further. Not wishing to put me and the baby at more risk than we already were.

"It would be easier to talk if you put the gun down first," he said in a measured tone.

"Fuck you! As soon as I drop this gun, you will shoot me. I'm not stupid."

Romeo sighed. "I didn't say you were. Look, I'm sorry it didn't work out with us."

"Why did you kill my baby!" she sobbed again "and why does she get to keep hers!?"

She moved her aim back to me, suddenly remembering I was still there.

King's stoney mask slipped for a split second when Hanna took a step closer towards me.

"Hanna, you know as well as I do that you weren't pregnant."

What?

"Shut up!"

Hanna wasn't pregnant, after all? The revelation was one that I desperately needed answers to. But all I could do in that moment was watch the events unfold.

King stepped forward again, one step closer to taking the gun from her.

"STOP!" She aimed at King again and they were back to stalemate.

The sudden noise of helicopters' blades thudding above the mansion halted their actions. Armed police officers surrounded the exterior, looking at us through the expansive window. "Police, Freeze. Drop your weapons!"

King, with experience on his side, did as instructed by

dropping his gun, where he fell to his knees with his hands behind his head.

"If I die, you die too Daddy." Hanna yelled over the thudding noise of the helicopter's engine.

I waited with bated breath as my heart pounded while I witnessed the father of my child, unarmed, knelt before Hanna's gun. God, please! Save him.

There was a gunshot; a loud sound that bounced around the room and then, almost simultaneously, there was a second shot.

Both Romeo and Hanna's bodies dropped to the floor in synchrony, thudding as they hit the ground.

No! No! *He's not dead. Right?*

Still on my knees, I was helpless. He can't be dead. Please no.

As soon as the gunfire silenced, the police stormed the room in large numbers, alongside several of King's men.

Time seemed to move in slow motion as Tommy ran towards me, scrambling to untie my restraints.

"Boss, are you OK?"

Once he'd freed my hands of the rope, I forcefully ripped off the tape from my mouth and gasped for air deep into my lungs.

Romeo! He can't be—

My first reaction was to reach him; hold him. He was lying on the floor, listless, in a pool of blood.

"Tommy, help us!"

My heart stopped beating when I saw Romeo's pale face as I scooped him into my arms. So much blood; too much blood.

"Tommy! Is he dead?"

"Shit," Tommy mumbled.

"What!?"

"I can't find a pulse."

BOOKS IN THIS SERIES

The king's empire series

Give Up On Me Part 1

Give Up On Me Part 2

Don't Give Up On Me Part 1

Don't Give Up On Me Part 2

Printed in Great Britain
by Amazon